KINGDOM COLD

THE COMPLETE COLLECTION

BRITTNI CHENELLE

CONTENTS

Kingdom Cold 1
Kingdom Soul 231
Kingdom Untold 407

KINGDOM COLD

A YA NOVEL

BRITTNI CHENELLE

I dedicate this novel to my father.
The man who saw glimpses of brilliance in me
before I did.

CONTENTS

1. Princess Charlotte 7
2. Prince Young 14
3. Princess Charlotte 19
4. Prince Young 23
5. Princess Charlotte 30
6. Prince Young 34
7. Princess Charlotte 39
8. Prince Young 44
9. Princess Charlotte 48
10. Prince Young 53
11. Princess Charlotte 58
12. Prince Young 63
13. Princess Charlotte 69
14. Prince Young 73
15. Princess Charlotte 76
16. Prince Minseo 81
17. Princess Charlotte 86
18. Prince Young 91
19. Princess Charlotte 95
20. Milly 99
21. Princess Charlotte 104
22. Prince Emmett 109
23. Princess Charlotte 114
24. Prince Emmett 118
25. Prince Young 122
26. Princess Charlotte 128
27. Prince Young 133
28. Prince Emmett 138
29. Milly 143
30. Princess Charlotte 147
31. Prince Young 151
32. Princess Charlotte 155

33. Prince Young 161
34. Princess Charlotte 164
35. Prince Young 168
36. Prince Minseo 172
37. Prince Young 177
38. Prince Minseo 181
39. Princess Charlotte 184
40. Prince Young 188
41. Prince Minseo 192
42. King Young 197
43. Queen Charlotte 200
44. Prince Minseo 204
45. Queen Charlotte 208
46. King Young 212
47. Queen Charlotte 215
48. King Young 218
49. Queen Charlotte 222
50. Prince Minseo 226

Author's Note 229

1

PRINCESS CHARLOTTE

Dying wasn’t my intention. Yet there I lay, ravenous— twelve hours into my hunger strike, certain I was already slipping away. The moans of my stomach howled for me to submit to the trays of food of every variety within an arm's reach. I swallowed a gulp of nectarous air, heavy with the aroma of my favorite dishes, as the servants marched them in one by one. My mother was not relenting, but neither was I. As I lay dying, I didn’t observe my life flash before my eyes, but rather the few hours that led me to this desperate act— and ultimately to my untimely demise.

"Married? To who?” I seethed. *It didn't even matter.* "Married!"

My mom, Queen of Besmium, let out a breathy sigh. "Honestly, Charlotte, can we skip the theatrics?"

I rushed closer to her. "I'm only sixteen. You said I'd have more time, until eighteen at least."

She crossed her arms. "And you would feel differently about marriage in two years?"

I opened my mouth to speak, but nothing came out. Tears

stung my eyes. I clenched my jaw, rage pulsing through me. *Was this a punishment?* Everyone knew I would make a terrible queen. I wasn't cut out for rules or duty. My parents were never able to conceive another child, so they gave in to the fact it would have to be me. Married off for an alliance. "No. I won't do it," I said.

"I wasn't asking your permission." Her gaze cut into my resolve but I refused to surrender the modicum of freedom I had.

"I won't say 'I do'," I said, locking my knees to keep them from shaking. *Marriage?* Even the word repulsed me. It sat at the back of my throat and I choked on it.

She stepped forward and leaned her face close to mine, her voice almost a whisper. "Could you be any more selfish?"

I swallowed back a wave of tears.

"Drethen marches closer every day," she said. "Without this alliance—"

I succumbed to sobs, melting like a wax candle at the end of a banquet.

This seemed to please my mother to no end. She watched my anguish, her eyebrow slightly raised. She did this after all her victories. Certainly, this was revenge for my disobedience. After what felt like one hundred years of silence she continued, answering the question I couldn't bring myself to ask.

"The Prince of Vires. Prince Young."

I choked. "The *Eastern Statue*? Did you know that's what they call him? They say he never smiles."

"Be grateful he's only a year older than you."

Her words hung in the silence like a thick fog, but instead of obscuring my vision, my mother had exposed herself. Her marriage had been arranged as well, and it was no secret that father was twenty years her senior. She pursed her lips as if she could somehow suck the words back. I studied her face but she spun away, taking her leave with poised, deliberate steps before I could respond, and left me there with the news.

I walked like the undead to my bedroom and collapsed on the floor. Milly, my lady-in-waiting, appeared.

"Is everything—"

"Corset off. "

Milly rushed over, her small hands unlacing my corset with quick, decisive movements. From behind me, all I could see of her was an occasional wisp of her summery hair. When she finished, she dropped down in front of me, as if my morbid energy was draining her.

"What happened?"

"Prince of Vires," I said as I buried my face in my hands.

She leaned forward, awaiting more information, as I remained motionless. Her eyes widened. "Marriage? But you're only sixteen."

I sat up and gave a hard nod, shaking a few of my dark curls from their pins. We sat there in silence. Each drape, chandelier, and ornately decorated vase screamed the same thing: my life wasn't mine.

I strained to remember him. I'd met Prince Young once. Dark hair and dark, almond-shaped eyes that curved in at the corners... But his face—I couldn't really recall it. I could only remember the feeling of him. He'd seemed so serious and miserable, even more so than the stuffy, political vultures that circled court. I hadn't given him a single thought since we met—until now. Now, all I could think about was his cold, heartless stature and a lifetime without laughter.

Milly wrapped her arms around me and pulled me in. She was a year younger and yet I'd always gone to her for guidance. She was beautiful, the kind that could rival any well-groomed royal, but that wasn't what I envied. Even as a paid servant of our household, she was in charge of her fate.

For the next few weeks, I tried to think of a way to sabotage the wedding. I tried running away but didn't make it past the courtyard before the guard caught me. I wrote a heartfelt and smartly worded letter to my father. He responded with a letter of his own, which read something like, "Tough luck…" Finally, I got the idea of going on a hunger strike.

Admittedly, I had expected my mother to give in much sooner, but I remained obstinate because she'd clearly expected me to do the same. The anger welled inside me, tightening my stomach, which only emphasized its emptiness. A fresh loaf of Sasha's wheat bread fluttered into the room on a silver tray. I sat up and stared as a servant placed the tray down beside me, the corner of her mouth turned up.

I leaned into the steaming loaf and breathed in its warmth, my will being sucked away like summer rain on dry soil. I eyed my chamber for servants, but I was alone. No doubt they were scheming to bring in the next temptation. My stomach ached for me to surrender. If I took a small bite from the bottom of the loaf, they'd never know. I lifted the loaf carefully and bit into it. My mind surged with delight and I savored the crunchy exterior and doughy flavor before carefully placing it back on the tray, bite side down.

I hesitated before I lay back down. Surely, my mother was evil for forcing me into such extremes. My father wasn't though. Why hadn't he intervened? Was the war with Drethen so dire that he was willing to sell his only daughter for a few extra soldiers?

I remembered that five years ago, when the war first started, the rhythmic clop of two hundred horses reminded me of the rain. I was eleven and my father knelt before me, for kings bow to no one but the daughters they love. He urged me to hug him goodbye, but I didn't want to—I hated goodbyes. I remembered how my mother pinched the back of my arm.

"Hug your father," she rasped, coldly. "You'll regret your poor attitude if he's killed in battle."

I hugged him. The trumpets sounded as he mounted his horse —taking his place at the front. After that, Besmium was always at war, and my father, the king, was always one goodbye away from being gone forever.

I reached over and ripped another piece of bread from the bottom of the loaf. I sighed as I popped it into my mouth.

No matter how many times my mother had prepared me for the news of my engagement, I still felt blindsided. Where was love in all this? Love was just this abstract concept for novels but unspeakable inside the castle. Not even my father said it. Maybe it was their way of protecting me from something I could never have. Marriage was the duty of every princess, and love was the cost.

I tore another piece of bread from the tray and rolled onto my stomach to avoid choking.

By the time I was fifteen, there was a party or tournament almost every month, parading me around like some trophy to be won. The other courtiers cooed over the high-standing men at court, but I never understood why. Sure, the idea of courting seemed fun enough. I could wear elaborate gowns and be whispered sonnets by handsome princes. But that's not how any of it actually happened. In the end, the choice was out of my hands. I'd marry whoever my father thought was best for the kingdom, and nothing about that seemed fun.

Throughout my early teens, I'd sneak out beyond the walls of the castle every chance I got to try to catch a glimpse of the world beyond. There, I saw children at play and parents home for dinner. There seemed to be a general warmth in the ordinary lives of Besmium's people that never existed in my world.

During one of my excursions beyond the wall, I saw a scattered batch of white wildflowers on the far side of a small stream. Their petals shone like pearls in the sunlight, each delicate flower lovelier than the last. I rushed over and lost my footing on a slippery stone. My legs flew from beneath me. I twisted to catch myself, landing with a hard scrape of stones against both palms and my knee. I cried out in pain as I scrambled for my balance, only to slip again, this time landing in the center of the stream. The cold water was a series of daggers on my skin. My vision turned to waves of white fuzz. Panicked, I pulled myself out and sat by the water's edge.

As I caught my breath, tears warmed my cheeks. I sat muddy, wet, and bleeding, the lesson learned: beautiful things could hurt. I felt a touch of shame as I trudged back to the castle. The independence my adventures had given me drained away.

I spent several fearful moments attempting to convince the castle guard that it was I, Princess Charlotte, who stood before him. By that time I felt as small as I'd ever been and certain I couldn't be lower.

That was the last time I was allowed beyond the wall without supervision. My mother put me under constant surveillance and conversations about my future as a wife became more frequent. Still, I hadn't expected the day to come so quickly.

I chewed thoughtfully.

My desire to live a different life from the one I was born into remained strong. Marriage seemed like the fatal blow to my freedom. All I wanted was to see the walls of the castle fall and to walk out with no title and no crown. Now that my engagement was official, I was certain my dream would never come to be. At the same time, I never considered what I'd lose, if it did. Still, would it be so bad if Drethen won?

I looked down at the empty platter in surprise. Did I eat the *whole thing*? I sat up, just in time to see one of the servants slip out of my room. Sure enough, minutes later, my mother strode into my chamber, her crown gleaming in the candlelight. She eyed the trays of uneaten food until her gaze landed on the empty tray beside me. Without a word she smiled, a searing and heartless grin that boiled my skin long after she'd gone. As helplessness overcame me, I scanned the room for the next tray I'd indulge in. There was no use resisting food now. I'd failed.

On the eve of the wedding, the prince was shown to my home at Hiems Castle. I could hear the distant *clip-clop* of his horse-drawn carriage as it pulled up outside. I stared into the mirror and studied my face. It was more than about accepting all the things I'd never get to experience—love, freedom, happiness—it was also about the things I wasn't ready for: a kiss, a consummation ceremony, and—above all—a husband.

2

PRINCE YOUNG

It was as if my life had finally started—an immense bolt of lightning that jogged me awake. I bowed deeply with gratitude, to my father. As I headed back to my chamber, my mind played her name in a constant loop. *Princess Charlotte of Besmium.* A princess, a kingdom of my own, an adventure in a foreign land. I barely made it inside my room when I was hit from behind and toppled to the floor. My brother, Minseo pushed my face into the carpet.

"Brother!" He laughed, berating me with a series of playful punches. I shoved him off. "I am definitely coming along for the ride." He beamed.

I nodded, instinctively suppressing my joy.

"Aren't you excited? You'll be King of Besmium!"

I stood, dusting myself off. "Yes, brother, but this is a serious matter."

He reached out and messed up my hair. "It doesn't have to be *so* serious."

When he was gone, I allowed my mind to race with the possibilities. Minseo was right, I was happy, so I should show it, but unlike him, years of scolding and punishment had taught me to hold everything in, and it was a difficult habit to break.

As the third prince of Vires, I was always destined to wed a kingdom. My father had done right by me, bartered me one of my own—a kingship. What I hadn't expected was to be matched with a western princess. I'd always assumed, based on the women they presented at court, that I'd marry an eastern princess. It seemed only obvious to join kingdoms that were closer. I'd never known anyone to marry outside of this region, and the thought that I'd someday rule as a western king thrilled me as much as it scared me.

I had no time to waste thinking about the princess in the weeks that followed. I studied western culture, etiquette, political tensions, and history—it was like I was starting over. I'd been trained to handle just about any political situation that could happen in Vires or its neighboring countries, but not even my father could have predicted that King Morgan of Besmium would make such an offer. My father explained that the opportunity was too good to pass up. It wasn't until I'd reached the transport ship and settled in for the long journey that my thoughts turned to Charlotte.

I remembered the first time I met her—Charlotte, Princess of Besmium. It was my first and only trip to Besmium or any western kingdom. I was overwhelmed by the foreignness of all the people I saw there. The women in my kingdom were beautiful—white skin, red lips, and hair as long and glossy as the tail of a fully-grown stallion. But the Princess of Besmium, like many of the courtiers in her kingdom, had a brown skin tone, which I'd only seen once as a child when the King of Besmium visited my father. I had asked to touch the king's skin, only to be scolded by my father, though I was too young to understand why. Charlotte's skin was lighter, a mixture of her father and the fair-skinned queen, but it was still unmistakably brown. I could see *that* clearly across the room.

I approached for my introduction. We bowed and she looked up at me. I froze. I tried not to gape at her, but I couldn't help but notice her caramel skin, which glowed a yellowish-gold in the candlelight; her black eyes, so round they made me freeze beneath their gaze; and her hair, which was curled into spirals. Then she was gone. My body pulsed. *Fascinating.* I wanted to see more of her, just to observe her features more closely, but my time had come and gone.

The swaying of the ship lulled me into a state between awake and asleep.

Charlotte curtsied. I took her hand and slyly whisked her out of the ballroom, making sure we weren't seen. Once in the hallway, I took a knee. "Charlotte, will you be my wife?"

She beckoned me to my feet and whispered, "I am yours." I pulled her face to mine and kissed her. I wrapped my arms around her, drawing her in closer and—

"Young?"

My eyes snapped open and I lurched to a seated position. My brother Minseo hovered over me.

"I've been meaning to ask, have you given any thoughts to your duties as a husband?" He grinned.

Disoriented, I ran my hand through my hair twice before I convinced myself I was awake. "Uh, yeah. I guess," I croaked.

"Have you thought about the, you know, the wedding night?"

Heat radiated through my cheeks. *Oh, that.* I turned away from Minseo so he wouldn't see the color searing into my face.

"You don't want to disappoint your new wife," he jested.

The truth was that I hadn't allowed myself to think about it. It wasn't really the type of thing you could prepare for. Although I knew the logistics of it, I'd never actually *been* with a woman. That was something that male royals in my kingdom did on their nineteenth birthday, as a sort of rite of passage. Since I was eighteen, it hadn't happened yet. Minseo had turned nineteen six months ago and had often requested the company of various women ever since.

"I know you're excited," he said, trying to read my expression.

Our brotherly dynamic changed when he turned nineteen. Suddenly he knew things, having experienced a world that I hadn't, and he relished every moment he could remind me.

"It's no big deal," I said, stretching my arms above my head. My voice was more convincing than expected.

"Good man. I'd hate it if my first time had to be in front of people. What an unusual tradition. To think I'll be there cheering you on the whole time."

My stomach tightened. "It's just a moment of discomfort."

He tilted his head back in a loud, open-mouthed laugh. "Let's hope it's more than a moment."

"All worth it for a kingdom."

His smile faded. Minseo was the second-born. Our older brother Sumin would inherit Vires when father got too old, and Minseo would never have a kingdom of his own. I'd hurt him. And worse, he didn't deserve it.

He gave a soft, unconvincing chuckle, his shoulders relaxed. "Yeah. Good luck with that."

Before I could form an apology, he had gone on deck and left me with my guilt. What's *wrong* with me? Was I already cracking under the pressure? Honor, duty, and respect—these were the values instilled in me as a child, the values that built eastern culture. Vires had proudly carried these for centuries and I was determined to do the same.

As we got closer to our destination, the nerves set in. It was like I was cycling through nervous habits, trying to find one that fit. I chewed my nails, I tapped my foot, I licked my lips. Minseo's presence eased me. He had a joke or game ready each time he noticed signs of nerves. I was glad he had come along. The carriage ride dragged, days blurring together as if we'd slipped into purgatory. Even Minseo's spirit dimmed. With each jerk of the carriage, I felt my home slip further away.

Our military escorts worried that we wouldn't reach the castle in time.

I punched Minseo on the shoulder, waking him suddenly. "What do you think'll happen if we're late?" I prodded. He scratched his head and grinned, "No doubt the king will marry off his daughter to someone else." He laughed. "I hear there are quite a few unmarried princes in Algony." I stared out the window of the carriage, imagining the worst, but it was the night before the wedding and our horse-drawn carriage came to an abrupt halt outside the stone gates of the Hiems Castle.

I stepped out of the carriage and stretched. I hadn't expected to be this tired or this sore, but my nervousness numbed it all. Minseo patted me on the shoulder and we readied ourselves to be received.

Woosh. Shloop.

A guard's voice rang out, "Arrow!" It hit the ground more than twenty feet away. In an instant, the guards had formed a circle around Minseo and me. They searched the dusky sky. I braced myself and suddenly understood.

This whole arrangement was a trap.

3

PRINCESS CHARLOTTE

The moment I let the arrow fly, I regretted it. It was as if it all happened in slow motion. I gasped and reached my hand out to grab it from the air, but it soared beyond my reach, landing on the ground several yards from the prince. What even *was* my plan? I kill the prince, then what? War? The fall of my kingdom? How could my parents want me to be queen when I couldn't make basic moral decisions, like don't kill my betrothed?

I leaned against the stone wall of the castle. It cooled my skin as I slid down, and I sank my face into my hands. I heard the commotion of the guard outside—the fear in their voices. What had I done? Before I knew it, footsteps filled the corridor and I was surrounded by my own castle guards. Hot prickly tears stung my eyes. I had no intention of putting up a fight—I was cornered and guilty.

"This is the most shameful thing you have ever done! What were you *thinking*?" My mother's voice was as shrill as it was strained—she clearly worried her voice would carry, making the combination sound like a dying animal.

"Where's father?" I croaked.

"He's trying to reassure your future husband that he's not under attack. This could mean *war*! How can you be so selfish?"

I gulped. "I—" The words stuck to my tongue. I was so stupid. Why couldn't I just be a normal girl? I closed my eyes, trying to remember what was going through my mind as I pulled the bow back. I was just tired of everything feeling so beyond my control.

She paced. "My daughter is a murderer. Where did I go wrong?"

"He didn't even—"

"What Charlotte? Die?"

I swallowed to meet the bile rising in my stomach. I felt like I was going to vomit.

The door swung open and my father strode in. His presence weakened me. I fell to my knees and sobbed as hot tears poured from my eyes and stung my face. I wiped them furiously, taking choppy laborious breaths. I braced myself for his rage but my father pulled me to my feet. I buried my face in my arm so I wouldn't have to meet his gaze. He wrapped his arms around me and pulled me into his chest. I whimpered as he rubbed my back gently. Being held by my father always made me feel like a little girl.

Several minutes passed without a word as my tears slowed and my breath evened. I pulled back, "Father—I'm so sorry. I didn't mean to—"

"I know, my dear." He dropped his arms and peered down at me.

"You do?" I sniffed.

"I trust you. Do you trust me?" he asked, the lines on his dark forehead deepened.

I nodded, a steady stream of tears still flowing.

His lips peaked up at the corners. "Then trust my choice here."

I wiped my snot on the sleeve of my dress and I could basically hear my mother's eyes roll across the room without even looking at her. I cleared my throat. "Does he still want to... I mean, will he still—"

"He will honor our agreement, but his guard and his elder brother have requested to stay here until things..." he scratched the gray stubble on his chin, "settle."

His voice was a warm blanket in my cold life.

My mother's voice interceded, "You have five minutes to fix your face and greet your husband in the grand hall."

I turned to leave.

"Charlotte," my father called, "try to think about what he's going through."

I nodded and headed to my chamber, and the more I thought about how much I must have disappointed my father, the worse I felt, but it didn't mean that I was ready to hand my life over to some stranger. My only hope was that Prince Young changed his mind about the marriage. A devious plan began to gnaw at the back of my mind. If he canceled the wedding, surely no one could blame him. Perhaps the prince would be my ally after all. Maybe I could *convince* him not to marry me. There wasn't much time—the wedding was tomorrow—so I'd have to talk him into leaving tonight at the banquet. I picked at my fingernails. Was this the arrow incident all over again? Father had forgiven me, a favor I knew I didn't deserve, but surely he couldn't blame me if the prince just left.

I pinched my cheeks and pinned a few of my curls out of my face, making sure I had no snot coming out of my nose or tear lines on my cheeks. My eyes were still red and puffy but it was starting to get dark and, with the low lighting, I was sure no one would notice.

Minutes later, I was standing face to face with a tall, dark stranger. His black eyes peered into mine. He smiled a devilish grin that shot flecks of mischief into his irises. His face nearly brushed mine as he bowed, never taking his gaze off me. He'd gotten too close on purpose.

My heart fluttered and I momentarily forgot my plan, my words, my name. A hot blush burned the insides of my cheeks. He oozed charisma, drawing me in. My heart thudded against my ribcage. There was nothing statue-like about him, except his perfect statuesque face. He waited for me to speak, glaring at my lips like I was a snack and he hadn't eaten in days. Electricity shot through me, shattering every cell of my body. All the determination to hate him melted away. I *wanted* him.

He cleared his throat. "Good evening, princess. I'm Prince Minseo of Vires."

4

PRINCE YOUNG

The moment that she turned away from my brother and looked at me, all the glitter in her eyes vanished. Her smile waned. Her posture slumped. She couldn't have been more obviously disappointed if she'd screamed it from the tallest tower.

My stomach tightened, but concealing my emotions was my specialty.

"Oh," she said, tucking a curl behind her ear. "I'm marrying *you?*"

Minseo choked, biting back his smile.

I stood paralyzed by humiliation. As I looked into her face, she did not resemble the foreign beauty I'd met once before, but rather a spoiled, selfish little princess who had already crossed enough unforgivable lines in the brief time I'd been in Besmium. This marriage wasn't going to be as fun as I thought.

"I'm Prince Young of Vires," I said, bowing deeply. My mind raced.

I'll never love you.

I continued. "It's an honor to meet you."

You tried to kill me.

She said all the words she was supposed to. She even apologized for “losing control of her arrow” but it was as soulless as reciting legislation. All the while, Minseo watched over my shoulder. My lips dried. I’d expected a significant amount of discomfort from this experience, but this was public humiliation. Charlotte was to blame for all of it. What kind of princess acted like this?

Later that night, the banquet bustled with elegantly dressed Besmians. The royal dresser had chosen a military-style jacket with a sash and a series of multicolored pins for me to wear, and I was finding it more constricting than the loose, soft-flowing fabrics that were commonly worn in Vires. I was glad, however, that at least my clothing didn't make me stand out.

Maybe it was the way that Charlotte was still sneaking glances at my brother, but I felt like everyone in the room *knew*.

Beads of sweat prickled my neck around my collar. I hadn't been able to keep my feet under me since I'd arrived. I'd been shot at and rejected. Whatever trace amounts of bravery I was clinging to diminished the moment she sat down beside me. I speculated on what trauma she had in store for me next. Poison perhaps? I eyed my cup warily.

After our brief introduction, Minseo had given me a few pointers, but the only one I could really remember was "smile". How could I? Her presence felt unpredictable, even dangerous. I could swallow my pride and ignore that Charlotte fawned over Minseo —I mean, what did I care? But this *was* a problem. Minseo was eligible and there was no logical benefit for either king to have me marry the princess instead of him. The wedding was tomorrow and at the rate things were going, I'd be on a ship home, shamed—and without any hope of ever being king. My father would be so disappointed. *One night.* I just had to charm her for one night. Tomorrow the marriage would be made official and my position here would be secure. Besides, I was every bit as good a man as Minseo.

Trumpets sounded, reverberating off the candlelit ballroom. Rows of servants filed in, carrying silver trays that they placed in rows before us. When the trumpets stopped, the servants lifted the covers off the trays, revealing an assortment of plain-looking food. Though the amount of food was immense, it didn't look very special or interesting.

The king and queen sat at the end of the table, more than twenty high-ranking members of court between us. Charlotte sat beside me but Minseo was halfway between the king and where I was. He was too far to talk to, but not too far to send him an occasional expressive glance. With the bustle of the chatting courtiers and the music from the band, they were far out of earshot, but they watched me carefully. Were they already not considering me? I turned to the princess, who was filling her plate with thick strips of chicken breast and dark purple grapes.

I summoned all my courage. "You look lovely this evening," I said.

The princess lifted her head clumsily, her mouth slightly agape. Eyes half open, her head bobbed back as a droopy smile stretched across her face. I looked into her eyes, a cloudy haze glossed over them. She picked up her silver cup and brought it to her lips, taking a long slurpy gulp before she plunged it back on the wooden table with a dull clank. "

Annnnnnnd she's drunk," I huffed under my breath. The dinner had begun maybe twenty minutes ago. How many drinks could she have possibly managed since sitting down beside me? I stared in disbelief though she didn't seem to notice. She shoveled chicken into her mouth using her fingers. This is a *princess*? I tried focusing on my own bland meal, but Charlotte started drawing concerned glances from the courtiers across from us. She swallowed too quickly and choked. In a fit of coughs, she proceeded to wash the chicken down with more wine, before laughing at nothing, ogling my brother, and then starting the process over again. I was going to let her continue. For all intents and purposes, this was exactly what I needed. With her so out of it and a little acting on my part, the king and queen would think we were having a good time. I could go on to marry her tomorrow, become Prince of Besmium, and eventually king, and my father would never have to know what a rough start it had been. Charlotte could drink herself into oblivion for all I cared—but then she sat up, her head swerving involuntarily. She let out a faint burp. For crying out loud, she was going to be *sick*. We hadn't stepped one foot on the dance floor and already my only option was to drag her out of here.

I stood quickly. "Miss Charlotte, would you care to accomp—"

She burped again, lowering her head to the table. I quickly picked her up and held her against my hip. There was a door at the opposite end of the table from the king. It seemed to be meant for servants, but it was my only option. She managed to get her feet under her and we were able to semi-inconspicuously slip out of the ballroom.

She led me through the dimly lit corridor, nodding her head in the correct direction whenever there was an option to turn. Suddenly, her knees buckled and she slumped down to the cobblestone floor.

The candles burned low, probably as a result of the servants being busy with the banquet. The cool archways, a dark gray contrast to the golden-flecked columns of the ballroom.

"Come on, Charlotte," I said, kneeling. I tilted her head up to look her in the eyes. "We're almost th—" I froze. A heavy stream of tears flowed down her cheeks, dripping from the bottom of her chin.

She sobbed. "I don't want to marry you."

It wasn't news, but I'd never seen a woman cry before. She seemed so fragile it made something ache at the bottom of my stomach. This was not the girl who shot the arrow or the girl who showed her disappointment upon our first meeting. This was someone new.

I sighed. "I know." I felt fear seep into my skin before my next question manifested. "Do you want to marry my brother?"

She shook her head. "I don't want to marry *anyone.*"

I nodded as her breakdown worsened. It was a terrible reality, but somehow it made me feel better. I hadn't exactly been a disappointment, she just didn't want any of this. I had a lingering urge to reach out to her, to wipe her tears, or hold her in my arms, but I didn't. I let her cry.

"I don't want to be a princess," she sobbed. "I just want to be free."

Afraid to touch her, I inched back and settled into a more comfortable position on the floor.

"I'm sorry this happened to you," I said.

"Stop the wedding then!" she cried.

My body stiffened. "I too am bound to honor my father's agreement."

She wiped her face and looked me straight in the eyes, her swollen cheeks red and brimming with emotion. "What do you want?" she asked.

I shook my head.

"My kingdom? You can have it," she breathed. "Let me go."

Frozen, I begged my body to tear my gaze from hers.

Her lips parted and she breathed in like it hurt, before she spoke. "Aren't you afraid of what you'll be giving up?"

My brow furrowed as I contemplated what she meant. I bit the inside of my bottom lip.

"Do you honestly think you could ever love me?"

The word “love” struck me, like an arrow masked by dusk.

She studied my face, my silence burning away her last seeds of hope. Her tears began to fall again, this time slow and sorrowful.

“I-”

"Charlotte!" a voice called.

I turned. A fair-haired girl cantered toward us and knelt in front of us, cupping Charlotte's face in her hands. A wooden cross swayed from her neck as she attempted to calm the crying princess. The girl quickly wiped away Charlotte’s tears and pulled her close. Charlotte's cries softened as the blonde girl rubbed her back gently.

I was having a day of new experiences and none were what I'd expected. Here I was, witnessing a kind of affection that wasn't shown in my kingdom. In fact, I'd never seen this kind of nurturing at all, not even from my own mother. It warmed me—entranced me.

The blonde girl lifted her chin, turning her face to me. "Your Highness!" Her voice, soft and musical. "Please pardon my rudeness."

"No—I mean, thank you. I didn't know what to do."

She nodded. "Will you help me get her to her chamber?"

I leaped to my feet and, with the help of the girl, we got Charlotte to her feet too. As we moved toward Charlotte's chamber, I felt a twinge of something stirring inside me.

The blonde girl spoke, "I'm Milly. I'm a servant here in Hiems Castle and Charlotte's friend."

"I'm Young," I said.

Milly giggled, warmth radiating from her smile. I turned to find her smiling widely.

I shook my head in confusion, "What? What's funny?"

Her laughter reached her pale, crystal-blue eyes. "*I* can't call you that."

"Oh. Well, maybe you can make an exception. Like you do for Charlotte," I said, biting down on my bottom lip.

She laughed. "Charlotte and I are close friends."

I pointed at Milly. "Exactly." For the first time since arriving in Besmium, I felt myself smile.

5

PRINCESS CHARLOTTE

I awoke with an intense throbbing in my head. My limbs were noticeably heavy, and every time I moved a fraction, I felt the threat of nausea clawing at my stomach. Flashbacks of the night before started coming back like puzzle pieces strewn across my bed.

I don't want to marry you.

I cringed and buried my head into my pillow as if I could suffocate the embarrassment out of me. My plan was ruined. Although my behavior had been humiliating, I doubt it was enough to scare the prince away. I was out of time. Behind the door, I heard my mother's shrill voice cry out, "Open the door, you idiot."

I rolled over as the guards pushed open the door, and my mother strode in.

"Get up," she said, her voice shrill and forceful. "Wash your face. Your father wants to have a word with you before the wedding."

I couldn't move. "Mom," I groaned, "I'm sick."

She sighed. "I don't care if you're dead, this wedding is happening today."

Ugh. I considered sitting up quickly and throwing up on her. Then she'd have to accept that I'm sick, but based on the rigidness of her movements this morning, I decided it wouldn't change a thing—barring a smidge of personal satisfaction. I forced myself to sit up and felt the forceful pulse of a headache as the room tilted into a repetitive loop.

My dad entered, already dressed for the wedding ceremony. "Charlotte," his voice boomed, "I'd like to talk to you." He sat down at the edge of my bed while my mother headed for the door. He waited for her to leave before he spoke again. "I want to tell you why I chose Prince Young."

It was almost enough to make me sit up, but I stayed put. As my mother shut the door behind her, a strange thought came into my head: Do they even *like* each other? Why did it seem like when one came, the other left? Was I doomed to suffer a similar marriage?

My father continued, jolting me from my thoughts. "As you know, I've had a very long-lasting friendship with the King of Vires. He is a wise man, able to appease his surrounding kingdoms with gestures of peace and fair political dealings." He scratched at his beard. "Because of this, his military has grown quite strong where ours has grown weak due to ever-present war. Reports from the front lines say the Drethen Kingdom is close to breaking through. Someday you and Young will take my place and I'd like to leave you in a secure kingdom. It's what every father wants for his daughter."

I sighed. "Father, I know."

"But what you don't know—is why I chose Young specifically." He paused and waited for me to respond. I didn't move. He had my attention. That was all I had to give. "I was in Vires about ten years ago, visiting the king, when I came across his three sons playing in the garden. The eldest, Sumin, was in a scuffle with the middle boy Minseo. Young, who was no older than eight, was sitting in the grass with his eyes closed, his face turned to the sun."

I sat up slowly, resting my head in my hand.

"As I got closer, I could hear the young boys arguing about which of them would be the king in their game. *I'm taller and I'm older,* Sumin yelled. *You always get to be king!* Minseo cried. Intrigued, I walked up to the youngest boy and asked him why he didn't want to be king. He blinked open his eyes in confusion, stood to face me, and said something along the lines of, 'Kingship is not a position that one can aspire to. You must be predestined or chosen. Do you see how they argue?' I nodded at the boy. He continued. 'It means they haven't chosen me, therefore I am not fit to lead them.' He took a seat. 'So I'll enjoy this fine weather until my time comes.'"

"What kind of eight-year-old talks like *that*?"

He tilted his head back in a wide, deep laugh that warmed me inside. "I don't recall his exact words, but the sentiment stood out in my memory. Besides, you're also a little..."

I shrunk. "Creative?"

He smiled. "Yes, creative. You just might be what each other nee—"

The door swung open and a guard rushed into the room, his face pale and covered in beads of sweat. He bowed, but not as low as usual. Out of breath, he handed my father a letter. My father opened it immediately while the guard caught his breath. My father's cheeks sunk in and his shoulders stiffened.

"What's wrong, father?" I asked. My heart thudded, matching the pace of the guard. Had Prince Young fled the kingdom from my drunken rampage?

"I—I have to go," he said. He jumped off the corner of my bed and headed for the door.

I stood up, feeling a surge of anxious energy rise to my chest. "Go? Go where?"

He shook off my question. "They've broken through," he blurted, half to himself. "You have to go too. To the southern castle." He mumbled something inaudibly, his gaze shifting back and forth. His gaze met mine. "Quickly. You must evacuate."

"What about the wedding?"

He shook his head. "The wedding is canceled."

6

PRINCE YOUNG

Everything was uncertain—my place in this kingdom, the future, and even our safety. The only two things I could really be sure of were that the kingdom was under attack and that the wedding was canceled. Drethen had broken through the front lines, and King Morgan of Besmium had gone to assist in the battle with as many Heims castle guards as he could rally on his way out. I wasn't sure exactly how close to the castle the battle was, but I did know the castle sat only a few days on horseback from the Drethen border. Which meant, if the king's men couldn't stop them, at best, we had only a few days to escape. At worst, a few hours. I stuffed the jacket and sash, meant for the wedding ceremony, into my trunk.

"Let's just go," Minseo said, pacing around the room.

I shook my head. "We can't just leave."

"We can. They canceled your wedding and this isn't our battle."

"If this attack was a day later, it would be our battle. Besides, we don't even know how bad this attack is."

"Did you hear the king? He said canceled. Not postponed, not delayed—canceled."

I knew he was right. This was a dangerous situation. We could get caught in the middle of a war without having any significant protection from either side. But was running away really *honorable*? If the king managed to negotiate peace, he'd likely resume the wedding. What would he think if his future king fled at the first sign of trouble?

Minseo continued, "I'll round up our guards and let them know we're heading ho—"

"I'm not going," I said, slamming my trunk closed. My words hung in the air between us.

Minseo stared at me in disbelief. His eyes narrowed and his chest puffed out. "You could *die*. We don't know how bad this is, or even how close to us the battle is."

"Why don't you go on ahead back to Vires?" I said. I stood and scanned my chamber for any more of my things. "You can tell father what's happened here and ask him if he'd be willing to send troops in support, despite the marriage contract's dissolution."

Minseo plopped down onto his bed. "You're my brother. I can't leave you behind. I'll send a message, but I'm not sure if there's enough time—"

A loud knock at the door captured our attention. Minseo leaped to his feet. We held our breath as we waited for the door to open as if about to find out that the sky had fallen. The queen strode in. Minseo and I froze. She'd hardly acknowledged us since we'd arrived, and now she barged into our chamber without introduction. It meant only one thing—bad news.

The queen's voice was forced and uneven. "Prince Young, our kingdom is not in the position to ask any favors of you. However—"

Minseo cut in. "Your majesty, we were about to send a message to my father, asking for aid in this conflict."

A glimmer of irritation flashed across her eyes, then she softened. "That's very kind. However, the king has asked something else of you, something of a different nature. He's asked that you and your guard accompany a small group to the Valor Castle in the south of Besmium. We can't spare our guards at the moment, and the king would like our daughter protected."

"Is the negotiation not going well?" I said, trying to grab clues from her stone-like expression.

She huffed. "The king takes every precaution when it comes to his daughter." She looked me up and down and added, "Although, I can't say I agree with all of his choices."

I bowed deeply, ignoring her attempt to fluster me. "I accept this quest, Your Majesty."

She returned the bow half-heartedly and hurried out.

I turned to Minseo. "Ready the carriage and the guard. Send out the message to father."

"Young," Minseo said.

"Make sure that everyth—"

"Young."

"What?" I asked, noticing the perplexed look spread across his face.

He chuckled. "You're not king yet."

I sheathed my sword and prepared for the mission ahead.

Adrenaline pulsed through me as we made our way through the castle. Everywhere I looked, servants and guards rushed about, carrying bags and weapons in every direction with profound urgency. I couldn't focus on the evacuation, not after the news that the wedding was canceled. I clenched my jaw in frustration. How was Charlotte taking the news? My thoughts flashed to the night before. *I don't want to marry anyone,* she'd said. I bristled at the thought that Charlotte might rejoice from this news, even if her kingdom was in danger. When my preparations had been made, finally, I had an opportunity to prove myself. I balled my hands into fists in anticipation. Only one part of this mission concerned me—the princess.

I hustled through the corridors of the castle to collect Princess Charlotte, remembering the way from last night. I knocked on the double door, my nervousness swelling. No response. I had my fist ready to knock again when one door swung open. In front of me stood the crystal-eyed blonde from last night. She clutched a wooden cross that hung from a bare string around her neck.

"Milly..." I said, the words barely a whisper.

She curtsied. "Hello, Your Highness. The princess has asked me to accompany her on this evacuation."

A voice shot out from behind her. "Vacation, not evacuation. My father will fix this. This is just temporary," Charlotte said, pushing the second door open.

I had to step back to avoid being hit. I nodded, my gaze darting between the two foreign-looking girls. I didn't know why, but a twinge of guilt settled at the bottom of my stomach. I turned my attention to Charlotte. "Charlotte, it is my intention to keep you safe during this evac—forgive me, vacation."

That afternoon when the sun was almost at its midpoint, the halls of the castle had almost cleared. I helped the two ladies into the carriage, which already held my brother, the royal dresser—Philip, and two other men I recognized as high-ranking members of the court. I was the last to enter. As I took my seat, my stomach clenched at the way Charlotte's gaze met Minseo's so quickly.

I settled in for the long ride as the horses neared the outer gates of Hiems Castle.

We were only ten yards away from the front gate when the first cannonball hit the castle walls. The horses bucked. The carriage shook, launching seven bodies into chaos. I glimpsed an orange orb crash beside the carriage as balls of fire rained down around us. The crackle of war sounded. The air filled with dust and smoke, filling my lungs and stinging my eyes. I choked. The world darkened as screams reverberated off every surface and rattled my bones. We scrambled to break free from the carriage just in time to see the walls of the castle crumble down around us, blocking our escape.

7

PRINCESS CHARLOTTE

The first sound I heard was the crack of stone hitting the castle walls. The second was the furious neighs of the horses. The carriage jerked. Our bodies tossed around in the cabin in a mess of limbs and colliding bones until someone's hands pushed me out onto the cemented ground. I crawled away, still in danger of being hit by the crazed horses and giant wheels. My head throbbed. A hot warm liquid slid down my forehead. Bodies lay around me as dark masses in the smoke and dust. The horses bucked until released from the rig. The carriage flipped as a ball of fire engulfed it. *Was someone still inside?*

"Milly!" I screamed. My body lurched toward the flames. Milly stood over me, pulling me to my feet. Relief washed over me and I squeezed her hand hard as if our locked hands could protect us from the attack like a child's blanket protects from darkness. Another flaming ball hit the ground a few yards away.

Young and Minseo propped up Phillip between them, then dragged him toward us—two Viran guards at their sides.

Minseo said, "Let's make a break for the gate. It's closer than the castle. If we make it out—"

Another ball of fire hit a few feet away, sending dust all around us, the heat of it on my skin. Milly let out a blood-curdling scream. She fell to her knees, covering her face with her hands. Young ran to us then lifted Milly's chin, looking her in the eyes. "Breathe," he said. "I need you to keep your head up. You can see them coming. You can avoid them. They're aiming for the walls, so as soon as we get away from them, this will be over."

She nodded and Young helped her to her feet, tears still streaming down her face. He wrapped his arm around her, turning his attention to our group. "Let's stay together," he said.

My gaze lingered on Young, who had his arm around Milly. Had I missed something? I shook the thought from my mind.

Minseo led the way, still supporting Phillip who limped clumsily at his side. Behind him were the two guards from Vires. Where were the other Viran guards? Dead? Mixed up in the attack? Young and I clenched Milly's arms as we ambled toward the broken gates.

Trumpets sounded behind us as Hiems Castle guards poured out of the castle we were fleeing. I felt my heart leap. We were *saved.*

"Young, behind us!" I yelled. “The guards!”

"Should we go back?" Young called, looking over his shoulder.

Minseo shook his head. "No, we're so close."

The fire in front of us surged upwards like an orange tidal wave. Heat licked out towards us like slithering serpents, biting at our cheeks. We turned away. Our path to escape engulfed in black and red. I gasped for fresh air but inhaled a gulp of thick gray smoke that scalded my throat.

We turned to Minseo who stood in stunned silence, watching our escape burn. The crack of fireballs ceased and the only sound was the crackle of the burning courtyard. Minseo turned with a look of terror so hair-raising that it made my stomach drop. "Run!" he screamed.

We turned and ran back toward the castle—toward the charging Besmium guard. The encroaching flames closed in, spreading faster with each moment. My body soaked in sweat as my lungs filled with smoke and dust, but I didn't slow down.

The northern wall collapsed, its broken stones raining into the courtyard inferno. I eyed the opening as my numb legs carried me towards the castle. Over the rubble, the silhouette of enemy soldiers sliding into the fray stopped my heart. Of all the years we'd been at war, I'd never actually seen an enemy soldier—until now. They leaked into the burning arena and began to engage with the Besmian soldiers. If they could hold them off a little longer, we might make it back to the castle.

The smoke obscured my vision, but I could hear the clang of metal, the cries of wounded soldiers. Nausea threatened to overcome me. A loud crack pulled my attention back to the northern wall. I glanced back over my shoulder to see a second chunk of the wall collapsed, this one bigger than the last. Blue-suited soldiers charged in from behind us. Exhaustion and oxygen deprivation blurred my vision. My legs slowed.

Drethen soldiers closed in from the left, and now behind us.

Just steps ahead. I focused on our salvation—our guards. My mind raced. *We're not going to make it.* I heard the furious howls of the blood-thirsty nation behind us as they cleared the crumbled walls and charged across the far end of the courtyard. *We're not going to make it.* I glanced back. *Minseo.*

Minseo, with Phillip on his back, was several strides behind—the enemy inches away. "Young!" I screamed.

He looked back. "Take Milly and get to the castle."

He unsheathed his sword and turned toward the battle. My leg muscles shook, threatening to give out, but we were almost there now. I didn't dare look back. I ran, my hand tightly gripping Milly's arm. The front line of Hiems guards parted to clear a path for us. *We made it.* With each row of soldiers we passed, we felt safer, but we didn't slow down or catch our breath until we reached the inside of the castle. The clash of the battle outside rattled the corridors. I toppled over in exhaustion, finally looking back. There was no sign of Minseo, Young, or Phillip in the sea of soldiers.

When we caught our breath, we raced through the corridor toward a tower staircase. The tunnels beneath the castle were our only hope now. I became increasingly aware of how empty the castle felt. Every guard had joined the battle at the front. I'd never seen the entrance hall so deserted.

An unfamiliar voice filled the hall. "Aye, you reckon we'll be heroes when we return home, mate?"

"You slob, the battle's not even over! Never count your women before they've been paid for." Laughter reverberated off the ceiling.

The enemy was *inside* the castle. I pulled Milly backward, now conscious of the scratchy chuff of our shoes on the stone floor. The Drethen soldiers were blocking our only way to the tunnels, and although I wasn't sure, it could've been the path they used to get inside. They were headed our way. I pulled Milly into the closest room, a medium dining room with a grand fireplace, and closed the door, locking it behind us.

The voices in the hallway grew louder. "Now what? We found a way in, so where's the king? Bet you I'd be promoted if I was the one to take him down. No doubt hiding like a rat in this dump."

"I heard we already got him. He came out to fight the battle and one of our boys got 'im."

A dull thud sounded. "You ninny. If they'd killed the king, why are we still fighting? Honestly, it's like I'm the only man here with any brains at all."

I gasped as my heart crunched in on itself, feeling like my soul briefly left my body and stabbed its way back through my skin one shard at a time. Was my father *dead?*

The soldier spoke. "Whatever, mate, I'm sure some of the king's whores are still somewhere lurking around the castle. You hear that, ladies?" he called. "Your king is dead! I'm your king now." They laughed.

The other chortled, "Don't be shy!"

Trapped like a thief in my childhood home, the walls caved in around me. My father's sudden departure. Something dark tore through me.

"This kingdom belongs to us now." His voice lowered, "But I'm telling you, I'm not going to live here," the soldier said, his voice just on the other side of the door.

My body shook with rage until an alarming calm took over. I walked over to the fireplace and pulled a fire-iron from the dying embers.

"Wh-what are you doing?" Milly whispered. "You can't go out there."

"Stay hidden," I said.

"You *can't* go out there," she said, squeezing my arm.

I shook her off and walked over to the door, unlocking it with a *click.*

"Yes, I can."

8

PRINCE YOUNG

I ran to Minseo, who was fighting back a large Drethen soldier. With the two Viran guards covering his sides, I clashed swords with the enemy, freeing Minseo's sword. He thrust his sword forward, stabbing into the enemy. Minseo pulled his sword free and stumbled back, bewildered. Several Besmium guards rushed over to us. In the confusion of the castle guards colliding with the Drethen soldiers, Phillip crawled toward the castle, but I never looked back to see if he made it.

I held my sword horizontally as a bearded soldier in front of me attempted to slice me in two. The clang of every weapon in the mass of soldiers and guards set my nerves on high alert. My life hung by a thread between inches of fatal attacks. Though we'd made it to the Besmian guards, it still felt like we were outnumbered. Drethen soldiers poured through the fallen walls. The red banners waved on either side of the castle entrance, but the Drethen soldiers continued to push forward and blue banners inched forward as one Besmian soldier fell after the other.

"We need to get back to the castle!" Minseo yelled. His gaze glued to the bloody tip of his sword.

He was right. Our movements were slowing. My limbs were shaking.

"Together," I called.

He nodded as we slowly inched backward, blocking the incoming attacks.

My father taught my brothers and me to wield a sword from a very young age. Sumin and Minseo started when they were nine and eight and I was only six at the time. However, my father knew once their training began, I'd never be able to sit idly by and watch. My mother protested but was overruled. I'd taken to it faster than my brothers. I loved the weight of the blade and the momentum that built every time I swung it. Over the years, my brothers and I got quite good, and we sparred as often as our studies allowed. I often wondered if I would ever have a need for my sword—other than the art form it had become. I believed the thrill of battle was my purpose.

An enemy soldier on horseback approached us as Minseo and I fought off a fresh wave of blue-adorned men. The soldier on the horse yelled, the soldiers in the vicinity halted and turned, all as one, to Minseo. My stomach dropped. They're after Minseo! A group of soldiers swarmed him. My focus intensified. *Not my brother.* I lunged at the closest soldier, my sword more determined than ever. My blade plunged into a soldier in blue. He looked me in the eyes, the paleness of them screaming the word *why,* the shock in his furrowed brow reflecting my own. My gaze darted back to Minseo, whose sword was wrenched from his hands. Desperate, I tried to pull my blood-stained sword from the soldier's limp body, but his essence suctioned onto it. "Minseo!" I screamed. Tears sprang to my eyes as adrenaline pulsed through my arms. I put my foot against the bloodstained armor and wrenched my blade from his flesh.

I snapped my attention back to Minseo. A group of Drethen soldiers dragged him, several men restraining each of his limbs, pulling him further from reach. His gaze met mine with a soft and relaxed expression that whispered, "I surrender." My stomach tightened. "No, brother." I sobbed. Don't give up.

Crazed, I swung my sword wildly. I'll save you. A Viran soldier grabbed my shoulder but I shrugged him off, leaping toward the enemy. Several more allied soldiers pulled me back. I searched the crowded field for Minseo but he was gone and there was an army between us. My body weakened. *I'm going to die here.* I glanced back at the castle. Behind the rows of red-suited soldiers was a line of blue flags. Are they coming from the castle? We're *surrounded.* Dazed with grief and exhaustion, I felt myself resign. I fell to my knees and let out an agonizing scream that drained me. If the castle was overrun, this battle was over.

My mind jumped to Charlotte. She was inside the castle and all her soldiers were out here. Before my mind could contemplate any of the worst-case-scenarios, my body moved. I couldn't save my brother, I couldn't save myself, but maybe I could save her.

As I approached the castle, I readied my mind and blade for another fatality. A cry of pain rang out and my gaze snapped to a youthful-looking Besmium guard, with several Drethen corpses strewn in front of him. I slipped through a cloud of smoke and felt the heat of a withering fire beneath my boots. I raced toward the guard, avoiding another fight if I could help it. The guard's eyes flickered with confusion as I approached him.

"Where's the princess?" he asked as he cleared a path for me.

Out of breath, I huffed, "The castle." I glared at the blue banners. "I think the enemy is getting in the castle some other way. She's in danger." I eyed the bodies around us. "Who are you?"

“Leon.”

I nodded, "Leon, get a group, as many as you can, and concentrate on reclaiming the castle. We can cut off their way in if we can drive them out. Once inside, I'll get the princess."

"Yes, sir," he said, turning back towards his unit.

"Leon!" I called.

He turned back to me, but the words stuck to the roof of my mouth before they finally emerged. "They took my brother."

Leon nodded understandingly and returned to gather his troops. Several minutes later he had gathered four soldiers to cut through the last line of Drethens. It didn’t seem like it would be enough. Surrounded by the enemy, fighting for their lives, Leon and the other Besmium soldiers rallied, pushing their way back to their castle. With each man they cut down, they freed a Besmian soldier to help them get me to the castle. Beside Leon, I fell into a rhythm, cutting through row after row of hostile enemies. I slammed my sword down, clashing it into the helmet of a Drethen. I leaped over him and hustled into the castle, knowing there would be more danger inside. I dashed through the hallway toward Charlotte's room. I didn't know where she would go, but it was one of the few places in the castle that I even knew.

I heard her voice in the corridor ahead. "Please don't hurt me."

My mouth dried as her fear rang through the halls.

A gravelly voice replied, "You hurt my friend, it's only fair."

I sprinted toward the voices when a metallic clang sounded. I clenched my jaw, dread seeping into me. A dull thud reverberated off the walls. She was dead. I was too late. Out of breath, I turned the corner to see two piles of flesh and blood on the floor.

The princess stood above them, unscathed, holding a blood-spattered iron rod still glowing red.

9

PRINCESS CHARLOTTE

The moment I saw Young, all the power I'd felt moments ago melted away. I was a blood-spattered princess standing amidst a murder scene, one I'd starred in. My gaze met his, and I searched for the horror I felt, in his dark eyes, but couldn't find it. I glanced over the gentle lines of his expression and drank in the easiness of his parted lips. He exhaled relief and I felt the sudden pull of my body towards him as I breathed it in. I couldn't discern how he could look upon me, with such reprieve, then I took a step forward. And another. He was my cage, my captor, the death of my freedom, but in one kind glance, in my darkest hour, he granted me a modicum of comfort. I ran to him and threw myself into his arms. I didn't care that he didn't embrace me. I didn't care that his body tightened with discomfort. He was *alive* and, to me, that meant that my father could be too.

"Milly's over here," I sniffed as I motioned to the door. I felt the pulse of my hand as I released the fire poker from my finger-numbing grip. It fell to the floor with a clang and I stared at my hands as they shook. Blood was everywhere. It dripped from my fingertips and pooled on the stone floor. As the adrenaline waned, the horror of what I'd just done sunk in. I bit back the urge to scream. I backed away.

"Hey," Young called, dragging my attention back to him. He shook his head. "Look at me."

My heart pounded as my mind slipped back towards the lifeless heaps on the floor, dragging my gaze to them.

"Charlotte," Young called, but he was a distant voice floating negligibly through the back of my mind. Young stepped in front of me, blocking my view of the corpses. He took a firm grip of my wrist as if to hold me to the earth. I felt the warmth of his breath on my forehead, and the steady beat of his heart as his chest pressed against mine. My body numbed. My gaze crept up to his chin and stopped at his lips. My breath synchronized with his. I lifted my chin, my gaze meeting his. His dark eyes peered down at me, black as a moonless night with just as many stars. I searched them for clues, but if he felt something, he showed nothing at all.

Feeling rushed back to my body all at once. I reached for my wrist and pried it out of his hand just in time to feel the bile rise from my stomach. I doubled over and vomited an acid more bitter than the emotions that caused it.

When I caught my breath, I stood, feeling a sense of frailty in my legs that wasn't there before. I looked up at Young. "Where's—"

"He's still out there," Young replied, his voice so even and smooth it sounded like a lie.

A voice shot out from behind Young. "Prince Young, you found the princess." A brown-haired boy in a soldier's uniform approached. He couldn't have been older than me. He had a baby face, softly curved features, and not a bit of hair on his chin. He looked more like a boy in costume than a warrior.

"Leon," Young said as he walked over to shake his hand. "Yeah, thanks to you."

Young turned to me. “Charlotte, grab Milly. I’m going to... uh,” he tucked his dark hair behind his ear, “clean up.”

I nodded and returned to the dining room where I knew Milly was hidden.

"Milly, it's me," I looked around. "It's safe." I said the words, but I wasn't sure how true they were.

Milly crawled out from behind a sofa. Her eyes widened. "You're covered in *blood*." She lifted her arms in front of her body and clutched the hand-carved cross hanging from her neck.

"No, it's okay. I'm fine," I said, moving toward her.

She backed away, terror still in her eyes. "You *killed* them?"

I shook my head. "N-no. I saved us. If I hadn't done that, they would have—" Blood. So much blood. I shivered.

"Passed by," she whispered.

"Milly..." Guilt seared my skin. It was the last emotion in the world I could stomach in this situation. I clenched my jaw with rage. They'd invaded my home, they might have killed my father, they could have killed us. I'd acted in the way that I thought was right, but looking into Milly's eyes, it was obvious she felt different. Doubt started to creep in. The guilt slithered down my spine as Milly backed away. She thought I was a monster and maybe she was right.

The door swung open and Leon and Young hustled in.

"Leon has a plan," Young said. He paused, noticing the tension in the room. His gaze moved from Milly to me. His eyebrow raised and he spoke, "That was a brave thing you did to save your friend, Charlotte." He turned to Milly, his jaw clenched. "Let's go."

I felt a warm vibration of gratitude pulse inside me. Before I could give it another thought, Young and Leon ushered Milly and myself out of the room and down the hallway. They carefully checked each corner before moving us along. I stared at Milly’s back and bit down hard on my bottom lip. I wanted to reach out to

Milly to tell her it was okay—to let her know we were in this together—but she wouldn't look at me. I saw the queasy look on her face when she'd seen the bodies of the two Drethen soldiers slumped into the corner in the hallway. It could take a while, but I'd get her back somehow—she was all I had left.

We rounded the corner to the staircase in the east tower. The stone platforms wrapped around the tower led up to several bedrooms, one of which I had used to shoot an arrow at the prince when he arrived, and another down to a tunnel below the castle that exited a mile in the opposite direction. If we could make it out, we'd have a decent chance of escaping.

I whispered, "I think they're getting in this way." Leon nodded and took the lead, followed by Milly, me, and Young just behind me. We descended the stairs into the poorly torch-lit tunnel. We paused at the entrance to listen for the enemy, but all we heard was the occasional drip of something leaking and the distant sounds of battle.

We hustled through, still on our guard. The darkness reminded me of the fear I'd felt as a child. My mind always twisted the shadows into monsters. Now, as I trudged along, the monsters took a new form. Did my mother make it out? Was my father really dead? I reached out for Milly's hair for comfort as it shone in the torchlight as we passed, but I stopped myself as I remembered Young was behind me. We walked single-file in a tense, uninterrupted silence the entire mile, expecting to hear someone shout. As we shuffled through the darkness, I picked at my hands, trying to focus on the faint light at the end as it grew nearer.

We stepped out into the sunshine. My eyes locked onto two men in blue standing nearby.

"Eh! Who the hell is that?" a scruffy Drethen soldier called.

Leon sighed with relief. "Only two."

His confidence put me at ease as the two soldiers approached us.

Young turned back to me. "Charlotte, you want to get this one or..." he trailed off.

I shook my head in disbelief. I would have missed it if I wasn't looking so closely, but unmistakably, the corners of his mouth tilted up just a smidge before he turned and readied himself for a fight. Was that a *joke*? Now? I felt something flutter inside me and quickly shook it off. I turned to Milly and pulled her into me, burying her face in my shoulder so she couldn't see. "Cover your ears," I whispered.

10

PRINCE YOUNG

Every step away from the castle, I felt a little safer and a little more panicked about leaving my brother behind. There I was guiding the princess of "Oh, I'm marrying you?" to safety, while my brother was being dragged into enemy territory, or worse. I glanced over at Charlotte, her arm wrapped tightly around Milly's shoulder. My gaze lingered on her blood-spattered dress. I had to admit, she wasn't exactly like my first impression of her. Even now as the glisten of fresh tears streaked her face, her strength was evident. She followed Leon and I with sure, decisive steps as she moved away from the only home she knew. Her gaze met mine. I flinched and snapped my attention forward.

We arrived at the forest's edge. The warm green of the trees and the lush fern-covered ground was untouched by war. The crevices of the wood teemed with life, unlike the death-stained castle we'd escaped. The sounds of war could no longer be heard, giving us the illusion of safety, but I knew that with two dead guards outside the castle, the enemy wouldn't be far behind. The birds chirped playfully unperturbed, and for a moment I felt myself yield to the serene environment. *Minseo.* A lump lurched to the back of my throat. My knees weakened. I clenched my jaw, hoping to bite back my tears until it was sore and I had to release.

We came to a slow-flowing river, its bank littered with wide trees that stretched high above us, impeding strands of the setting sun.

Still battling my urge to cry, I knelt beside the river, dipped my hands in, and washed my face. I scrubbed at the dried bits of blood on my hands and drank until I was certain I'd suffocate. Leon slumped against a large tree. I could see the exhaustion in his movements but he continued to smile, a trait that perplexed me. The girls exchanged solemn looks by the river and whispered, but I was happy to not be a part of the conversation.

After a few short minutes, Leon rose. "Follow this river," he said. "It should take you about five days on foot." He ran a blood-stained hand through his brown hair. "You can see the southern castle from this river."

I leaped up. "You're *leaving?*"

He smiled widely. "Yeah. Did you think I forgot about my *other* mission? Prince Minseo." He rested his hand on my shoulder. A rush of emotions hit me in waves. Relief, gratitude, hope. I shook his hand and he turned to leave. I wasn't sure if he was too late to help Minseo or what difference one soldier could make, but having someone like him looking for my brother gave me hope. I'd seen firsthand what he could do.

"Be careful." I shook his hand, suppressing my urge to bow—my kingdom's custom.

He huffed. "*You* be careful." A devious smile flickered across his face. Confused, I followed his gaze to Milly and Charlotte. Leon smirked and headed back towards the direction of the castle. I felt a pang of embarrassment. That kind of sexual joke reminded me of Minseo, though it wasn't a social norm in Vires. If Leon did rescue

Minseo, they might just get along. I waited for the warmth to dispel from my cheeks before turning back to the girls.

"Is he coming back?" Milly asked as she instinctively reached for her cross.

I shook my head. I didn't want to tell her that Leon was going to try to find Minseo. "We are going to the southern castle without him." Her eyes bulged. Milly was right to worry. She and the princess would be safer if Leon stayed with us for the journey. I chose to let him go for Minseo. "It'll be fine," I added. "I'll keep you both safe."

Milly's face went white. "How much farther do we have to go tonight?"

I eyed the direction we came from. "The farther the better."

She dropped her head. She lifted her dress slightly, revealing a disproportionately swollen ankle. "I need to rest."

Charlotte gasped and rushed over. "When did it happen?"

Milly shook her head.

"Let's cool it down in the river," Charlotte asked, supporting Milly's weight on her hip.

"Young," Charlotte said, tucking her hair behind her ear. "I was wondering if you could give me a few minutes to help Milly and wash some of this bl—" Her gaze flickered to Milly before falling back to me, "to wash some of this dirt off my dress?"

"Ah." Leon's joke jolted into my mind, searing my cheeks with warmth. I nodded. "I'll go see if I can find anything useful in these woods. I'll be in earshot though, so if anything happens just yell."

I turned into the woods and headed down river, debating whether we should put more distance between us and the battle or if we should camp here for nightfall so Milly could rest her ankle. Both were risky. Small bushes sprinkled the forest and were filled with black-colored berries that were familiar to me. They were also a common berry in Vires but were usually too bitter this time of year. Maybe with the change of climate… I popped one into my mouth and immediately crunched down on the stone-like bead. I spat it out almost immediately, but the bitterness of its skin lingered. *Fishing it is.*

I picked up a branch that split at the end and sat down beside a tree, sharpening its edges with my dagger. I'd most likely need a fire to cook the fish, but it might make us more vulnerable to attack. I clutched my stomach; we needed our strength. I'd been hunting and camping in Vires so often it felt like second nature, but it had always been for leisure and never with other people depending on me.

The sun hung low in the sky and began to set the sky ablaze with a sweltering orange—my mind heavy with thoughts of home—of Vires. I dusted myself off and carried my makeshift spear toward the river.

The river flickered orange as it licked its rocky banks. Tree branches stretched out over it, dropping leaves and branches into the current to be swept away. I breathed in the calm of the slow-moving current. My mind drifted back to Minseo, the fear in his eyes as they pulled him away. A shadow moved in the corner of my vision, drawing my full attention. I choked. Charlotte's bare shoulders glistened in the final rays of sunlight. I ducked behind a tree to block my vision. I thought I'd gone far enough away, but the river's current must have slowly guided her in this direction. I could even hear the scratch of Milly washing Charlotte's dress in the distance, though barely. My heart raced and I struggled for breath like I'd been chased by something.

I bit down on my bottom lip, afraid she'd hear me. She hadn't screamed. I didn't think she saw me. I planted my feet firmly on the ground, determined to hold my position, and closed my eyes, leaning back against the tree. Images of her glistening shoulders and her brown skin replayed in my mind. What was I *doing*? I listened for the sound of her moving through the water but heard nothing but the steady gurgling of the river as it flowed. Then I heard a soft splash. She was getting closer.

Surely I should make sure that she's okay. It was my job to get her to the southern castle safely, and that meant making sure she didn't drift too far. I reasoned with myself that I'd only look for a moment.

I knew that what I was about to do was wrong, but I couldn't find a way to talk myself out of it.

I turned to move but froze. Sharp, cold steel pricked my throat.

11

PRINCESS CHARLOTTE

I hadn't bathed in a river since I was a young child. Feeling the pull of the current relaxed me. I let myself drift along and tried to bury the feeling of looming danger and my fears about my father. I clenched my jaw and promised myself that what I'd heard wasn't true and that I'd see my father again.

"Madam!" a boisterous voice called. I dropped like a stone, hiding my shoulders and my bare body beneath the water. The voice continued from the dark of the forest. "I caught this deviant trying to catch an eyeful. He is subdued. I recommend that you adorn your clothing so that you may thank your hero."

I waded through the water towards Milly, who was already limping in my direction, my dress in hand. She shielded my body from the direction of the voice as I slipped into the damp fabric. A soldier? Drethen? How many were there?

I cleared my throat to alert to him that I was decent. "Where is Young?" I called. A broad-shouldered man walked out from the forest's edge. "Worry not, madam. You are safe." His icy blue eyes glistened, his white smile radiant, his blonde hair glossy. He was beautiful—and yet, he set off every alarm in my body.

I thought of how I'd reacted negatively to meeting Young the night before. How I'd seen Young as the chain that would lock me in the castle forever, but the man standing in front of me was different. Each brazen move of his body whispered one thing: *predator.*

The way he puffed up his chest when he spoke reminded me of the way many high-ranking politicos carried themselves at court. Using her wiles to control men with inflated egos was an area where my mother excelled. I once asked her why she didn't yell at these kinds of men or kick them out of court to knock them down a bit. She'd taken me by the chin and warned that men's fragility was dangerous when threatened, but easy to control when stroked. I didn't understand her at the time, but since that conversation I'd noticed that she handled tense situations with a smile, a complementary attitude, and an innocent but seductive gesture.

I curtsied. "Brave hero. Thank you for your assistance." I eyed the forest for Young. "Ugh."

My gaze landed on Young, who rubbed his head and stumbled forward in a daze.

I turned my attention back to the stranger. "This man here is my guard, merely charged with watching over me. I am certain if he was watching, it was in my best interest."

The blonde man looked unconvinced. We gazed at each other for a moment and it dawned on me that he wasn't aware who we were. I reasoned that the more we blended in the better.

He chuckled in a manner that felt insulting. "Ah, I love the naivety of women."

I cringed. Young stepped forward but the stranger casually blocked Young's path with his sword. I gulped as Young shook his head, disoriented.

Who was this strange man? He was wearing a green tabard over his armor. Not Drethen then. His accent was unmistakably Algonian. I huffed. "Regardless, please return my guard to me so that we may resume our journey."

His eyebrows raised. "Perhaps you would benefit from keeping more moral company."

"Generous hero," I said, my voice as hard and thankless as my mother's. "Have you heard that Hiems Castle is under attack by the Drethen army?"

He scoffed. "A woman shouldn't burden herself with such serious issues." Heat rushed to my face. He continued. "If you must know, I was summoned to offer my assistance as a gesture of alliance from the great kingdom of Algony."

All at once I understood. I didn't want to believe it, but he was just as the other courtiers described. Under my breath, my voice whispered, "Which means you're..."

A bright smile beamed from his dimpled cheeks. "Yes, my fortunate flower, I am Prince Emmett of Algony."

My stomach dropped. It was okay as long as he didn't know who I was. Something wasn't sitting well with me. Where were his guards? Who summoned him? How did he get here from Algony so quickly?

He continued, "I understand your shock and wonderment."

Young shook his head.

Emmett continued, "But it is customary for a peasant to bow to royalty once they reveal themselves."

I bit my tongue and began to curtsey.

Young's voice shot out. "Enough," he said as he knocked Emmett's sword out of his path with his own. He re-sheathed his sword. "You dare speak with the Princess of Besmium like this, you arrogant—"

His gaze caught mine, freezing him in place. *No.* Emmett's face lit with understanding as he dropped to one knee. "My princess, if I'd but known—"

My eyes narrowed. He'd believed that rather quickly. Was he *looking* for me? "So, you see why it's imperative that we make it to the southern castle in a timely fashion?"

Emmett rose and turned to Young. "Which means that you must be..."

Young bowed. "Prince Young of Vires."

"Yes... Vires." Emmett nodded, circling Young like a vulture. "Such an unusual choice the king made to turn to a distant kingdom for military assistance, especially with Algony just to the west. Now with Hiems burning to the ground, his kingdom may fall before your Viran forces arrive." He scoffed. "To think he refused my offer to take the young princess's hand, and yet, here I am to save the day. I really am a saint." He brushed a strand of his golden hair out of his eyes.

Young's expression was neutral. If Emmett had upset him, he didn't show it. "We'll be going."

“Princess,” Emmett said, “where’s your guard?”

I said, “I could ask you the same.” Emmett smiled, flashing his glistening white teeth.

“Well, good day to you,” Young said with a bow and a glare. He turned and began trudging through the greenery towards Milly and me.

Emmett scoffed as he disappeared behind a large patch of shrubbery. A moment later he reappeared, pulling the reigns of a restless horse before mounting it. He turned the horse toward the Hiems Castle and I felt the tension ease.

Emmet's voice rang out, "Vires, what a joke."

Young stopped.

I could taste the tension rising. "No, Young," I whispered.

He turned back to Emmett. "I am the future prince of

Besmium. I will give my life to protect it. What I don't understand is why *you* are here."

Emmett's eyes darkened as he turned his horse around with the grace of a dove. "So..." I felt the menacing nature of his words before he even finished. "What you're saying is..." a confident hand slid breezily through his silky locks, "you're not married."

12

PRINCE YOUNG

Killing was wrong. I knew that. Sure, you can defend yourself, but there had to be a better way to resolve a conflict with someone you don't like. I knew all of this, and yet I couldn't escape the nagging voice in my head that screamed, "Find a cliff and push Emmett off of it."

For one, who even was this guy? Secondly, something was off. He just happened to show up in *this* forest, all alone. Even the timing seemed too convenient. I didn't trust him. I'd doubt he was even a prince if he hadn't been barking orders at me from the moment he sucker-punched me with the hilt of his sword.

Despite a significant amount of protestation, the moment Emmett realized the throne was up for grabs, he was irrevocably tied to our quest to the southern castle, Cadere. For three days I had endured his boorish comments, his braggadocious prose, and worst of all, his attempts to court Charlotte. I'd hardly slept. I didn't trust Emmett to be alone with the girls, and I could feel the lack of sleep putting me on edge.

The fire crackled and snapped as the sun began to set on the river's edge. I tossed some dry branches into the fire and it sparkled with dancing embers, a brief show of gratitude, before simmering back into its steady form.

"My radiant flower," Emmett called. I cringed.

"I'm here," Charlotte said, stepping into the fire's light, Milly at her side. She smiled brightly, twirling her curly hair around her finger.

Emmett approached. "It's time for the hunt." He gestured to me. "One of us must stay behind to defend you helpless womenfolk, while the other finds us dinner. Who do you delegate to this task?"

I didn't budge. He gave this speech every night, and every night she responded the same way. As I suspected, she smiled and said, "Surely I can put my faith in you to find us something to eat."

His dimples deepened. "Fear not, princess, I won't fail you." He smirked at me.

“Emmett,” I called, the suddenness of my voice surprising myself. “Uh…” I continued zealously toward him then pulled him out of earshot of the girls. “Can I talk to you for a minute?” He eyed me warily.

I sighed, “Look, maybe we got off on the wrong foot.”

He grinned. “Come to your senses, have you?”

“I appreciate that you’re risking your life to help us reach Castle Cadere.”

He puffed up his chest. “And I appreciate you knowing your place.”

I swallowed my response and the empty air hung between us. “I’m betrothed to Charlotte and, when we reach the castle, I intend to marry her.” I held his gaze, though my stomach turned from how adamantly I’d meant what I’d just said. A glimmer of firelight glinted across his eyes. He tilted his head back and laughed, open-mouthed and loud. His gaze landed heavily back on me and I felt my cheeks burn red.

"You're serious?" He wheezed. "There is no conceivable advantage you have over me."

I shifted my weight. "I-I don't see it that way."

"Your military is too far, your personality is dry, and…" He covered his mouth with his hands. "Just look at you." He grinned. "And more importantly, look at me."

I blinked with disbelief.

"Fair skin, eyes the color of beryl stone, golden locks."

I huffed. "So, I imagine in your world that's superior somehow?"

"In every world that's superior."

"You do realize that Charlotte doesn't have any of those traits, right?"

"And I'm willing to overlook that. Do you see how generous I can be?"

I leaned closer to him. "I think you're vastly overestimating yourself and underestimating me."

"Please, you look like the stable boy who washes the weapons for the child of my sparring partner."

I smirked. "Want to try again?"

"Your arms are like the string on my…" He nudged a rock with his foot. "Whatever, I should get to my hunt."

"Have at it," I said, heading back towards the fire.

He disappeared into the woods, but I could still hear the loud crunch of his footsteps. As soon as he was out of sight, Charlotte's demeanor changed. Her smile faded, her posture slumped, and she released the strand of hair she often twirled. Charlotte sat a few paces away from the fire and Milly made her way around it, taking a scat beside me.

I couldn't help but glare at Charlotte. Emmett had barely been gone five minutes and Charlotte was already missing him. Why was she acting like this? It was all over her face. A sliver of doubt crept in that maybe Charlotte was more attracted to him than me, plus he showered her with compliments—but it just didn't seem possible for any woman to be interested in such a deplorable man. Yet here I was, witnessing it all. She clearly liked him, reciprocating everything he threw at her. Emmett had given the same treatment to Milly until he'd realized she had no title or ranking, then he basically pretended she didn't exist for the past few days. Charlotte didn't even seem to mind. Where was her loyalty? I didn't care if Charlotte was interested in someone—even if I was obviously a better man—so why *him*?

I puffed up my chest to make myself look bigger, and instantly deflated. I'm an idiot. I felt the warmth rush to my face, hotter than the heat coming off the fire. Milly's hand touched mine, jolting me back from my thoughts. "You're doing great," she said, the fire's light illuminating her yellow hair.

I pulled my hand away.

She continued. "Prince Emmett is difficult to tolerate."

"Yeah, he's been pretty rude to you."

She turned back to the fire. "To you too, and you've managed to stay calm. Charlotte appreciates it."

I gazed at Charlotte through the fire. I knew she couldn't possibly like Emmett, but I just needed to hear it confirmed. "I'm sure they'll be happy together."

Milly snorted. I turned to her. A bright smile spread across her lips. Her eyes searched my face for something, but when she didn't find it her smile waned. "You're serious? Okay, you should talk to Charlotte."

"What is it? Just tell me." *Confirm it.*

She shook her head. "It doesn't seem like my place. Just go talk to her for a minute."

I let out a labored sigh and made my way over to Charlotte, my legs jellied as I neared. The fire popped and released a handful of yellow embers into the sky. I sat down beside her, suddenly hyper-aware of my hands and where I should rest them. On my knee? Should I clasp them together? She turned to me and smiled, flashing a glimpse of her pearly teeth, but there was no joy in her eyes. I felt unsettled at the bottom of my stomach and I studied her face for clues. She crinkled her forehead for a second before returning to her smile. She was unraveling. "Charlotte," I whispered. The first few tears fell to her cheeks and she covered her face with her hands.

I froze. I didn't know how to comfort her. I didn't even know what was wrong. She seemed just fine yesterday. Not happy, but fine. Why suddenly when I sat beside her did she fall apart?

"My father," she sobbed, "my mother... the kingdom." I could barely make out what she was saying, but I understood the feeling. *My brother.* She weakened me and I swallowed back my urge to cry with her. It had been a hard few days. I wondered if that had something to do with how she was acting toward Emmett. Was it possible that she was *afraid* of him?

She slumped into me, her curls falling over to tickle my cheek. I felt her sniffle against my chest, my pulse rising with each stifled breath. “Charlotte,” I whispered. My heart slammed against my ribcage, and I worried she could hear it. Here we were again. The wet of her tears soaked through my shirt. “Charlotte,” I began again. The fire raged in front of us, suddenly heating my whole body. My mind flashed to what I’d said to Emmett about marrying her. He was wrong about me. I was more than he knew, and as Charlotte nestled closer to my chest, I thought I might be more than I knew too. I stared in silent observation, frozen until I felt the rare urge to wrap my arms around her like Milly had that night. I lifted my arm and stopped a few inches away from her shoulder. What was I doing? I didn't know how to comfort her. She'd just lost her whole family. Panic surged through me. I leaped to my feet. Charlotte jolted back, gazing up at me with widened eyes and confusion.

"Milly," I called, "Charlotte needs you."

13

PRINCESS CHARLOTTE

I was alone. That was clear to me now.

For a second, it felt like Young was an ally in all this. He had understood, he had taken my side, and he hadn't left me throughout this whole ordeal—until now. I'd let myself fall apart for a moment and he'd proven to be no more substantial than Emmett. Milly had always been a pillar of comfort in my life, but ever since the incident, when I was forced to kill those men, Milly hadn't felt like a person I could count on.

Milly rushed over to me and dutifully put her arms around me. But I could tell it was more out of habit than anything else and I didn't need it, not out of obligation. I didn't need a servant or a prince, I needed a friend. I shouldn't have let myself cry. My parents would want me to keep going.

The orange glow of the fire seemed to suck the sunset out of the sky. Emmett shortly returned with the carcass of something and proceeded to roast it on the fire, taking the silence as his cue to regale us with stories of his past adventures. Normally this would annoy us, but tonight it was a welcome distraction.

"And when I was just four years old," Emmett boasted, "I climbed to the top of the tallest mountain in Algony on my own, with nothing but a small blade and the will to look down-"

I felt Young's gaze on my face across the fire.

Emmett's voice rose. "Then at the tender age of seven, I departed from my beloved kingdom in search of..."

I willed myself to continue to listen to Emmett—anything to avoid looking at Young. I didn't want to see his false sympathy. I didn't want to see him mouth an apology. I wasn't angry, just done.

"Where I pulled the sword Excalibur from a large rock."

My gaze drifted up along the fire's edge, drawn like a ship caught in the tide. I felt myself losing an internal battle against my own curiosity.

"... but I had no interest in their filthy kingdom," Emmett continued.

I surrendered. My gaze met Young's and I held it, challenging him to look away.

"I merely returned the sword back to its stone, and I've been told it's still there."

I felt my skin prickle beneath his unwavering stare. He gave nothing away. Something hot radiated from my forehead down to my chest as if my body understood his message but my brain didn't know how to translate it.

"Princess Charlotte," Emmett said, blocking my line of sight to Young and the edge of the fire. I felt cold on my face where Emmett had snuffed out the fire's light. "Weren't you listening?"

I sat up straight. "Uh... yes. The uh... mountain—"

Young interrupted. "Charlotte seemed enthralled by your tale of Excalibur." I nodded as Young continued. "It's no wonder you've left the princess out of breath. I bet you have another fine story to tell."

Emmett beamed. "Of course she loves it." His chest puffed up and he sat back down an equal distance between Young and me and began prattling on again. I was struck by the word princess as it came off Young's lips. It was something I was called by most people but Young hardly ever said it. He usually called me just Charlotte, so hearing princess from his mouth sounded like an insult and not a title.

When Emmett's storytelling finally exhausted him, he walked back over, motioning to Milly to leave my side. She got up and took a seat beside Young on the other side of the fire. I knew I had to muster whatever energy I had left to keep Emmett appeased.

Emmett leaned in close. "Fair Princess, did you enjoy your dinner?"

"Very much," I said with a smile.

"Only the finest for a woman in my company."

I was worn out from playing this part, but I could feel the girl I was a week ago telling me it was exciting. I was starting to realize things were more fun before they were real. Suddenly, I was being courted. I was speaking to a handsome prince around my age. It was a scenario I'd often fantasized about while waiting for my parents to decide I was old enough to be courted. Although courting in my case was never going to be more than meeting a man my parents had already agreed to bind me to. I didn't want to be married. Not yet. But this part, the courting, seemed glamorous. I guess I never imagined it would be so much work or with someone who so severely repulsed me. There was nothing romantic about it. It was politics for the sake of survival—just like everything else in my world.

I pulled a strand of my hair out of my face. "You have quite a gift for storytelling."

I heard a laugh across the fire. Milly leaned into Young with a bright smile and tucked a strand of her summery hair behind her ear. I could hear a wisp of her voice across the fire, but I couldn't make out what they were saying.

Emmett said, "Thank you, Princess. I have quite a life."

I nodded. "So that stuff is all true?"

My eyes wandered back to Milly as she giggled once again. Her laugh was so infectious it made me smile too. I wondered what was funny.

Emmett sighed. "Well, it's mostly true. Embellished in some areas as all great stories are."

"Yes, it sounds like it takes a lot of skill," I said.

Young's laugh floated across the fire, grasping my attention. It was a sound I'd never heard before, and I realized I'd been listening out for. The moment I heard Milly laugh, I'd been dreading it, and somehow it was worse than I expected.

14

PRINCE YOUNG

I knew I'd messed things up with Charlotte. It only took me a moment of her reaction for it to click. I'd tried to signal my apology to her by the fire and to assist her with Emmett, but this morning she wouldn't even look at me. Lucky for me, Milly seemed to be in good spirits. At least *she* didn't hate me.

Emmett watered his horse as I scouted ahead. I lumbered through the forest, the gentle rustle of the trees, carried the foggy haze of early morning. With the sun not high enough in the sky to warm the air, I felt a chill similar to the feeling of stepping into the coolness of the river. The area ahead of last night's camp was not as densely wooded, and the forest floor thrived with overgrown ferns and shrubbery. I made a mental note to tell our group to step carefully through them and also noted a patch of plants I thought might be poisonous.

"Prince Young!" Milly called, a sound that snapped me out of the sereneness of the forest.

I felt my stomach tighten. I gripped my sword and turned back to her direction. I mentally prepared myself for battle. I'd gone too far. My pulse rose up to my throat. I sprinted but my legs couldn't carry me fast enough. Then I saw her.

She stood in a clearing by the river, her shoulders relaxed and her smile sunny.

"What's wrong?" I huffed, surveying the area.

Confusion wrinkled her forehead then dispersed into apology. "Oh, nothing's wrong. I just wanted to check on you."

I spent a moment suspended in awkward disbelief. "I'm fine" I croaked, still catching my breath. I felt a hint of relief when it sunk into my brain that nothing was wrong, but now I'd have to scout again, and I'd lost so much ground already.

"How did you sleep?" she asked.

"Oh, I uh... I didn't really sleep." The concerned look on her face said she needed more information. "Emmett. I mean, just in case."

Her smile returned. "Ah. That's very kind. You know, now that you mention it, your eyes look kind of red." She squinted and walked toward me—analyzing my face.

This whole conversation was a complete waste of time. I looked for an opening to politely escape.

"Milly!" Charlotte called, stepping into the clearing. She froze when she saw me, for a moment that felt like it dragged. Her gaze crawled from me to Milly and stayed there.

This was my chance. "I should finish scouting before we get going." I turned to leave and neither of them seemed to mind.

The rest of the morning went smoothly enough. The girls kept to themselves. Emmett insisted the plant that I thought was poisonous, wasn't, so he rubbed it on his chest to show us how confident he was that I was wrong. I'd only seen him scratch there twice but I was certain the reaction would kick in soon.

We followed the river for several hours as the forest thinned around us, and then in the distance we spotted the peaked towers of Castle Cadere. Relief washed over me.

"It was so close to where we camped last night," I said. "We probably could have made it."

Charlotte looked like she was fighting the urge to sprint to it—her eyes widened and her pace quickened to a canter.

Each step up the hill revealed more of the castle, like its towers sprouted out of the grassy mound. It was unmistakable. We had made it. We hustled up the hill, the deadened thud of Emmett's horse climbing like a heartbeat, rising as we neared.

As we reached the top, we could see more—a grand structure that rivaled that of Hiems, with red flags waving. Once the princess was safe inside, I'd finally return to the north and join Leon in finding my brother.

The last few strides up the hill simultaneously pushed all the air from my lungs and put my plan to find my brother on hold.

When we finally saw the base of the castle, my heart sank. Cadere was surrounded by an army even greater than what I'd seen of the Drethen army. Soldiers, catapults, archers, generals, all stood ready for battle. The unmistakably green uniforms were just like Emmett's and told me three things. First, this army didn't belong to Besmium. Second, I had underestimated Emmett. Third, Charlotte had to marry him or we were all going to die.

15

PRINCESS CHARLOTTE

One look at Emmett's smug expression and my recognition of the same green present on his crest was all it took to realize what was happening. Instinctively, I reached out and grabbed Milly's hand. This wasn't the haven I'd allowed myself to believe was waiting. How long had Emmett been planning this? Was he looking for *me* in the woods?

"Look, Princess," Emmett said with a sly grin, "my reinforcements have arrived. The castle is secure."

I gulped. "How did they know to come here?"

"I sent a messenger to deliver word to my general a few nights ago, during my hunt. Some of my men were a mile or so away the whole time. I told them not to be seen, so I could see your reaction," Emmett replied. He leaned forward and looked at Young's face before chuckling to himself, "Totally worth it."

I shot a look at Young. His furrowed brow and gentle frown at the corner of his lips told me he was as frightened as I was. In the back of my mind, I regretted my choice to let Emmett hunt alone.

It would have been better to keep an eye on him. Despite all the posturing he displayed about how safe we were, it was clear that his army was a threat. The castle was surrounded—a trap—and we were walking right into it. We could make a break for the forest, but they had horses. We wouldn't get very far. But that wasn't the only problem; something else pulled me toward the castle, the possibility that my parents had somehow made it here too. Emmett had us.

Emmett strode confidently in front of us, confirming that he too knew we had no hope of fleeing. Young's face calmed as we approached the army, but his hand rested on the hilt of his sword. Milly fiddled nervously with her cross. As we followed Emmet past the first few rows of iron-plated men, it occurred to me that I had neither a sword nor a cross to comfort me, and I wondered what it was I was holding onto. I approached the last major stronghold of my kingdom and felt my hope drain away as I swallowed the realization that it was already lost.

It was clear that the soldiers all admired Emmett. They bowed deeply, and some cheered like they were welcoming a hero back from war. The excitement and joy of their army was unsettling. They were victorious; their prey was surrounded, and there hadn't even been a battle. Milly squeezed my arm and leaned closer to me.

As we walked through the courtyard, now filled with Algonian soldiers, I remembered the summers I spent here with my father. Warhorses sipped water around the pond where we used to skip rocks. Beneath the blooming marigold trees were pitched tents and crackling fires, with smiths hammering at the edges of heated blades. Besmium's forge was crawling with foreign troops, the red uniforms all replaced with green. On the grassy fields where we once found pictures in the clouds, monstrous catapults were partially constructed and ominously aimed at the castle. How long had they been here? A month? Longer?

I shook with rage as the reality of how much I'd lost set in. Just days ago I knew my father was alive, the war was just the weather and not an actual threat, and I felt safe. Now Besmium was in trouble and Algony circled it like a hawk. The doors to the castle were more than ten feet high, yet they seemed smaller than I remembered. Trumpets sounded as the doors unbarred, the way they always did, but it seemed inappropriate for prisoners to celebrate. A long line of Besmium guards stood at attention to welcome us. The castle doors closed behind us with a loud boom.

My gaze locked with Young's and in that instant I hoped we had the same crazy plan. We strode in behind Emmett, Young's gaze locked on mine. He nodded and at once I pulled the dagger he'd given me and held it against Emmett's throat. Young pulled his sword and held it at his back.

"We got him!" Young called. Milly screamed and jumped back.

I was right. He *did* have the same plan. Emmett froze. Young's gaze met mine, triumph beaming from his eyes. We'd done it. My heart swelled with gratitude as it thudded wildly in my chest. We could use Emmett as a hostage to make his troops retreat. I gazed into Emmett's face and saw nothing but a calm smile and crystal blue eyes. He reached up to his chest and scratched it. I glanced around the room to find the Besmium soldiers with their blades drawn, surrounding Young.

"W-why?" I stammered.

"Charlotte," a familiar voice said.

My heart leaped. I lowered my knife. Young's gaze burned my cheek as he kept his sword pointed at Emmett. I turned slowly to the voice. She stepped forward, her rigid features, her dark hair pinned back. Tears pricked my eyes, my body weakening. *Mother*.

Her eyes followed the dagger in my hand. "Put the knife down," she continued. I tried to slide the dagger back into my belt, but my hands were shaking. I dropped it and ran to her.

"Mom," I cried. "You made it. Is Father—"

"I don't know," she said stiffly.

I nodded, holding back tears. "We," I sniffed, "we need to take Emmett hostage. He's their prince. They'll have to leave."

The queen walked slowly toward Emmett. "Young, it's alright. You can drop your weapon." Young hesitated before lowering his sword and bowing to her.

"Apprehend him." Before the words finished leaving her mouth, the guards had Young restrained and they'd begun to shackle his arms behind him.

"No, Mom!" I called. She ignored me and bowed deeply to Emmett. He reciprocated and turned his attention to me.

"Relax, Princess," Emmett said. His voice slithered down my spine. He chuckled. "Women's minds are so cute. You seem to have the wrong impression about my soldiers. They're a wedding present."

I stumbled back. He continued. "Your mother has agreed to allow me your hand in marriage."

"Young," I said. The name suffocating me. "What about Young?"

My mother sighed. "He tried to kill the future King of Besmium."

Rage began to boil inside me as everything sunk in.

"The council will decide his fate," she said. "Don't worry, though, we can't go around hacking off princes or we'll never have peace. He'll most likely be sent back to Vires."

As they dragged Young away in chains, I felt myself detach from my mother. I was an orphan. Tears of hate burned my eyes until I squeezed them shut and tried to picture what my father would say. *Take a deep breath.* I clenched my fists as tightly as I could manage. This was wrong. It wasn't good for Besmium and it wasn't what my father wanted. And Young—how could I let him spend the night in the dungeon? What was my mother thinking? How long had she been planning this? I scanned the Besmium guards, all in my mother's control. Emmett was untouchable. I'd have to play the part of an obedient princess until I could find another way to turn things in my favor.

16

PRINCE MINSEO

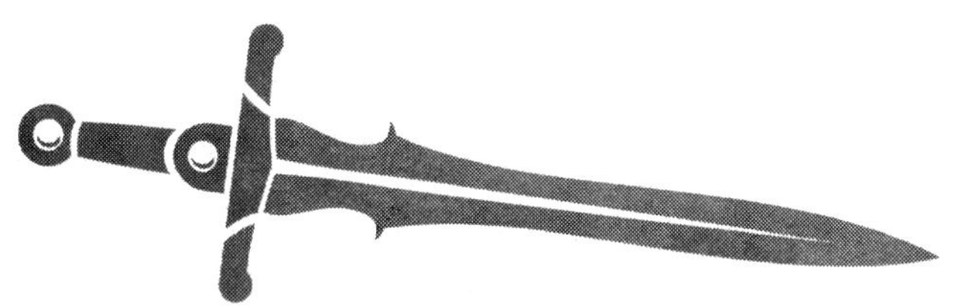

It's my fault Young is dead.

Imprisoned, it was easy to lose track of the days. How long had it been since I was pulled away from him? Days? Weeks? The image of my brother's face remained in my mind. The fear in his eyes haunted me. When the Drethen soldiers dragged me to their army camp, I'd waited up all night. If Young was still alive, the enemy would likely capture him. When he didn't arrive, I feared the worst. Still, I wanted to believe he'd escaped.

The Drethen army camp was unlike any I'd seen. I'd spent some time with my father among the Viran troops and always admired their efficiency and their loyalty. The Drethens were different. They were not an organized and well-led group poised for war but rather a drunken and obnoxious horde. The air was filled with the sound of fistfights and war songs and smelled of body odor and fiery liquor—a scent that burned my nose until I acclimated. I was chained to a tree, limited to a radius of a few feet. The iron chains dug into my wrists from their weight and blistered my skin.

Captain Trisby was in charge of the camp. A broad man with a thick beard that went down to his chest. He ordered the men not to harm me, but I didn't have much faith that they'd obey.

On the third day of my incarceration, Captain Trisby and a few of his soldiers sat down beside me, the heavy stench of booze around them. "To our honored guest," he said, raising an oversized goblet to his lips. He moved clumsily toward me, huffing as if each step drained him. He held the metallic cup in front of me. "Here, old boy," he said, pushing it against my lips.

I welcomed it. The liquid scorched my throat, a vile taste that differed from what I drank in Vires. I nearly choked but gulped back another burning mouthful. It was a brief distraction from my wrist pain.

"Oy. We got a real man over here!" the captain called. His soldiers burst into cheers and laughter. He pulled the goblet away but took a seat nearby. The booze hit heavily in my chest and I began to feel a dull haze creep up the back of my neck. An hour passed and, as the soldiers got drunker, they forgot I was there and occasionally let slip information about the battle.

I felt the sting of the irons on my bare wrists as I listened to their voices in the moonlit forest.

A coarse voice I recognized as Captain Trisby floated by me. "I heard the lieutenant is transferring Besmium's king to our camp in a few days." My stomach dropped. This was *bad.* The king was my brother's only hope and a man my father trusted.

"Ain't he dead?" another soldier replied.

"Not yet. I hear he's bleeding, though. Doubt he'll live 'til he makes it here."

"Why they movin' him?"

"Because our men lost Hiems. Had to move back a few of the camps," Trisby said. A fleck of hope swirled around me. If my brother had made it back to the castle, there's a chance he could have survived.

"Eh. When he gets here, I'll kill him myself."

Within a few hours, most of the soldiers were asleep. They slept where they dropped like stray dogs without a home. A small rotation of guards kept watch, but they were also drunk and no more aware than if they were sleeping too. I knew if I were to escape, night time would be best, but not tonight. Tonight I needed rest. I closed my eyes and leaned my head back against the tree.

"Hey," a voice whispered to me. I froze. "Are you Prince Minseo of Vires?" I didn't recognize his voice, but his accent was unmistakably Besmian. "Yes," I whispered back. "Who are you?"

"I'm private Leon," he said. "Your brother sent me to—"

"My brother's alive?" I shouted. *Too loud.*

A soldier rolled over and tossed an empty bottle in my direction. It landed a few feet away. He rolled back, settling to sleep.

"Sorry," I whispered. There was no response. "Are you there?"

"I'm here," Leon whispered. "I'm going to get you out of here. Are you able to run?"

A wave of relief hit me. I *could* run. I could run all the way to Vires if he cut me loose. I was going to get my brother and go home.

Leon tinkered with the lock on my wrist and, with each click, I felt the hope of escape. "My battalion is only five or so miles away from here. I was scouting the enemy camp when I saw you chained to this tree," he said, his fingers working quickly. "The king is dead and your brother escorted the princess to the southern castle."

The lock clicked louder. The metal clasp released my left wrist. Adrenaline surged through me as Leon moved to work on my other wrist. "The king is only injured," I said. "I heard a soldier say he's being moved to this camp in a few days."

Leon froze, his gaze locked on mine. "The king's alive?"

"Yes." I shook my right hand to hint at him to hurry and unlock it.

"I'm sorry," he said. "If I let you go now, they won't bring the king here."

"No. No. Listen, unlock this. We'll get your army, we'll save the king."

Leon dropped my wrist. The iron chain dug sharply into my raw wrist. "Just hold on a few more days."

"No!" I called. I felt my voice elevating too high. "My brother needs me," I said, closing the gap between us.

Leon backed away. "Lower your voice. Your brother is strong. He'll be fine and so will you for a few more days while I rally my troops."

He turned to leave. "No, Leon!" I called. "Don't do this! We'll find—"

"Well, well, well..." Captain Trisby stepped out of the darkness and into the moonlight. "Looks like we got ourselves an enemy soldier."

Leon drew his blade. The captain lunged forward, his sword meeting Leon's with a resounding clang. It was a noise that was likely to wake a least a few more soldiers. I shook the chain around my wrist to see if Leon had loosened it. If I could escape I could help him, but the clasp remained tightly fastened. Once again, I found myself watching helplessly. Leon was on his own—just like my brother. But with one hand free I had slightly more reach.

I grabbed the chain and hustled around the tree, giving myself an extra foot of slack. A soldier lay in undisturbed slumber a few feet away. If I lay on the ground, my legs might be long enough to reach his sword, but I'd risk waking him up. *Hang on, Leon.* I shuffled to the ground and as quietly as possible dug my heels into the ground by the sword, the clash of the battle behind me clawing for my attention.

I dragged my heels on the ground behind the sword and pulled my knees in. It moved a little. I repositioned my legs and tried again until the sword came into range of my free hand. I lifted it. The weight felt unnatural in my left hand. I positioned myself as close as I could get to the battle but was too far away to help. I considered throwing my sword, but it would be a long shot with my non-dominant hand and I might hit Leon.

I knew I wouldn't be able to cut the chain with the sword, but I had to try anyway. The blade slid along the chain with a sickening screech. I wasn't generating enough momentum. I shook my bound wrist with frustration.

"Uhh!" Leon shouted, grasping my attention. He had fallen to one knee. If I was going to save him, it had to be now. I eyed the sword and my already damaged wrist. The sword wouldn't cut the chain—but it wasn't my only way out. I lifted my sword and braced myself for pain.

17

PRINCESS CHARLOTTE

I lay my head back and closed my eyes as my lady's maid, Glenda, poured another pail of hot water into my bath. The heat mixed in with the cooled water from previous pails, prickling my senses. I exhaled deeply. I was drowning in chaos and had no idea how to pull myself out.

My nose filled with the scent of lavender as Glenda added more oils to my bath. I had to admit, I'd missed being a princess. Five days in the forest felt like an eternity. I shuddered at the memory of sleeping on the cold ground, feeling hungry, and the bugs I'd felt crawling on me. Feeling lost scared, and anxious without a comfort in the world, except one.

A surge of guilt hit my stomach as my mind drifted to Young. I'd only gone to the dungeons in this castle once as a child. According to my father, it was dangerous and, therefore, forbidden. Regardless, one day I convinced a guard to give me a few minutes to explore. I remembered it was dark, cold, and foul-smelling—so I'd left quickly and never returned. It was hard to think about Young being kept there. We'd been through a lot in a short time. He'd taken care of me that night I drank too much and protected me and Milly from the battle at Hiems. He'd taken my side when Milly was afraid of me and delivered us safely to Castle Cadere. My mind flashed back to his dark eyes illuminated across our campfire. I felt a nervous flutter at the pit of my stomach. Why was he doing all this? Regardless of his motives, somewhere along the way, he'd become my ally—my only ally. It was possible that my mother had good intentions. Maybe she even thought she was doing what was best for the kingdom—but her scheming put us in greater danger than before. She imprisoned someone I cared about, and I needed to stop her.

"Miss?" a soft voice said. My eyes opened to Glenda sheepishly hovering above me. "Shall I heat some more water?"

I sat up quickly. "N-no. I'm just about done," I said. I was clean, but I still felt disgusting. I didn't know how to wash away the things I'd done, the blood on my hands since the Drethen attacked, or the mess that my life had become.

I opened my wardrobe and waded through the dresses that hung there, then stopped when I came to a silver one I remembered from last summer. I loved the way it flowed in the breeze, a trait that most of my dresses didn't have. I slipped into it with ease but noticed it was a bit snugger on my chest than it was a few months ago. Had I really changed so much?

"That's lovely, miss," Glenda said, fastening the clasp in the back. "I've always admired that one."

"Thank you," I said, clipping my curls back and out of my face.

The corridors of the castle were packed with soldiers. Some were Besmian and others Algonian, but all of them seemed to be under my mother's thumb. Everywhere I went, they followed. They even waited outside of my chambers. I was not allowed outside the castle or near the dungeon, nor was I able to send letters—but that's exactly what I needed to do.

When I thought about everything at once, I shut down, so I'd planned to take it one step at a time. Today I'd write a letter to the King of Vires, and tonight I'd find a way to send it.

The day went by as a disconnected blur. I blocked out the meeting with the Besmian council and my mother's plans for the wedding. Even Emmett didn't seem to need more than an occasional nod to keep him satisfied as he droned on about his plans for "his" new kingdom.

All day I arranged the words for the letter in my head.

Dear King, one of your sons is believed to be dead and the other imprisoned. Please send help.

No.

If you don't send troops, you'll have lost two sons for nothing.

Ugh. That was worse.

King Lee Won of Vires,
Besmium is under the attack of Algony and Drethen, our neighboring kingdoms. My father is believed to have fallen in the course of battle. The attacks interrupted the wedding agreement previously set forth by you and my father. We are surrounded by the Algonion army under the understanding that I'll wed Prince Emmett of Algony. I humbly ask your assistance in...

I crumpled the practice parchment that I'd been jotting down ideas on all day and tossed it into the fire. I couldn't risk anyone finding it. I pulled out a fresh piece and quill and began again.

Besmium is under attack by Drethen, and my father, the king, is missing.

I want to honor the agreement you made with my father. To do this, I need you to send as many troops as you can spare to Besmium's southern castle. These are uncertain times, and without your help I'm not sure how much time Besmium has left, but I will fight alongside your son and your kingdom until I draw my last breath.

Sincerely,

Princess Charlotte of Besmium

Satisfied, I slipped the letter into an envelope and sealed it with a few drops of wax and my family seal. Now all I needed to do was find a way to get it to Vires.

I slipped out of my dress and into my nightgown, allowing the mental exhaustion I felt to sink in. I lay in my bed and listened to the sound of Glenda's footsteps as she hustled around the room.

I couldn't trust the guards with the letter and I wasn't sure if any of the servants would be willing to disobey my mother, their queen. Not even Milly seemed like a realistic option. I couldn't risk anyone warning my mother because my plan would only work if I convinced both her and Emmett that I wanted this wedding to happen.

I sighed. "Father, I need help."

I listened for his response, half-expecting the low hum of his voice to fill the air around me, but it didn't. "Glenda?" I called, listening for her footsteps, but there was no reply. Before I could call her again, I drifted into a heavy sleep.

A loud knock at my chamber door sent a fierce panic through my body. I sat up in the darkness, the fire by my bed a glowing pile of ash, and waited for Glenda to get the door. The knock sounded again, an alarming thud, the same pace as my heartbeat, and forced my body out of bed and across the room. I opened the door. A Besmium guard with a steely expression and rigid jaw line stood at the door.

He bowed. "Your Highness, this thief claims you've given her this item. Say the word and she will be removed from this castle," he said before pulling a woman into the doorway.

"Glenda," I whispered.

Glenda sobbed heavily as her tears dripped from her chin onto the silver dress I wore earlier. Why had she taken it? Why was she *wearing* it? Her wet eyes pleaded with me for mercy. She slouched and winced every time the guard moved her arm.

I cleared my throat. "I apologize for this misunderstanding. I gave this dress to Glenda and asked that she contact the dresser to make another like it. This one has gotten a bit tight," I lied.

"Why is she wearing it?" he asked, unconvinced.

I laughed. "How is it you've lived in a royal castle all these years and know nothing about how women's clothing is made?" I turned to Glenda. "Glenda, if the dresser has what they need, I'll need you in here immediately to start my bath." I pulled Glenda from the guard.

"Yes, Your Majesty," she said while slipping past me into my chambers.

I turned my attention back to the guard. "Thank you for your diligence. However, there is no problem here."

I closed the door behind me. Glenda knelt on the floor, tears still pooling in her eyes. "Thank you, miss. I-I was getting it washed and I just wanted to see what it would feel like," she sniffed. "I swear I wasn't going to take it. You lied for me, Princess. I-I won't forget this."

I walked to my bed and pulled something from under my pillow. "Actually, I need something," I said.

"Anything, miss," she said, her face brightening.

"I need you to deliver a letter."

18

PRINCE YOUNG

"Imprisoned in the kingdom that I was meant to rule," I huffed. "What a king I turned out to be."

My body ached as another hour in my dimly lit cell crept by. If I passed the time standing, my legs grew tired. If I sat on the damp floor for long enough, my extremities would numb. Either way, the time in my windowless cell dragged into a timeless nightmare from which I could not escape. Luckily, the dungeons in the southern castle housed a bizarre collection of characters to entertain me. From what I gathered, the more serious criminals were sent to the prison near Hiems Castle, leaving this dungeon for people who committed petty crimes like thievery, or forgetting to bow to a high-ranking member of the council.

Despite its dark, barren appearance, the dungeon was the center of information and drama in the castle. Guards used the tunnels to share their secrets and bribed prisoners to share things they'd heard. All I had to do was wait until I heard something I could use. Most of the information was useless—a cook ran away with a guard, or the gardener hid things for people in the garden.

Finally, I heard my first news about Charlotte. A servant had attempted to steal a dress from Princess Charlotte's room. It wasn't much to go on, but just hearing her name gave me hope that if anything newsworthy happened, I'd hear about it—for a price.

I crawled toward the left wall of my cell and pressed my ear to it. "Balzar," I whispered. "Do you have anything new today about the princess?"

I heard the shuffle of his feet as they dragged across the stone floor. "So eager," his weary voice rasped. "What have you to trade?"

"Nothing," I sighed.

"Then I have nothing to tell," he replied. I knew what he wanted—secrets. But the ones I knew could worsen the situation, even get me killed.

"My brother Prince Minseo of Vires was taken at the battle of the northern castle," I said.

Balzar chuckled. "That's old news, hardly worth the breath it took to spit it." He paused, waiting for a response I was reluctant to give. He went into a coughing fit and then wheezed, "What else you got, kid?"

I searched my recent memory. There was one thing that had been on my mind recently. Of course, I had no proof to support this, and worse—though it could be considered treason—it was newsworthy.

"I have something."

Without ever seeing his face, I could feel Balzar smiling on the other side of the wall. It's too big to say aloud—I'd have to whisper. I waited until I heard his breath. "Get on with it then," he spat.

"If I do this, I need you to tell me everything you know that relates to the princess from now on." I waited, unsure if he'd heard me. His voice floated through in a faint wisp. "If I decide your news is worthy," he said.

"Promise me you'll give it a fair judgment."

"You have my word," he said.

"And that you won't tell anyone I told you."

He laughed. "You don't become the center of castle news by selling out your informers," he said smugly.

"Okay," I said, being careful not to raise my voice. "In the battle at the north, we were completely surrounded. Drethen soldiers attacked the front gate before we could escape. I spotted more inside the castle. We took an underground tunnel out of the castle only to find it guarded by more Drethens. We barely made it out alive, and journeyed straight to this castle, arriving a day ahead of schedule."

"Though this story is interesting, it isn't news," he scoffed.

"Wait! Wait!" I called. "I wasn't finished." I lowered my voice. I whispered so softly that I worried he didn't hear me.

After a moment he whispered back, "You're sure she was at the northern castle that day?" he asked, his tone lit with intrigue.

"I spoke with her myself."

"Interesting," he said. His voice rang with a mischievous hum.

"Now, tell me what you know," I insisted.

He sucked in my request through his nose and pursed his lips, considering if what I offered was suitable payment.

I nervously picked at my fingernail, trying to force him into submission with my silence.

He sighed. "The princess plans to have ten thousand white roses at her wedding ceremony. Also, she's asked her betrothed to go on a hunt for the feast afterward. She plans to invite all the soldiers from Algony as well."

My mind raced. Why was she planning the wedding? What was she doing? Had I been wrong about her? "Th-this information is useless," I said, breathing out my frustration. "Guess you're not the center of information after all."

"I have more," he said, his words pulling me back to the wall.

"This little tidbit cost me more than your life is worth. The maid that was caught stealing from the princess, she called in a favor to have a letter delivered."

My pulse quickened. "To where?"

"Vires."

I settled back into my cell as the hours blurred together. Charlotte sent a letter to Vires? She must be planning something.

A loud creak and a flood of light indicated someone approaching. I backed away from the wall, lay on the floor, and listened to the distinct click of jeweled shoes on the stone floor as they grew closer. The sound stopped in front of my cell. I opened my eyes and stood to see the queen. "Your Majesty," I said, bowing.

She spoke, "I'm terribly sorry for these horrid conditions. As soon as the wedding is over, I'll send you straight back to Vires where you belong."

"Thank you, Your Majesty," I said. She crossed her arms and her face darkened. "I was hoping I could get a second helping of lunch today, Your Majesty."

Her shoulders relaxed. "Ah. Certainly," she said, dropping her arms. Her gaze drifted to her right to beyond what I could see from my cell. "Balzar," she said. "Has the prince given you any information?"

My stomach tightened. Of course she knew about the information trade going on here. That's probably why she put me here to begin with. I searched my cell for something I could use as a weapon.

Balzar's voice echoed off the walls. "I don't think he said anything worthy of your time," he said.

I froze. He'd been a man of his word after all. I felt relief flush my cheeks.

"That's just it," the queen said. "It's your time I'm concerned about. I'll trade you what you know for your freedom."

19

PRINCESS CHARLOTTE

With the letter on its way to Vires, hope blossomed inside me. I was no longer marching toward my marriage to Emmett but toward freeing Young and taking back my kingdom. All I had to do was stall the wedding—an easy task that only required me to make up time-consuming requests. Emmett saw these requests as his opportunity to win my affection and my mother never got suspicious. After all, these kinds of demands were not too out of character for me. But one thing did weigh heavily on me: Milly. Since we'd returned to the castle, she'd disappeared from my life. I figured she'd changed her duties for a while to get some rest after our journey, but when a week went by and I still hadn't seen her, I knew something was wrong. We hadn't seen eye to eye lately. Recent events showed me just how different our morality was, but she'd been there through it all. She understood and I missed her.

I told my mother I was going to speak to the cook, Sasha, about the wedding day feast, but I was hoping Sasha could tell me where to find Milly. The servant's quarters were poorly lit and sparsely decorated. It was another part of the castle that royals rarely visited, but I knew them well. As a young girl, Milly would bring me here to help me hide from my mother, or skip my lessons. It was hard to believe that now Milly used these halls to hide from me.

"Your Majesty," a servant said, bowing deeply.

"I'm looking for Sasha," I said.

"Kitchen, last I saw, miss," she said, wiping her dirty hands on her apron.

I hustled down the hallway to the kitchen and turned the corner. I expected to see Sasha there, bent over the stove with permanently rosy cheeks, but instead I saw Milly washing dishes by the window. She stared out as she scrubbed her soapy hands against a metallic pot. When she didn't notice me come in, I considered turning back, leaving her in peace. I put my hand over my chest to steady my heartbeat. If I'd learned anything in the last few days, it was that friendship was more than just the good times. I stepped into the light of the kitchen.

"Hey, Milly," I said.

Her face paled. "Charlotte. What are you doing here?"

I tried to imagine her tone was welcoming. "I've missed you."

She turned back to her dishes. "Is there something you need?" The pot she was washing was clean, but she kept scrubbing it as if she hoped to wash away her problems with it.

I shivered under her cold tone then took a few steps closer. "No, I just miss my friend."

She continued to wash, without speaking. I put my hand on her shoulder. "If I've done something wrong to you, please tell me."

The pot landed with a clang at the bottom of her washing pail. "Everything's wrong," she said, shrugging my hand off.

"I know. The situation is bad, but I'm trying to fix it."

She glared. "That's just it. Every decision you've made has made things worse for everyone." I stepped back as she continued. "People are killing people and you are at the center of it all."

"Yeah, but—"

"Wielding a sword, taking hostages. That isn't you. I know you. You'd never hurt anyone. You certainly wouldn't ki—" She covered her mouth with her hand. It shook. She dropped her hand and took a sharp breath. "Prince Young is in the dungeon!"

Sasha entered the room with a cheerful smile that quickly faded. She turned and hustled out.

I shook my head. "Look, Milly, you're like a sister to me—"

"Stop!" she yelled. "I am not your sister." She stepped toward me, her brow furrowed, her eyes a burning blue. "Sisters don't blindly serve other sisters. You don't take care of me, you don't ask how I feel, and you don't know who I love. You're a spoiled, selfish princess who has run our kingdom into the ground in a matter of days." Tears pooled in her eyes.

My heart ricocheted off my rib cage. I swallowed her words. "Fine. Who is it?"

"What?"

"Who do you love?"

"I-I was just—"

"Say it aloud, Milly," I demanded. She choked on her tears, turning back to the window. I continued. "There are a thousand reasons why he'll never be yours—none of them are imposed by me."

She cried into her hands.

I continued. "I didn't start this war."

She turned back to me, her face and eyes pink. "Yes, but you can end it," she said. "Promise me. Promise me you'll marry Emmett. I can't tell if you're really excited about this wedding or if you have something planned, but promise me right now you'll go through with it."

"Milly, I can't just—"

"For me," she said while wiping away her tears and moving closer. "If we are sisters, do this one thing for me."

It was a promise I knew I couldn't keep. It was also in support of her fantasy that I shouldn't indulge. Yet, as she cried in my arms, I couldn't form the words to disappoint her. I said nothing.

After that, she returned to my quarters as my lady's maid. She never mentioned what passed between us, or how she felt about its resolution. I no longer knew if she was still my sister, friend, servant, or if she were merely keeping an eye on me to see if I kept the promise I didn't make, but either way, having her close put me at ease.

That night, I opted to eat my dinner in my room. Milly hurried to the kitchen to fetch it while I pondered the things she said. She had been right about a lot of it. Had all our conversations been about me? How long had she felt that way? I made the decision to prepare a royal bath for Milly as a tribute for her friendship.

A little later, Milly returned to my room before I could adequately fill the tub.

"Surprise!" I grinned. "It's for you."

Her pale face and crystal eyes glistened with horror. She spoke, her shaky voice uneven. "Prince Young has been found guilty of treason and sentenced to death."

20

MILLY

Charlotte did her best to comfort me, but I knew her too well. She was as scared as I was.

I didn't even deserve her concern. I'd scolded her—a royal. The closer we'd grown, the deeper the discord between us crept. She could have had me beheaded for less, yet, late into the night, she wiped my tears and promised me she'd save him. But no matter what she said, one truth remained. Young was in danger.

I plopped onto my stiff bed in the servant's quarters, attempting to quell the storms that raged inside of me. My mind replayed the moments I'd shared with the prince as I prepared for my dream to be snatched away by death.

He was not the first prince I'd seen. I'd served many when they were guests at Hiems. They were needy, shallow things with no love for God or others. A visiting prince once scolded me and refused to sit because he claimed his chair was dusty. Young was different though. He looked at me with eyes that were soft and kind and saw me not as a servant, but as a girl. It was a definition with which I hardly defined myself.

After that, I prayed every night to take away the feelings I harbored. I asked God why he'd burdened me with this love if it was so *impossible*. I begged for answers.

One night in the forest, Young sat beside me, our campfire burning like my feelings. He nodded his head toward Emmett and Charlotte on the other side of the fire. "Do you think she could someday love him?" he asked.

His question was so absurd that I said, "It's impossible."

Staring into the fire he said, "Nothing's *impossible*."

Even though we laughed, I couldn't help but feel like this was God's reply. There I was, despite my birth, sitting next to a prince as equals. I made a secret vow that night and pledged myself to him. I couldn't tell him now, but perhaps someday I could and maybe he could love me too.

It was obvious that Charlotte didn't feel like I did about Young. I hurt at the memory of Young being treated so poorly by her. She tried to kill him, showed interest in his brother, and hated the idea of marriage. Still, sometimes he watched her. She had a kingdom to offer him, while I only had my feelings. Once the jealousy began to set in, I found it difficult to eradicate. Last night I found myself trying to convince Charlotte not to marry him, and this morning I was depending on her to save him. Love was maddeningly irrational. Even so, I couldn't trust Charlotte to save Young. What could she do? Did she even care? I'd have to watch him die—unless I did something myself.

I got to my knees, pushing my palms together. "Almighty Father, I have done my best to serve you graciously and thank you for your many blessings. You taught me that all life is precious, an idea that I've protected even through these times of war." My heart raced as I formed the rest of my prayer. "The only thing stronger than the promises I've made to you is the vow I made to dedicate myself to love. I ask that you turn away from me now." I clutched my wooden cross and yanked it from my neck. It landed with a clunk and slid across the stone floor. "My new God and guiding force is Young. I ask that you be merciful in your deliverance and that you consider your part in the events that led me here."

I had no choice but to kill the queen myself.

The sun peeked over the horizon, indicating that I might already be too late, but I didn't care. I had to do everything I could to save Young. I sprinted through the hallway to the servant's garden. I knew I'd find nothing useful there, but I had heard of one thing near the back of the castle: a very poisonous pink flower called Oleander. I didn't remember where I'd heard about it, nor did I know if it was really poisonous. What I did know was where pink flowers grew outside of the castle and that, for the moment, it was my only hope. I knew it was crazy. I knew that there was probably a better course of action out there than chasing a could-be poisonous flower, but the hope of saving Young was all I had left.

I spotted the pink flowers in the leafy passage between the servant's garden and the back of the castle. I reached for them but froze. I didn't know if they were poisonous to the touch. It seemed silly that a flower so lovely and innocent could be something other than that—proof that this flower and I were made by the same God.

I took several flowers, using my dress as a barrier between my hand and the potential poison, making sure that no one was around to see me. But I was alone—not even God was watching.

I rushed to the kitchen to join Sasha in the breakfast preparation. I was late, but she didn't so much as make a face in disapproval. She was kind that way. We prepared the queen's breakfast as usual. When Sasha was far enough away, and humming along to a familiar tune, I pulled the flowers out of my pocket, being very careful not to touch them. I chopped them so finely they could have been mistaken for a bit of dust on the corner of the table. I closed my eyes, my heartbeat in my throat. I swallowed down my nerves. With the knife, I pushed the flower dust into the queen's wine. I placed the cup onto the tray, dropped the knife into the washing bucket, and turned back to collect the tray.

I froze. Sasha faced me, holding the queen's breakfast tray out for me to serve— wine and all. I studied her face, the guilt seeping in, blurring my vision. She *knew*. My breaths felt strained as I pushed them out in slow hot bursts. I took the tray and headed for the door. She didn't stop me. It must have been all in my head.

I pictured Young alone and afraid as I made my way to the queen's bedroom. I pushed open the door.

"There you are," the queen said, her voice chilling my bones. "Is it my imagination or is someone running late this morning?"

How fitting that she waits for me, her deliverer. I held the tray steady, willing my arms to stop shaking.

I bowed my head. "I apologize, Your Majesty."

I laid the tray before her. "My, my, my. How lovely you've become!" She raised the cup. "I remember the first day they brought you to us in the northern castle." She sighed, bringing the cup to her lips. I froze—my attention bound to her mouth.

She sipped. "Now you're practically a woman."

I did it. I did it. I *killed* her. I bowed and turned toward the door. "Wait," she said. "I should thank you for being such an important person to my daughter."

I wanted to run to the door—a mere ten feet from freedom.

"Have some wine."

I turned slowly. Did she *know*? Could she taste it?

"That's very kind, Your Majesty. I am but a lowly maid. I can't drink the queen's wine."

She grinned. "I insist." She took a big gulp. "It's delightful, you'll love it."

I lifted the cup from her hand and held it to my mouth. *So this was God's answer.*

21

PRINCESS CHARLOTTE

The moment I woke up, I knew something was off. I must've fallen asleep while comforting Milly because I wasn't sure when she had slipped out. I rushed to get ready and hustled into the hallway. The sun was high in the sky, splashing a cheerful yellow onto the usually gray walls. Servants rushed around the hallways, carrying large white floral arrangements, no doubt preparing for the wedding which was set to begin in a week or two, depending on how quickly things came together. I headed for the servant's quarters.

"There you are, Princess."

My stomach tightened. I turned to see Emmett, an arch of white roses framing him for a moment before the servants carried it past.

He smiled brightly. "I feel I haven't been able to spend much time with my beloved since we arrived." He plucked a white rose from a passing bouquet and handed it to me. The acid in my stomach bubbled but I feigned a smile. He continued. "Can I interest you in a walk on the grounds?"

Only a few steps from the servant's quarters, my escape, I glanced over my shoulder. "I-I... I have to—"

He moved closer. "Surely you can spare a moment, Princess."

I stepped back. "Actually, I have to—"

"I insist," he said sharply. His ocean blue eyes darkened, sending a pang of fear through me. I took it and my hands instinctively clenched, causing the thorns from the white rose to prick me. On the surface, Emmett was a handsome and charming prince, but in a moment of disagreement, the predator within glared through.

It was obvious to me that he was used to getting what he wanted, a trend I promised myself I'd break for him—but for the time being he had to believe I'd go through with the wedding. I had to play his game, but he was just a pawn and I wanted to find out if I had what it took to be a queen.

I smiled and took his arm. In an instant, the predator dispersed and the charming prince returned. Although, people who are only charming when it suits them aren't charming at all. He led me down the corridor.

"Penelope, I need that dress mended before tomorrow," I said to a passing servant. I turned to a patrolling guard nearby. "Charlie, there's this drumming sound outside my chamber at all hours. Can you investigate?" They were false requests, but I needed someone to know that Emmett was taking me. I wanted someone to know which direction we went.

"You are a busy girl, aren't you?" Emmett said. "Might I suggest you take a short break?"

I gulped, too unnerved to meet his gaze and face the beast buried inside him.

"Yes, my dear," I said as we slipped to a quieter part of the castle. If I screamed, the echo would carry. Someone would be able to hear, but then what? I needed Emmett to believe I wanted to marry him. There was no Plan B. I needed to buy enough time for

Vires to respond. My muscles stiffened as Emmett pulled me into a dark stairway. We walked silently down and up to a door that was familiar, though I couldn't remember what was on the other side. Emmett opened the door and gestured for me to enter. *This was it.* No one could hear me from in there.

The door closed behind us and I stood at the edge of an overgrown atrium. The sound of running water pulled me toward the atrium's center. A small stream flowed through it, with stone bridges providing passage around the gardenesque courtyard, which was surrounded by castle walls on each side with green leafy plants crawling up each wall. The streams flowed through barred tunnels beneath the castle walls. The light came straight down from the open air above, and sunlight beamed through the long leafy branches of an overgrown willow tree. Dark purple flowers lined the stream. Why hadn't I remembered this place? It was like a dream.

In my amazement, I'd briefly forgotten the dangerous situation I was in. This garden was secluded and I didn't want to imagine the kinds of things Emmett was capable of. I spun to find Emmett kneeling before me.

"Princess," he said, grabbing my hand. "I never did get the chance to ask you officially to be my wife." He reached into his pocket and pulled out a small box. My heart crashed into my ribs repeatedly. He opened the box to reveal a pink diamond the size of his irises. Of all the horrible scenarios I'd imagined, it had never occurred to me that Emmett might actually *propose.* My mind flashed to Young, sadness clawing at my stomach.

Emmett gazed up at me with sincerity. "Will you do me the honor of becoming my bride?"

It was a beautiful proposal in a secret garden. Heat rushed to my face, filling my cheeks with a pronounced red. I couldn't help the overwhelming feeling of flattery and the way my mind continuously tripped on the word *wife*. My next move was clear—easy even. I'd simply accept his proposal and stall the wedding until the Viran troops arrived. Only I couldn't. Something about his sincerity made the lie seem unfair. I stared into his blue eyes, hoping to get a glimpse of the beast, but all I could see was the serene blue of the autumn sky on a cloudless day.

"I realize that you're in a difficult position here, Princess," he said. "But I promise to protect you and your kingdom until my dying breath."

Somehow his speech made me feel like *I* was the monster. I couldn't bring myself to form the words. I nodded. What was I *doing*? Emmett smiled brightly and slipped the ring onto my finger. He stood and pulled me into his chest, locking his arms around me. I felt a pang of guilt. I was a liar, but his embrace was comforting, the warmth of his body making me realize that I'd been cold moments ago. My thoughts returned to Young, who was sitting in a dungeon that very moment, and I wondered how I'd feel if it was him who proposed instead. My cheeks burned.

Emmett pulled away without letting go and smiled down at me. My stomach dropped. He reached his hand up and gently brushed my cheek with his thumb, his gaze drifting down to my lips. Fear tore through my body as I felt his grip on my waist tighten. Would he steal my first kiss? He held our bodies together as he leaned in, his lips just beyond mine. His breath was warm and sweet. My body pulsed, my head dizzy. Suddenly his lips were on mine. His tongue slipped into my mouth as his body tightened. I could've pushed him, I could have told him to stop, but I was overcome with the need to know more. The excitement thrilled me, the sensation so dangerous and new. My mind sounded with alarm, even disgust, but my curiosity got the best of me.

"Charlotte?" someone said from behind me. Emmett and I leaped apart. We spun to see Milly standing in the doorway to the atrium. She bowed. "Your Grace, the queen has requested your immediate presence in her chamber."

Had she seen? The blush of her cheeks said she had. Milly's gaze surveyed our faces for clues but not even I knew what happened. I turned to Emmett, who laughed shyly before gesturing for me to go.

I bowed and hurried away with Milly. As the door closed behind us, I wondered what story I'd tell her. My world was expanding and I hadn't yet figured out my place in it. Emmett had brought nothing but horror into my life since I'd met him, but somehow that didn't taint the memory of my first kiss. I blushed every time I looked down at the pink diamond on my finger.

"The date's been set," Milly said as we hurried through the corridors.

I shook my head. "The wedding?"

Tears welled up in her eyes. "No, the execution." She buried her face in her hands. "They're going to kill him tomorrow." She looked up at me. "*Do something.*"

22

PRINCE EMMETT

Nothing virtuous about that princess. It's possible her mother had lied. I sat in silence in the atrium for several minutes after the princess left, but even in the open air I found it difficult to catch my breath, and I couldn't regain full strength in the back of my knees. Perhaps I needed to get beyond these walls. I headed out to the back of the castle where I'd run into fewer people. I didn't feel like talking.

Behind the castle, there was a fair amount of open field, with several scattered camps packed with patrolling soldiers. Even so, the majority of the army was at the front of the castle, leaving me to roam in peace. The climate in Besmium was similar to that of Algony, but today it felt hotter somehow. Was I ill? One thing I knew for sure was that I wasn't feeling this way because of Charlotte. If I'd learned anything, it was that women were interchangeable.

I sighed and lay in the grass, the late afternoon sun casting a refreshing bit of shade. I knew that the princess wouldn't be able to resist my charms. She'd fall victim to my will eventually, just like all the simple-minded women-folk of Algony. So, what was my problem?

A soft humming sound alerted me to a nearby presence. A red-faced servant in the unappealing end of her prime dug up several patches of a soft pink flower. I watched her for a minute—it was such a shame to watch her destroy such lovely flowers that I almost felt compelled to say something. I took a deep breath, attempting to exhale the memory of my kiss with the princess. Perhaps I needed to remind myself who I was. I needed to replenish the feeling of power that came so naturally to a man of my caliber. I got to my feet and puffed up my chest before strutting toward the servant.

"You there," I called.

She looked startled, her forehead crinkling. "Your Highness," she said, curtsying. I gagged. She looked older up close, with laugh lines around her eyes and her mouth. What did she have to be happy about?

"What do they call you?"

"Sasha, Your Highness. I'm the head chef." Her hands were covered in dirt, her apron covered in grease. There was a matronly charm to her; however, I quickly concluded talking to this woman could do no good—by comparison the princess was a goddess.

"Forgive me, Your Highness. I must get back to work." She turned back to the flowers.

"Of course," I nodded while turning to leave. The scrape of Sasha's shovel stopped me. *Irritating.* I turned back. "Why is a chef out here in the gardens, murdering an innocent flower?"

"I uhm..."

Too late. Her brief hesitation was enough. She rambled on but I blocked her out and took several steps closer to the flowers. They really were beautiful. Their pointed petals had a dangerous beauty that I appreciated—appreciated but didn't recognize. For such a beautiful flower in a climate similar to that of Algony, it was strange that I'd never come across it before. My eyes widened as I recalled it.

"*Oleander*," I whispered under my breath.

The chef's face turned porcelain white.

I smiled so big it stung my cheeks. "What an interesting kingdom this is." I waited—watched her crumble beneath my gaze. She wouldn't dare lie to me. "Who is it for?"

She visibly shook. "Your Highness, you have the wrong idea. I'm merely trying to prevent—"

"So *someone* used this flower for its purpose, then?"

She shook her head, desperation in the flare of her nostrils. "No, sire."

“So they tried? And you're out here getting rid of the evidence."

She nodded somberly. "Who took the flower, servant?" I loomed over her, using my size to intimidate her.

She lowered her head, closed her eyes, and prepared herself for pain. "Tell me!" I barked, grabbing her arm. She remained motionless. I tilted my head to the side to observe her. She was willing to die to protect someone. I respected that. I released her arm. "Will you at least tell me who it was intended for?"

She bit down on her bottom lip. A loud pop sounded from where my hand hit her cheek. I looked over my shoulder, but no one was around. She buried her face in her hands.

Her posture slumped. "The queen," she sniffed through tears, keeping her gaze from mine.

"Well, we can't have that, can we?" I said, pondering the possibilities. My tone wasn't convincing. Any idiot could see that my situation would be significantly improved if the old bat were killed off. Especially now that I've sufficiently won Charlotte's affections. Still, the flowers were a good tool to have on hand for later. "I'd like every single one of these flowers transported to my chambers for safe keeping."

"Yes, Your Highness."

"And servant," I added, "it's in your best interest not to mention this conversation to anyone."

I headed back into the castle, my mind reeling with excitement. Things were finally starting to get interesting. *Someone* was trying to kill the queen. I hustled into a side entrance and headed to my chambers.

"Your Grace." I turned to see Draven, my mousy advisor, standing just outside my chamber.

"Not now, Draven," I huffed, pushing past.

"The queen has requested an audience with you."

I stopped. "Fine. Where is she?"

"The throne room, sire."

Without another glance back, I headed to the throne room. I pushed through the double doors, ready to see the queen, and froze. Charlotte stood in front of me, her befuddled expression implying she was as surprised to see me as I was to see her. I bowed too deeply and too quickly. What was wrong with me? She curtsied, smiled softly, and walked past me into the hallway I'd just left.

"Welcome, Prince Emmett," the queen said from her throne. Her voice carried through the gold-lined room. She motioned to the guard, who left and pushed the heavy doors shut behind them. "Come here, we have much to discuss."

I eyed her warily. "Is this about the princess?" My throat went dry.

"Yes. Charlotte has requested to move the wedding to tomorrow," she said, brushing a pin-straight strand of hair out of her face. A wave of weakness hit my knees. I *did* leave an impression on the princess... naturally. The queen continued. "It seems she doesn't want her big day to be overshadowed by the execution."

"Yes, that makes sense," I replied lamely.

"Of course, I told her it would be impossible. You promised you'd find my husband before the wedding. That was the condition of our agreement and your betrothal to Charlotte. Have you forgotten?"

"No, Your Majesty. I sent a unit of soldiers ten days ago a little after I delivered the princess. I received word five days ago that they have the king in tow and will be arriving here tomorrow afternoon."

The queen stood, a glisten of light in the corner of her eye. "He's alive?"

"Badly wounded, Your Majesty, but yes, alive."

She slowly sat back down on her throne, the strictness of her posture melting away.

"Then the wedding will be tomorrow evening then?" I prodded, hoping she wouldn't note my eagerness. Her eyes were glazed over in a way that suggested she was more within her thoughts than in the room.

"Your Majesty," I nudged a little louder.

Her face brightened. "Yes, of course. Let the servants know. The wedding will be tomorrow."

"And the execution?" I asked.

She paused, clicking her fingertips on the armrest of her throne. "We'll let Charlotte have her special day, but rest assured, when the sun rises the morning after the wedding, Prince Young will be dead."

23

PRINCESS CHARLOTTE

A fleck of scattered light tickled my eyelids, waking me like a soft whisper, welcoming me to the dawn. I traced its source to the white ball gown in the center of my bedroom. It stood erect on its own, maintaining its rigid and elaborate shape. Droves of white fabric draped in layers filling a full skirt and endless train. Tiny hand-sewn porcelain beads scattered along the bottom of each layer and across the ornately beaded bodice, with a low dipping neckline and off-the-shoulder sleeves. Beside the dress was a small table with long white gloves and a glittering tiara.

I circled the dress several times, leaping over the train in the back each time. It must have taken many sleepless nights to complete on time, but here it was. It was the loveliest dress I'd ever seen in any royal event anywhere. A month ago, I would have squealed and called Milly to help me put it on, but this wasn't just a fine dress, it was a wedding dress, which meant this was my last day to save Young.

I headed to the armory. The hallways of the castle were quiet and still. I must've been up earlier than I thought. Suddenly, Emmett's voice filled the hall. I stopped and hid behind a column.

Emmett's voice rang out from the castle's entrance. "Tell McCaffrey I'll need him to go with me to fetch the king. He has five minutes."

"Yes, Your Highness," a soldier responded before their retreating footsteps and the silence that followed indicated they'd gone.

Their fading footsteps and the preceding silence told me they'd gone.

I felt the strength drain from my legs. Did he mean *my* father? Tears stung my eyes. I pushed my weight against the column until I caught my breath. My father's *alive*. I took a deep breath, but I wouldn't let myself believe it until I saw him. I wiped the tears from my eyes and continued to the armory.

The royal armory was much smaller at the southern castle. Still, it was packed with enough weapons and armor to fully equip Emmett's entire army twice. The quartermaster was an elderly man with tattered hands.

"Your Highness," he said with a bright grin. His smile was pleasant, despite the fact he was missing most of his teeth. "It's been some time since you've come down here."

I smiled, straining to remember his name, but I couldn't. "Uhm, I need a sword," I said.

His smile drooped, framing his mouth with lines much akin to ripples in a lake. "What is the occasion?" he asked, looking more concerned.

"A wedding gift for my new husband," I said.

Dread filled the shopkeeper's eyes. "I hope it's not for the wedding *today*." He shook his head. "I wish you'd come sooner. I could have commissioned a sword fine enough for Prince Emmett, surely I have nothing on hand of that caliber."

I sighed. "Please, if you had commissioned it, he would have found out about it. Will you just show me what you have?"

His smile returned. "Of course, Princess. Right this way." He led me through the rows of helmets to the swords in the back.

The collection was incredible, even to someone who didn't care much about swords. Each sword varied in size and had a unique case that complemented its design. Some were dipped in gold and displayed on a red velvet cloth, others had jeweled hilts and rested on white silk, but my gaze was immediately drawn to a huge broadsword that had a ruby-studded dragon wrapped around the top of it, acting as the hilt. Despite its size, I'd have no problem concealing it in the folds of my dress.

"That one," I said.

"Fine choice, Your Majesty," he said, lifting the glass case, placing it aside, and handing the sword to me.

The sword was even more intricate up close, with carvings and patterns all the way down the center of the blade. For my purposes, though, it was too heavy. I'd never be able to pull it out and swing it before I was stopped. I needed something lighter.

"Do you have something smaller?" I asked, feeling a wisp of sadness as the shopkeeper gently lifted the sword from my hands.

"S-smaller?" he said, "Surely the prince—"

"For me," I said flatly.

"Well, this sword comes with a matching dagger," the shopkeeper said, placing the sword gently back in its case and leading me past the swords to the daggers. He picked up the dragon dagger, a marvel—with equal detail as its larger counterpart. He handed it to me. A surge of power rushed through me, followed by a wave of fear, though I wasn't scared of Emmett. I was afraid of myself, who I was becoming, and the terrible things I was planning to do.

"Will it do?" the shopkeeper asked, regaining my attention.

"Oh, yes, it's pretty," I said.

The shopkeeper laughed, a wide-mouthed grin that exposed his bare gums. "Yes, very pretty."

"I'll take them both," I said, heading for the door. "Have them both sharpened and in my chamber by noon today," I said, half calling over my shoulder.

"Would you like me to have them gift wrapped, Princess?"

I smiled. "That won't be necessary."

24

PRINCE EMMETT

One little errand was all that remained between the Besmian throne and me.

I mounted my horse and trotted into the palace courtyard to meet McCaffrey. I had hundreds of soldiers at my disposal but didn't need their protection. I had ten men waiting at our destination a mile outside the castle but, more importantly, I had McCaffrey. We were unlikely to meet any Besmian soldiers as they'd all been sent to the north to recapture Hiems. I needed a calming presence, and McCaffrey was my go-to man for that.

The sun was peaking over the horizon, mixing with the morning dew to create a pink color that reminded me of the poisonous flowers I had hidden in my chamber. McCaffrey came into view as he made his way around a catapult. His hair askew, he was hunched over his horse as if he were asleep, and his droopy-eyed expression said the same.

"Morning, Your Highness," he croaked. He looked like he hadn't been to sleep for the night, but I'd seen him in much worse shape than this. At least he wasn't vom—. As if he read my mind, he leaned to the side of his horse and made a deep gargling sound. He raised a hand to me. "Just a burp," he said, his horse fidgeting nervously.

I sighed. "We're off then."

We rode away from the palace and finally into the forest where, only a few weeks ago, I'd saved Charlotte. I knew the path well and as the sun rose in the sky, the path only became more obvious. This final task was almost too easy, just like winning Charlotte had been. She was a worthy reward for ruling over Besmium.

Once McCaffrey adjusted to the early hour, he began chatting voraciously, covering all manner of topics. Despite his constant warbling, I listened with a mild intent—it was enough to distract me and keep my mind from the excitement of my plan coming together. An hour and a half later, when we neared the rendezvous point, not even McCaffrey could keep me calm. I wanted to burst through the wood to the clearing, collect the king, and return to my new home to claim my bride. We neared the clearing and I hurried through the surrounding bushes.

I froze. All ten of my men were tied to trees scattered across the clearing. Some were bleeding, some weren't moving—the king was gone. My stomach dropped. McCaffrey and I hopped off our horses. I hurried over to the closest soldier.

"Where's the king?" I shouted, grasping at the ropes.

"Behind," he gasped

I turned to see a single Besmian soldier holding a sword to McCaffrey's throat. A second man stepped out from behind a tree with an arrow cocked back and aimed at me. *Prince Young?* I gaped. No. It wasn't him. He was a bit taller, with longer hair—still, the resemblance was uncanny. Must be the other Viran prince.

I cleared my throat. "I think we've gotten off on the wrong foot here."

The Viran prince spoke. "I don't think we have. It seems like you and your men are trying to kidnap the King of Besmium. Whoever you are, that's an act of treason. Give me one good reason I shouldn't put this arrow in your head right now."

I spoke carefully. "I was attempting to rescue the king. I was planning to return him unharmed to his family at Castle Cadere."

The prince considered my words for a moment before gesturing to the other man. "This here is Captain Leon of Besmium. We will return the king. Just... collect your men and be on your way."

The prospect of presenting the king to the Queen of Besmium and fulfilling our deal was slipping through my fingers at an alarming rate. Everything I'd built in the last few weeks was on the verge of being destroyed by this man with an arrow. If I was a few feet closer, I could destroy him with one swipe of my sword, but perhaps this situation called for a more diplomatic approach. I chose my words carefully. "How about a trade. The king for your brother."

His face paled.

Leon scoffed. "We'd never consider such a deal." But it was clear from the prince's expression that he did not fully agree.

I had them. "I am Prince Emmett of Algony. I've been summoned by the queen herself to retrieve her husband the king." I focused my attention on the prince. "Prince Young of Vires has been found guilty of treason and is to be put to death tomorrow. What I am proposing is most beneficial to everyone here. You release the king to my care. Me, my injured men, and both of you will all accompany the king back to safety at the castle. When we arrive, I will personally see to it that your brother is released, and you and your brother can return to Vires unharmed."

The prince turned to Captain Leon. Each moment of silence drudged on, tempting me to just draw my sword and end it.

Finally, the soldier nodded. I exhaled my anxiety. The plan was back on.

"Wonderful," I said. "Now show me to the king."

25

PRINCE YOUNG

Still alive, then.

At least I thought I was. It was hard to tell with the days dragging on as they were. Why hadn't they come for me? After my sentencing, the other prisoners were afraid to talk to me, like my looming death was a contagion. From the moment I found out I was going to die, I hadn't been able to stop thinking about Vires—its mountainous landscape, it's spring cherry blossom trees. I'd made the decision months ago that I would move to Besmium, take the crown, and likely never return, but now it was certain. I'd never see my kingdom again, nor my brothers, nor my father.

Maybe my ambition was to blame. If I'd been content as the third prince of Vires, if I'd never wanted to be king, I would still be in Vires and Minseo would be alive. I closed my eyes and rested my head on the cold dungeon wall. What would Minseo say?

Don't give up, Young, I imagined. *It's not your fault.*

"Brother, wake up!"

An eager voice woke me, to find Emmett standing beside

Minseo outside my cell. For a moment, I thought I was dreaming, but in a few short seconds, I realized my brother was actually there. My heart slammed into my ribcage. *Minseo*. Dazed, I leaped to my feet and pulled my brother into my arms, three iron bars between us. I choked back tears as I struggled through the bars, to clutch him tighter. I put my forehead to his and felt the splash of his tear on my cheek, turning me into a blubbering mess.

Emmett cleared his throat.

Minseo and I jumped back, wiping our faces. Emmett stepped between us and unlocked the cell. Minseo's shoulders relaxed. He turned to Emmett. "Just like that?"

Emmett grinned widely but his gritted teeth made me believe witnessing our reunion made him uncomfortable. When the gate opened, Minseo rushed in and hugged me again, then looked me over, like a mother after her child comes home for the day. Relief surged through me. I tried to choke back another wave of tears, but it was no use, my brother was *alive*. He wasn't just alive, he was here—saving my life.

"I must ask a favor," Emmett said.

Minseo turned back to Emmett. It was hard to see in the darkness of the dungeon, but I thought I saw traces of tears still on Minseo's rigid cheeks.

Emmett continued. "You may collect your things and rest in Besmium until tomorrow, but I must ask you to not attend the event this evening."

"Event?" Minseo asked.

"My wedding to Princess Charlotte," Emmett said. Minseo's gaze darted between Emmet and me before it finally came to rest on me. Sadness spread across his face. His lips tensed, his eyebrows slightly raised. His sympathy was unsettling. He searched my face for my reaction—but this was old news to me.

I smiled, placing a reassuring hand on Minseo's shoulder. "Let's go home," I said. Minseo hesitated for a moment, like he wanted to say more but didn't. Instead, he pulled me out of the dungeon cell, notably keeping his body between Emmett's and mine.

We were given our own quarters and allowed to bathe. Minseo told me the story of how he'd nearly been forced to chop off his own hand, and I filled him in about Emmett and our time in the forest. By comparison, my last few weeks seemed uneventful though the exhaustion and hunger I felt said otherwise. I was happy to learn that Leon had assisted Minseo in his escape and I was eager to find him and thank him.

"Actually," Minseo said, "Leon refuses to leave the king's side."

"The king's *alive*?" I choked, reaching out for a chair to plop into.

Minseo tilted his head to the side as if I'd missed a crucial part of his story. "Yes, Leon and I traded the king to get you out of jail."

Excitement overflowed from within me. "Charlotte's going to be so happy." I turned to find my brother looking somber. He nodded, but I could tell that once again he was swallowing his words. "It's okay, Minseo. I'm alive. We can go home to Vires. You did that."

He feigned a smile, given away by the pity beaming at me through his sorrowful gaze.

"Let's get some food and find Leon. That way we can leave for Vires nice and early tomorrow." I peeked my head out the door to try and find someone to bring us lunch, but the hallways were empty.

I called over my shoulder to Minseo, "They must all be preparing for the ceremony. Hold on." I hurried into the hall and toward the servant's quarters.

"Hello?" I called, but there was no reply. I headed toward the grand hall, making sure to take the side corridor to avoid being seen by anyone going to the event.

I froze. Standing right there, on the other side of the corridor, was Charlotte. My hands began to sweat and my legs grew heavier with each endless second. I couldn't breathe. She wore a white flowing dress that cinched in her waist. Her brown skin was luminescent, her curls pinned out of her face. Suddenly, as if she felt my gaze brush her shoulder, she turned to me.

I tried to bite back the audible gasp that slipped out and quell the electricity that tore each cell of my body apart with every step closer she took. She smiled so brightly that I almost felt myself smile back. Forgetting herself, she threw her arms around me and buried her face in my neck. My body went rigid. Instinctually, I took her by the waist and eased her away from me. Her face glittered and I wondered if she had been crying. She wiped her eyes.

"I thought you were going to be executed," she said, her white ball gown swaying with each tiny movement of her body.

"Me too," I said, my gaze traveling around the angelic princess. "Minseo saved me."

She covered her mouth with her hands. "He's alive! That's great. My father is here in the castle. He's hurt, but he's alive."

I nodded. My gaze lifted from her waist to her chest, up to her collarbone, her neck, and finally met her eyes. The sudden dread of silence sunk in. "You make a beautiful bride." My eyes widened.

She smiled softly, and all at once I could see the same sorrowful gaze that Minseo had given me. "Thank you," she said.

I prepared myself to tear my gaze away from her, trying to drink in every detail of her and capture the memory before I left, but she reached out and touched my wrist, sending sparks radiating up my arm.

"I-I..." she stammered. A faint pink blush wisped over her cheeks. She continued. "I guess I won't be needing this."

She reached under the outermost layer of her dress, digging underneath for something. She seemed to be struggling, but I wasn't sure how to help her or what she was doing. I mean, it wasn't like I could reach in there and assist her. Finally, something unhooked from her waist and from under a fold of white fabric she pulled out an ornately-decorated sheathed broadsword.

The handle of the sword was a dragon covered in red rubies. It was much too large and heavy to be concealed in a dress, or so I thought.

"I guess I don't need this anymore," she said, handing me the sword. I eyed her dress, wondering what other mysterious objects were hidden in there.

"Why do you have a sword in your dress?" I asked, unable to fight a smile from stinging my cheeks.

She laughed. "I was going to save you."

"Were you going to stab him at the altar?"

She bit her bottom lip, biting back a smile.

I gaped. "*That* was your plan?" I whispered, checking the empty hallway for listeners.

She pushed my shoulder. "It wasn't Plan A."

My smile dimmed. "What were you going to do about his army after you killed him?"

"I hadn't gotten that far," she said, putting her hands on her hips.

I nodded, attaching the sword to my belt. "Well, thank you, Charlotte, for the sword and your reason for having it."

I turned to leave, glancing back one more time. "Got anything else hidden under there?" I asked.

"Matching dagger," she said with a sly smile. With each step away, my breathing became more labored. I shook inside. How could it be unbearable to be near her and worse to walk away? It was hard to believe that this was goodbye, that after everything I had to just go on living my life in Vires as if nothing happened. As if my entire world hadn't been changed forever.

I left the corridor, heading straight back to my chamber. I wasn't hungry anymore—in fact, I felt sick. I hoped Minseo would know what to do or what to say to make my chest stop aching.

26

PRINCESS CHARLOTTE

The moment Prince Young turned away from me, I felt a swirl of emotions I wasn't expecting. How could I feel this sad when everything had worked out perfectly? Young was safe, my father was home, and when I said "I do" in a few hours, Algony's army would clear out Drethen. My kingdom and everyone I loved would be out of danger. I never wanted to be a wife, certainly not Emmett's wife, but it wasn't worth losing anyone else. Besides, Emmett had given me such a beautiful proposal and that kiss... I wondered what it would have been like to kiss Young. I shook the thought from my head. I was so childish. Everything was fine. So, why did I feel like crying?

I decided I'd given my father enough time to rest and headed to his chamber. As I approached the double doors, I noticed the guards had their ears against the door.

"What's going on?" I asked. The guards jumped back into a straightened position. "Leon!" I said rushing over. "You're alive."

He bowed and pushed a brown strand of hair out of his eyes. "I'm happy you also arrived safely."

The other guard looked like he was asleep on his feet. "That's McCaffrey of Algony," Leon said. McCaffrey slouched against the door.

I considered asking what was wrong with him, but I didn't care enough. "What's going on with my parents?" I asked.

He smirked. "Want to take a listen?"

I gasped in excitement. "Can I?" I rushed to the door and put my ear to the crack. I could barely make out the words.

"Well, what was I supposed to do?" my mother cried.

"Honor the agreement," my father said weakly.

"If I had, you'd be dead."

"I was also rescued by a prince of Vires. What kind of king backs out of an arrangement this important? Furthermore, Emmett of Algony is the worst kind of man. Are you really willing to vouch for him?" Even in anger, my father sounded much weaker than normal.

My mother's voice cracked. *"I'd stake my life on it."*

I pushed myself away from the door. I wished I didn't hear that. My corset dug into my sides. Emmett *was* the worst and Young didn't deserve how this turned out. I knew all this already but hearing it from my father made it seem worse. I gasped for air. There was no way I was going to last in this dress until the ceremony. There were several more hours until it started. My parents had some business to work out, business that I didn't want to be a part of. I'd buy myself some time to plan and marry who I had to marry. For now, I just wanted to be out of this dress. I hurried to my chambers, half expecting to see Milly there, but the room was empty. I swallowed my disappointment. All the servants must've been busy making the feast or setting up the grand hall. I was sure Milly was with Sasha trying to prepare enough food for the council and nobility that would be in attendance.

I reached around my back to try and unlace my corset myself. Not even close. There was no way I was getting it off. I tried reaching one more time, but this time I wound up making myself light-headed and out of breath. A thud sounded on my door. My shoulders tensed. I hoped it was one of my maids—I needed to get out of this thing. I hurried to the door and pushed it open. Prince Young stood in my doorway.

"Charlotte," he said. I looked into the hall behind him to see if someone else was passing, anyone who could help me—but it was only him.

"Please pardon me for coming to your chamber. I wondered if I might be able to have a word with you before the—"

Grabbing him by the shirt, I pulled him into my chamber. "Get in here," I said, shutting the door behind him. I took two steps toward the center of my room and said, "Quick, untie it. Help me take this off."

"Well... this is going better than expected," he said, half under his breath.

"Hurry, I can't breathe," I shouted.

Young's hands moved clumsily over the ribbons. "Sorry, I've never done this before," he said, "Uh-uhm. I mean—"

"That's okay. Neither have I," I said without thinking. What did I even mean by that?

"How do I do this?" he whispered.

I said, "Just try to loosen it. I just need a deep breath."

He pulled at the ribbons and I felt a slight release around my waist. I exhaled. "So, what was it that you wanted to talk about?" I asked as he continued pulling aimlessly at strings behind me. He let my question hang there. I wasn't sure if he would answer.

"I wanted to know if you're happy with Emmett."

I opened my mouth to answer. "A-"

"No, that's not what I wanted to say. I guess what I mean is, do you still want to marry me? No, I guess you never really did want to. What I'm trying to say is, I miss Vires."

My heart thudded and I felt my corset tighten.

He continued. "Now that I'm free, I can return there, but for some reason I can't—and I think that reason is that I want to marry you. Still."

My heart slammed into my ribcage. Was this a proposal? I turned to face him, holding the front of my dress up with my arm. It made no sense. "Why? There's barely a kingdom left. You know what Emmett will do if I don't go through with this."

"I don't care." He stepped closer. My eyes disobeyed me and my gaze slipped to his lips for a fraction of a second. His eyebrow raised slightly. He'd noticed. As if he was reading my curiosity, he leaned in.

The door swung open, "Brother! Emmett is headed this— Oh," Minseo said, eyeing my half-untied dress. I sprang back from Young in a panic. Minseo grinned. "Wow, that really went better than I expected." My face exploded with heat.

"Minseo, she can't breathe. How do I untie this?" Young said, gesturing to my back. With three quick fluid motions, Minseo untied my entire corset. One thing was clear: Minseo *had* done this before.

Minseo turned to Young, "Emmett is coming. Hide." The Viran princes dove behind a lounge chair on the far end of my chamber, just as a knock once again sounded on my door.

"Getting ready," I called. Emmett peaked into the room. He grinned widely at my unlaced corset. "Is this a preview of tonight? Don't worry about the audience, Princess, I'll handle everything." I'd almost forgotten about the consummation ceremony until he mentioned it. *Ugh.* Dread pulsed through me. He stepped up behind me and tightened my corset as quickly as Minseo had loosened it. *Ah. Not his first time either.*

"You look stunning," he said, heading for the door. I felt a rush of relief because he hadn't spotted the princes. A chill went down my spine as my mind contemplated what might've happened if he'd discovered them alone in my chamber, especially since I was half-naked when he arrived.

"Oh, Princess," Emmett said, turning back to me. My stomach dropped. He continued, "I've been thinking about that kiss." He ran his hand through his hair. "I'm excited for tonight," he said, and with that he left my chamber, closing the door behind him.

Afraid to move, I concentrated on my, once again, restricted breathing.

"You *kissed* that guy?" Young asked, stepping out from behind the velvety lounge chair.

"Yes," I said flatly. I had no explanation. "I-I." My cheeks burned hot with guilt.

Minseo put his hand on Young's head. "It's not a big deal."

Young headed for the door. "I'm sorry to have taken up so much of your time," he said, his gaze glued to the floor. The door closed behind him.

What was *happening*? How had I lost this much control of my life? Once the parade of princes left my chamber,

I slumped into my bed and cried. I wasn't sure what I was crying for anymore. I sobbed into my pillow until, somehow amidst the chaos, I drifted off to sleep.

27

PRINCE YOUNG

"Young!" Minseo called. I kept walking straight into my chamber. "Young!" he said, grabbing me by the shoulder. "You're not seriously mad about the princess kissing Emmett, right?"

I scoffed. "Of course not."

"Good, because not twenty minutes ago, you told me she was going to kill that guy to save you. Remember that?"

I put my hands in my pockets. "I don't know."

"You don't know what? Why're you so angry, brother? You'll soon feel better once we get to Vires. Soon enough you'll turn nineteen, and after you've been with a few women, you'll forget all about the princess."

I turned away from Minseo. "I'm just not—ready. I can't just go back."

"Brother, it's over. She's marrying Emmett."

I clenched my fist and I felt something hot bubbling inside me but said nothing.

Minseo continued. "Is this about the kingdom? Father will find you an—"

"It's not," I said, unwilling to listen.

He stepped back. "So all of this is about the girl."

"It's about keeping my word."

"Brother, we're surrounded by Algonian soldiers. You think he's going to let you storm the wedding, take the throne and the girl, and walk out of here alive? This is over. We're leaving tonight."

I inhaled sharply. "You should go," I told him.

Minseo shook his head. "Don't do this. Don't die for a girl. Come home."

I couldn't look at him, so I looked down at my feet, but even without looking at him I could sense the pain I was causing him. "I'm sorry," I said. "I'm staying, but I think you should go. Tonight, while you still can."

We walked in silence back to our quarters. I sat on my bed examining the dragon sword Charlotte had given me. Minseo was afraid, but he knew he couldn't change my mind. I understood everything he said, I even longed to see Vires, but somehow I was tied to Besmium now. I needed to know Charlotte would be okay. I had to do whatever I could to protect her from Emmett.

My brother was going back to Vires. The only one I was putting in danger was myself. I could live with that.

Several minutes passed in frigid silence before my brother's voice broke it. "This is ridiculous! Stop being childish," he yelled. "Father would be ashamed. This kingdom is worthless and Charlotte is nothing but a pathetic, helple—" My fist collided with his jaw before I knew I'd even crossed the room. Minseo dropped his hand from his mouth, a crimson stream of blood flowing from his lip to his chin. His gaze cut into mine, a glimmer of sadness in his eyes that told me it wasn't my punch that hurt him most.

My brother packed his things without a word. It was hard

knowing that he was leaving. I glued my attention to my sword until Minseo stood at the door of our chamber, a bag slung over his shoulder. He cleared his throat. "Please, Young?" he said, making my chest ache. He sighed, "I just got back."

I wanted to go with him. To see my kingdom and my family again. I wanted to apologize to Minseo and make things right, but I couldn't leave Charlotte. She was willing to kill Emmett to save me. Now I would do the same for her. "I'm sorry, brother," I said. "I'm staying." I heard the door shut and the reality of my choice weighed heavily on my shoulders. There was no escaping Besmium now.

I changed into my finest clothes. After all, I *was* going to a wedding. I tied my new broadsword to my belt and headed toward the grand hall. Leon was standing near the entrance. "Leon," I called. He grinned with his whole face. "Your Majesty," he said, bowing before looking me up and down. "I hope you're not planning on crashing the wedding," he chuckled. When I didn't respond, his smile faded. "No, Young. That's a bad idea."

"Where's Emmett?" I asked, ignoring him.

"What did your brother say about this?"

"My brother's gone back to Vires. He left a few minutes ago."

Leon shook his head, his eyes widened in understanding. "It's suicide."

"Where is he?"

Leon took a deep breath, his eyes as heavy with regret as Minseo's.

"Leon," I said, "I have to do this."

He nodded solemnly. "He's in the atrium. It's at the end of the east wing, down the stairs."

Before he could say another word, I hurried toward the atrium. I sprinted down the dimly-lit staircase, skipping stairs as I went.

Finally, I stood outside a large wooden door. I pushed the door and stepped outside into a green garden courtyard.

Emmett stood on a bridge toward the middle of the atrium, seemingly enjoying the temperate weather. He turned to me, a soft smile on his face. "Ah, " he said moving closer. "I suppose you've come to bid me farewell."

"I've come to challenge you," I said.

He blinked at me dumbly.

"For Charlotte's hand in marriage."

Tension closed around the atrium like a thick fog. I felt sweat begin to bead on the back of my neck. Emmett stared at me for several moments before a look of understanding flashed in his blue eyes. He threw his head back and let out a loud, breathy laugh that echoed off the walls of the atrium.

"Go home, kid. You're going to get yourself killed." He chuckled, wiping tears from his eyes.

I clenched my jaw and drew my sword. "I'm a better man than you."

"Seriously," he said, still smiling. "Don't make me kill you. I have a lot on my plate. I'm getting married today." He ran his fingers through his golden hair.

He wasn't going to agree. I had to find a way to antagonize him. "It sounds to me like you're afraid."

"Afraid?" he scoffed. "I could eat you," he said, erupting back into laughter. I wasn't getting anywhere.

The sun began to dip behind the castle wall, casting its final beam of light directly onto my sword. The red rubies scattered red light around the garden, like blood splattered across a war-torn forest.

"Actually," I said, turning the sword over in my hand, " Charlotte gave me this sword about an hour ago."

Emmett's smile faded. "Shut up."

He pushed past me and headed to the door to the castle. I was losing him. If he didn't accept my challenge, I'd have no chance of stopping the wedding.

I ransacked my brain for one last bit of ammunition as he reached for the door. *Ah.* A pang of guilt hit my stomach before the words even came out. "Corsets," I huffed. "Am I right?"

Emmett stopped with his hand on the door.

I gulped, trying to keep my voice as even as possible, but my fear started to creep in. "Those things are a pain to unlace." I feigned a laugh. "You weren't even a little suspicious."

Emmett turned back to me, a fierce darkness in his eyes, like a summer storm about to break. "If you want to die so badly, I accept your challenge."

28

PRINCE EMMETT

They were all lies, everything he implied. One look at him and anyone could see the man didn't have it in him. Still, the thought of him and Charlotte together made hatred surge through me. I didn't care what Young said, there was no way the princess would ever choose a man like him over a man of my caliber. Who did he think he was? It was true that Vires had an impressive military, but the location barred them from being a threat or ally to anyone in this region. Not to mention Young himself—weak, scrawny, and barely man enough to grow facial hair. What was he thinking! To challenge me? I settled on the possibility that he'd been so ashamed of losing his contract with Besmium that he was choosing suicide over returning home. If that were the case, then this was a mercy killing—a perfect way to stab away my wedding jitters.

I glared at Young from across the atrium. He was on the bridge, a higher plane than me, but it didn't matter. I was unbeatable. I could tell by the way he held his sword that at least he'd held one before. I scoffed, unable to believe his arrogance.

He swung carelessly. I easily avoided his attack and he'd left himself open. I was going to end this with one swing. I raised my sword above my head and veered it down from above him. He blocked it with the flat of his blade. He was *fast*; it didn't matter. The sheer force of the impact knocked him down to his knees. I pressed down and he collapsed beneath the weight. I raised my sword once again and swung down for the finishing blow. He rolled to his right, off the bridge and into the water. My sword sliced into the wooden beams. I tried to pry it out but it didn't budge. Again. The wood splintered. One more, the sword dislodged, sending shreds of wood flying. Spinning around, Young charged me. I dodged his advance, his blade slicing past me, knocking me off balance.

He *was* good—I swept his leg out from under him—but *I* was better. He slammed back onto the bridge, his sword sliding out of his damp hand. I stepped on his chest as he swatted at my boot helplessly. This was the end. At worst, I'd get a little blood on my boot and have to dip it in the stream. It had been useless for him to challenge me. It was obvious before we started. He had no chance at all. I brought my sword down.

"Wait!" a voice called.

I paused, tracing the sound of the voice to the door to the castle. McCaffrey stood in the doorway, his hand outstretched, his mouth agape, and his face stark white.

"Not now, McCaffrey," I said while lifting my sword.

"Don't, sire! Prince Minseo has returned..."

I shook my head. "I didn't know he'd left. This is a fair duel. Why shouldn't I finish it?"

"Prince Minseo has returned with the Viran army, sire. I feel it's in your best interest, duel or not, to let the other Viran prince live."

It was impossible. Vires was too far. They would have had to be summoned weeks ago. Minseo hadn't even arrived until this morning. Young had been in prison. That meant—*the princess.* I staggered back breathlessly. She doesn't want me?

"H-how many?"

McCaffrey shook his head, alarm flashing in his eyes. "More than us."

My boiling blood seared my skin from the inside. My body shook. *Charlotte.*

"Sire," McCaffrey said. "We must retreat."

"N-no. The wedding. It's—" Young got to his feet. Stunned, I stared at Young, staring back at me with fear in his eyes, so weak and helpless. Would the king just hand the throne to such a man now? Someone I could destroy this very moment. I *would* destroy him this very moment. No, I'd destroy them all. If I couldn't have Charlotte, no one could. If I didn't sit on the Besmian throne, no one would. I hustled past Young with half a mind to impale him on my way, but I had a better idea.

I returned to my quarters out of breath and snatched the pink flowers, with a gloved hand, from behind the curtains where I'd concealed them.

"McCaffrey! Get the carriage ready. Start moving the troops!" I shouted.

In his contorted expression, I noticed what, to him, must have looked like a crazed, unraveling man with a fist full of pink flowers. No one would make a fool out of me. I stormed to the kitchen, ready to cut down anyone in my path. I'd find something to put the flowers in, and as they dined and celebrated their victory—I'd wipe out the entire Besmian royal family, the council, and half the nobles in one night.

The kitchen was empty. Not a soul or a servable food in sight. The dishes were stacked high in the sink, but nothing was cooking. I must be too late. There were four large barrels at the far side of the kitchen that seemed to be pushed forward from their usual resting place. I peered in to see a black liquid. Sticking my face near one of the barrels, I sniffed. *Wine*, perfect. I ripped the pink flowers into the smallest pieces I could manage with frantic, shaky hands and dumped them into each of the barrels. I stood back, pleased with my work.

"What are you doing here?"

I looked up to see the middle-aged woman from the garden. Her face was even redder than usual. She took one look at me, and then at the wine, and realized what I had done. I clutched the hilt of my sword. Without a second thought, I raised it and ran it through her. Blood spattered and she made a feeble gurgling sound before the light left her eyes. I dragged her body around the corner. Someone would find her, but it was unlikely that anyone else knew about the flowers—there was no reason to suspect the wine. Before I left, I spotted a streak of the old chef's blood across the floor. I grabbed a ladle and scooped some wine from the closest barrel and poured it over the blood to make it look like the blood was just spilled wine. Happy with my work, I darted out of the castle.

I marched with my remaining men as nearly all of them were already outside of the courtyard. They must've begun retreating hours ago. I passed row-by-row of Viran soldiers all uniformed in yellow—with some indistinguishable symbol on their chests. I tallied the number of soldiers I saw there. I'd triple my own numbers and return. I'd slaughter every last one of them, all of them. As I passed the last row of Viran soldiers, I was greeted by Prince Minseo.

He smirked a victorious grin that made me impulsively reach for my sword. Instead of drawing it, I smiled. "Enjoy the party," I said.

He waved. "Don't worry, I will. So sorry you couldn't make it."

I vowed to myself that they wouldn't get away with this. I wouldn't rest until every last person in that castle died, whether it happened tonight or tomorrow. I'd get my revenge.

How dare they humiliate Prince Emmett of Algony like this! How dare *she*.

29

MILLY

Where was Sasha? I wondered as I scooped a spoonful of rice onto the serving plates. We'd been in the kitchen together cooking all day, but since we moved the food we'd prepared to the grand hall, I hadn't seen much of her. At first, I didn't mind her absence. She'd been especially harsh towards me since the poison incident with the queen. I was grateful to her for switching the cups and knew I deserved every bit of her anger towards me. I would have been executed for treason if she'd told anyone, and she could be too for keeping my secret. Still, I relished the hours I was out of her company.

I never realized how many servants there actually were in Castle Cadere until today. Since I'd arrived here, we stuck to our usual routines and designated areas in the castle, but today was Charlotte's wedding, and everyone was either in the grand hall or the chapel trying to get everything ready for tonight—except Sasha. Another hour passed and I still hadn't seen her; perhaps we'd forgotten some of the food in the kitchen. I headed through the poorly-lit servants' quarters toward the kitchen. Many busy people rushed past carrying strings of flowers, plates, and cutlery. Droves of decorations, trays filled with candles, ribbons, and lace fabric to decorate every inch of the hall. I'd never seen an event of this magnitude in my lifetime.

Just as I turned the corner to the kitchen, I ran straight into a server carrying a large tray with three golden goblets. He swayed backward. The goblets wobbled, spilling a few drops of red wine onto the tray.

"Oh," I said. "I'm terribly sorry." I paused for a minute as the boy composed himself.

He exhaled, "It's alright. No harm done."

I stepped aside to let him pass. "Wait," I said, remembering what Sasha told me earlier. "We're not meant to serve wine until after the ceremony. No exceptions," I said.

"I know," he said, "but this is a special request from the king himself. Some pre-wedding toast with the groom, no doubt."

I nodded and turned into the kitchen to look for Sasha. I stood stunned in the doorway of the kitchen.

Impossible. Who could have done this? The sink was piled high with every dirty cooking utensil in the entire castle. Surely, I'd have to be the one to wash these while everyone lays down to rest tonight. But I suppose no one would miss me if I washed a few of them. I plunged my hands into the soapy water and scrubbed. I pushed myself to increase my speed with each dish, timing myself in my head. I started grabbing dishes from the countertop and tossing them into my bucket. One by one, they splashed in the water. I yanked a large pot near a bag of potatoes and tossed it into my washing barrel. The bag toppled over, sending stumpy brown potatoes rolling across the kitchen floor. *Great.* I wiped my hands on my apron and chased after the scattered spuds, grabbing as many as I could and tossing them into the sack.

One particularly ambitious potato rolled a little farther than the others toward the back door of the kitchen. I reached out of the dimly-lit kitchen toward the dark hallway and grabbed for the potato. It didn't move. I could tell by the weight of it I hadn't grabbed the potato, despite its similar brown color. I moved toward the object. I gasped as horror pricked into me like a thousand needles. *Sasha.* I fell to my knees, shaking her body with my hands. I rolled her over to find a look of pain frozen on her stark white face. She was covered in wine.

"Sasha, what's wrong? What happened to you?!" I screamed, but she didn't move. Her lifeless gaze chilled me. "Sasha!" I shook her hard but she didn't move. I pulled my wet hands back and held them towards the light. It's not wine, I gulped. *Blood.* I shrieked a horrible sound as the realization dawned on me. Sasha was dead. My mind reeled.

I pressed my hands together. "Oh, heavenly father, please guide Sasha safely through the gates of heaven where she—" I choked through my sobs, my ears still ringing from my scream. "...where she will be welcomed into your loving arms." I wanted to continue, but I couldn't think with the sound of a wailing girl reverberating off the walls around me. I cried for help but no one came. Half-delirious, I pulled myself away from Sasha's body, a mass now as lifeless as a sack of potatoes. I stepped into the kitchen to find myself covered in blood. Red everywhere. My vision blurred and whitened as I struggled to stay on my feet. I stumbled and caught my balance on the edge of the wine barrel. I put my weight on the barrel and rested my head on the side. Taking a deep breath, I closed my eyes.

When I opened them again, I felt my senses intensify. The red of the wine was crisp—the smell stung my nose with an astringent aroma. I stood quickly then leaned in once again to get a closer look. Unmistakably, there in the wine were the floating petals of the Oleander flower.

Sasha knew about the flowers. She'd switched out the poisonous wine that I'd tried to serve the queen and scolded me for the attempt. She'd saved my life that day. I never told her that the queen forced me to drink it as well. However, one thing I did know was that this wine was *poisoned*. Luckily, we were instructed not to serve wine until after the ceremony, with no exceptions... except. My eyes widened. The king!

I sprinted out of the kitchen and toward the king's chamber.

"Help! Help!" I screamed. Now that I was closer to the grand hall, someone might hear me. Several servants rushed to silence me, but they stopped when they saw me—a hysterical blood-covered freak show.

"Wh-what happened child?" another servant called as a crowd began to form around me.

"Sasha's been murdered. The wine has been poisoned. The king is in danger!" I screamed.

The next hour went by in a blur—servants rushing in every which direction, Sasha's body being carried out of the kitchen, and the doctor being called. Everyone was asking me things, but I couldn't hear them.

Sympathetic hands removed my bloodstained clothes and washed me. Afterward, I began to hear their voices again and the truth began to reveal itself—the Viran army had arrived. Prince Young had taken Emmett's place as Charlotte's groom, and Sasha—the wine; it was all Emmett's revenge. Young was too nervous about the wedding to drink the wine but the king and Minseo both had. The doctor wasn't sure if either would make it through the night. I replayed the news in an endless loop until I settled on the only comforting thought I could manage—that Young was okay.

30

PRINCESS CHARLOTTE

My father was murdered on the night of my wedding.

"The king is dead," the doctor said, removing his gloves. "I gave him the antidote, but he was still too weak from his injuries to recover."

"No!" I screamed, leaping out from the corner where I was hiding. "You," I cried, pointing at my mother. "You told me to let him rest. Now I'll never see him again!" She turned to me with wet eyes.

"I hate you. I hate you," I choked. She reached out to me and I braced myself, ready to push her away. My mother wrapped her arms around me and pulled me into her chest as my limbs jellied. The wet of her tears soaked into my shoulder and I couldn't remember the last time she'd held me that way. It was the kind of hug my father gave, and in it, I felt everything my mother couldn't say to me. *I'm hurting too. You are my only family. I love you.* But she wasn't my father. In fact, she'd stolen the last moments I could have had with him. I pushed her away and hurried out of the room.

I wasn't permitted to go in the king's parlor where my father's body was, but the doctor handed me a letter written by the king to me before he died. *A letter*. I held it to my chest as endless tears fell down my cheeks. It was all I had left of him and that thought alone prevented me from opening it. All my father was—reduced to one piece of parchment.

The doctor loomed over Minseo. He'd also received the antidote, and while his condition was far from stable, he'd survived an hour and a half since he'd been poisoned, an hour longer than my father. I knew Young would be there beside his brother, but I wasn't sure if it was appropriate for me to go to him. Who was I to Young anyway? I wasn't his wife yet; perhaps a friend. It didn't matter. I was all he had right now and I wanted to be there for him. I slipped a peek in the mirror, only to find my face red and puffy from crying and then felt stupid for checking. I hastened out of my chamber.

There were two Viran guards outside Minseo's quarters, their faces stoic, their features unmistakably Viran. I lost my nerve as I approached and turned to walk away. Young stood in front of me, sending a tingling sensation that started from behind my eyes and spread to my cheeks.

He spoke, "I went to check on you."

I nodded, feeling a heaviness in my chest.

He continued, "I'm sorry about your father."

I held out the letter sealed with my father's stamp.

"He wrote you something? Heh... what an amazing man he was."

I nodded, forcing myself to break eye contact; if I hadn't, I would have begun to cry again, and once it started, it was difficult to stop. We stood in silence for a moment. I imagined he was waiting for me to say something, but I was afraid of what I'd say.

"Must be overwhelming getting that letter. Give yourself some time, Charlotte."

I sniffed. "This is all that's left of him."

"No," he said. "Every moment you've ever spent with him is what's left of him. That's just a letter."

I stared down at the crinkled paper in my hands and let my mind dance through my memories of my father. After several seconds, Young grabbed my hand.

"I have to go check on Minseo."

He lifted my hand to his lips and kissed it before sliding past the Viran guards into Minseo's chamber, closing the door behind him.

It was a kind and simple gesture of comfort and somehow it helped a little. Had I really come here to comfort Young? Or did I come here because I knew he'd comfort me? I hadn't asked him how he was feeling, or even about his brother. More importantly, he didn't bring those things up either. He wasn't thinking of himself, nor his brother at all. Just me.

I returned to my chamber, my mind drifting from my father to Minseo. Every time someone knocked on my chamber door, my stomach tightened. I worried for Minseo and I worried for Young. Several servants came knocking on my door to check on me, not Milly though. I'd been told that Sasha had also been killed. Milly had found her and discovered the poison in the wine. I wanted to run to her, to throw my arms around her, but everything was broken, and each piece too sharp to mend.

I was certain that finding Sasha the way that she did had pushed her beyond what she could take. To think she had the piece of mind to report the wine afterward. I knew she needed me, but I couldn't help her—not now. Not while the news of my father's death still stung my heart with each beat.

Worse were the rumors. Whispers among the servants suggested that Emmett was to blame, but I knew for sure. It was him. Another knock sounded at my door as panic surged. *Minseo.* This time my mother strode in, a somber energy slumping her posture like I'd never seen before.

She lay beside me. "I've decided to proceed with the wedding tonight."

I sat up. "W-What? But father—"

"I know," she said as she looked deeply into my eyes. For the first time, I noticed the age lines setting in around them. She was getting older, and she looked like she'd been crying as much as I had. She sighed, "That's why. Your father wanted this union. He trusted Prince Young."

I felt an ache inside that was unrelenting. I wasn't sure when, but things with Young had changed. I remembered what he'd said, in my chamber earlier that night about how he still wanted to marry me. I relived the flood of emotions those words unlocked. He was my ally, and like my father, I trusted him, but I somehow couldn't find it in me to be happy about this marriage. In fact, with my father gone, I couldn't find it in me to be happy about anything.

31

PRINCE YOUNG

I put a damp cloth on Minseo's head. "Hang in there," I whispered. What happened to him wasn't my fault—yet, somehow, I blamed myself. He'd wanted to leave this kingdom more than anything and now he couldn't. He must've run into the Viran army on the way out and decided to lead them here. Once again, he'd saved me. I knew somehow it was Emmett who'd poisoned the wine. I made a silent promise on my brother's life that next time I faced off with Emmett I wouldn't lose. I'd make him pay for this.

"Sir," a voice said from behind me, "Captain Leon is here to see you."

I nodded and the guard opened the door, allowing Leon to pass. Leon stepped forward. "I'm sorry about your brother," he said, anxiously shifting his weight from one foot to another.

"Thanks," I said. "He'll be fine." I didn't believe it, but I wanted it to be true.

"I was sent to inform you that the queen wishes to proceed with the wedding."

I stood. "But Minseo—and Charlotte's father."

He shrugged. "I think that's why. This kingdom needs stability. She didn't want to delay it anymore."

"What does Charlotte think about this?"

Leon scratched at his eyebrow. "I... have no idea."

My face reddened. Of course, she was upset about her father. I guess I was just worried that this would make it worse.

Leon asked, "Uh, do you want me to go ask?"

"No," I said. "But what was her mood like when she told you?"

Leon bit back a smile.

I shook my head, hoping it might hide my embarrassment. "I have to look after Minseo."

"He needs to rest. You go on, I'll look after him tonight while you're away," Leon said.

I turned back to Minseo. He was breathing weakly and his skin was deathly pale. It was difficult seeing him like this. I needed him beside me to talk me through everything. I needed him to make witty comments about my marriage or my new kingdom. I needed him to antagonize me about the consummation ceremony. "Don't die," I said. "I need you, brother."

"They're waiting for you out there. Better get going," Leon said.

Two hours later, I stood in front of an altar—an ornately decorated platform dripping with golden cups, flickering candles, and velvet cushions. There were endless rows of pews with white ribbons and roses draped across each one. The announcer called the names of the nobles and council members in attendance one by one as they came in, but I'd been standing up front for over an hour, and my mind had blocked out the announcer half an hour ago. The council members stood out to me as they were all wearing similar red robes. I'd heard plenty of things about them, their judgments, and their law enforcement tactics, but this was the first time I'd been able to put a face to them.

Despite the hundreds of Besmian guests that were arriving, I felt alone. On the other side of the castle, my brother was fighting for his life. My parents and my eldest brother had never planned on making the trip here for the wedding. Most of my soldiers were stationed outside the castle, or, in some cases, getting settled into their new quarters. Despite the wedding, I felt defeated. I couldn't beat Emmett, I couldn't keep my brother safe, and I'd been met with trial after trial since I'd arrived. In a room full of strangers, I longed for some piece of home, or even just someone who *knew* me.

The music changed to a pleasant and flowing organ tune that I'd never heard before. The double doors swung open and Charlotte stepped through. Without her father to walk her, Charlotte walked the hundred-yard chapel on her own.

I'd loathed every moment I stood at the front of the chapel alone, but Charlotte's long walk to the altar must've been worse. Every soul in the church watched her, and why wouldn't they? Her tearful eyes glistened, her cheeks pink from crying, her curls straying free from her pins. Yet, she was the loveliest princess there'd ever been.

She stepped up onto the altar, gifting me a small smile. The pain in her eyes was so vividly obvious it hurt to look at her. I wanted to tell her it would be okay. I wanted her to know I understood. I willed her to hear these messages with my gaze but had no way of knowing if she'd received them.

The ceremony was in Latin, a language I didn't understand. The guests stood and sat many times throughout at the request of Besmium's religious leader. Charlotte and I each lit a candle and fed each other bread and white wine. It all happened in a blur—slipping by like a falcon passing the mountain's peak. I tried to focus, to be in the moment, but before I could grab ahold of it, it was over.

"You may kiss the bride."

What? Oh. Looking down at Charlotte only made me more nervous. I felt the burn from the attention of three hundred people on my face, but the more I hesitated, the weirder it became. I leaned in, barely brushing her bottom lip with mine.

"I now pronounce you husband and wife," the director said.

I was flooded with relief. This time, Charlotte and I would make this walk together. I felt a surge of adrenaline as she gripped tightly onto my arm. After everything, we'd made it. I didn't know exactly what lay ahead of us. But I felt like it couldn't have been worse than what we'd already faced. We were headed to the grand hall for a feast, although I didn't feel much like celebrating and I couldn't imagine Charlotte wanted that either. I felt drained and wanted nothing more than to lay down to rest.

Suddenly, I remembered. A nervous energy seethed through my body with alarming force. How could I possibly rest? The council members would all be there at my bedside tonight. Charlotte would be in it.

The consummation ceremony was hours away—and I could barely even kiss her.

32

PRINCESS CHARLOTTE

I was allowed to change my dress before the banquet. With the ceremony over and the majority of the grand hall ready for the feast, there was plenty of help this time. As an amber-haired lady's maid unlaced my corset, I remembered how Young had struggled to unlace it earlier—and how Minseo hadn't. I stepped out of my dress and felt the drafty castle air brush my legs. I rubbed my line-printed waist with my fingers, the marks from the corset a semi-permanent design on my body, then begrudgingly slipped into my reception dress. This one was much more free-flowing, with a large ribbon that went around my waist synching in the dress and tying in a bow at the back.

My mother entered my chamber. "Daughter," she said. "Tonight you will become a full woman." *Oh God.* I turned away hoping that she'd stop, but she didn't.

"The consummation ceremony is essential. It's the last step in binding the marriage—and as a woman, you have certain obligations."

"Mom, please. Stop."

"You're a wife now. You will also soon be queen."

"Mom, stop. Now."

"It's your duty to produce an heir and reestablish Besmium as—"

I couldn't take another word. "Seriously. I was going to go through with it, but now I'm reconsidering it."

She ignored me, grabbing me by the chin and kissing my cheek. "I'm so proud of you," she said. Then she left my chamber, a grimace of pity on her face before she stepped out.

I tried to push the consummation ceremony out of my head, to focus on what was ahead—the feast—but I simply couldn't.

I adjusted the top of my dress but quickly stopped, wondering if what I hid underneath my garments was okay. I'd never given much thought to my body before. It seemed normal enough to me, but I'd never tried to compare it to other girls' before now. What would Young think? One thing I was certain about was that I didn't want my body to be seen. My mind raced. And worse than seeing my body is what would come *after*. Would it hurt? Would I need to stop? With so many people watching, the best I could hope for was something quick and ordinary. A standard experience. Dread seeped in. What if I *enjoyed* myself? Every moment I thought about it, I would bring new worst-case-scenarios to light.

Young sat beside me at the reception and I couldn't help but sneak glances every chance I got. Why didn't he seem nervous? Why was he eating so much? Should I eat more? What if my stomach bulged out? He was calm and at ease, his posture confident and his demeanor pleasant. It unsettled me. I considered drinking wine to relax, but it didn't feel like a safe option. Even after we had been assured that the white wine had been tested for poison and no traces found, most people seemed to be avoiding it.

Not to mention, the last time I drank too much wine I'd made a fool out of myself in front of Young. It seemed unnatural that these celebrations continued as they'd been planned as if my father were in attendance. Life just cruelly kept moving, without even pausing to mourn a fallen king.

"Without further ado," the announcer called, "the Prince and Princess of Besmium will share their first dance."

Young helped me to my feet. My cheeks flushed with color as the entire room put down their cutlery and watched us take our positions at the center of the grand hall. Young pressed his body against mine, palming my right hand in his. His grip was tighter than I was used to, but once we started moving, I was grateful that I didn't have to guess where he was leading me. He swept me across the dance floor as the band filled the room with a symphony of flutes and violins, Young's steps precise and graceful. He spun me, turning my body outward and pressing his chest against my back before continuing the dance from this position. The onlooking nobles applauded as Young strung my body around the room with long, sweeping strides. He spun me back to face him as a hint of a smile appeared on the corner of his mouth, and I felt something warm stir inside. *This isn't so bad,* I thought. Perhaps tonight wouldn't be so bad either.

When the final dance ended, I knew it was time for the final ceremony of the night. The dance had quelled many of my fears, but they all rushed back as I entered the royal bedchamber and had my maid slip my dress off to leave me in only an undergarment. It was a thin, loose-fitting cloth that could be easily removed. It was not like a corset, required no practice or experience, and was virtually see-through from close proximity—it was my last layer of armor, and as I stood by the bed, waiting for Young to arrive, I could feel the presence of the rest of the counsel chattering quietly on the outskirts of the room. The bed was already turned down, a thin white curtain, made from a material that was not unlike my undergarments, was drawn, separating the bed from the rest of the room. The candles were burning low, and in this amount of light I was certain I'd only be a blurred shape to the onlookers—but Young would see everything. He'd *feel* everything. I gulped a mouthful of stale saliva.

Young entered the room, skyrocketing my pulse. I took a deep breath and felt tears prick my eyes. I wasn't *ready* but it was too late to back out. He entered the bed area, taking special care to fully close the sheer curtain surrounding the bed. He pulled off his shirt. A fierce wave of fear and excitement tore through my stomach as the yellow candlelight illuminated his bare chest. His muscles were defined peaks and valleys across his body, which surprised me, but I wasn't sure what I thought a man would look like shirtless before now.

I held my breath as he grabbed my waist and pulled me close. Tears spilled from my eyes as one emotion eclipsed all the others—fear.

He pulled my body to him and I felt my chest brush against his. He put his lips to my ear and whispered softly, "It'll be okay. I promise."

I nodded but fought my instinct to flee. I wanted to lock myself in my room and never come out. I needed more time. My mother was wrong; two more years might have made a big difference after all. Young took my hand and I sat down on the bed. My heartbeat in pace with my thoughts. With his palm, he eased me back onto the bed. He wrapped his arm around me and moved me onto the pillows.

I pressed my knees together with all my strength. He leaned in, his body pressing on mine. A fleeting wave of relief hit me as I realized he couldn't see my body from his position on top of me.

"Trust me," he whispered.

I clenched my eyes shut as his fingers brushed down my exposed leg to my knee. I felt my body shake as I allowed my knees to separate.

He used his knees to separate them further. *This was it,* I thought as I braced myself for pain. Young slid his hand over my mouth with one hand. *What is this?* With his other hand, he ran his fingers across my ribs. It tickled, and an involuntary laugh burst from my lips. Young tightened his grip on my mouth, muffling my laugh. *What was he doing?*

He tickled me again, each time muffling my laugh into a labored groan. He increased the intensity on my ribs. I thrashed to free myself from the tickle torture but he locked my body down and continued the cycle. I felt myself begin to sweat from his unusual game. After a few short minutes, he took his hand off my mouth, he kissed me on the forehead, and lay down beside me.

He faced me, his bare shoulders under the covers of the bed. My wrinkled brow prompted him to hold his finger up in front of his lips. I didn't dare speak, catching my breath as I waited for the answers. Sure enough, in minutes, I heard the onlooking counsel members' footsteps as they left the room until we were finally alone.

We lay in silence for several minutes before we broke it.

I spoke first. "You faked it," I said.

He adjusted his pillow. "Yeah."

I smiled but my wrinkled brow remained. He continued, "You've been through a lot today," he said.

"But I felt you... You were ready."

His face reddened as if I'd struck him. "Yeah, sorry about that. I've never seen... I mean, you were practically naked."

I was overcome with relief and gratitude. "Thank you," I said, burying my face in his chest. He hesitated, but ultimately wrapped his arms around me. I snuggled in close, feeling the warmth and safety I'd been longing for all day. Young's body tightened.

"Woah!" I said, louder than expected. "You're still... ready."

He let go, giggling to himself. "You're still naked."

33

PRINCE YOUNG

I awoke beneath a tangle of curls. I pulled a few strands out of my mouth and sat up to free myself from the rest. Charlotte lay asleep beside me with her mouth open as a steady stream of drool stretched between her cheek and her pillow. *My wife*. I felt a warm sensation in my chest. This was how I'd start every day for the rest of my life. I knew I should move, I had things to do, but instead, I lay there beside her in our haven soaking up the softness of the moment.

Last night, I'd been anxious to hear a knock at my door—afraid to hear bad news about Minseo, but somehow, with the exhaustion of the day, and Charlotte's even breathing beside me, I'd drifted off to sleep.

The castle had rooms designated specifically for married couples, so I slipped out and headed to my old chambers, where my things were still kept. I'd change for the day and then head straight for Minseo's room. I swung open my wardrobe and slid out of my nightwear before reaching for my royal blue coat.

"You're meant to wear black," a voice said from behind me.

I turned to see Milly and quickly covered myself with the blue coat. "What are you doing here?" I asked.

A hint of blush pricked her cheeks with pink. "I am to tell you to wear your black coat."

My stomach dropped. "Minseo—"

"Oh no. I'm sorry. Minseo is okay. Well, not good, but he's alive. There is a funeral for our fallen king this afternoon."

I sighed with relief but instantly regretted it. "I'm sorry, I just—"

"I understand." She tucked her golden hair behind her ear. "You were worried about your brother."

I nodded. "Exactly," I said. Today was meant to be my funeral. If my brother hadn't always shown up to save me, it very well might have. With the funeral happening later today, I knew this would be a difficult day for Charlotte. I wasn't used to consoling her—or anyone. I guess I didn't know how and with my brother in his current condition, I wasn't sure if I was in a place to help anyone.

An uncomfortable silence set in. My hands grew stiff from holding the jacket over my exposed body. "Uh..." I began. "I'll wear the black one then. Is there anything else?"

Milly smiled. "Here, I'll help you," she said, hurrying toward me.

"That's not necessary," I said, but she ignored me. She pulled out my black coat and held it out for me to exchange it with the blue one. I gulped, suddenly aware of what she was trying to do. I reached for the black coat and yanked it toward me before handing her the blue one. She'd resisted handing it over but wasn't prepared for me to use so much strength and was forced to let it go without getting a look at me. She stood there, stunned.

"Charlotte is my wife," I said flatly.

"Of course," she said, bowing deeply. "I only want to serve." She turned to leave. "If you need anything..." she took a breathy sigh, causing her chest to rise, drawing my attention to it, "just let me know." Then she was gone. What was that? Afraid she'd return, I dressed quickly. I needed to see Minseo.

Several Viran guards stood around the room where my brother rested when I arrived. They were younger than most of the other soldiers, no doubt friends of my brother, but I didn't know them well. They stood to attention as I entered, but there was a somber softness in their eyes that worried me.

Minseo hadn't so much as moved since the antidote had been administered. I sat at his bedside, feeling more hopeless than last night, as I examined his pale skin and nearly lifeless body.

I looked down at my hands. The cuts from my battle with Emmett were already healing. I wondered if my brother's internal wounds were healing as well.

"Dressed in black, I see," Minseo whispered. "I'm not dead yet."

My throat tightened. Minseo's eyes were slightly open and a hint of a smirk rested on his left cheek. The guards rushed over, all laughing and greeting Minseo all at once.

"Water," he choked.

The doctor, who was waiting nearby, rushed over, a bowl of water balanced in his hands. I moved aside. The doctor lifted Minseo's shoulders and poured the water carefully into his mouth.

The doctor turned to me. "He's not out of danger yet. He needs to rest."

I nodded, but my body wouldn't let me walk out of the room. I couldn't leave my brother there.

The doctor cleared his throat and the guards hurried out of the chamber. Still, I wanted to stay at my brother's side.

"It's okay, brother," he whispered. "Go." His voice was so weak his words only made it harder to go, but my brother had given me an order and, for once, I obeyed.

34

PRINCESS CHARLOTTE

The morning after my wedding, we buried my father. The details about Emmett—what he'd done—started being pieced together, and another war seemed imminent. I eagerly agreed. Our king had been murdered—my father—taken from me.

More than once my mind slipped to a dark place and I couldn't help but wonder if it had all been my fault. Perhaps I'd pushed Emmett too far. I pretended. I *lied*. I made him believe I'd marry him, and all the while I was moments away from plunging a dragon-hilted sword into his chest on the altar. I was a monster, and in all my scheming, I'd forgotten something important—Emmett was a monster too.

As I slipped into the black gown laid out for me, my mind raced. I really *had* planned on marrying Emmett, hadn't I? After I knew Young was safe. I had no way of knowing that Vires received my letter, or that they'd arrive before the wedding.

My eyes felt heavy with sadness. Sasha had been killed by

Emmett too. My heart ached for Milly. Sasha was family to Milly and many others, but she would not receive a grand funeral like my father. I knew she deserved one, but today I had no energy to fight for justice. My grief manifested like exhaustion and I could hardly bring myself to say my final goodbyes to my father.

No amount of reasoning made me feel any better. The church was filled with genuine sadness and the soft hum of whispered memories between the nobles who'd spent time with my father. I walked down the aisle that I'd walked the night before, this time in black—looking for a familiar face, looking for *Young*. My mother stood at the front of the church, her face covered by a black veil that ended below her shoulders.

My body numbed as I approached the casket. My limbs grew heavy with grief. My vision blurred. I needed to sit, or I might— I felt the gentle grip of a hand on my forearm. I turned to see Young, his gaze fixed on me. "Are you okay?" he whispered. I shook my head, so he grabbed me by the waist and supported most of my weight as he gently led me to our seats near the front of the church. As soon as I sat down, I felt better. Just a few deep breaths and the dizziness wore off.

I sighed with relief. "Thanks," I said, squeezing Young's hand. We'd been married for no more than twelve hours and he'd already saved me twice. I owed him more gratitude than just "thanks", but it was all I could muster under the circumstances.

I scanned the rows of people dressed in black. Did any of them really *know* my father? Was this just some kind of political event for them or just an excuse to wear their fine black garments? Anger filled my body. Had anyone here ever heard the sound of my father's laugh? Did they know he loved to look at constellations?

I hated the formalities of the life I was born into. It all seemed rehearsed. Fake. After the service, several nobles were selected to speak about my father. I readied myself for the politics. For the kind words meant only to gain my mother's good favor.

The first, a raven-haired woman with a sharply pointed nose told a story about how my father had personally assisted in rebuilding a bridge in her province after a particularly bad storm destroyed it. She went on to say that my father was the kind of king who cared enough to help his subjects, even if it meant rolling up his sleeves.

I was moved to hear a story about my father that I'd never heard. I felt the glow of pride at the heroic deeds my father did for so many. The next speaker told a different anecdote. Again, it was a story I'd never heard but spoke of the many incredible traits my father possessed.

Five more speakers told their story, each lovelier than the last. An unsettling thought weighed heavily on my mind. Maybe *I* was the one who didn't know my father. My mind tore through my memories searching for something, something he'd told me about himself. My heart tightened as the realization settled in. We'd only ever talked about *me*. Tears burst from my eyes and my body shook as panic settled in. I didn't know my father. There were a million things I wanted to ask him. I needed his advice. I wanted to hear his opinions, and now that chance would never come. I spent the precious moments of my father's life telling him about my day and complaining about my problems.

I buried my face in my hands to muffle the crying. I thought I had more time. I thought he'd always be here. Regret clouded my thoughts like a thick mist on a foggy shore just before dawn. I'd left the letter he wrote me locked away in my chamber and it took everything in me to keep from leaping up, running out of the church, and reading my father's final thoughts to me.

I had one more chance to know my father. It was as if I'd asked my father one question about him after all, perhaps the most important question given the circumstances. *Father, if you knew you were dying, what would you want me to know?*

35

PRINCE YOUNG

Charlotte worried me. She was suffering—barely able to stand or keep from crying. The hardest part was I couldn't fix it. I could only watch her endure it and that was dizzyingly frustrating. The funeral was arduous—an endless amount of emotional daggers being hurled at Charlotte continuously. I knew it wasn't intended to be that, but from where I sat, I worried it would be too much for her. I felt her pulse quicken with each new story. I figured Charlotte wouldn't want to fight the crowd to get to the exit, so I planned on waiting for the chapel to clear out a bit, but before I could tell her, she vanished into the crowd of people. I wasn't sure if I should give her space or make sure she was all right.

When I didn't see her at the banquet, I knew she'd gone back to our new chambers. I slipped out of the banquet room and followed her. As I turned down the corridor, I could hear the sniffle of a woman weeping. *Charlotte?* At the foot of Charlotte's chamber door, the queen of Besmium sat, tears and snot lining her face. I ran over, half expecting a pool of blood. Nothing but steel could take down someone so strong. As I neared, I saw no sign of pain on her face, only sadness. I knew I wasn't close enough to her to even attempt to comfort her. Physical pain was so much easier. I secretly wished she'd just twisted an ankle or something.

"Your Majesty," I said.

With a flick of her wrist, she dismissed. Good enough for me. I turned to leave but her voice stopped me.

"It's my fault he's dead," she said, her words slurring together like a linked chain.

I crouched down to her eye level, the sudden aroma of stale wine hitting my nose. "I think—"

"I was the one who told Emmett to come here. If I hadn't, my husband might be alive."

"We can't know the future. We can only do our best in the moment." It was not an empathetic speech. It wouldn't mend her wounds, but those were the facts and I hoped they could at least eliminate some of her guilt.

The queen sat in silence and I eyed the door behind her, wishing I was on the other side. Finally, she got to her feet and patted me on the back. She turned away from the chamber door and headed down the hallway.

"Don't you want to talk to Charlotte?" I called.

She continued walking and called over her shoulder, "You go ahead."

"I don't know what to say," I spoke while catching my breath, but she was already gone.

I pushed open the chamber doors, feeling the same adrenaline as on the battlefield. Charlotte sat at the foot of our bed. *My wife.* The moment I saw her, the peaceful feeling I'd relished this morning returned. She stared down at the king's final letter, but her gaze wasn't moving. I sat down beside her, lifting the letter from her grip. I read it to myself.

Dear Charlotte,

My time in this world is coming to an end. I feel I've lived a full life with many adventures and you, my dear daughter, were my most precious. Since my return, your mother has filled me in on your actions since my capture, and I must say I am proud of you. It doesn't matter who you marry, I am certain you will make an incredible queen of Besmium and with this knowledge, I can rest well.
You are my greatest accomplishment.

With love,

Your father

Charlotte leaned her head on my shoulder and cried. I put my arm around her and gently rubbed her back. She buried her face in my chest. I was grateful that I didn't have to say anything. Without thinking, I kissed the top of her head, drinking in the sweet aroma of her curls.

She leaned back, her gaze meeting mine. It startled me, but before I could say anything, she leaned in and kissed me. Her lips pressed against mine, a sharp jolt tingling violently in my chest and spreading throughout my entire body. I wrapped my arms around her, dizziness fogging my thoughts. Her soft lips pressed warmly into mine. Her curls tickled my cheeks, then she pulled away.

"Thank you," she said, stepping back.

I stood. "No, thank you for that. That was... I mean—"

She giggled and a rush of heat hit my face. "I mean," she said, "thank you for being there for me today. I don't know what I would have done without you."

I stopped, unable to respond.

She smiled, but it faded quickly. "I'm going to go find my mom. Will I see you at the banquet?"

I nodded. She walked over to me and pulled the letter from my rigid fingers, and then she was gone. Overwhelmed, I slumped back onto the bed. Grief was a formidable dragon to slay.

36

PRINCE MINSEO

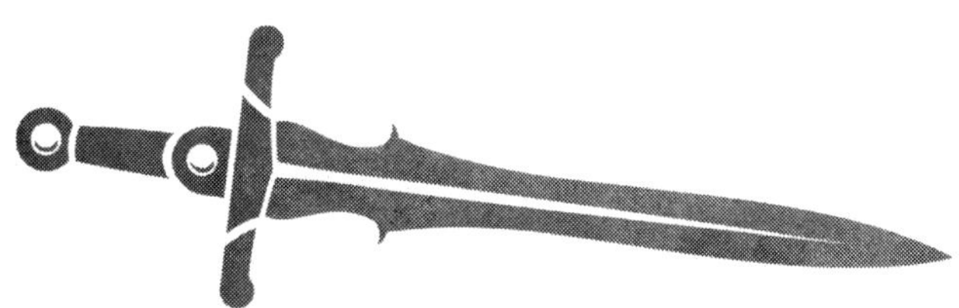

The evening after King Morgan's funeral, I was drifting in and out of consciousness when I realized Charlotte stood beside my bed. Alarmed, I sat up and glared at her. What further chaos was this woman going to bring down on me?

"Prince Minseo," she whispered.

It was strange to hear my name said with such a foreign accent.

She stepped closer. "I'm sorry this happened to you."

I opened my mouth to speak but the burn of the antidote still lingered in my throat and churned my stomach. *Evil witch.*

"Don't speak," she said. "You should rest. I'm sure you're angry with me. I just want you to know I'll make this up to you." Her eyes glistened. "I'll visit you here every day until you're well again. Anything you need, I'll make sure you have it."

Don't bother. But she'd already sat down beside me and began to read a chapter of some adventure story, and before I knew it I'd drifted back into deep sleep.

Princess of destruction, I seethed the next day, hoping she wouldn't return, but just like she'd promised, she came, with a bright smile and a book. With each passing day my hatred for her abated and I began to see what my brother must've seen right away.

It took almost three months for me to get my strength back. I spent most of that time in bed, some days only able to get up and walk around for a short time. I'd missed my brother's first few months of marriage. Young would come by and chat with me sometimes, filling me in on things I'd missed, but Charlotte never missed a day.

It only took a week for me to realize that I looked forward to her visits, and a week more to realize I needed them. Sometimes she'd read to me, sometimes she joked with me, and when I was finally able to walk, she'd walk with me. I'd never spent so much time with one woman before and I felt my weakness for her growing each time she'd laugh or when she twirled a curl around her finger. There was a warmth about her that I wasn't used to and a nurturing presence that wasn't commonly shown in my kingdom.

I didn't understand why at the time, but I'd rigorously questioned my brother about his wedding night and the consummation ceremony until he'd admitted that he'd faked the whole thing. I promised him I wouldn't tell. It was a promise I'd easily kept, but it changed the way I thought about Charlotte. Somehow, it meant she didn't belong to him.

It didn't help that Young spent weeks at a time away from the castle. Now that Drethen had retreated out of our territory, he'd helped rebuild the northern castle and set out across the kingdom to recruit and train new troops for Besmium. He seemed to be acclimating nicely to his new role and gaining the trust of the queen and the rest of the council, but more importantly, it left Charlotte mostly to me.

There was a clear line between the thoughts I had about Charlotte and what I could share. I knew what was at stake. I knew that if I slipped, I'd destroy my brother. I hadn't so much as hinted to Charlotte how I felt, but I had begun to admit to myself that I had feelings for her. Feelings I never had before, and each day they became more difficult to bury.

One afternoon, Charlotte arrived waving a leather-bound book over her head.

"It's here!" she said, the brightness of her smile filling me with warmth.

I reached out to touch her face but caught myself and ran my hand through my hair instead. "Your favorite? *Dragon's Breath*?" I said, trying to match her enthusiasm.

"*The Dragon's Call*," she said, sitting beside me. "Which means that your brother could be back today or tomorrow." Her leg touched mine as she grinned, her eyes dimming as she wandered through some hidden memory. She always looked that way when she thought of my brother. My cheeks burned hot and I lay back on my bed.

Charlotte leaned over me. "Are you okay?" She put her hand to my head and a jolt of energy shot through me. The urge to touch her was maddening.

Her eyes widened. "I'll fetch the doctor." She stood, but I grabbed her wrist.

"Wait! There's no need for that. I just need to rest a moment."

She sat down again and, in a moment, the dreamy, far away look returned to her face.

I was happy my brother was returning, wasn't I? It was just that my time with Charlotte was nearing its end. I spent three months in recovery, three months with Charlotte, and if I was being honest, my strength had nearly returned. Still, I remained bedridden, too afraid to break from this routine. Even so, this time with her didn't seem like it would be enough for me much longer.

I sat up and put my hand down flat on top of the book. "How about we forget the book today. I think some fresh air will do me some good. Why don't we go outside and I'll show you how to use that dagger you love so much?"

"Really?" She beamed. It may have been the spell she cast on me, but I loved the way she lit up about things, like she'd had a hard year and looked for any excuse to be happy.

The temperature in Besmium had dropped a lot in the last couple months. The air was crisp and refreshing—too cold if you weren't moving much. But this was combat training and in the midday sun, I knew we'd be alright.

"Huah!" Charlotte swept the dagger through the air.

"Better, but your stance is still too weak," I said. I positioned myself behind her and kicked her left foot out, widening her stance. Then I pushed down on her waist, lowering her center of gravity.

"Ahh," she said, "I feel it. That's better."

I went to release her, to fix the form on her arms, but couldn't let go. Had I planned this the entire time? Was this whole combat idea an excuse to touch her? A practice swing of her dagger brought me back to reality.

"Yes, exactly," I said, recovering. "Remember, you'll typically be fighting someone taller than you, so swipe up at this angle," I said, thrusting my dagger upwards.

I stepped away and stared down at the ground. Disappointment seared into me. What was I doing?

"Is everything okay?" Charlotte asked, noting my obvious mood change.

I nodded. "Yeah, just tired is all. Maybe I pushed myself too hard." I lied. I needed to get over this—to forget about her.

A few months ago, I encouraged Young to return to Vires and to leave Charlotte here. I'd told him to spend the night with a few other women and he'd forget all about her. The better man had already won. Perhaps it was time I returned to Vires—I chuckled. Or spend the night with a few women.

"Milly!" Charlotte called, interrupting my thoughts. Charlotte ran over to a pretty, yellow-haired servant girl and threw her arms around her.

"Prince Minseo!" Charlotte said, turning to me. "Come meet my friend Milly."

A *servant girl*? Back in Vires, I would have never even considered it, but I was desperate to let go of Charlotte and this was the only idea I had. "Milly, is it?" I took her by the hand and kissed it.

37

PRINCE YOUNG

The more time I spent in Besmium, the more I learned there were still troops throughout the kingdom, but they were poorly organized. Teams of troops patrolled Hiems Castle and weren't reassigned after the Drethen army broke through. The borders seemed too big for the number of available troops, and the contact between outposts was infrequent. The council delegated most of the travel work to my men and me while Charlotte stayed at Castle Cadere to watch over Minseo. In just three months, we'd begun to put the pieces of Besmium back together, but I missed Charlotte when I was away.

Captain Leon dismounted his horse and tied it next to my camp near Hiems. "Your Highness, a letter came for you."

My stomach dropped. *Charlotte.* One thing I'd learned in this kingdom was that no news was good news. I tore open the letter, my fear spilling onto the wrinkled parchment.

Prince Young,

I hope this letter finds you well. The council and I are very pleased with your work around the kingdom, and as such, have decided to bring forward the coronation next week as planned. Your father, the King of Vires, has been made aware and set out early last week. He is expected to arrive in the next few days with your mother, the queen. Your eldest brother will not be in attendance.

Sincerely,

Her Royal Highness, the Queen of Besmium

I exhaled relief. It was *good news*. I looked up from the letter to find Leon biting his bottom lip. I laughed. "It seems we've both been conditioned to expect bad news." I handed him the letter. "Worry not, my friend. There's to be a party."

Leon skimmed the letter then grinned. "Home at last."

It had been a no-brainer for me to select Leon as my right hand; he had proven himself a loyal warrior and gained my trust. However, it took several months to realize just how good a choice he'd been. With each visit to an outlying outpost, it became increasingly obvious that not all the soldiers felt comfortable being led by a foreign prince. Selecting Leon had sent two distinct messages to the kingdom. One, I didn't intend on favoring the Viran soldiers. And two, I had Besmium's best interest in mind. The counsel admired my political know-how, but I didn't feel I deserved their praise—I'd chosen based on trust, not politics.

It felt good to be returning. Home was the southern castle now. I'd always assumed we'd eventually return to the northern castle, but it was still undergoing repairs. After seeing it in my travels, I had a hard time believing that Charlotte or I would ever want to move back there. It was a mausoleum—littered with the memories of the massacre that still lingered within each cracked stone.

A few days later, my company arrived at the southern castle. Trumpets sounded as we rode up to a red-carpeted entrance framed by several lines of soldiers. Poised to attention, they formed a path to the palace like brightly-colored statues. It was a stark contrast from arriving here surrounded by Emmett's men.

I dismounted my horse and hastened in. I had to see Minseo. Charlotte had written me, explaining that he was doing well, but I had to see it with my own eyes. I sprang up the grand staircase and hurried straight for my brother's chamber. A Viran guard stood outside his door. As I neared the chamber, I heard the muffled sound of a woman's cries. I gulped. It was a sound I'd heard outside Minseo's chamber before, back in Vires. Once I'd forced Charlotte to replicate it. In fact, it sounded exactly the same.

I backed away from the door as I tried to swallow the horrible thought before it manifested, but it was too late. My mind replayed the moment Charlotte first met Minseo, the glimmer in her eye. A sharp pang of fury tore through my body, my temperature comparable to the sun's surface. I gripped at the air, stumbling mindlessly to my chamber. Tears stung my eyes as the wind departed from my lungs with no hope of returning. I pushed open the door with far too much force and slammed it shut behind me. *How could she?* I leaned back against the door and slid down to a seated position, burying my face in my hands.

"Young?" Charlotte's soft voice called from the other side of the chamber.

I exhaled a taste so sweet that the Viran persimmons would've been envious. I sat frozen in a perfect world before allowing the guilt I'd earned to settle in.

"You're back!" Charlotte said, running toward me. She got to her knees and nuzzled her head under my arm, forcing it around her. "Are you okay?"

Overcome with relief, I pulled Charlotte onto my lap and hugged her. She froze as if she'd expected me to pull away, as I'd done many times while I was getting to know her.

However, today was different. I'd doubted her, and I'd doubted my brother. That thought alone meant I didn't deserve them, but for the moment it didn't matter. Sometimes terrible things happened that no one deserved, so why shouldn't the opposite be true once in a while?

38

PRINCE MINSEO

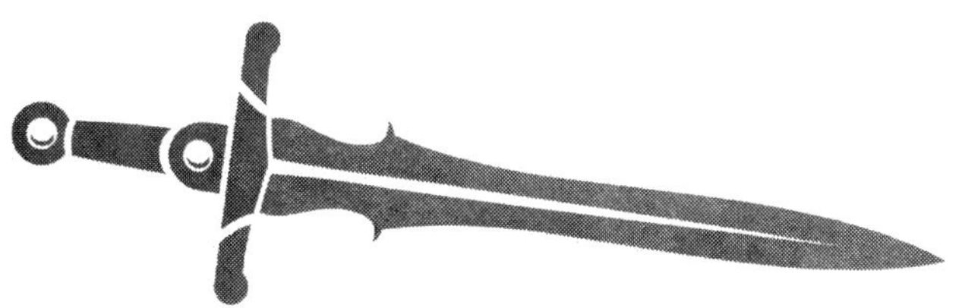

I felt disgusting. Now, it was painfully obvious that Milly would never be able to help me forget about Charlotte. Milly was too easily convinced. She hung on my every word and breathed truth into my every lie. Despite the impossibility of the words I told her, she lay beside me gazing into my eyes with a girlish grin. I turned over, unable to look at her any longer. Every moment with her only made me miss Charlotte more. My body ached with longing, an unquenchable thirst. This was not the outcome I had planned, but it hadn't been for nothing. Milly made me certain of something—I only wanted *Charlotte*.

I couldn't dress fast enough. Without a word, I hurried out of my chamber, leaving my mistake behind in my bed. I needed to be alone to think. Had I been wrong all this time? Women had always been interchangeable in my world, so why couldn't I trade Charlotte for Milly and feel satisfied? *Unless.* I stopped. Turned. This time headed for Charlotte's chamber.

It was unlikely that she felt the same way. I *knew* that. I just couldn't kill the seed of hope that grew within.

My heartbeat doubled my footsteps as I pushed open the door to Charlotte's chamber. A surge of energy exploded through me. *This was it.*

My stomach clenched as I stood face to face with a part of the plan that I hadn't considered.

"Brother," Young shouted, his eyes beamed excitement. He laughed, throwing his arms around me. "It's good to see you on your feet again." He nudged me with his elbow, waking me from my trance-like state.

I faked a laugh, noting his mischievous smile. Ah, *Milly*. "Yes, yes. That's what the real thing sounds like." I felt bile rise up in the back of my throat. I'd already forgotten about Milly. I didn't like that Young knew about it, though he probably didn't know it was Milly in my bed this morning. I hoped she'd left my chamber by now. "So, I take it you've been back for a while," I said, forcing my attention back to Young.

"Just a few minutes. I went to see you first, but you were busy. Glad to see you're back to your old self."

I smiled, my gaze stealing quick glances around the room, looking for Charlotte.

"Actually, brother," Young said, "you don't look that well after all." He reached out and touched my forehead with the back of his hand. "You're a bit warm. Your cheeks are flushed, and if I'm not mistaken, you're quite a bit less talkative than usual."

I laughed. "This is the glow of a job well done," I said with a conscious effort not to picture Milly. "Has our father arrived yet?"

"Not yet, but any minute now."

"And your—" I knew the word. *Wife*. But my mouth wouldn't say it. "Charlotte?" I said.

"You just missed her. She went to see the queen."

I put my hands on my hips, hoping to relieve the heaviness that plagued my arms.

Young patted me on the back. "Well, I hope you cheer up before the party tomorrow. You're more than a bit depressing today." He turned to leave the chamber. "I'm off to bathe and rest a bit before father arrives."

I felt like a spy. Every passing thought was a betrayal of my brother. I shouldn't have allowed myself to feel this way about Charlotte—his *wife*—but I was a man in love, and my brother was just a boy with a crush; a boy who'd faked the consummation of his marriage. What did he know about the depths of adult love? Besides, she would surely reject my feelings, and when that time came—I'd surrender.

I stood alone in my brother's chamber for a moment before springing back to life. *Parchment*. I scoured the room to find some. Now that Young had returned, it would be difficult for me to get Charlotte alone to tell her how I felt. I'd write her a letter and slip it to her in passing. I just needed parchment. I didn't find any on the desk and started hopelessly pulling open drawers.

"Guards! Help, there's a thief in my chamber."

I turned to see Charlotte standing with her hands on her hips. She smiled playfully. My stomach dropped. This was my chance.

39

PRINCESS CHARLOTTE

"Uh, hey Princess," Minseo said, dropping something made from dark fabric into the open drawer beside him.

"Is there something I can help you find?" I asked, noting the disarray of my desk.

"Parchment," he sighed.

What was he doing here? I walked over to my cabinet and opened it, exposing four drawers inside. I peeked in the first and found nothing. I wondered what he'd say if I started going through his things. I slid open the second drawer and pulled out a blank piece of parchment. "Just one?" I called over my shoulder.

"Yes."

My heart leaped as Minseo's voice came from directly behind me. I hadn't heard him cross the room. I turned, handing him the parchment, instinctually backing up into the cabinet.

"Thank you, Princess."

I'd spent a considerable amount of time with Minseo over the last few months, enough to know something was off. He reminded me a bit of Young, despite what I'd originally thought. I closed the cabinet and slipped out from between it and Minseo.

"Is there anything else?" I said, trying to ease the tension.

"Actually, yes," he replied while pushing his hand back through his hair. "I—" He stopped. His eyes glistened like something lay hidden behind them. In a blink, it was gone. "I wondered if we were going to get the chance to finish that book. The dragon one."

A wave of relief washed over me. "Oh, right." I wandered over to my desk and picked up the leather-bound book. "Here," I said, handing it to him.

He took the book but lingered a few seconds too long. He laughed. "I can't do this." He shook his head and traces of the Minseo I knew returned. "I'll write it then," he said. "When the words come, I'll write it." He turned and started walking toward the door.

I followed. "Minseo? Is everything—"

He closed the door between us. *Odd.*

As I straightened up the things that he'd displaced, I thought about the cause of his strange behavior. Had he still felt ill? My heart sank. I had seen him spending time with Milly; perhaps he'd developed feelings for her. I made a mental note to gently ask Milly about it, although if it were true, I had every reason to worry about her. My mouth dried with anxiety. No. I *knew* Milly better than anyone in the world. She'd never get involved with him. The feelings she had for Young were different, and I was certain she had put all that behind her by now.

I hoped that things with us had gone back to normal—to the way they were before. On the surface, they looked normal enough, but there were things we hid from each other now, topics we never discussed. I was starting to wonder if I knew her at all.

The next day, the King and Queen of Vires arrived. Young and Minseo had spent all morning and part of the afternoon with him, and I'd heard by rumor that they had brought along an unexpected guest.

"She's beautiful," Glenda gushed. "A princess, all the way from Ryosun. That's even farther than Vires."

"Do you know why she's here?" I asked as Glenda laced the corset of my coronation dress. "For Minseo. The King of Vires is trying to arrange something."

My thoughts flickered to Milly.

"—the loveliest thing I've seen. Skin of porcelain and all," Glenda said as she tied the last of the ribbons.

Curiosity clawed at my belly until, at last, we were finally introduced just outside of the chapel.

I curtsied to the King of Vires. Nerves overtook me. I was used to meeting kings, but this was my new father-in-law. He was a small man compared to my father. His gentle, soft-looking skin and kind eyes matched his rather pleasant demeanor. The queen remained a step behind the king, but whenever he spoke, her gaze softened. I could tell in an instant that they were more united than my parents had been. Minseo's posture was slumped with disinterest, or perhaps he hadn't slept enough. He stood several paces away from the rest of his family—and the princess.

That's when I saw her—the Princess of Ryosun. Pure white skin. Black waist-length hair that shone with every tilt of her head and flowed delicately with every move. Her eyes as dark and secret-filled as Young and Minseo's, and similar in shape.

Young leaned closer and spoke in his kingdom's language. I'd never heard him use it before, not even when conversing with Minseo. The princess smiled shyly and bowed deeply to me—a bow only reserved for men in my kingdom.

I found it difficult to look away. She moved gently—gracefully. Her agreeable nature and calm disposition lured in the gazes every man that passed. Despite my best effort, I was unable to stop comparing myself to her, my opposite in nearly every feature. She made me feel like a little girl again, how I'd admired the courtiers with their pink cheeks and rose-stained lips—with one difference. The sickening ache that radiated from the bottom of my stomach to my chest every time Young spoke to her. They shared similar cultures and language. Those were things I could never give him. I wondered if meeting the Princess of Ryosun had made him regret his choice.

40

PRINCE YOUNG

My family stood together outside the church, soaking in the sun before we were forced inside by the ceremony. Everyone seemed reluctant to enter, so we remained there chatting. Charlotte and the queen had joined us, but outside of introductions, they had remained quiet. I'd expected a bit of awkwardness between our two families. My parents and Charlotte's mother. But I was too excited to see everyone together to be the bridge they needed me to be to bring our families together.

As I gazed into the aging faces of my parents, I realized I'd been homesick. A familiar sense of comfort consumed me, reminding me of my life in Vires. It felt nice to speak in my original Viran language, though I didn't know I'd missed it.

My parents were *here.* I'd known they were coming and still felt surprised to see them. Was it because I thought I'd die before I saw them again? What I hadn't expected was for them to bring the Princess of Ryosun along. She was beautiful—the kind of woman Minseo and I always imagined we'd marry, but based on

Minseo's lack of eye contact and cold responses, he wasn't interested.

My father must've noticed too because his posture stiffened. "At least be *polite*," he whispered to Minseo, his voice somehow dripping with daggers in his soft tone.

Minseo rolled his eyes and walked a few more steps away from the princess and the rest of us.

I pitied her. She came all this way for him to not even give her a chance. I cleared my throat. "Princess, how do you like it in Besmium?"

"It's quite beautiful," she said, her voice musical like a wind chime.

"That's wonderful. Was the journey here long?"

"It was quite manageable," she said, smiling softly.

If I'd asked Charlotte a similar question, she might tell me a lengthy and dramatic tale of her misfortunes, but Princess Mina was nothing but agreeable. In minutes of small talk and replies filled with rainbows, I was bored. My gaze wandered back to Charlotte, her face riddled with befuddlement. Had I been speaking Viran with Charlotte standing right here?

Before I could translate, the queen of Besmium spoke. "Your Majesty," she said, gesturing to my mom, "there are some members of my counsel that are eager to meet you." She turned to Princess Mina. "We've also never hosted a royalty from Ryosun. We would be delighted if you could squeeze a little politics in before the coronation." My mother, Mina, and Charlotte disappeared into the church—leaving us to enjoy a couple more minutes of sunlight.

I turned to my father and froze. His cold stare sent an instant chill down my spine, and for this rare moment, he looked like a king. I traced his frosted gaze to Minseo.

"Minseo. Get over here," he demanded in a tone that set my teeth on edge.

Minseo's posture straightened and I knew my father's transformation affected Minseo too. He walked over like a man condemned.

"Princess Mina of Ryosun has agreed to become your intended."

Minseo nodded. "Yes, sir."

A vein popped out of my fathers' temple. "Then why do you mistreat her?"

"I do not love her."

My stomach tightened. I admired my brother's courage for such an answer, but I feared for him.

My father thrust his arms into the air, causing Minseo to flinch. "How could you learn to love her if you do not give her a chance?"

"I don't want her," he admitted.

I sucked in the silence through my nose but was too afraid to exhale it. My father finally shattered it. "Immediately following your brother's coronation, you will return to Vires, where I might beat some sense into your corrupted mind."

With a huff, the king turned and hurried into the church.

I turned to Minseo, feeling the heat of his pain from where I stood. Was he in love with someone? I'd heard him in his room with someone. Could it be *Milly*? That was the only explanation. It was obvious he wasn't ready to return to Vires; his feelings bound him to Besmium as mine had. He had no choice but to obey. My father was a king—in a minute's time, however, I'd be a king too.

I put my hand on Minseo's shoulder. "I'll talk to him."

He looked at me and I could swear I saw pity beaming from his sorrowful gaze. Maybe it was just sadness. One way or another I'd find a way to help him.

As the coronation began, I contemplated all it meant to be a king. I pledged myself to Besmium, and that meant that I could no longer consider Vires my home. I took Charlotte's hand as we knelt together at the altar. We'd gotten into this together, and I knew we'd remain that way. She was the loveliest queen I'd ever seen. Too young perhaps—we both were—but it was our actions that had allowed Besmium to heal these last three months, and everyone, the council included, wanted to move forward.

The priest said a prayer and placed a golden crown on my head, its weight a reminder of the burden I would carry until my death. The Queen Regent of Besmium placed a crown on Charlotte.

A swell of pride filled me. I'd done it. I was finally the King of Bes—

The church door swung open and an audible gasp from the crowded pews reverberated around the vaulted ceilings as a bloody figure stumbled in.

41

PRINCE MINSEO

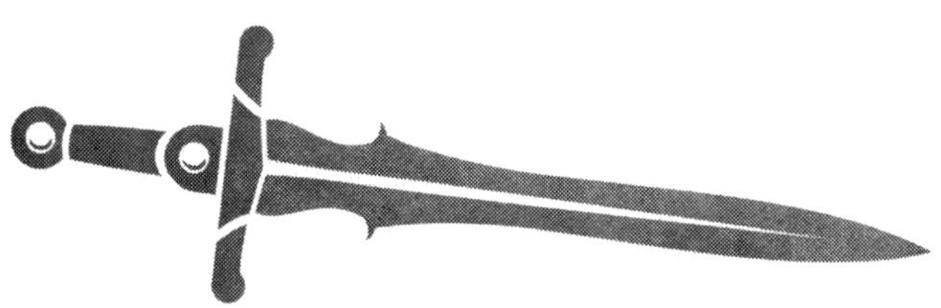

My heart ricocheted off my ribcage as I sprinted across the church to the blood-concealed figure. Each step brought me closer, his shape becoming more familiar. Pushing past the nobles all straining to get a better look. I collapsed onto my knees and cradled the fallen soldier in my arms. "Leon!"

I scanned for his injury but there was too much blood, most of it coming from his left side beneath his ribs. His pulse weakened. "What happened?" I gasped. "Wh—Who did this to you?"

He opened his mouth to speak but no words came through. Nobles crowded around as his body shook. "Who did this, Leon?" I whispered, as his breathing grew more labored.

"K—" He huffed.

Tears blurred my vision, sprinkling his cheeks as I watched helplessly. Fear radiated from his body. I couldn't make myself ask again.

"It's okay, Leon. Just rest."

He turned his gaze to me, the light in his eyes fading. "K—King Emmett of Drethen," he said.

The salt of my tears lingered on my lips as I forced myself to take a deep breath. All at once, he was gone. I froze, holding the empty shell of my friend.

Whispered conversations scattered about the church. The council, adorned in their red robes, pushed their way through the assembly and stood beside me.

One of the councilmen, a thin man with a pointed nose, stepped forward. "Did he say King Emmett of Drethen?"

I nodded.

He continued. "Perhaps he meant to say Algony."

A portly noblewoman chimed in. "No, sir. Emmett's a fair few siblings away from being King of Algony."

The thin man replied, "We can't trust the accuracy of a dying man's ramblings."

"His name was Leon," I said too loudly. "He used the last of his strength to deliver that message."

"Pardon me, Your Highness, I meant no disrespect," he said, shifting his weight nervously to his other foot. "Is it possible that Emmett married Princess Margaret of Drethen?"

The council went quiet. An inaudible panic filled the room.

Charlotte spoke, "They're coming for us." Before then, I hadn't noticed Charlotte and Young standing beside me. She continued, "Young, take your brother and a unit of soldiers and go find out where Leon was scouting last. If Emmett is leading his attack from Algony in the south, they could be here already. Same with Drethen in the north." Then she turned to the council. "You, write letters informing all the posts to allocate their men to either the northern or southern borders. We'll treat this as two separate wars. " She pointed at the portly councilwoman. "You evacuate the King and Queen of Vires, as well as Princess Mina."

There was so much to do but I couldn't move. I didn't want to leave Leon behind. My father pulled me away, leaving Leon to lie lifelessly on the church floor and me covered in his blood.

My father turned to me. "You can still return to Vires. This is not your war."

"I'm staying," I said, unable to offer more of an explanation.

A musical voice piped up, "Then I'd like to stay as well." I turned to see Mina bow deeply to my father.

"I cannot allow that," he said, his voice stern and kingly once again.

"With all due respect, Your Majesty," she said, "my place is here beside your son."

My father's gaze stung me with a warning before a robed council member whisked him away from the crowd. Charlotte called after them, "Head northeast and you should avoid all conflicts—" Her voice broke. Her body swayed.

Charlotte toppled forward. Vomit erupted from her in two strong heaves. Instinctively, I reached out to her but stopped, as my brother's arms were already around her.

"Call the doctor!" he shouted. A surge of fear washed over me as Charlotte's face paled. Young rubbed Charlotte's back and whispered in her ear until the doctor finally pushed his way through the crowd. The doctor put a withered hand on Charlotte's forehead, then waved over his apprentices to help him move her to her chamber. I studied the doctor's face for clues of what might be wrong, but if he knew, he gave nothing away.

Young remained still as a statue as Charlotte was carried back into the castle.

A gentle hand rested on my shoulder and I turned to see Mina standing above me. What a nuisance. It was too late to send her off with my father and now she was in the way. I stood. "Stay with Charlotte's mother."

"But I must stay beside—"

"No." I turned away. "You must do as I ask."

Without another word, she vanished into the crowd.

Young prepared for the mission ahead. Servants rushed around, prepping our horses and packing provisions, but there was still something I needed to do.

I slipped into my chamber and pulled out the parchment Charlotte had given me. I wasn't sure if she or I would survive the night. More than ever, I burned for her to know how I felt.

Dear Charlotte,

I've fallen in love with you. You're the reason I can't return to Vires.

Love,

Minseo

It was all I had time for. I folded it quickly, not bothering to seal it, and headed to her chamber to check on her. I hustled through the crowded hallways. There were people rushing everywhere, but no one spoke. Fear was a thick fog that engulfed Besmium and we all disappeared into it.

I flinched as Milly stepped in front of me. I was on edge. Everyone was. "Not now, Milly," I said, trying to pass her.

"I want you to have this," she said, holding out an embroidered handkerchief.

I needed to end this. "Milly, I don't want this."

She tucked a golden strand of hair behind her ear. "Well what do you want?"

"It's not you. It'll never be you." I pushed passed her, rushing to Charlotte's chamber. I hurried in to find the doctor sitting nervously beside her bed.

"What's wrong with her?" I asked.

He sighed. "I can't be sure just yet. She's resting. Will you stay with her while I get some more water?"

I nodded, feeling relieved to have a moment alone with her without asking. Charlotte lay sleeping with beads of sweat dotting her forehead. I brushed her cheek with the back of my hand and whispered, "I'll save your kingdom."

I slipped my letter underneath her pillow in hopes that when she woke she'd finally know the truth.

42

KING YOUNG

Everything fell apart at once. Leon dead, my home under attack, my parents forced to flee, and my Charlotte... that's what scared me most of all. As I stepped into the courtyard, a breeze of virulent wind left the kingdom cold and surmounted the warm sun we basked in at the coronation.

I mounted my horse and shook with anxiety as Minseo's horse remained riderless. After several minutes, he sprinted down the stairs of the castle and mounted his horse. We rode to the soldiers to find out which direction the attack came from. Each step felt like a betrayal to Charlotte. How could I leave her now?

I turned to one of the castle guards. "The moment you hear news of Charlotte's condition, send someone to find us straight away." Minseo paled. He must've been worried too. I secured my ruby-studded dragon blade on my belt before we set out.

After a brief interview, the courtyard soldiers all agreed on the direction that Leon rode in from; we'd start there.

I clenched my jaw to suppress the fear I felt swelling inside me. Emmett was out there. It was him or me this time.

I turned to Minseo but didn't see any trace of fear in his broodish gaze. "This is a scouting mission only," I said, hoping only to comfort myself. "If we're not careful, we could easily end up like Leon. We know the enemy is close by, so we shouldn't be caught off guard." I considered taking a few more men with me, but I wanted to move quickly without being seen and needed every available man here at the castle—where Charlotte was.

Sensing my fear, Minseo smiled. "Long live the king."

I smirked, overcome with gratitude. I had my brother with me this time and that came with a comfort I felt nowhere else in life.

We headed back to the forest, the warmly-colored trees hardly resembling what they had looked like in the spring. Every so often, we'd stop, hide, and listen for the sound of Emmett or his men. We rode in silence as there was too much at stake. Death hid behind every tree trunk, waiting for us to drop our guard so he could claim us.

The forest was distressingly clear. No woodcutters or animals about. No commoners out for a late afternoon stroll. It was as if the entire world had stopped to watch the battle ahead.

The *clip-clop* of horses in the distance floated around us, making my hair stand on end. We froze just to be sure it wasn't our horses we'd heard. I held my breath, hoping for silence. *Click-clop clip-shloop*. Nope. Minseo and I searched for cover but found none. Which direction was it coming from? We turned our horses around, ready to race back to the castle. The sound grew louder.

Minseo exhaled loudly. "It's one of ours," he said. Relief poured into me. Minseo ran his hand through his hair, a sure sign he was relieved too.

A Besmian soldier rode into view from the direction of Cadere. He was a guard I'd seen around, with a distinctly curved mustache that rested on his upper lip as if it could be blown away by the slightest breeze. "Sir," he said, "there's news of the queen." I dismounted my horse and Minseo followed.

My eyes widened. "What is it? How is she?" I asked. I braced myself for pain, the kind that didn't heal and had no remedy.

He shifted. "Perhaps you should read it yourself, sir." He held out the unsealed letter.

My stomach dropped. The news was too horrible for him to speak. She's *dead.* The wind pushed against me, a lump rising in the back of my throat. Unable to grab the letter, I clutched my stomach and hunched over.

Minseo snatched the letter, his gaze oscillating rapidly back and forth across the parchment. "*Impossible,*" he whispered. "Th-the queen is with child." He turned to me, his eyes a cyclone of terror and confusion. He scrutinized my reaction, but I was frozen.

I inhaled a sharp gust of air, tears stinging my eyes and laughter burst out. My cheeks stung from smiling. "She's okay," I breathed. "More than okay, she's—" I looked up at Minseo, his cold stare a monument of agony.

He spoke, "It's impossible. You faked the ceremony."

Tears rolled down my cheeks. "I did, but since then—I mean, I guess it's not exactly *impossible.*"

Minseo drew his sword and swung, splitting the corner of a nearby tree with a loud snap.

"Minseo, stop! Emmett could hear—"

He turned away. "I don't care!"

I shot forward and reached out for his shoulder. "Minseo, what's wrong? What happened?"

He spun and held the sword to my throat. "I challenge you," he choked.

43

QUEEN CHARLOTTE

"I'm pregnant?" I asked, rubbing my stomach in suspicion. "Yes," the doctor croaked. "Congratulations, Your Majesty."

My cheeks burned as my body filled with a flutter of nerves and excitement. My mind flashed with memories of the last few months. How I'd been so afraid of the consummation ceremony that Young faked the whole thing. How we'd grown closer each day. We rebuilt this kingdom and our lives together until one night Young finally returned from spending a few weeks away. I lay beside him unable to sleep. His breath evened, so I knew he was asleep or nearly there. "Young, are you awake?" I whispered. I held my breath and waited for him to stir but he didn't. *Perfect.* There was something I wanted to say to him, but I hadn't mustered the courage when he was awake. "Young," I whispered, "lately I've been feeling like... Well, what I mean is when you're close to me like this, I feel this ache inside and I think it's because I'm in lo—" Young's palm cupped my cheek, startling me. My pulse raced as I remained frozen halfway through the word. He guided my face down to his and tasted the last two letters on my lips. It was the key that unlocked the final door between us. Without hesitation, or fear, he pulled me in for more, but the more we took, the more we craved until every unspoken word between us had been tasted or felt.

It all happened on its own.

Even the memory of it permeated adrenaline into my body, sending shocks of tingly electricity through my extremities.

I wanted to run to Young, tell him everything and see his reaction. Somehow, I thought it might help me determine what *my* reaction was.

Now felt like a terrible time for him to leave me alone. I looked down at my stomach. Only I wasn't alone—not anymore.

The doctor gave an unconvincing smile. "It's probably best if you rest a while," he said before exiting my chamber. I sat back and sighed. A *baby*.

I vaulted up. Yeah, right—*rest*? With the kingdom under attack? This was not the world I wanted to bring my—I gulped—*baby* into. Despite all the things I'd lost these last few months, I had so much to live for, so much to *fight* for. I inched up to my mirror and pinned my curls out of my face. I looked very much like the bratty teen that had protested her engagement, but in almost every way I wasn't her. I was queen, I was a wife, and now I was a mother. I gripped my dagger. I was battle-tested, I had killed, I had survived. The only thing that limited my abilities was my fear—and I wasn't afraid. Not of dying and certainly not of Emmett.

I headed to the courtyard fueled by a new purpose. As I neared, the commotion of a conflict hung in the air. I burst through the door to see a crowd of Besmian soldiers huddled in a circle. At the center, two men brawled, their fists colliding with each other's faces sporadically.

"Hey!" I called. The crowd turned, sending each soldier to

attention. "What's going on here?" The bloody men at the center of the circle hung their heads.

An older man stepped forward. "Leon was the leader of the southern unit, but he never named a successor—or even his second in command." He scratched his thick beard. "These two men believe they should be the new leader."

I put my hands on my hips. "Listen, gentlemen," I said, projecting my voice as much as I could, though my throat was still raw from vomiting. "I can imagine why Leon didn't feel any of you were ready to lead. Here you are, fighting each other over a title, while the enemy is practically knocking down the castle door." I scanned their faces. "What good is your title when your kingdom burns to the ground? Do you want to be a hero? Then, for God's sake, act like a hero." A frost-cold wind pushed through the courtyard. "There are three outposts a reasonable distance from here with reinforcements. I need those men delivered to this castle in less than three hours. Understand? Three hours."

The old soldier finally spoke, "What happens in three hours?" The soldiers' gazes scorched my face.

My voice broke. "There might not be a castle to come back to."

He nodded, the deep lines on his face drooping. "Then I'd better let someone else take this."

"I'll do it, Your Majesty," a voice called from the crowd. A fair-haired man with a split lip stepped out of the center of the circle, blood dripping off the bottom of his chin. "I apologize for my behavior earlier. I can make it back in time."

I eyed him warily. "Which outpost?"

"Any," he said, bowing deeply. "Let me make it up to you."

I nodded. "Make it up to your own men. It's their lives at stake if you don't make it back."

He mounted his horse. "I'm headed for Magnolia."

A tall man with several medals stepped forward, pulling

another decorated soldier with him. "I'll take Begonia and Gresham said he'd take Calla."

Instinctively, I put my hand on my stomach. "We're counting on you."

The three soldiers raced to their assigned outposts, but even if they made it back, I worried they'd miss the bulk of the battle ahead. "The rest of you, gather every soldier on the premises. We're going to back up the King and the Prince of Vires."

The old soldier pulled on his graying beard. "Excuse me, Your Majesty. Not to cause waves, but who will be leading us?"

I clutched the hilt of my dagger. "I will."

44

PRINCE MINSEO

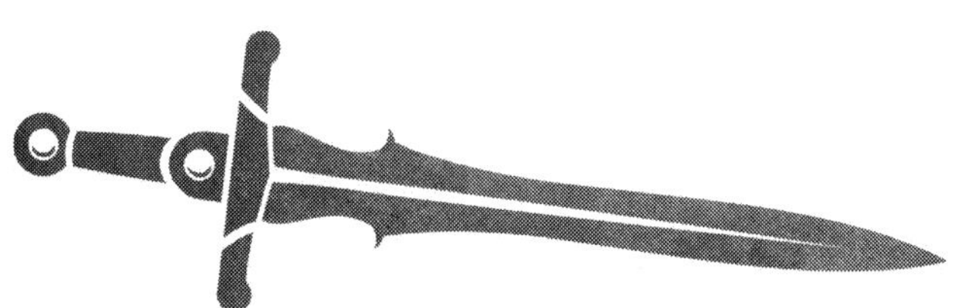

I held the edge of my sword to my little brother's throat, my body shaking. What was I *doing*? I didn't want to hurt him, but my body wouldn't lower the blade. I knew none of this made sense, but I didn't care. I was a mess of adrenaline and rage.

Young's gaze remained transfixed on me, a glimmer of sadness in them that I'd never seen before.

"Why, brother?" he whispered.

The wind knocked out of me. "Charlotte," I said, pressing my sword against the soft of his neck.

The soldier who delivered the message lunged at me.

"Stay back!" Young shouted. "Don't interfere."

The guard stumbled back as if he'd been struck.

My brother's gaze returned to me. "I'm in love with her," he swallowed, prompting my blade to cut him slightly. "I can't let her go."

Rage tore through me. "Then raise your sword."

"I won't," he said. He stood up straight, daring me to cut him further. "Who are you?" he asked. He pushed me back with the flat of his blade. "The heroic older brother or the wife-stealing villain?"

I shook my head. Small white flakes of snow fluttered down around us.

He continued. "Oh, you don't know?" he said, wiping a drop of blood from his throat. "I suggest you figure it out quickly. You're putting us all in danger."

"Raise your sword!" I shouted, tears stinging my eyes.

His sword landed with a thud on the ground, a snowflake dissolving on the blade. "Even if you love Charlotte," he said, stepping toward me, "you love me too."

I inhaled his words and they stung my lungs.

Emmett stepped out from behind a tree. *"What a touching speech,"* he said. I clutched the hilt of my sword and my pulse raced. Of course he would show up now.

He continued, "No doubt arguing over Charlotte." Young picked up his sword and pointed it at Emmett, but he didn't seem to notice or care. Emmett sighed. "I felt something for Charlotte too, once upon a time," he said.

"Are you alone?" I called, scanning the empty woods.

He ignored me. "She has this quality about her, doesn't she? She can make you believe whatever she wants you to believe."

Young shouted, "Enough!"

Emmett continued. "She doesn't lie, exactly—she just implies things." He turned his attention to me. "I mean, here you are fighting your own brother over her, and has she ever actually told you she loved you?" His gaze moved from me to Young. "What about you?"

Young clenched his jaw.

Emmett huffed. "I didn't think so."

"Where's your army, Emmett?" I asked, stepping between him and Young.

He laughed. "Not three seconds ago you were about to kill him. Now you're trying to protect him? Make up your mind, Prince of Vires."

In the distance, the rhythmic clop of horses moving toward us echoed. They were *coming*. If we left now, we could make it back to the castle and our army before Emmett's men arrived—but I wasn't sure we'd get another shot at Emmett, not like this.

"Young!" I called. "Get out of here."

I clutched my blade. In my periphery, I could see Young and the castle messenger mounting their horses. Emmett smiled, amused by the prospect of battle. His confidence unnerved me. I analyzed his broad shoulders. I'd lose if this fight came down to strength alone. I needed to knock him off balance, and with Emmett's army growing closer, I had to be fast. "Young, go!" I shouted over my shoulder.

"Let him go, brother," Young said.

"Did he let Leon go?" I said. My mind was already made.

I charged toward Emmett, his army a cloud of thick dust in the forest's horizon, coming into view. I tallied the number of soldiers with a glance. Forty, a hundred, perhaps more. It was about as many as we had at the southern castle. The full Algonian army must've been a bit behind. Even so, my window to defeat Emmett was closing fast. Emmett drew his sword with a fluid motion, as if his large broadsword was an extension of his arm. It was now or never. I lunged forward, slamming my sword down on Emmett. He blocked, sending me stumbling back. Young rode his horse between us, holding his arm out. "Get on!" he yelled.

I spit on the ground and grabbed his hand, thrusting myself onto the back of his horse. We rode back toward the castle. *Shloop.* An arrow landed on the frozen ground. I turned to see Emmett, another arrow already nocked on his bow—but Emmett was a swordsman through and through, and for the moment, we were out of his broadsword's range.

"You should have let me try to beat him," I told Young.

"I couldn't let you die," he said.

"We're not going to get a better chance than that. With his army's support, he'll be unbeatable."

"He's already unbeatable."

"And now, because of you, he's alive in your kingdom. Who else will you allow to die while you try to protect me? Charlotte? Your baby?"

Young rode on silently. I wasn't sure if I could have defeated Emmett, but the small chance we had was gone now.

Our northern army was almost equal to that of Drethen's. Emmett and one hundred of his men were here, near the southern castle. At best, we could hold them off for a good while, but when the rest of Algony's forces arrived, Besmium would fall and my brother, Charlotte, and I would fall with it.

45

QUEEN CHARLOTTE

Come on, Young, I pleaded with the universe. Where are you? I rode my horse through the empty forest. The thud of the Besmian soldiers riding behind me soothed me. With each stride deeper into the forest and no sign of Young, I worried that Young may have met the same fate as Leon.

In the distance, a hooded figure on horseback, followed by two soldiers in green, drew nearer; their deep green uniforms an effervescent contrast to the wintery landscape. *Algonian soldiers.* I forced myself to refrain from looking back over my shoulder to my men. Though we outnumbered the three strangers thirty to one, I felt an upsurge of fear. As I approached, the hooded figure dismounted his horse. I breathed a puff of white vapors and clutched the dagger beneath my shawl. My men drew their swords but the mysterious figures didn't draw theirs. The man threw back his hood. *Emmett.* My stomach dropped, but as I looked into the face I'd dreaded to see, I realized it wasn't Emmett's. This man was slightly taller, with similar features and a thick but light-colored beard on his wide, double-cleft chin.

"Your Highness," he said, bowing deeply. He eyed my men. "My apologies. I was not expecting to see you away from your castle." He lowered his voice. "What luck," he said, half to himself, "I am Prince Ezrah of Algony, the second son."

I eyed him warily.

"So, you're what the fuss is about?" His gaze traveled up and down, like a vulture swooping in on its prey. "I've seen prettier."

If I closed my eyes, he almost *was* Emmett.

He continued, "I've come to deliver a message from the king."

I nodded, unnerved by his likeness.

He opened a crinkled letter and read aloud. "To her royal highness, Princess Charlotte of Besmium. Algony does not support the actions of King Emmett of Drethen. Emmett is allowed to oversee a certain amount of our military forces but when he returned to Algony to ask for military support and explained how he's been using our resources, he was refused. Some of his soldiers defected to Drethen in order to follow him, but this does not reflect the attitude of the Algonian counsel. The disgraced son of Algony is in no way associated with our kingdom. We cannot condone joining in a war and risking lives over some..." he scoffed, "romantic feud. I wish you well in your upcoming battle but cannot lend my support to either side. Sincerely, King Ethen of Algony, the first son of Jarvan."

I dismounted my horse. "How many men does he have?"

"From Algony?"

I nodded.

"A few hundred, but he claims to have a thousand coming from Drethen."

My stomach tightened. "Is that true?"

"Apologies, Your Highness, I don't know. I suggest you clear these woods before he arrives," he said, mounting his horse. "Rejoin the rest of your military. Your battle has nearly begun."

His words echoed in my head as he rode away. *The rest of my military?* It was obvious that Algony didn't know how depleted we were. If they did, they probably would have supported Emmett. The majority of Besmium's southern army was at my back, and Prince Ezrah had assumed it was a mere scouting troop. One truth was indisputable: the moment I married Young instead of Emmett, I doomed my father's kingdom.

I looked over my shoulder at my soldiers. Their somber expressions all seemed to suggest the same thing: we were all going to die today.

I turned my horse around to face them. "Listen, we don't know if any of this is real. If Emmett had a thousand soldiers coming from the north, we would have been notified by now," I said. "Besides, one Besmian soldier is worth more than ten Drethen soldiers." I scanned the faces of my men and saw defeat conspicuously dripping from their sunken faces.

A middle-aged soldier cleared his throat. "Maybe we haven't heard anything because everyone to the north is dead."

A weight pressed in on my chest. This was my last semblance of home and I'd die protecting it. Why wouldn't they? Was I the only one that hadn't given up? I knew we didn't have a great chance of winning, but as long as I had breath in me, I'd fight. I straightened my posture. "Emmett is here near the southern castle. He's got only a few hundred men. So, we cut the head off the snake, and while the rest scrambles and dies, we hold our kingdom." I rode my horse through the soldiers, each bowing as I passed. A new surge of energy circulated the group. One drop of hope was all it took to draw the life back into Besmium's last warriors. "Let's head back to the castle," I said. "We'll have an advantage if we're ready when they come."

A gruff man called from the back of his horse, "But what about the king?"

I smiled, the fear inside me draining as I filled with something stronger—something indestructible. "He knows the way home."

46

KING YOUNG

As my brother and I rode toward the castle, I felt the threat of Emmett's army behind us. They were almost here. I started to wonder if the north was really under attack again and, if so, if they were holding up against the Drethen army. Had I underestimated Drethen the way I'd underestimated Emmett?

We rode through the outskirts of the castle grounds, my mind focused on making it back to Charlotte and our baby. A gust of frozen wind chilled my bones.

We'd almost made it to the castle, just in time. Emmett's men fusilladed from the edge of the forest, but I didn't want to think about what was behind me. Just ahead was Charlotte. If I could just make it to her, I knew everything would be okay—even if these were our final hours. I felt the frantic energy surge through me as we made our final approach. "Archers," I breathed. "We need to get archers ready."

Before I could put together a plan for rounding up enough archers to buy us time, I saw them step forward. Row after row of bow-slung soldiers readied themselves for the approaching army.

They lined the top of the walls like gargoyles, ready to protect their home. *Charlotte*. Where had they all come from? How could she've managed to rally so many since I'd left only a few hours ago. A glimmer of hope began to take form inside me. Even Minseo seemed to gain energy as we neared the walls of our salvation. As Minseo and I rode through the outer gate, the soldiers closed and fortified it behind us. Red and yellow uniforms cut through the grayness of the sky and castle walls as Viran and Besmium soldiers alike joined together to defend Castle Cadere.

I dismounted my horse and pushed through the rows of soldiers, feeling more triumphant with each one I passed, but the mood inside the castle walls didn't reflect my own. I didn't pause to observe more closely. If I had, I would have noticed that the soldiers had already been to battle. They'd already been defeated.

I raced into the castle, ready to congratulate my queen on a job well done. I knew that this new surge in troops meant Charlotte had given us a chance, and a chance was all we needed. I hurried to her chamber.

"Young," a voice called behind me.

I spun around to see Milly. "Where's Charlotte?" I asked, half out of breath. Her eyes were heavy with despair and I braced myself for an onslaught; retribution from my laxity over the past few months. We had been friends once, and now we were as disconnected as two ships passing—bound for different lands.

"She's in the throne room," she said, sadness dripping from her lips.

"Thank you," I replied. I paused for a moment. I wanted to say more—to apologize for the way everything happened—but there was no time. Emmett's army would reach the castle in minutes, and once the fighting started, the chaos would make it difficult to find Charlotte. I headed back toward the throne room, once again leaving Milly to fend for herself.

I pushed open the doors to the enormous throne room to find Charlotte sitting on the golden throne. She wore her ceremonious crown and her face was as expressionless as a stone carving. Relief poured into me. She was alive, she was carrying our child, and thanks to her fast thinking we stood a shot at winning this battle.

"You did it," I shouted as I raced toward her. "How did you manage to get so many soldiers here?" She remained frozen.

I reached her throne on the other side of the massive hall and leaned in to kiss her. Her lips brushed mine but she didn't move. She didn't embrace me the way she'd done after each of my past missions. What spell was this?

I tried again, this time willing her back from her motionless state with my love. A single tear slipped down her cheek.

She whispered, "I'm sorry I failed you."

My stomach dropped. "Failed? No. You've done so well. Th-the soldiers—"

"They're from the north."

All at once, I understood. We'd already lost.

47

QUEEN CHARLOTTE

It was the first time I'd ever sat on the throne. It was a place I'd always avoided. Maybe I'd known all along I'd fail as a leader. Now, all that was left of Besmium hid behind the castle walls, and I longed to remain here—on the throne—a little longer.

Young lifted my chin. "It's not your fault."

I sighed. It was a beautiful lie. In the palm of my hand, I felt the scratch of crinkled parchment. I tightened my grip. Young reached for my hand and pulled the note from it.

"*Dear Charlotte,*" Young read, "*I've fallen in love with you.*" His voice trailed off to a whisper. "*You're the reason I can't return to Vires. Love, Minseo.*"

"You see?" I sniffed. "I'm the reason he's here. I'm the reason you're here. I'm the reason they're all here."

"Do you love him?"

The suddenness of the question threw me. It was as if we were unwittingly having two different conversations at oncc. I gazed into his eyes and saw fear brimming at their corners. I shook inside. *He didn't know.*

My heart thudded in my chest to match the pace that my mind raced, looking for the words. How could he not know? Each breath Young took was what made my soul breathe. I collected his words. I memorized each moment we spent together so that I could re-live them later in his absence. Each smile was my purpose —a drop of heaven shredding every obstacle that life presented into a fine, golden dust. He didn't know. If I were to return to the moment we'd met, knowing what I stood to lose—I'd choose him again. I'd watch everyone I loved die. I'd watch my father's kingdom burn. Fueled by his motionless gaze, an electric pulse tore through me. Had I known how much I loved him until now?

This war. This life. It was not something that happened. It was my choice. No matter what lay ahead, I knew I'd choose Young every time.

I didn't have time to explain it all. I stood and leaned in. My lips brushed his, sending chills through my body. I wrapped my arms around him and slid my fingers into his hair. He stepped back in surprise, but I didn't let go. He wrapped his arms tightly around my body, pulling me off my feet. I wrapped my legs around him. He turned, walked us back to the throne and sat, pulling me onto his lap. He deepened the kiss, separating only to kiss my neck or my jaw. I held him close, willing the ecstasy he'd given me back into his body with every delicious kiss. I needed him to know. Our child would be loved. He bit down on my shoulder, sending a gasp through my lips. My body temperature rose as Young did as he'd always done—turned the arrows and the armies outside the walls to fine, golden dust. There was no war. Only love. Just my husband, our child, and a world of glittering gold.

The doors to the throne room swung open. "Your Majesties!" a guard said, rushing into the hall. "They've penetrated the outer wall." I pulled my lips away from Young, but not my gaze. He smiled at me softly, and with that smile my life's purpose had been completed. I was ready to die. I stood, drew my dragon dagger, and turned toward the open door. The sunlight streamed into the throne room, spilling on the floor. Young took my hand and kissed my palm. This was not goodbye. My recent losses had taught me something that I believed to my core: love was immortal.

48

KING YOUNG

As I walked with Charlotte toward our certain death, I'd never felt more alive or more in control of my destiny. My time was almost over, but I had two things left to accomplish before I died. One, find Minseo and say goodbye, and two, somehow sneak Charlotte out of here.

The roar of battle echoed off the walls of the corridor, along with the clang of sharpened blades against steel armor. Besmian soldiers rushed through the hallways toward the western entrance.

"They're in the castle!" a bloodied soldier cried, his eyes wide as he toppled and gasped his final breath. I drew my dragon sword and headed toward the direction he'd come from, making sure to keep Charlotte close behind me.

I heard footsteps approaching from around the corner. This was it. I raised my blade, ready to strike. A figure turned the corner, the gleam of his armor refracting light around the room. I brought my sword down but he blocked it, leaving me vulnerable for counter strike. I braced myself. "Brother," he gasped.

I stumbled back. "Minseo?"

He was so covered in blood that if he hadn't spoken, I might not have known it was him. "They're in the castle," he said, out of breath. "They—" He stopped, his gaze drifting past me to Charlotte. His voice softened. "They killed Charlotte's mother. Princess Mina too."

Despite his breathlessness and the blood splattered all over him, Minseo didn't appear to be injured, but if the castle was as lost as he said, we had less time than I thought. There was no time for grief. My mind locked on my last remaining goal. *Charlotte.* I couldn't let her die here. I couldn't let our baby die. "Help me get her out, Minseo," I pleaded. Given what I learned the last few hours, I was certain he'd agree. I reached my hand back and felt the warmth of Charlotte's hand as she took mine.

"Where?" he asked. "The castle is overrun."

My heart ricocheted off my ribs as I ran through every possibility. Finally, the answer hit me. "The atrium."

Minseo's eyes brightened with hope and the three of us hurried through the corridors, stopping only to cut down an enemy soldier in our path. Step. Step. Step. Slice. Step. Step. Slice. As I fought in sync with my brother, I recalled how we used to imagine battles just like this. Our swords pierced a soldier's armor and the battle began to feel as make-believe as it was when Minseo and I were kids. We were untouchable. Each move created in the imaginations of innocent children practiced in adolescence and mastered at this moment.

We reached the door to the atrium, yanked on the handle, and hurled ourselves inside.

"Quick," I called to Minseo. "Help me pry loose one of the drainage bars." I leaped into the water, the current pulling at my knees. "She can swim across to the other side and escape." Minseo and I gripped the iron pole. We put our feet against the stone wall and strained to bend it. It curved slightly. "That's it," I called. "Let's go again."

As I pushed the bar, my mind turned to a memory I had from a few months ago, where I lay with Charlotte beneath the oak tree in the courtyard.

"Do you ever wish you were just normal?" Charlotte asked.

I liked the weight of her head on my arm. "What do you mean?"

"Like, not royalty. Just an ordinary person."

"I wish I was taller," I joked.

She rolled toward me, her gaze meeting mine—urging me for a real answer.

"I guess I never thought about it," I said. "It's like wishing to be a bird or a fish. You are what you are." Her gaze drifted up to the tree. I pulled her close. "I would never have met you if I wasn't born a prince."

She smiled. "If we were commoners, we could have peace. We'd only have our own lives in our hands. We could spend every day like this."

Every ounce of my life energy poured into moving that bar. *Please.* The bar gave way, bending enough for Charlotte to easily fit through. Relief shot through me. She was going to be alright; they both were. I turned to Charlotte but shot Minseo a quick look. He smirked and pulled himself onto the bridge, to give me a moment to say goodbye to her.

I ran my fingers through Charlotte's hair and put my forehead to hers.

Tears dripped from her chin. "If I could go back, I'd do it all again the same way," she said.

"So would I," I breathed.

She pulled away. "I-I can't leave you here."

I brushed away her tears, memorizing every detail of her face. "You have to. You need to protect our child."

She nodded, wiping her face, her dark eyelashes sprinkled with droplets. "Have you thought of a name?"

"Morgan, like your father."

She nodded. "And if it's a girl?"

I shrugged. "Morgan-a?"

She laughed and sniffled, "That's terrible."

"I kind of like it."

Minseo cleared his throat. "Young, why don't you go on ahead with her. I'll meet you later."

I smiled. "Nah, if the King of Besmium doesn't die, they'll keep looking for us. It's better if I stay."

He kicked a small stone off the bridge. "You really think they can tell us apart?" He smiled widely. "Consider it a wedding present."

The door to the atrium swung open. Out of instinct, I pushed Charlotte into the drainage tunnel, hoping to conceal her. I leaped up to the bridge beside Minseo.

Milly stood in the doorway, her icy gaze transfixed on Minseo. "Emmett," she called, "I found them."

My stomach dropped.

Minseo's eyes widened. "Wh-whose side are you on?"

She smiled. "Not yours, Minseo. It'll never be yours."

A sword shot through Milly from the back. Her face whitened. Her eyes dimmed before she even fell to the ground. Emmett stood behind her and, with difficulty, wrenched the sword out of her fresh corpse. "Well, I hope she didn't think she was on *my* side," Emmett said with a smile.

49

QUEEN CHARLOTTE

Three strides. That was how far I made it through the pipe's rushing water before I turned back. The clash of weapons echoed through the drainage pipe as I forced my way against the current back toward the atrium. *Young, stay alive,* I pleaded as if he could hear me. Baby or not, I couldn't walk away from this. I peered into the dusky atrium, only to watch Minseo and Young fly back at the swing of Emmett's broadsword. They got to their feet and lunged at Emmett only to be knocked back again.

I crouched down, concealing my body in the frigid water, before venturing out of the pipe. I didn't have the courage to fully submerge; I needed to keep an eye on Emmett. The battle drew all his attention, giving me a window to reach the bridge without anyone noticing. I gripped my dagger, now wet, but I knew it would never slip from my determined grasp. Emmett was going down. He'd taken enough from me. I was going to make him pay for all of it. I waited for the fight to bring him close enough, running through the dagger training Minseo had given me.

Finally, above, I felt the heavy stomp of Emmett's boots on the bridge. *This was it.* I took a deep breath. Readied my attack. *Clang.* A cry of agony rattled my bones. It was unmistakably Young. My body shredded as if punctured by an ocean of needles. I had to get in there, now! I thrust myself onto the bridge. I rushed at Emmett, slashing at his face with my blade. He hadn't seen me but moved in time to escape the full force of the blow. He turned to me, his expression changing from surprise to amusement.

"This day just keeps getting better," he said with a smile. I wasn't in the mood to talk. I leaped forward waiting for his blade to descend on me.

"No, Charlotte!" Young screamed.

Like clockwork, Emmett swung his blade down. Instead of jumping back to avoid it, I pushed my dagger into Emmett's chest.

In astonishment, Emmett dropped his sword and wrapped his arms gently around me. I took a slow breath in as my frozen body began to feel the warmth of Emmett's blood run down my right arm, where my dragon dagger still remained buried in his breached chainmail. The blood dripped steadily from my elbow, but I was too afraid to let go. My gaze crept up from the bottom of Emmett's chin to his lips, and finally his pale blue eyes. He stood and held me, a kind warmth in his eyes as they faded. Enraged, I pulled out the dagger and plunged it into a new spot on his chest. He toppled forward, spitting blood as his weight fell on me. I snatched my dagger and jumped back, allowing Emmett's body to land with a thud in front of me. His lifeless body lay face down in front of me, but I couldn't stop. I wanted the pain he'd caused me to stop. I stabbed his corpse for my father. Again. Again. My mother. A warm hand gripped my wrist, gently pulling the dagger from my hand. I balled up my fist and punched Emmett. Again and again. Minseo kicked my dagger off the bridge and into the water then pulled me off of Emmett.

"Charlotte, it's okay," he breathed. "You saved us."

I turned to see Young, kneeling, both hands pressed against his leg. "Young," I called, stumbling to my feet only to fall again in front of him.

"You were so brave," he said, attempting to hide his pain. My gaze went to his leg, blood gushing through his fingers.

"Young, oh God," I cried, reaching out to help him apply pressure.

"Charlotte, listen," he said, his voice low and even, "I can't go with you."

"N-no," I sobbed. "We've done it. Emmett's gone."

"Yes, Charlotte," he said with a smile. "You made sure of that. Listen, you need to get out of here. Go through the pipe with Minseo. If I die here, they might not pursue you."

"You're crazy if you think I'm going to leave you here."

Young's gaze moved to Minseo, but they didn't speak.

"No!" I screamed as Minseo pulled me away. "No!" I thrashed my body around to break free, but it was no use. "Wait!" I yelled. "Wait! Young, I love you."

"I love you too," I thought I heard him say.

Minseo dragged me through the water and into the pipe. He pushed me against the wall, covering my mouth. I heard the slam of the door opening as my screams brought several soldiers to the atrium. I listened, my heart bursting from its cage, my eyes blurred with tears.

"King Emmett's dead," I heard someone say.

“Where’s the Queen of Besmium?” a soldier shouted.

Minseo started pulling me down the pipe.

“Long gone,” Young said.

An unfamiliar voice laughed. “She’s here. Check the pipes.”

Minseo pulled me faster now, trying to get us deep enough not to be seen.

A cry of pain rang through the pipes and the clash of metal echoed. “Get him!” a soldier shouted.

As Minseo pulled me farther, the sounds grew fainter.

“I said get him!”

The commotion stopped. “Good, now kill him.”

“Wait, check the pipe first.”

Minseo covered my mouth and stopped breathing as the soldier peered into the dark pipe.

A voice rang out so clearly through the blackness, it was as if the soldier stood beside us. “I don’t see a thing, sir.”

“Forget it. She probably is long gone. Why are you smiling? You’re about to die.”

No. I thrashed, but I couldn't get enough leverage in the water and Minseo was prepared. “Because I’m happy,” Young said, his voice carrying through the pipe and to my ears like a soft whisper. With one final clang of the sword, my heart stopped. Young was gone.

Why had I survived? All the strength I'd built over my lifetime melted away. After the soldiers cleared from the atrium, Minseo carried me through the pipe to the lake where it let out.

Young was gone. Besmium had fallen. I walked beyond the walls of the castle with a title I never wanted: *widow*.

Minseo got us safely out of the kingdom and asked me to join him in Vires, but I'd had my fair share of kingdoms and castles. When he was certain that I'd never agree, we went our separate ways.

The pain I’d caused remained fresh and my mind became an endless cycle of the same question: *What was it all for?*

Until the day I found my answer.

50

PRINCE MINSEO

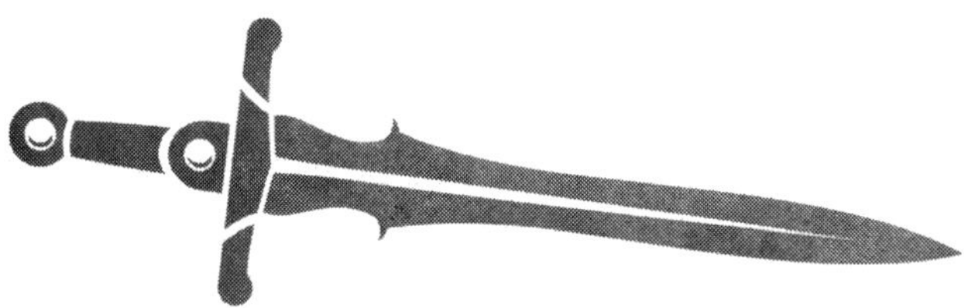

Little brother,

It's been five years since I last saw your face and nearly the same since I've seen your Charlotte. I know this letter is an exercise in futility, but it helps to quell the near constant need I have to speak with you again.

I take comfort in knowing you died without regrets – a death that has taught me much about how to appreciate life and its fleeting moments.

After I lost you, I was as broken as Charlotte and quickly realized that I was not whole enough to console her. I offered her refuge in Vires and, when she refused, I regrettably took my leave without regard for her safety or the cold of the winter that followed.

When I'd finally accepted your passing, I sought her out—though I must admit, I never expected to find her. I found it difficult to gather information about her whereabouts without revealing her former identity. My travels brought much news. What was once the land of

Besmium had been swallowed by Drethen, only to be renamed Camelot and ruled by a teenage tyrant named Arthur.

After many months of fruitless searching, I finally found Charlotte. I was relieved to find that she was not the dead-eyed widow I'd abandoned, but a woman of grace and silent strength. She sang while she cooked and spent long stretches of time in her garden. She picked wild flowers by the river and gazed up at the stars. When she speaks of you, she smiles to herself then looks off into the distance, as if she's waiting for you to arrive at any moment. Or perhaps she's waiting for her time to come so that she can be reunited with you in the next life. Through all the loss she suffered, she somehow became more.

Your young daughter, Morgana, glitters with all the charisma and poise of royalty and all the mischievousness that you and I possessed in youth. When Charlotte's gaze fell upon her, I saw in her eyes the glimmer of love that I'd only ever seen when she looked upon you. Though Charlotte prefers to remain tied to the simple life she's grown accustomed to, I will return to visit your daughter as often as time allows. And if Charlotte permits me, I'll bring her lavish gifts and toys from Vires. Though she was born untitled, she'll remain a princess in my eyes.

Morgana is true joy embodied, and it seems her most treasured moments are spent listening to tales of her father's adventures. Can you believe it—she has your smile.

With all my love,

Minseo

AUTHOR'S NOTE

I hope you enjoyed Kingdom Cold. While it's still fresh in your mind I'd love to hear your thoughts.

You can review Kingdom Cold HERE.

Thank you!

Get ready, here comes Kingdom Soul.

Kingdom Soul

A Kingdom Cold Novel

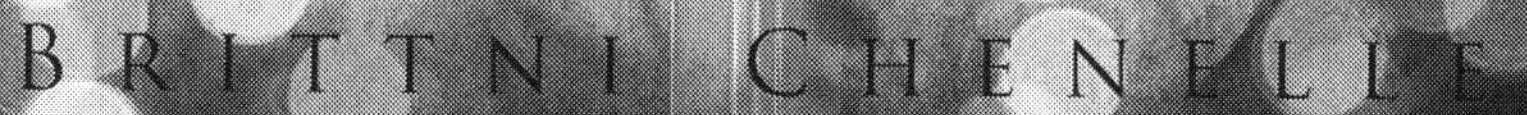

I dedicate this novel to my mother,
the woman who never gave up on me when I struggled to read and write,
and who's always lifted me up with her endless love.
You are the armor that makes me feel brave.

CONTENTS

1. Minseo 237
2. Charlotte 243
3. Minseo 249
4. Charlotte 254
5. Minseo 257
6. Charlotte 260
7. Lancelot 264
8. Minseo 268
9. Merlin 273
10. Minseo 279
11. Charlotte 283
12. Lancelot 288
13. Minseo 292
14. Charlotte 297
15. Merlin 305
16. Minseo 311
17. Lancelot 318
18. Minseo 322
19. Merlin 328
20. Charlotte 331
21. Lancelot 335
22. Minseo 339
23. Merlin 343
24. Charlotte 347
25. Minseo 351
26. Lancelot 357
27. Minseo 360
28. Charlotte 364
29. Minseo 369
30. Lancelot 374
31. Merlin 377
32. Minseo 381

33. Charlotte 384
34. Merlin 388
35. Charlotte 392
36. Lancelot 395
37. Minseo 399

Author's Note 405

1

MINSEO

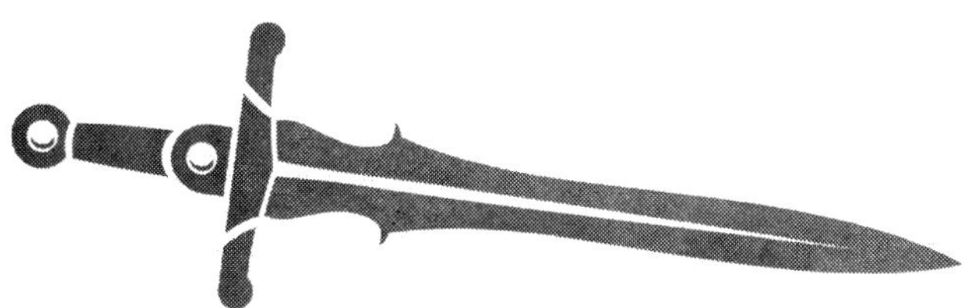

Every night, when I close my eyes, it's the same. Rushing water, my body pushed against Charlotte's, my hand tightly pressed against her mouth, and the clanging of metal that ended my brother's life.

I've been drowning ever since. My screams smothered by the waves, my movements slowed, and my tired arms unable to break the surface before another wave crashes down, tossing me through the abyss.

Year after year slips by, but the memory returns like an echo. Again and again I wonder if Charlotte hears it too, wherever she is.

I awoke to what felt like the gentle kiss of fingertips on my cheek only to discover the white petals of the cherry blossom tree had floated through my open window. The morning's golden rays granted me a moment of peace before my mind acquainted with the world the way it was. A world without my little brother.

I dressed quickly, unwilling to break the silence and hoped to sneak out before my attendants arrived. The sunlight seeped through the hanji walls, meaning it might already be too late to leave unnoticed, but all I could hear outside was the rustle of the cherry blossom tree.

I slid the door open and stepped onto the clay platform below.

"My prince, shall I fetch your breakfast?"

My heart leapt as I eyed the kneeling servant, Mingee. "Don't bother," I barked.

Mingee bowed and closed the door to my bedroom as I turned toward the palace. "Sir," she said, her voice breaking. She shrunk beneath my gaze. "His Majesty wishes to see you in the throne room."

I could have kicked her, and the thought lingered in my mind for several moments before I dismissed it and turned away. I needed to get out of here before she further burdened my morning. I eyed the castle walls, wondering how big of a deal my father would make if I ignored his request and went into town. But the throne room wasn't far from the front entrance, and I was in no mood to battle.

I walked past a series of buildings, each made from wooden pillars and clay-tiled roofs with elaborate, brightly-colored woodworking designs framing each pillar. The clouds hung in the sky like spun sugar, pink from the sunrise still caught in them. Beyond the palace walls, mountains reached above, like walls of a fortress. The most striking element of Vires this season was the cherry blossoms now in full bloom. Still, the wind carried a bite of frosty air that tossed the white petals like snowflakes in a storm. I shivered as I passed the rooms of my mother and older brother Sumin, and I stopped when I reached Young's. His attendant waited outside his bedroom like he'd wake up and ask for breakfast. My father was a senseless man. Almost five years later and he can't even reassign the staff.

I stepped to the edge of the palace lake, my father's throne room platformed at the center of it. The lake, sprinkled with white petals, thrashed with a sudden gust of wind. The petals caught the morning light like stars twinkling in the night, like there was something left on Earth to celebrate. I crossed the stony gray bridge and kept my head down until I knelt at my father's feet.

"Rise, Minseo." I stood up to find my father perched on his throne in his red hanbok, with golden designs that weaved up his sleeves and a slender black hat atop his head. I bit back a smile; he looked like a great stuffed bird on a nest.

"There is a strategy session this evening. It's time you attend," he said, his gentle voice whispering around the room.

"I can't. I have plans to meet Junho at the—"

"That wasn't a request!"

I wrenched my hands, suddenly aware of the cold glares from around the throne room pricking my skin. Hanbit—the king's advisor—and a slew of guards I used to train with bristled.

I bowed. "Forgive me, Father, I only meant my presence at these meetings in the past haven't—"

"It's time."

I clenched my jaw and bowed before turning away and making my exit, swallowing the truths I couldn't speak. He still had attendants outside my dead brother's room and somehow believed I was the one who needed to move on. I exhaled my frustration through gritted teeth and reminded myself it wasn't his fault Young died; it was mine. On my way out, I caught a flash of Jay Hyun, a soldier I'd once been close with. If he wasn't working, or if I wasn't inappropriately headed to drink first thing in the morning, I might've considered inviting him. He bowed to me as I left the throne room and stepped back out onto the stone bridge.

A few hours later, I slammed down my empty ceramic cup. "More!" I bellowed, my head bobbing back and forth at the table.

Junho lay his chopsticks on his bowl of rice before reaching for the bottle of rice wine we call makkoli. "Shouldn't you sober up a bit before the big meeting?" he asked.

"More," I commanded.

Junho sighed and picked up the bottle, pouring the white liquid while his opposite hand lay politely on his chest. "You know, man, maybe he's right. Maybe it is time."

I slammed my hand on the table, rattling the dishes and sending one of my chopsticks flipping through the air and onto the floor. The clatter cut the babble of the other customers and drew their eyes to us. I raised my hand to wave away their attention and the room soon buzzed once more. Junho's face reddened, but it might have been that way from the makkoli.

"You and I both know those meetings are pointless. What is the intent of having a great army if you can't use it to avenge your son's death?" I groused. "The man is a coward." I reached for my chopsticks, but one was still on the floor.

Junho nodded, his eyes flickering toward another table. "That may be true," he said, pouring himself a shot, "but how are you going to change that if you never attend the meetings?"

"Your Highness," a mousy voice whispered. A woman, who appeared to be in her late fifties, held out a new pair of chopsticks.

"Thank you," I said, trying to dismiss her with my tone. I turned back to Junho who held out his shot glass. "Gombe," I said, clashing my glass into his. Just as I was about to throw back another shot, I noticed Junho's eyes flash back toward the table to our left.

I lowered my drink. "What are you looking at?" I asked.

"Oh," he said, "I think I know that guy." The corners of his mouth turned up. "Don't look."

I turned.

"Don't look!" he whispered sternly. He concealed his face in his hands.

The other table had three Viran men sharing a pot of Mayon-tang, a red fish soup, and drinking makkoli. Judging by the quality of their clothing, they were upper-class citizens, and the three empty makkoli bottles on their table indicated they'd likely been there as long as we had. Two of the men chatted loudly, but the youngest man on the far side of the table who seemed to be in his early twenties quietly and conspicuously stared down at a small plate of kimchi.

"Stop looking," Junho said, drawing my attention back. Junho dug into the fish with his chopsticks, pulling out the meat of the jaw muscle, my favorite, and stuffing it into his mouth. "Look," he said, "it won't be as bad as when you first returned home. It was all so fresh. Nobody blames you for losing it as you did."

"You're killing my buzz."

Junho's gaze drifted to my left once more, and I snapped my head to look. The three men rose from the table, scrambling for their wallets. The young man smiled shyly at Junho before his gaze met mine, and he quickly turned away and hurried out of the restaurant.

I shook my head and turned back to Junho. "Does that guy owe you money or something?"

Junho shook his head. "Should we get you some water?"

"Nah," I said, picking through fishbones to get some meat. "It doesn't matter how many meetings I go to. My father will never attack Camelot."

"What about Charlotte?"

I halted. He must have been drunker than I thought to mention *that* name. My mouth dried. "What about her?" I spat.

"She could still be out there."

Charlotte was certainly dead, and I didn't appreciate Junho's mention of her. For almost five years, I've tried to overcome losing her. At first, I tried convincing my father to allow me to seek revenge. When he refused, I tried the company of other women, but there was no antidote to be found in my bed. No, antidotes came in bottles. Drunk, celibate, and numb, I'd drunk nearly every day to drown out those memories, and I endured headaches and nausea all so that names like hers never drifted in. The room spun, but with one mention of her name, I was transported to five years ago, when my wounds were still bleeding and her tearful eyes turned from me that final time. Anxiety pooled beneath my skin as I felt her name reverberate around the room. Surrounded, my only option was to escape the restaurant and get some air. I stood, dropping silver coins onto the table in front of Junho. "Don't be a fool."

2

CHARLOTTE

I watched intently as four-year-old Morgana threw a handful of dead orange flowers in the air. "And then the witch blasted the king with another fireball!" Her soft round face was bright with excitement. She shouted as she leapt to the other side of the room, picking up a strategically placed stick.

"Nooooo!" she called back in a deep voice as she waved the stick in the air. "Her power is too great. Now I must die!" She dropped to the floor only to bounce up and race to the other side of the room. "Next, I'll go rescue the—"

Gabriel clapped his hands loudly, interrupting. Morgana opened her mouth to continue, but I joined in with Gabriel, clapping and cheering. Morgana's wrinkled forehead smoothed as she forgot all about the second part of her show and beamed with pride, her smile bright even with a missing front tooth.

I bit down on my bottom lip to refrain from laughing. This was the tenth play Morgana had put on today. "What an exciting story, my love," I said, scooping her into my arms.

"Brava!" Gabriel said, tickling Morgana who squirmed out of

my grasp. "Time for bed," he said, chasing after her. I watched them play. Morgana looked too much like her father to be mistaken for anything other than Viran. The only bit of myself that I saw in her was the wild mop of curls on her head and the face she made when pouting. Even her skin looked more like Young's than mine.

I was sure people suspected Gabriel was not her biological father. Gabriel's skin was a warm chestnut brown a bit like my father's, but his had red undertones. Mine was a lacey brown with a distinctive yellow that shone brightest in the sun. Both were several shades darker than Morgana.

Biological or not, I could hardly remember a time before our family of three. The past was filled with days I didn't relish to reminisce and these last four years had changed me from a broken girl to a strong woman.

Gabriel entered the room, his bulky frame strong and muscular. He kept his hair short, but the waves of his naturally curly hair were still visible. He had a thick black beard that framed his kind eyes beneath the wide ebony eyebrows above, but his most striking feature was his curly eyelashes that flitted with every smile. I often found myself wondering how a man so intimidating in both size and features could also be so beautiful.

"She's promised to go to sleep now," he said with a chuckle.

"Did you triple check that all the candles are—"

"Char," he said, putting a hand gently on my shoulder. "It's been two years. I don't think there will be another incident." His gaze was warm, his charcoal colored eyes gentle—like the breeze on a hot summer day—and his eyelashes like the rays of the sunrise in a world with a blackened sun. He pulled me in and I buried my face in his chest, letting myself relax. Some families are made and others found. From the day we met, Gabriel felt like he belonged with us—cosmic restitution for a lifetime of sorrow. Even as strangers, we forged a haven for Morgana with the shattered pieces of our former selves. But one shadow from my past lingered, threatening all we'd built, and I couldn't hide from it in Gabriel's embrace.

My calm shattered as a flash of orange light shot through my memory and sent a cold shudder down my spine. "Regardless," I said, pulling away, "I better see if there's any news." For the last couple years, worrying had become routine. I grabbed my cloak and headed for the door.

"Ask Lynn if she's got any leftover scones," Gabriel said.

"Will do," I called over my shoulder. I closed the door behind me and took a deep breath; the cool air still tangled with the last bit of winter. As I moved toward the center of town, I looked back at my peaceful cottage tucked away on the outskirts. We were safe; he wouldn't find us here.

I scurried by the other cottages as I went. I heard the chatter of the townspeople and saw the glow of the torch-lit streets ahead, but it wasn't until the dirt paths became cobblestones that I considered myself in town. I heard the clop of horses on the hard stones and hustled toward the tavern on the west side of the square: Blue De Loon.

The tavern sat alongside a busy street and was always packed with locals, mostly due to the friendly barkeep Lynn who had an affinity for baking that brought people together like nothing else. Still several blocks away, I could taste the sweet, doughy scent wafting through the air. My mouth watered. Lynn's cooking drew a bizarre mix of locals to the tavern, but that made it a good place to gather information. If *he* was still looking for me, Lynn might have heard something.

I pushed open the doors of the tavern, and the rush of sugary air hit my face. I was not surprised to find the tavern filled with boisterous people, goblets of ale on each table with plates of half-eaten scones and cookies. There was hardly an empty seat, except for the few vacant stools at the bar. Lynn rushed about refilling the goblets, her fluffy hair pulled into two puffs on her head. She looked up from the keg and smiled at me, motioning to an open stool at the bar.

A crash on my left sent my hand instinctively to the dragon-hilted dagger I kept hitched to my belt. A handsome brown-haired man with silver strands in his beard bent down to retrieve his spilled goblet. His gaze met mine, and a twisted smile grew at the corners of his mouth. I rolled my eyes and took my seat at the bar next to an old man who seemed somewhere between asleep and awake.

Lynn rushed over. "Charlotte!" she said, her voice muffled in the noisy tavern. She reached over the bar and hugged me with her free arm, two full goblets of ale in her opposite hand. "I'll be right back," she said, rushing out from around the bar and toward the tables in the back.

"Charlotte, eh?"

I turned to see the old man grin with a toothless smile. "I like that name. It reminds me of the former Queen of Besmi—"

"Sir," I jabbed, "mind your words carefully." I scanned the tavern.

The man threw his head back and laughed, his white hair only present just above his ears. "I'm too old to be shipped off to one of the king's camps. I'm above the law."

"He can still kill you."

He took a gulp from his goblet. "Just this morning I met a baby with the same name." He looked up at me, a glimmer of mischief in his eyes. "Guess you can kill a kingdom in body but not in soul."

Yep. He was going to get us both killed. I lowered my voice. "Excuse me, sir, have we met before?"

"In another life, perhaps." He stood and thumped three copper coins onto the bar before grabbing his jacket and heading for the door.

Lynn rushed over, her hair buns bobbing with each step. "Sorry about that. So, what's new?" Lynn's bronze skin accentuated her beautifully curved nose.

"Who is that man? I've never seen him in here before."

She traced my gaze to the old man who just pulled the tavern door open and headed out into the night. "He said his name was Morris. He's friendly, don't you think?"

I nodded. It wasn't a familiar name, but it certainly seemed like he knew who I was. I tried shaking the encounter from my mind. I hated thinking about Besmium; it made me think about all I'd lost. *Who* I'd lost. Still, whenever I thought of Young, I felt a stab of sadness that never dulled. Most days I could carry it, but on the days I couldn't, I was grateful to have Gabe be there for Morgana.

The word Besmium wasn't illegal, but Camelot's King Arthur loved taking prisoners, and he or his soldiers didn't need much of a reason to take anyone in. Because of this, I hadn't needed to face the mention of it often, just when one of the drunk patrons at the tavern got bold and reminisced. There was usually a guard or two around to end it quickly.

However, I couldn't escape the dreams. Dreams don't care about death or distance. Some mornings I'd wake up with Young's kiss still on my lips and have to relive his loss when my mind turned to the morning once more. Each night that he returned, I'd fall for the illusion, and each morning he slipped away again.

"You having some ale tonight?" Lynn asked, already filling a goblet and placing it in front of me. Before I could answer, the bubbles of the crisp ale tickled my throat.

"Atta girl," she said, and I felt the color return to my cheeks.

"Have you heard anything?" I asked before swallowing another mouthful of ale.

She shook her head. “Not about *them*. All anyone can talk about is Camelot's new alliances. They’re saying Algony agreed.”

My eyes bulged. “That’s impossible. Algony would never agree to that. It must be a rumor.”

Lynn shrugged. “As for *them,* no news is good news. If they’d been spotted near town, someone would’ve said.”

3

MINSEO

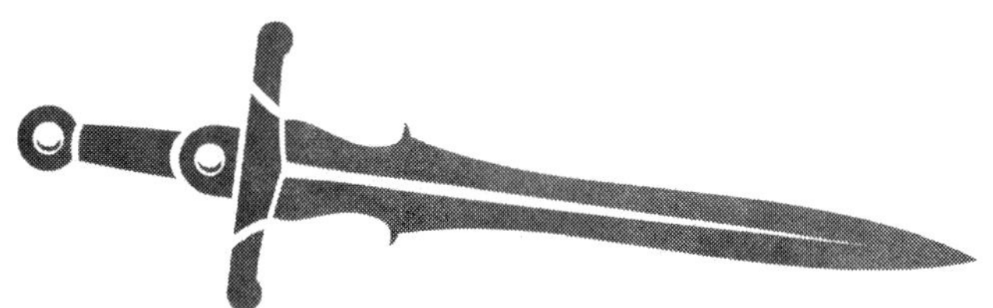

I stumbled through the double doors of the council hall, alarmed to see my father already seated at the head of the table beside my older brother Sumin. Why hadn't I expected to see *him* here? Mr. Perfect, here to witness another breakdown. Ever since I'd caused a scene at the meeting, after my return five years ago, Sumin kept his distance. It was like grief was a virus you could catch, and I was its host. When we crossed paths, he just stared down at me with the same stern look in his eyes as our father. A look that whispered, *You're the reason Young is dead*. The room echoed with the sound of my footsteps and hummed the whispered disapproval of the council members. I took my seat on father's left side, the makkoli from earlier turning in my stomach. Even with liquid courage, I was unable to meet the king's gaze.

After several painful moments, my father cleared his throat. "You may begin."

A white-haired official who wore a silky orange sash over his hanbok bowed and turned to address the table. "The first order of business is to discuss the matter of succession. Prince Sumin and his wife have yet to produce an heir." I couldn't see Sumin from his position on the other side of Father, but I felt a twinge of joy to learn he wasn't as perfect as he pretended to be.

The official continued. "It's time to start considering other options."

My father waved his hand. "He's still quite young," he said, "Send the doctor to visit the couple and find out if there's a reason for the delay. What's next?"

It was faint, but I heard Sumin whisper "thank you" to the king.

The official with the orange sash bowed and continued. "As you know, Camelot is a growing concern. They've acquired many of the adjacent territories as allies, including their newest conquest, Algony."

The room erupted into panicked chatter but one voice rose above the rest. A young, red-faced council member shouted, "There's no way that Algony would ever enter into such an arrangement. Not after their disgraced son, Emmett, had a hand in the creation of Camelot."

A thin, sunken-cheeked official interrupted. "What are the benefits of joining these alliances? It must be very tempting for so many territories to have conceded."

The room fell silent and all turned to Hanbit, who wore a blue sash, indicating his position as the king's advisor. He blanched at the sudden attention and flipped frantically through his notes. Hanbit was well-known and intelligent but lacked the nerve for public speaking. "A-A-According to our spies, Camelot offers nothing but the opportunity to trade with them and in r-return g-gains favorable trade rates and control over the allied k-kingdom's military."

The red-faced man spoke, "Are they fearful of losing their throne if they don't agree? Like Besmium?"

I felt the gaze of several of the council members on my face; they must've feared I'd react to the mention of it, but I was only there because I had to be, and I planned to keep my head down until the meeting ended. Still, the word stirred up something iniquitous inside me. Something I'd been avoiding for the past four years.

My father's soft voice rose. "It appears that we don't have all the information on this matter, and with the acquisition of Algony's military, it would be unwise to attack Camelot. We should focus on building up our forces in case they offer us an alliance and countermeasures need to be taken. We must never agree to enter into such an unfavorable situation." He straightened his posture. "And you," he said, motioning to Hanbit, "increase the number of spies in Camelot and increase the regularity of their reports."

Instinctively, I scoffed, garnering an uncomfortable amount of attention from the attendees. My father leaned in. "Care to share your thoughts, Minseo?"

A dull headache began to throb behind my eyes. *Don't say anything, Minseo. Just shut up and get through the meeting.* I felt the words forming on my tongue and bit down to stop them from coming out. *Damnit.* "I think now is the perfect time to attack. If Camelot is acquiring allies, they're only going to get stronger. Just look at how much they've grown in the last five years alone."

The man with the orange sash spoke, a flash of defiance in his eyes as he addressed the room. "Attacking on their land will give them the upper hand. Due to our location, it would be difficult to transport troops and supplies."

I held his gaze and was surprised when he didn't waiver beneath it. My absence from the meetings had negatively affected my credibility, but it wasn't going to stop me. "Difficult doesn't mean impossible. We need to show them that they can't just take anything they want—that they can't get away with what they've done," I said, slamming my fist on the table. The smack of the table silenced the room, and I moved my gaze from one member of the council to the next.

My father leaned in, the sternness of his face absent from his voice. "Revenge will only lead to more death."

I straightened my posture, feeling disapproval ready to spring from the lips of every council member in the room. "All the more reason to attack."

My father sighed, his irritation marked by a hard line across his forehead. "Enough, Minseo." He turned to the other council members. "Is that all that's on the agenda for today?" he asked.

A frazzled Hanbit pulled on his blue sash and shook his head wearily. "There is one more thing…" His gaze moved to me. "But, perhaps now isn't the best time to speak of such m-matters."

My father waved his hand dismissively without so much as a glance in my direction. "He's fine, he's fine. Go ahead."

But I wasn't. I was fuming, unable to live with the fact that my brother was taken from me by a teenager who earned a throne in some ridiculous contest.

A lump in Hanbit's throat rose and fell before he spoke. "Apparently, there are rumors that the former queen of Besmium, Charlotte, still lives, and that the king's men, barring one incident, have had difficulty locating her."

My body pulsed. She's *alive*?

The rooms buzzed with questions, but they blended together like a dizzying smoke. The thought rang in my head again and again. *She's alive?*

The red-faced man shouted,"Does that mean the child lives as well? That could solve our succession problem."

Another voice interjected. "We could send a small party to try and retrieve them."

She's *alive*.

"Out of the question," the bold man said. "The girl made her choice long ago. Any interference on our part could be seen as a declaration of war with Camelot."

She's alive and I abandoned her.

4

CHARLOTTE

I knelt beside the magnolia tree, the buds already pink but not yet open. I traced my fingers across the ridges of Young's name. I'd chosen a tree near my home to carve his name. A place I could visit him and sometimes talk. This was the place where I gave myself time to turn grief into memory. When we moved to flee capture by Lancelot and his companion Merlin, I had to choose a new tree, but it wasn't like Young was buried there. I shuddered to think his body still lay in the atrium where he fell, beneath the ruins of the what was once Cadere castle, but there were many thoughts I dared not dwell upon.

"Papa!" Morgana said, hugging the tree. She sat down beside it and prattled a nonsensical story with no foreseeable end. I smiled, feeling the warmth inside push back the cold of the afternoon. I lay back against the tree and closed my eyes. Morgana's voice faded until the only voice left to hear was my own.

I walked through an empty, gray world that seemed to be made up of the absence of everything. I held out my hand and pushed through the dull, colorless particles and watched them swirl around my hand. Lucid, I looked out into the vacant space. *"Young,"* I said, and there, through the gray mist, I saw his silhouette. Relieved, I sprinted forward through the clouds toward him. The mist swirled around my ankles and brushed against my cheeks. Breathlessly, I pushed through, the shadow of him never growing closer. My legs weakened, but I didn't slow. I wouldn't. Not when he was so close. "Young!" I screamed. A hard gust of wind pushed through, slicing the mist. An empty gray space, with no discernible horizon line, lay before me.

"Charlotte!" Young called, his voice muffled. I stopped, unsure if the wind was knocked out of me from my run or from his voice. Behind me? I turned back and, in the distance, I saw a figure running towards me. "Charlotte!" he called.

I tore toward the figure, unable to breathe or blink for fear I'd miss him. I ran, my hands outstretched as his face came fully into view. First his dark eyes. His high cheekbones cutting through the remaining strength in my legs. His round lips, a dash of pink in this gray world.

Even as he yelled my name, his eyes had the calm, soulful glint in them that others get when staring out into the ocean.

A few yards away, I could see tears on his cheeks as he reached for me.

A gust of wind shot between us, pushing us further apart. I covered my face with my arms and felt myself slide back on the smooth gray surface. My eyes stung. "Young!" I called, my voice muffled and lost to the wind.

"No!" I screamed, unable to open my eyes in the monstrous gusts. "I love you. I love you. I love you," I shouted. The wind cut, and I stood alone in grayness once more. "No," I whispered. "I love you." But he was gone.

I stood shaking.

"There you are," he said from behind me. But before I could

turn, his hands were on my waist. He spun me and pulled me tightly to him, his mouth hot on mine. He buried his face in my neck, his tongue sliding up it and sending a chill through my body. I held him so hard it hurt. He pulled me off my feet and I wrapped my legs around him. He lay me on the ground and pressed his body to mine. His lips parted from mine as he whispered, "I love you too." I ran my thumb across his cheek and stared into his eyes as the mist around us turned from gray to gold.

My heart thundered against my chest, and I was certain he could feel it because I could feel his. His hand moved from my body to my hair.

Hot tears stung my eyes as I erupted into sobs. He kissed my jaw and laughed. Wiping my eyes, warmth radiated from his body.

I awoke beneath the shade of the tree, my eyes dry. The golden glow of the sun hovered as it threatened to set. Morgana was still midway through an endless story.

He was gone, and once again, the pain of his loss was as fresh as the first time. I clutched my stomach to keep from screaming. The agony was as much a part of me as my pulse. I exhaled the worst of it, the memory of the dream evaporating into the orange glow.

I could almost feel his kiss on my lips. Instead of crying as I used to, I smiled.

I thought a "thank you" to him for visiting and stood, rubbing my cold arms.

"Say goodbye to your father, Morgana," I said. Morgana stood and took my hand. "Bye, Papa," she said. "I'll tell you the rest later." She tossed her hair over her shoulder and we headed back to town just in time to see the sunset.

5

MINSEO

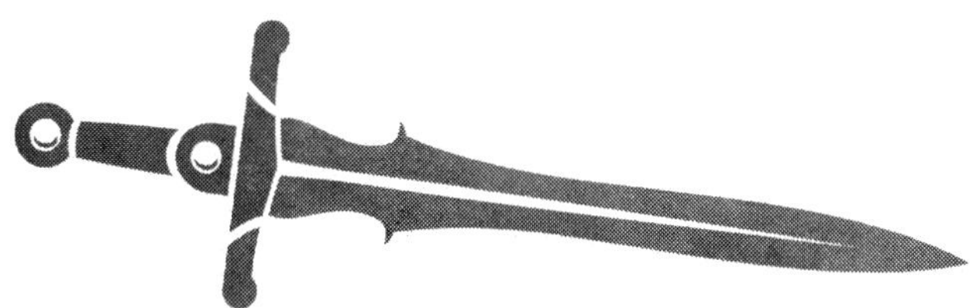

My heartbeat drowned out the sound of my father calling my name as I leapt from my seat and ran towards the door. I had to find her. I burst into the cool night air. Lanterns flickered along the bridge, illuminating the white petals that sprang off the nearby blossom trees and settled on the surface of the lake like freshly fallen snow.

"Get my horse!" I called to our stable keeper. Breathless, my vision blurred. *Get it together.* I'd need to prepare for the journey, supplies, I'd probably need to convince Hanbit to come so I could use his leads about her whereabouts, I'd need Junho and a small team of soldiers, maybe even Jay Hyun. It would take days, several days to prepare at least, but I reeled. I needed to move, to think, to be out in the fresh air. I looked up to the silvery half moon—she was out there.

I was jolted from my trance by the *clip-clop* of my horse's hooves on the rough path. My stable hand breathed heavily as he bowed and handed me the reins. I mounted my horse and felt a flicker of something warm inside, something I thought was gone. "Thank you," I said.

The stablehand recoiled and stepped back. "You're welcome, Your Highness."

I rode towards the front gate, suddenly conscious of how I'd treated everyone for the past few years. It was a miracle I still had a friend left. Without even realizing it, I headed toward his home.

The cold of the winter was over and the blooms of spring brought new life. I rode through the gates, through the dirt roads. Clay-tiled homes nestled behind their walls, the streets still alive with people rushing about, enjoying the fine weather, even in the lantern-lit night. "*Charlotte*," I whispered into the empty air.

Then I saw her—soft brown skin, dark secret-filled eyes, spiral curls. My cheeks burned, and she was just a girl then. Now she was a woman of twenty-one at least. I felt fire kindle in my chest, the one I'd lost all those years ago. In the four years since Besmium fell, I hadn't requested the presence of any woman to my chambers. I hadn't courted, and my mother knew better than to attempt another arrangement. I spent my time convincing myself Charlotte had died that winter until I believed it, and then I forced myself to forget.

I was nothing but the shell of Prince Minseo of Vires until moments ago when Charlotte re-entered my world—sparking my light. Now the blood coursed through my veins once more.

Vires was home, and when I had returned broken and lost, I vowed never to leave its borders again. How quickly I turned on that vow as I raced through the night.

I pulled on the reins, slowing my horse as my mind crawled towards the somber truth. I'd made other vows. I vowed to my brother I'd protect Charlotte and vowed to Charlotte I wouldn't leave her alone. I'd broken those as well. I stopped my horse. My mind flashed to Charlotte's cold expression shrinking into the distance as I rode back to Vires without her. She hadn't shed a single tear that day. It was entirely possible that she'd never forgive me. I dismounted, unable to take a step forward.

My horse stirred, sensing my uneasiness. I exhaled all the hope I'd allowed myself to build in the last few moments. I ran my hand through my hair and felt my eyes prickle. She'd never forgive me. I swallowed a mouthful of shame, the acidic taste still lingering on my tongue, and tilted my head back. I stared vacantly at the moon and sighed. My gaze drifted down to the ground below like blossoms on a windless morning. A gust of wind pushed at my back.

Then a thought hit me so hard it pulled the breath from my lungs. *What about the baby*? If Charlotte was alive, the child might be out there too. *Young's* baby. I stepped forward. My mind spun with the thought. A part of my brother was still in this world. I pulled myself back onto my horse and, before I knew it, I was riding full force toward Junho's house.

I looked up at the cherry blossom trees, the ones I'd miss this year. There were so many buds that hadn't yet opened.

6

CHARLOTTE

I pushed open the tavern door and stopped, my hand immediately moving to my dagger. It wasn't that the tavern was packed with dozens of soldiers in blue or that there was barely enough room to stand. It wasn't the roaring laughter or general chaos. What unsettled me was the smell; Lynn hadn't baked today. In all the time I'd known her, she'd never missed a day of baking. I couldn't see her from the door. Just an army of soldiers at play. I should leave, I knew that. Not only was I a woman in a tavern with sixty drunken men, but if Lancelot and Merlin were among them— I shuddered. Still, Lynn was in there. I knew she could take care of herself; she was a tough person, but she hadn't baked and that worried me.

I put up the hood of my shawl and made my way to the bar.

I saw an opening and moved my body into it, only to be shoved out by a large man with thick black hair on his arms. "Wait your turn." he barked, shoving me back from the bar without even glancing in my direction. I pushed back into my place, prompting the man to turn to me with such force he nearly knocked over the soldier on the far side of him. His face was lined with a snarl until he saw me. "Oh, I'm sorry, m'lady," he said and sheepishly retreated into the crowded room—ale in hand.

Pleased, I scanned the bar for Lynn. She darted in from the kitchen, slinging ale across the table so quickly the other bartends stood back, so as not to get in the way. *Of course, she's fine,* I breathed. She probably didn't have time to bake, that's all. Relieved, I turned back to the exit. It didn't seem like I'd have much time to check in today, but I could always return tomorrow. For now, getting as far away from anyone who could recognize me was the top priority.

"Hey, I know you," a man said from behind me. My stomach tightened. I turned to see he was slightly familiar—a regular at the tavern. Handsome, with a sandy brown beard that was sprinkled with gray. He swayed before he stood and slunk towards me. His voice carried, drawing the attention of several soldiers. "I heard a rumor…" He swayed forward, the ale on his breath stinging my nose. "I heard that husband of yours likes the company of other men." I turned back towards the door and started pushing my way to it. His wide arm wrapped around my waist and pulled me to his body. He lowered his mouth to my ear and slurred, "Let me show you what a real man can do."

I sighed. If I attacked him, I'd draw too much attention, and if I drew blood, I could be arrested and dragged to one of Arthur's camps.

I twisted his wrist and felt his knees buckle from the pain. I leaned in close to his ear. "If you ever touch me again, I'll kill you." I released his wrist and saw him rub it as I pushed the door open and headed back into the night.

I walked home slower than usual and had to admit to myself that I was shaken. Not by the drunk idiot, of course, but by the rumor. It was happening again. Just when we'd finally settled in.

After Besmium fell, I'd taken odd jobs and relied on the charity of some citizens who were still loyal to my father to get through the first winter. Morgana and I moved a lot in those days, as not to burden any one person too much. That's when the notices went out that Arthur was taking prisoners and putting bounties on members of the council or any dethroned royalty. There wasn't anyone I could trust, and the people who'd been helping me could be punished if it was ever discovered. I decided to take Morgana and head for a new town farther away from where Hiems or Cadere once stood.

Minutes after we arrived, I saw Gabriel bloodied and on the ground as a group of thugs beat him. Their words as they struck him reflected that of tonight's rumor; *Fairy, priss,* they'd said. Instinctively, I stepped in without a plan and an infant in my arms. What could I do? I could no longer use my name and former title to aid him. They'd probably drag me in for the bounty if I did. Instead, I introduced myself as Gabriel's wife, and after some convincing, they let him go.

To this day, I've wondered what exactly it was that thrust me into action, but if I had to guess, I'd say it was this light he had inside. This joy that couldn't be extinguished. Even as they wounded him, he smiled. It's the kind of light that people who live in darkness seek to destroy and, though I sought to protect him, he became the haven who rescued me.

As we grew more familiar and decided on an arrangement where we would live the lie that brought us together, I never was able to ask him if any of it was true; it didn't matter. From that day forward, he'd been a teammate and father figure to Morgana. I'd always assumed he might talk to me about it when he was ready, but he was eager to hide his past—and so was I. I realized through our unspoken understanding that we had already given up on a happy life, but together we could make a peaceful one. I thought it would go on like that forever, but after a year, the rumors about Gabriel started up again. We'd discussed it and decided to move to another town for our safety. We packed as much as we could and planned on leaving in the morning. That night, two seemingly unrelated tragedies occurred: Morgana's bedroom caught fire, and we came face to face with the man tasked with my capture—Lancelot of Camelot.

7

LANCELOT

My nose prickled with the overwhelming scent of lavender. The unearthly fog swirled around me in a purple cyclone. I listened intently for footsteps, relying on the one sense she hadn't hindered. A shadow moved through the fog, but I knew better than to attack the first time she showed herself—she'd gotten me with that one the week before. Impatient, I gripped the hilt of my sword.

"Merlin," I called into the darkness, "when am I going to be in a situation where I'm surrounded by violet mist?"

I spun in time to block her kick from connecting with my face. I stumbled back, tripping over a stump that sprouted from nowhere, sending me crashing to the ground. The newly forming tree snaked its vines tightly around my wrists and locked me in place. The mist dispelled and Merlin stood over me, sword pointed at my throat. Her rich umber skin was beaded with sweat, her bold lips continually drawing my eyes against my will.

"And this is why Arthur won't knight you."

I seethed, ripping the vines out of the ground and tearing them from my wrist. "We can't all be the king's favorite. Besides, it was your stupid vision that got me assigned to this quest in the first place. If not for you, I would have made knight years ago."

She lowered her sword, pushing her mint-green braids over her shoulder to her back. "If you hadn't let Charlotte get away two years ago, you'd be a knight."

I stood, rubbing my sore wrists. "You say that like you weren't the reason she got away."

She rolled her eyes. "I told you there was a baby close by."

"I don't care! Kill it." I pushed past her, ignoring the disgusted glare she shot me. I marched towards the forest edge and headed for the inn.

"So, I guess we're done training for the day?" I heard her call.

I huffed. How dare that insolent witch insult a future knight of Camelot.

I rummaged through my trunk, pulled out a piece of parchment, and headed to my desk where my ink was kept. Knighthood wasn't any closer than it had been years ago, and I was growing restless. I needed them to respect me—all of them.

I took a deep breath, sighed out my frustration, and pulled the image of my beloved into my mind.

Dear Gwen,

Not a day goes by that I don't miss your bright smile. I promised you that I'd complete this quest and be knighted, but neither of us could have predicted it would take so many moons to complete. But worry not, my love for you is as true as the day I bid you farewell when you cried in my arms. Once I'm knighted, I'll have the means and the title to marry you at last and we can finally be together, and I promise on that day, I'll never leave you again. I've not received any of your letters as of late, but with

Merlin and my location changing so frequently, it's not surprising they've not found their way to me yet. Even without them, I can feel your love. Also, please keep an eye on Arthur, will you? Make sure he doesn't get himself in any real trouble. Apart from you, he's the closest thing I have to family. And please congratulate him on his new alliance with Algony.

With love,
Lancelot

I sat back, resting the quill in the ink pool. I read the note over. A knock on my door startled me. "Come in," I yelled, my voice cracking. I quickly folded the letter. Merlin walked in, her dark brown skin still shining with sweat. Her green braids were loose and danced around her body, bucking off her lower back as she took a seat on my bed. "Look, I'm sorry about earlier. I shouldn't have said that. I was just trying to motivate you."

I turned towards the window.

She walked over, putting her hand on mine. She lowered her voice. "Of course Arthur will knight you. Don't worry, we're going to capture her. I'm here to help," she said. I met her gaze, her facial features softening her eyes beaming with the light of a woman in love. I knew because that's how Gwen looked at me.

I pulled my hand away, and her gaze moved to the letter.

She turned away. "Oh, is that for Gwen?" She faked a smile. "Bet she misses you." Her smile was bright, but the light in her eyes was gone. Merlin was the only known magic wielder in Camelot, and Arthur was obsessed with finding more for his army. Because of this, Arthur allotted her more freedoms than most, and I wondered how Charlotte still managed to evade. I grew ever more suspicious that Merlin was somehow hindering progress for her own purposes, and she'd noticed the tension.

Even so, I had to admit Merlin was beautiful. Enough to draw the attention of everyone she passed and garner us a bit of a reputation. Soldiers in Arthur's army were many and nameless—kingdomless even—but everyone knew Arthur's knights, and it was nice to hear my name among them, even if it was only mentioned as Merlin's partner.

I'd been tied to her for so long. I remember how envious I'd once been of her abilities. It took almost two years to realize just how much of a burden they placed on her and how much in the way of family and companions she'd lost as a result. But even if my heart didn't belong to someone, I couldn't surrender it to Merlin. That's what it would be, a surrender. I couldn't bear the thought of a life where I followed her lead and trailed behind her. My growing indifference about her powers had brought us together. Our differing genders pushed us apart because, even with Merlin's beauty and talent, there would never be any other woman for me but Gwenevere, and Merlin knew that. Still, every once in a while, I saw hope in her eyes, and most of the time I didn't stop it. I needed her to help me find and capture Charlotte, and nothing was going to get in my way.

8

MINSEO

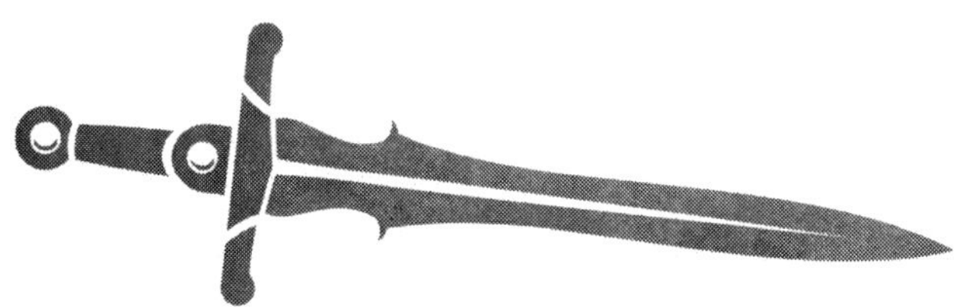

The carriage jostled as it moved along the stone-speckled path. The horses jerked the cabin with each step, and my lower back cramped from sitting for so long. I didn't care, though; I was glad to be off the dreaded sea. I hadn't recalled this journey taking so long when I traveled to Besmium with Young. I eyed Junho warily as he slept as soundly as a man in his own bed. I don't think Young ever slept soundly after my father told him he would marry Charlotte. Beside Junho sat Hanbit, a quill and leatherbound book of parchment clasped between his slender fingers. While I was certain his intel would help us locate Charlotte, his character made me doubt if having him along was worth the torment. He had this odd habit of whistling when he was uncomfortable, as if a tune would drown out the ramblings in his head. We'd asked him to stop dozens of times, but every time he'd lose focus, he'd begin again. The man couldn't help it. After the first few days, we learned to tune it out, but every now and then, my mind would tune into the high-pitched melody and disrupt my peace. Once given my father's permission, Jay Hyun had also agreed to accompany us on our journey, but he marched along the other soldiers outside the cabin.

My guilt lay just beneath my skin as I recalled my father's expression when he asked me not to go to Camelot. I'd hurt him. In his eyes, I could see he was certain that I too would be killed on the unholy land that now belonged to Arthur, but I had no choice. The moment I found out Charlotte was alive, I'd made up my mind to go. No one, not even the King of Vires, could stop me.

When my father was certain he couldn't persuade me to stay, he made me promise I'd bring Charlotte and her child back to Vires where we could protect them. I tried to imagine a Vires with Charlotte in it but couldn't. Apart from Junho, Hanbit, and Jay Hyun, my father sent ten Viran soldiers to accompany us on this quest. It was enough to make sure we were well protected without seeming like an act of war against Camelot. With a multitude of lengthy travel days under our feet, we were all a little irritable and in need of rest.

The carriage bumped up onto a smoother surface, a more level road. I knew we must've been close to a big town. *Finally*.

I pulled back the curtain and a white beam of light poured in, waking Junho. He scowled unpleasantly. I peered outside, pleased by the stone-built structures and angular rooftops which were a stark contrast to Vires. Even the people who roamed about seemed to be of every complexion and creed, no doubt an advantage of Arthur's takeovers. The last time I was in Besmium, I spent my time in the king's castles or as a prisoner of Arthur's Drethen army in the woods. This was the first time I'd spent any real time in a city outside of Vires.

We approached a wooden sign that read: *Welcome to Galvon*. I'd never heard of it. It wasn't one of Camelot's famous cities like Bullhorn, or Rowendale, but from the small window from which I observed, it was huge.

The architecture was simplistic. In Vires, we considered the designs and spent many years constructing palaces and temples that would last. Structures our kingdom could be proud of, that travelers came to admire. There was nothing of that scale in Galvon, but the sheer quantity of structures built in such close proximity gave the city spirit that tempted me to leap from the carriage and explore. The farther in we went, the tighter the streets between the buildings were, and I wondered what might happen if we came to an impasse with another carriage.

Our carriage stopped. "Excuse me, madam," I heard a Jay Hyun say. "You're blocking our path."

It was all the reason I needed. "I'm not missing this," I said, pushing the door open and stepping out into the stale sunlight.

"Forgive me," a woman replied. "Are you from Vires?"

I hurried past the horses to see her. There, in the center of the road, was the most unearthly figure I'd ever laid eyes on. She was tall, almost my height, with toned muscles and a powerful stance. Her cool black skin shone in the sun like she admitted light, and long, sea-foam green braids flowed from the top of her head and past her waist. Each tiny movement sent a wave of green locks dancing around her like the ocean's constant clash against the shore. She wore armor, but based on the scarcity of it, I'd say it was for style and not protection, a trend that had reached Vires as well. She had many rings on her fingers beneath each joint, and more around her wrists and arms. As I drank her in, my gaze settled on her lovely top-heavy lips. My first instinct was to kneel. *Who is she? A goddess perhaps?* Jay Hyun hadn't answered her, and I assumed he was struck with similar thoughts.

I stepped forward, mustering my voice to sound strong. "Yes, I am Prince Minseo of Vires."

Her gaze shifted to me, making me feel small and weak. Her eyes lit up. "A prince of Vires," she said, stepping forward. My guards drew their swords. She stopped, eyeing them suspiciously. "And what business do you have in Camelot, Minseo of Vires?"

"Merely traveling to admire the great kingdom of Camelot."

She put a hand on her hips, weakening my nerve. "There are a lot of guards here for a mere vacation."

"Yes," I said, trying to blink out her obvious beauty. "I lost my brother to this land."

She tilted her head, observing me, her dark eyes moving down my body and back up to my face.

"May we pass?" I pushed.

She didn't move; my presence bothered her in some way. Would we have to fight her?

"Merlin," a man called. I squinted into the light to see a heavily armored man approaching. Even with armor, I could see he had powerful shoulders. As he neared, I saw the hazel-green eyes that were as clear as the evening. His square jaw made him look older from far away, but when he stood next to the goddess, I could see a touch of childhood still holding his features. He might have been striking, though not conspicuously handsome, if not for the woman beside him.

At most, he was in his late teens, and it seemed they were traveling alone, which eased me a little. If this came to a fight, we could easily overcome them with our numbers.

"What is this?" the boy asked, his gaze bouncing between Merlin and me.

"I'm not sure," she said. "My most recent vision was... undetermined."

He sighed. "Let's go." He turned and started walking in the direction from which he came. Merlin smiled, but a sparkle in her eyes alerted me to danger. She held out her hand, prompting my guards to raise their swords. She laughed mischievously. "It's a gift for the prince. A little piece of home." She opened her hand to reveal a small, pink cherry blossom.

I froze. Did she want me to take it? I inched forward but felt someone take a hard grip of my arm. I turned to see Junho. He shook his head. Merlin smirked and dropped the cherry blossom. It floated beautifully from her hand to the earth below. In an instant, the small blossom melted into a pink liquid, soaking into the ground. We watched it in awe as Merlin turned and followed her companion. One root at a time, in a matter of seconds, a cherry blossom tree sprouted from the ground. It thickened, quickly prompting the horses to inch back nervously. Bigger and bigger the giant trunk stretched, each branch weaving into the air and sprouting thousands of pink blossoms.

Impossible. Yet there it was, happening before my eyes. There was no such thing as magic. *Is this some kind of trick or did we just encounter a witch?* Perhaps my original assessment of 'goddess' was more accurate than I thought. I'd just witnessed the divine.

I stood beside Junho, frozen in silence as we tried to process what occurred. There, in front of us, stood a cherry blossom tree that rivaled the beauty of those in Vires, though moments before it was just a bud in Merlin's hand.

Even without trying to process the enormity of what she'd just done and what it meant for our world, I was looking at a new issue. She'd blocked the main road, and it might take several hours to cut it down and clear the mess away. We had the option, of course, to backtrack and go another way, but since she'd gone through the trouble to delay us, I wanted more than anything to continue.

9

MERLIN

"What was that about?" Lancelot spat.

I sighed. "You couldn't tell who they were?"

He gulped his ale. "Virans?" His sandy brown hair was unkempt, his pale skin heavy with exhaustion. This quest was wearing him down. His strong jaw clenched as he anticipated my answer.

I ran my finger along the rim of my ale, picturing the face of the stunned prince."That was Prince Minseo of Vires."

Lancelot slammed his goblet on the table. "You think he's after Charlotte?"

My eyes drifted to his near-permanent frown. I pulled a quill and paper from my bag. "Obviously."

"We should have killed him on the spot! Why did you—" His voice faded away. I reached into my mind's eye and let a memory that wasn't mine flow through my body and concentrate on the hand that held my quill. My hand moved, but I could no longer see the paper, the quill, or the tavern, and Lancelot may have been a thousand miles away from how scantily I could feel or hear him.

When my hand once again belonged to me, I blinked the bar back into existence, handing the note to Lancelot.

Dear Charlotte,

I've fallen in love with you. You're the reason I can't return to Vires.

Love,
Minseo

Lancelot looked up from the note. "Wasn't she married to the other brother?"

I shook my head. "The point is he loves her. If they've arrived here after all these years, they could have information about where to find her."

Lance nodded. "And we can follow them."

"Exactly," I said, brushing my braids over my shoulder.

"So, what was with the tree?"

I smiled, fiddling with my rings. "A message for the King of Vires."

I put my head down on my arms. That *was* a big tree. Perhaps I shouldn't have overdone it and conserved a little more energy. I eyed Lancelot, but he didn't notice. He drank his ale and chipped mindlessly at the wood on the bar.

He was a powerful swordsman, maybe the most skilled Camelot had to offer, but he paid no mind to battle strategy or planning. Arthur was right to deny him a knighthood. Not to mention his mind was poisoned with love from that snake Gwenevere. I never understood what the big deal about her was anyway. Beautiful? Yes, but empty-headed as a ceramic vase. Above all, I hated the way Lance looked when she didn't write.

When I first volunteered to accompany Lance on his knighthood quest, Arthur refused to let me go. He needed the world's only battle mage by his side. He considered me his greatest asset, and it was an honor to serve him. But I couldn't pull my thoughts away from Lance. He wasn't especially kind to me, just the opposite. He didn't mind me at all. He gave no special attention or courtesy. He never gawked at my unusual appearance or inquired into the extent of my power. Some might have even considered him unkind, but I loved the way he made me feel ordinary.

Surely, if I traveled with him, he'd see I was more valuable than Gwenevere. I meditated on a solution every spare moment. Out of my desperation to join him, a blurred vision pushed through. A drop of magic in Charlotte's royal blood. The promise of two battle mages at his side convinced Arthur, and I'd been beside Lance ever since. Even so, Gwenevere still held his heart.

If I captured Charlotte, I'd be the one who helped him reach his dream. When he returned to simple Gwen, he'd see her for what she was, and he would see me as his champion.

I often wondered what it would feel like to be loved that way. The way he loved Gwen. He pined for her, lived his life for her—I think that's why I'd taken to him. I believed that if he was capable of that kind of love, perhaps one day, if I remained by his side, he'd look at me that way. It was ridiculous, of course, and the more I watched him fawn after Gwen, after all these years, the more my hope waned.

I felt my eyelids get heavy from the ale so I sat up, just in time to see Minseo barge into the tavern with his strong-postured friend and a weasel of a man who held a quill to paper like he needed to document each move the prince made.

I sighed. Of all the taverns, he chose this one. Maybe my vision had more credence than I'd originally given it.

The prince's gaze brushed over us, and he hesitated to enter, eventually taking a seat near the back of the tavern. Several guards joined him a few minutes later, but since it was only half of them, I assumed they were still clearing away the tree.

It felt unusual not to interact after we'd made such a fuss earlier. As if we were off duty. That was just fine with me; I was too drained to put on another show.

Several hours passed and the tavern filled. Every so often, the prince's friend would come to the bar and order another round of drinks, using a guard's help to deliver the sloshing goblets to their table. Despite the fact we'd started drinking earlier, Lance seemed to try to keep pace with the prince, his words starting to slur. His head bobbed as he recounted Gwen's beauty in an endless droll I tuned out. What a bizarre four years it had been since we'd set out on Lance's knighthood quest.

One blurred vision started it all—more of an inkling, that the former Queen of Besmium, Charlotte, was still alive and possessed magic blood. But Arthur had taken every vision and request seriously since he saw me cast my first spell. I relished every moment Lance and I spent together, and I had Arthur's quest to thank for it.

As I watched the foreign prince drink with his comrades, I wondered what it might be like to belong to such a happy grouping. My family had cast me out for the unique abilities Arthur welcomed, and since then, my abilities were the only things people knew about me. Except for Lance. He was the only one I felt *knew* me beyond just my power. He knew my weakness. He *was* my weakness. But even he had a way of reminding me how lonely life actually was. I think, of all things, the loneliness was the biggest surprise life had yielded.

"Merlin, was it?" a voice piped from behind me. I turned to see the prince, red-faced and grinning like an idiot. *Intriguing*. "So, are you a witch or something?" he said, a Viran accent present that wasn't earlier.

I winced. "I prefer the term mage," I said, stretching my shoulders back.

"Is your hair really that color or did you do that with magic?"

"That's a rude question. Are you a stick person or do you detest manual labor and exercise?"

To my surprise, Minseo of Vires threw his head back and laughed. "I've been going through something."

An honest answer. Just when I thought I had him figured out. Delighted, I leaned forward. "So, tell me what you're *really* doing in Camelot."

He took a seat beside me, his confidence much more prince-like than before. He almost looked charming. "What else can you do with your power?" he said, his eyes lingering on my shoulders. *He's unbelievable.* I contemplated if I should strike him or allow him to entertain me for a while longer when Lance stepped between us.

"Why don't you go back over to your table? She's not interested."

My heart leapt as Lance puffed up his chest. Was that jealousy? I put my hand on Lance's shoulder. "That's okay, Lance. He's not bothering me," I lied.

Lance turned to me slowly. A thousand questions reflected in his hazel eyes.

"See?" Minseo said, patting Lance on the opposite shoulder. "We're fine here."

Shit. In one fluid act, Lance's fist connected with Minseo's, cheek splitting it along his cheekbone. I turned, and the swords of five Viran guards pointed at our throats. I channeled my remaining energy to the bottom of my lungs and pushed the guards across the room with a gust of wind.

I pulled Lance to the door and shoved him out before turning back to the stunned guards. "I'm terribly sorry, Your Highness. My friend has obviously hit his limit. I will take him home immediately." The wide-eyed prince brought his hand to his bleeding cheek.

"That wind thing was impressive. Are you coming back after?" he asked.

Unbelievable. I left the tavern, pulling Lance along with me. At least I didn't have to worry about retaliation. In fact, it seemed Prince Minseo of Vires could be the key to getting everything I've ever wanted—both Charlotte and Lance.

10

MINSEO

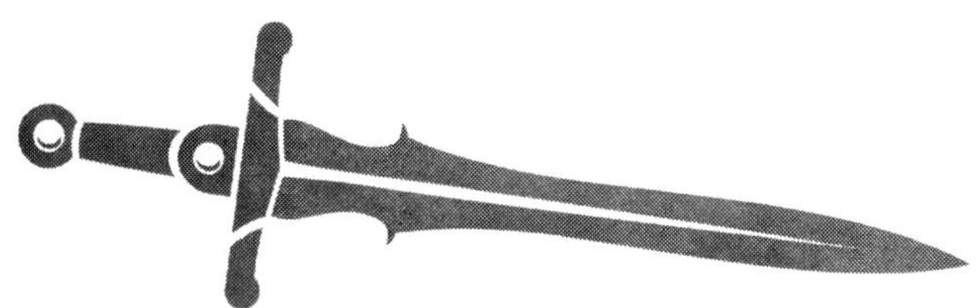

We stayed at the tavern until the tree was cleared, the room whirring with the excitement of witnessing Merlin's power firsthand, Junho, Hanbit, and Jay Hyun acting out the scene and arguing over its details. It was a sealed room and she'd conjured a wind powerful enough to push most of the ale off the tables, even in the back of the tavern.

Instead of being angry about their spilled drinks, the guests gushed about their experience. Even strangers outside of our company joined us to swap stories about the king's favorite new weapon. She had garnered a reputation for being unpredictable and her unique appearance, highlighted by her green braids, made her easy to identify. It was as if the force from the gust came directly from her soul. Was all of Camelot this interesting, or did I have a habit of finding trouble?

I leaned back in my chair, entertained. They were the kind of stories anyone might have dismissed as fantasy, but it was undeniable now. I wasn't sure what to do with this new information. I wondered what my brother would have said if he'd seen the magic up close. He'd no doubt be searching for a logical explanation, a hidden device.

"And her companion," a red-bearded man said, his dark eyes gleaming with delight. "Lancelot. He's on a knighthood quest."

I shook my hair out of my eyes. "What's that?"

"That's how we do things here in Camelot. Certain soldiers are given the opportunity to win a title and become a noble family after completing a trial set by our king."

I laughed. "*Win* a title?"

He scratched his beard. "It's how Arthur plans on spreading out the new wealth. It ain't natural for a kingdom to grow so quickly, if you ask me. And on the backs of prisoners no less."

"So what's this guy's quest?" I asked.

"Not sure. But I'll tell you what, knighthood quests are supposed to be completed alone. The fact that he's got a witch helping him means it's probably something crazy, like slaying a dragon or something."

I smiled with delight. "Hey, don't joke about dragons. Earlier today, I was sure magic was just a myth."

The bar shook, and for a split second, my mind stuck to the word dragon. But a heavyset bar patron pulled himself off the floor, brushing the ale off his shirt. He waved off our attention and the tavern returned to normal. *Dragons*. What a thought.

Hanbit's whistling started up again, a clear sign he had checked out of the conversation. I turned to him, hoping to distract him long enough to spare myself the sound.

"Any news? I received word yesterday that Camelot means to ally with Quembly."

"Really? That far north?" I supposed they had some decent mountains up there, some mining camps, but that was as far north as Vires was east. Surely Arthur wasn't planning on stretching his reach that far. How long until he went after Vires? I needed to find Charlotte and get out of here.

"Is the tree cleared?" I asked Jay Hyun. "Almost, Your Highness," he said as he and two other guards dragged in three huge velvet sacks.

"What's in there?"

Jay Huyn reached in, pulling out a handful of pale pink blossoms. "Part of the tree," he said, his eyes holding a touch of green in the tavern light.

"Why are we keeping the tree?"

"Sir, it's only part of the tree. You know," he scratched the back of his head, "since it was made with magic. We figured we should take it back to Vires, to see if there was some kind of trick to it." I nodded, and the soldiers carried the bags out to the carriage.

"We should get moving," I said.

Jay Hyun nodded, and I was surprised by his eagerness because I'd remembered him to be a man who frequented bars in Vires. He sat down beside me and leaned forward, his cheeks red from ale. "Your Highness, shouldn't we rest for the night?"

I shook my head, feeling the world lag behind, weighed down by my alcohol consumption. When did I get this drunk? I suppose from all that posturing with Lancelot. "If they'd meant to follow us, now is our best chance to put some distance between us and them." I sighed. "I'm tired too, but it looks like that Lance guy will be out for the night. I've never fought a magic wielder before, and I'm not sure if, even with our superior numbers, we'd be able to take them down. Merlin is too much of a wild card. We can't risk it."

After a momentary pause and an exasperated groan, the soldiers one by one prepared for the long night ahead, some putting down their nearly-full ales in one shot.

We had no leads to go on, and we hadn't even given this city a look yet, but something about being in proximity of Merlin and Lancelot unsettled me. She'd reminded me that anything imaginable was possible, starting with the most ridiculous. So I made a snap decision; our next city would be decided by fate. Hanbit whistled mindlessly from the corner as we came up with our travel plan. Junho and Jay Hyun held up a hand-drawn map of Camelot against the tavern wall. The cities listed were just the ones the bar patrons could think of off the tops of their heads. The place where one man met his wife. Another man's favorite city for fishing. They were so sloppily placed on the map, it resembled more of a list than anything else. I unsheathed my dagger and aimed at it.

"He's too good at this. Make him close his eyes or something," Jay Hyun said.

"Hello," Junho interceded. "You realize he's throwing that dagger at *us*."

Jay Hyun's eyes bulged. "Aim true, Your Majesty."

With one throw of the dagger, we loaded up the carriage and rode through the night, and I wondered if it was the last I'd ever see of the strange enchantress. I didn't know why, but I hoped it was.

11

CHARLOTTE

"She's finally in bed," I said, scanning the room for Gabriel, but the room was empty. A knock banged from the door, and I opened it to find Lynn, hair puffs and all, a basket of baked goods slung across her arm.

Before I could greet her, Morgana's tiny footsteps came blasting toward us. "Lynn!" she said, jumping into Lynn's arms, nearly knocking the basket over.

Lynn spun Morgana. "There's my little princess."

I clenched my jaw. "Any other nickname, Lynn. So what are you doing here? No tavern tonight?"

She nuzzled Morgana. "I took the day off and Gabe called in a favor." I must have looked puzzled because she added, "For your anniversary."

She stepped aside, and there stood Gabriel in his finest clothes holding a fistful of yellow wildflowers. His dark features and sunny smile warmed me.

"Wow, Gabe. This is so…" *Unnecessary.* "Sweet." I turned back to Lynn. "Are you sure this is okay? You never take time off."

She tickled Morgana, who squealed and squirmed from her arms. “I’m overdue. Besides, it’s been too long since I last spent time with my little pri— I mean monster.”

“Thank you so much, Lynn,” I said, kissing her cheek. “Anytime. Now go, so Morgana and I can have a tea party,” she said. Morgana’s face lit and, within moments, she was pushing me toward the door, her curly hair bouncing with equal enthusiasm.

As Gabriel and I strode along the cobblestone streets of the city, it was as if we’d just met all over again. We chatted as we always did, avoiding any heavy conversation—nothing important. Except, I felt it coming. When we’d first come to this arrangement, I feared Gabriel would ask too many questions about my past, but he didn’t and I knew it was because he had his own secrets to protect. But now I could feel the questions coming. I could feel his intentions pressing down on our small talk.

We stopped into a restaurant, a nice one, and I worried that my dirt-hemmed dress wouldn’t be suitable for somewhere so nice, but we didn’t eat there. In fact, Gabriel merely spoke to a servant and was handed a large basket that the server made look heavy. Gabriel took the basket out of the restaurant and we headed out of the city. On the outskirts, we came across a small pond. Normally, it was too small to be striking or even noticed, but tonight it seemed infinite as it reflected the star-speckled sky and orange crescent moon. We took a seat silently beside it, and Gabriel pulled a small candle from the basket and lit it before he broke the hush.

“Part of the reason I wanted to do this tonight was to talk to you about our arrangement. Please understand that this all is coming from a place of love. We never talked about what this plan would mean long term.”

My eyes moved to the flickering candle, unsure if it would stay lit in those first few gusts of wind. “I mean,” he took my hand, “what happens if you fall in love with someone?”

I laughed. "Is that what you're worried about? Don't worry, love is over for me."

"Forever?"

I nodded.

"I think that's a mistake," he said.

I froze. Where was this coming from? "Are you in love with someone?" I asked. He put his hands up defensively. "No, no, but if I ever get the chance to, I'm going to take it… and I want you to do the same."

"You're free to go, of course, whenever you want, but I can't love. Not anymore."

He nodded solemnly. "I think you're too young to just give up on it altogether. I mean, I know your husband died in the war, but maybe if you told me the whole story, I could understand."

I looked up at him. I had spent the last four years trying to close that book, and here he was asking for me to open it. My mind raced with recollections I hadn't dared revisit. My parents. My unusual childhood. My friend Milly. A kingdom at war. An arranged marriage. Two princes. Poisoned wine. Emmett. And Young, my lost love. My stomach clenched. "No, I can't."

He reached out and touched my face. "I'll go first. There was this man, Raj."

My eyes widened. As I'd suspected, the rumor *was* true. After four years, he was taking this leap? I found myself drawn in—finally uncovering the mystery of my angelic partner. If he'd hidden it, I knew this story wouldn't have a happy end. Could it be that, without words, we'd bore something in common all this time? Something we've been helping each other overcome?

He continued. "He was beautiful. Radiant like the sun itself." He smiled, his eyes glazed over with memory. "He taught me how to be a great merchant, but really he taught me how to connect with people. It was only a matter of time before the rumors started to circulate. When two souls are that connected, it's obvious to the world."

"What happened?" I asked, entranced.

He looked down at his hands. "One night, he didn't return home. I waited for a few hours, and when he didn't show, I set out to search for him. Not an hour later, I found him half-alive." Gabriel's eyes teared up, a single tear breaking onto his lap near our hands. "He died a couple of days later from his injuries." He laughed, startling me. "Do you want to know what he said to me in his last moments?" I nodded, unsure if I really did want to know. "Worth it."

Gabriel beamed at me, love still alive in his eyes. Water droplets clung to his thick eyelashes. His energy flickered out, and he continued, "After that, I went looking for a fight, and I found one. I was ready to follow him, to die like he died. If he was executed for our love, then I too would die by his side. That is, until a teenage girl intervened."

I reached out, wiping the tears from his face. I buried my face in his chest. He wrapped his arms around me, the warmth reaching all the way to my bones.

I was glad I'd stepped in that day. Glad to have Gabe in my life. He always felt like the only person in the world who understood me, and now I knew why. He wept for several minutes and I bit back my urge to cry. Finally, he pulled back and spoke to the top of my head. "So, please— just tell me one thing. His name," he said. "We can sort this out together."

His story rattled me. The look in his eyes… it was how my eyes had once looked. Gabriel and I had something important in common all these years, something that silently held us together. Something I'd only guessed at, until now.

"His name, Char," he pushed.

I swallowed and let his name slip from my lips like my soul from my body in death. "Young," I whispered.

His arms slowly loosened around me, but I didn't move. "That's a Viran name..." I felt my breath leave my lungs, "which means he was King Young of Vires." My breathing toiled in my chest, heaving as the words lashed me. "Which means you are not Charlotte of Camelot." He lowered his voice. "You're Queen Charlotte of Besmium."

After several minutes, he laughed and tightened his grip on me. "Actually, if I think about it, it makes perfect sense."

"Why?" I asked, his laugh easing me.

"Because you can't cook at all."

We laughed together, the final wall between us falling away like one of Lynn's crumbled scones. We were husband and wife, or as close as we'd ever be. It was all I wanted. Like I'd told him, love was over. I was happy to have a home, happy to belong somewhere. I was certain I'd live the rest of my life in this safe, comfortable world we'd built together.

Until a week later, when, like Raj, he didn't return home from work.

12

LANCELOT

I awoke with the scratch of dry air like knives on my bare throat. "Water," I croaked. I blinked my eyes open, the sun piercing into my head like the lances the knights used at Arthur's tournaments. "Merlin, water!" My voice rattled my brain in my skull, and I closed my eyes to rest. The door swung open and I heard the shuffle of small footsteps near. Definitely not Merlin.

"Your lady said she's going out to train. Told me you'd be in this kind of mood."

I heard the clang of tin. I squinted to find a small, gray-haired inn keep with a cup of water. I reached for it and embraced the cool liquid as it eased my throat. "More, please," I said, but the inn keep had already begun to pour another cupful.

"She's not my lady," I said. The inn keep's wrinkled eyes blinked with disinterest. "That girl, Merlin. She's not my lady. I have someone at home—"

"You should get some rest," she said. "I'll come back in an hour to check on you."

I slunk back into bed, feeling the spin of the earth heavily to my left. Even so, that water had done me some good.

When I awoke again, I felt more alert. I sat up and there, reading in the corner, was Merlin. She didn't seem to notice I'd woken, or maybe she didn't care.

"What happened to the Viran prince?"

She looked up from her book, her glittering eyes setting me at ease. Everything was back to normal.

"They're gone. They must've known we were going to follow them. They snuck off while you were passed out."

I lurched forward. "Do you know where they're going?"

She looked at her nails. "Not a clue."

"That was our only chance to find Charlotte. How could you let him go?"

"Here we go..."

I pulled myself out of bed and walked over to intimidate her. "If I didn't know any better, I'd think you didn't want us to find her. That way you could keep me away from Gwen."

She picked at her nails and, without looking up, the brightest smile crossed her face. Cold, I looked down at my naked body. She tried to stifle a laugh, but it came shooting out of her nose. I ran over to the bed and ripped a blanket from it, wrapping it around me. Merlin was nearly in tears from laughing.

"Why am I naked?" I barked.

She sighed, attempting to bite back her joy. "You threw up on your clothes." She fell into another bout of laughter. "I had them washed." She pointed to the closet door where my clothes hung neatly.

I shook with a mixture of rage and embarrassment. "Why didn't you put me in something else?"

She snorted. "You wouldn't let me."

I sat down on the bed and sighed; my embarrassment lifted my rage. "So the prince is gone?"

"Look," she said, "don't lose hope."

"Charlotte is an extremely popular name, that's why our leads always come up as dead ends, but how often are there Virans in Camelot, let alone a group of ten Viran guards and a prince?

"It'll be no time at all before we get word of their whereabouts."

She was right. Still, it was my fault they got away in the first place. Had Prince Minseo planned this? At least I'd cracked him across the cheek. Royalty or not, this was Camelot and I'd soon be a knight.

"Hey, Merlin," I said, still unable to look at her. "Did anything happen last night?" I tightened the blanket nervously. *What would I tell Gwen?*

She stood and headed for the door. "Of course not." She tossed her braids over her shoulder. "Except…" My stomach tightened. "You said something cruel."

My brow furrowed. It was an unusual thing for her to say. I said cruel things to her all the time. What could I have possibly said that hurt her worse than usual? My curiosity overtook my fear of her answer. "Wh-what did I say?"

She sighed. "You called me beautiful," she said as she left the room and closed the door behind her. I was an ass. Merlin always got the brunt of my frustration. Yet every day she stayed beside me. *Cruel.* That's the word she used. She was beautiful. I was sure everyone who passed her thought so, but was it so cruel for me to say it? Her beauty was as factual as a name. Not a word of flattery. Was it because I'd only said it when drunk?

"Wait!" I leapt up and pulled the door open. "Merlin." She stopped and looked over her shoulder at me. "You are beautiful."

She smiled, but her eyes were heavy with sadness. Then her

gaze drifted down. *Crap.* I grasped at the fallen blanket, wrapping it better around my waist.

She waved her hand and started down the stairs. What was I doing?

13

MINSEO

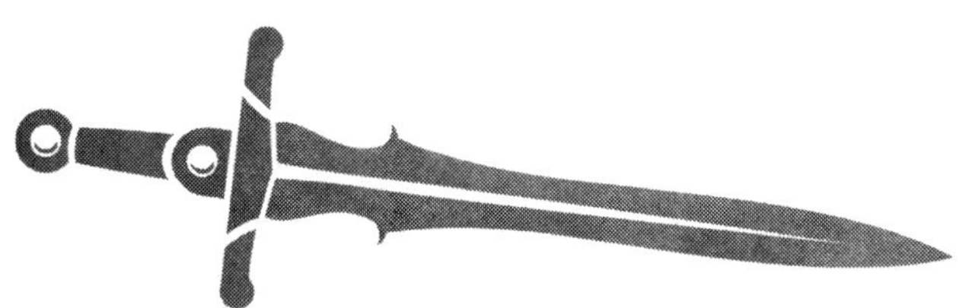

"Ugh," I moaned. "Wellwood isn't nearly as nice as the other city, in both size and quality. I mean, did you see our inn? Don't they know I'm royalty?" Hanbit rolled his eyes, his lips already pursed to start whistling again. "I mean, is there even a tavern here?" I said as we walked along a row of worn-down businesses. We came to a square with slightly better upkeep, and a soft gust of wind filled my nose with a sweet scent that made my mouth water. *A bakery.* I followed the scent until I stood outside a business called Blue De Loon, but when I entered, it looked more like a tavern than a bakery.

A woman with two piles of curls on top of her head and a well-curved nose wiped the bar with a cloth.

"Is this a bakery?" I asked, wandering in.

She looked startled to see me, but I'd been getting that reaction since I arrived in Camelot. "It's a tavern," she said, "but I also sell baked goods."

I turned to Junho. "Let's get some sweets and go."

"But weren't you looking for a tavern?" Junho asked, looking around the empty room.

"I'm not feeling the wholesome environment," I said as the barkeep set out several trays of baked goods. I picked up a bread puff and popped it into my mouth. Surprised by the sweet cream inside, I savored it, prompting Junho and Hanbit to do the same. "We'll take the tray," I said. The barkeep's eyes lit as she scrambled to find a bag for the puffs. Junho fished in his purse for the coins.

"Excuse me," the barkeep said. "Are you Viran?"

I nodded, eying the last of the puffs as she shoved them into a bag.

She handed them to me. "And what brings you here? Surely, there are bigger cities for touring. Bullhorn perhaps?"

"I'm looking for someone. A woman named Charlotte." The barkeep lowered her eyes and began counting Junho's coins. Suspicious, I pushed. "Do you know someone by that name?"

"Ah, yes sir," she said. "There are many women in this kingdom with that name."

When she was certain she had the amount she needed, she handed a few smaller coins to Junho then handed the bag of puffs to me.

Hanbit leaned in. "Perhaps I can carry that for you, sire."

"Not a chance," I said, and we left the tavern.

The spirits of my men and I improved as we passed around the puffs and walked. Had it looked this nice before or were the delicious cream puffs coating my perception?

We strolled along the suddenly charming streets of Wellwood until a voice cried out in pain, pulling me from the puff-induced trance. I hurried around the corner, my soldiers close by. There was a crowd of men huddled in a circle. Another cry burst from the middle. "You damn fairy!" a man yelled and kicked a bloodied figure on the ground. Before I could react, Junho drew his sword and barreled into the crowd. *Shit.*

I pushed through, my guards on my heels. Junho stood at the front of the crowd, between the man on the ground and the angry mob.

"What is this?" an angry, red-bearded man called.

I reached the front. "What is this man's crime?" I called.

Junho shook and shouted, "Disperse, this man is under our protection." I heard the word Viran bouncing through the crowd, but they didn't appear to be backing down. What was Junho *doing*? It was out of character for him to intervene, so why now?

"Junho," I whispered, "what are you doing?" His gaze met mine, an intense fire in them I'd never witnessed. I didn't understand, but I knew he had his reasons. Friendship often didn't need a reason to act.

"You're surrounded," I called, motioning to my guards at the back of the crowd. "If you leave now, nobody has to die." Slowly, the crowd tallied the number of guards and eventually dispersed, grumbling under their breath as they went. When they cleared out, Junho knelt and assessed the beaten man's injuries.

"What's going on, Junho?"

"Let's take him back to the inn and keep guards outside, just in case someone in that mob follows us."

"Junho," I repeated, "what's going on?"

His gaze met mine. "This man needs our help."

I'd never seen him with so much conviction, yet he hid his reasons. Was there something I'd missed? Sure, someone was in trouble, but it wasn't our fight. For a moment, as he frantically worked to save this stranger, he reminded me a bit of Young. Yeah, he probably would have charged in the same way.

We struggled to get the man to the inn. He was muscular and

tall, each of his limbs like a tree trunk. After some time, we were able to get him into our carriage, and with the help of Jay Hyun and two other men, we carried him into the inn. I called a doctor to treat his injuries, but it wasn't promising. The man was bleeding and bruised; the doctor predicted he wouldn't make it through the night.

Hour after hour, Junho stayed by his side, a brutal sleepless evening where Junho acted as if his presence beside the man was the only thing holding him to this world. I began to worry about *his* health when he wouldn't eat. His face paled, his eyes tense—I lay awake waiting for bad news that never came.

In the morning, the injured man regained consciousness long enough to tell us his name and for him to whisper the words, "My wife", before falling back to sleep. I'd expected such a promising sign to ease Junho a little, but he still refused to rest. I couldn't get him alone to talk, but I noticed his gaze had changed from concern to anger.

A few hours later, a commotion outside set me on edge. Jay Hyun ran in, blood dripping from his bottom lip. Out of breath, he said, "It's the wife— she's crazed."

I stood to the side, biting back laughter. Who was this crazed woman that struck Jay Hyun?

As she barreled in the room, my heart stopped. *Charlotte*. Her golden-brown skin shone, her curly hair pinned up on her head, but still, her curls swirled around her like black smoke, moving of their own volition. Her cheeks were red, but I couldn't tell if it was from running or crying. Her dress, a tattered, stitched-together heap of cloth that may as well have been a silk-spun ball gown by the way it hung on curves that had never been present when I knew her. My legs jellied.

Charlotte's gaze was locked on the injured man, her eyes fierce. A glint of wetness shimmered on her lashes, her unreasonably tawny eyes ablaze with strength. My pulse restarted when I caught a glimpse of her pink and floridly curved lips.

She heaved her face and arms onto the injured man's chest, waking him. He wrapped his arms around her and she wept, her curls bouncing with each gasp of breath.

14

CHARLOTTE

As Gabriel's arms wrapped around me, I felt relief fill my lungs. He was alive. But that calm feeling quickly succumbed to rage. *Who did this?* It had been so long since I'd let my emotions get the better of me, but nothing had compared to the fear I felt when Gabriel hadn't returned home. He'd just told me the story of Raj, and I knew when he didn't return from work that something must've happened. I whispered a silent thank you to Young for keeping him alive.

"Charlotte," someone said from behind me. I glanced over my shoulder and froze. My body surged with numbness. *Minseo.* I wiped my tears and stood to face him. "Your Highness," I said, curtsying. Some habits *were* difficult to break. "Are you responsible for his injuries?"

"Charlotte," he said, stepping towards me. My hand moved to the hilt of my dagger. Arms wide, he walked up to me, reaching for me. In an instant, my dagger was at his throat. He froze.

I had gone weak in the knees from his smoldering looks once upon a time. His prominent eyes were dark and mischievous. They had long, sharp angles and a heavy lid that accentuated the darkness of them. They whispered secrets, ones not asked to know. But I'd been thrown by them before, I even thought he eclipsed his brother when we'd first met. Something inside me wavered, perhaps just from seeing a familiar face, but I quickly crushed it. I could still see the dashing prince in there, buried beneath his tousled hair and stubbled chin. His once muscular frame was worn and lanky from inaction, his posture slacked with defeat and heavy with grief. I gazed at him, noticing the dark circles around his eyes. I bet, like me, he hadn't had a good night's sleep since Young died. But none of that warranted sympathy. In fact, I could probably slit his throat right now and not lose a bit of sleep over it.

A Viran guard I hadn't noticed put his sword to my back, but I didn't care. I glared at Minseo. "Did you have something to do with my husband's injuries?"

A drop of blood slipped from Minseo's neck, but he didn't flinch. Still, pain echoed in his dark eyes. I felt myself weaken as I noticed traces of Young in his features—the same nose, the same cheekbones, similar eyebrows.

"Minseo saved him," a voice said from behind me. "Your husband, I mean." I turned to see a man standing beside Gabriel's bed.

When I turned back to Minseo, there was so much hurt and sadness in his eyes that a touch of satisfaction filled me long enough to lower my dagger and sheath it.

Without another word, Minseo turned and left. Guilt seared my skin, but in a few short seconds, it transformed into boiling wrath. *How dare he!* I stormed out of the room and followed Minseo into the street.

"What did you think?" I yelled at his back as he paced through the street. "That I'd just welcome you back with open arms?" Several bystanders stopped to listen.

He turned. "I thought you were dead."

I caught up, stopping in front of him. "Yeah, I get why you'd think that. I was alone, pregnant, never lived outside the castle, approaching winter, and you left me there to die."

Minseo sucked in his words.

I gritted my teeth. "You thought you'd just, what? Walk back in my life and be welcomed like a hero?"

"Maybe welcomed as an old friend."

"Friend? Are you serious?" I laughed at the absurdity. "There's only one thing I can think of that could make you a bigger ass than you already are—and that's come back after all this time—after I'm already okay."

He tossed a shaky hand through his hair. "Charlotte."

"Where was this friendship when I'd just lost my whole family? I don't need you anymore."

"I need you," he said, his voice so gentle it would have made my teenage heart flutter. But those days were long gone—dead and buried with the rest of my past.

"Ah. This again. If I recall, you wrote me a letter once, remember?" Minseo's gaze softened. I continued. "You said you loved me." Tears glittered in his eyes but none fell. My mouth dried as I stepped closer, lowering my voice so only he could hear it. "You know *nothing* about what it means to love someone."

All the softness in his eyes vanished. He stepped closer, his chest so close I could feel the warmth of it. "Me?" He scoffed. "How long after my brother died did you replace him?"

Crack. He stumbled back, stunned. His hand rushed to his cheek. My palm stung.

He nodded and looked around the crowded square, his eyes glazed over with sadness.

"Do—" my voice cracked, "do what you're good at and return to Vires."

I turned away, feeling a heaviness in my chest that I hadn't felt in many years. It might have seemed heartless to some, but what heart did I owe to Minseo of Vires? What heart could anyone expect me to still have after all I'd lost?

When I returned to the inn, I knew they'd heard. The guards avoided eye contact, and one of the men looked as if I'd struck him as well.

Gabriel sat up. "Char, are you okay?"

I faked a laugh and a smile. "Of course I am. Are you okay? I was so worried."

Overwhelmed and constantly checking the door for Minseo's return, I decided to get some air. Gabriel had fallen asleep and I wanted him to rest before we tried walking home.

Not a moment after I stepped outside, I knew I was headed to see Lynn. I didn't know how upset my run-in with Minseo had made me until I looked at her. Her eyes widened. "Are you okay?" she asked.

The bar was empty except for a man sleeping in the corner and a bar hand who rushed in and out of the kitchen preparing for the night rush.

I threw myself into a bar seat and nestled my face in my hands. "No," I said. "Gabe was attacked."

"What?" She dropped her washcloth. "Why? Is he okay?"

"He's recovering. I should be able to take him home tonight."

"I'm sorry, that's a lot."

I nodded. "Yeah and… he was saved by someone from my past."

"Like an ex-lover?"

I shook my head. "No, definitely not. But I think he was here in Wellwood looking for me."

Her eyebrow rose. "*Definitely* not?"

"I just..." I put my hands on my hips and stretched my back. "I'm so angry. How can he even show his face here? You know?"

"Nope. There's clearly more to this story. I'll grab you an ale and a cookie and we'll unpack this."

"Thanks, Lynn." A thud on the door drew our attention, and I looked up to see Minseo fumbling with the handle. I leapt over the bar and lay flat on the floor behind it.

"It's push," Lynn yelled. I could hear the long, inconsistent steps of a drunk man walk into the bar.

"Ale," he said.

Lynn said, "Right away." She knelt next to me on the floor. "Is that him?" she mimed. "He's hot," she mouthed, fanning herself with her hand. She pulled an ale mug off the shelf next to me, filled it with ale, and handed it to him.

"Tough day?" she asked.

I reached my hand out to hit her ankle. What was she doing? I eyed the kitchen; if I crawled quietly enough, I could probably make it without being spotted.

"The worst," he said. "I got kicked out of the tavern across the square."

I began my crawl, inching towards the door.

"Bennigans?" Lynn asked.

"I don't know," Minseo slurred. "And the only woman I've ever loved…" I froze. "...is married to this other guy." He slurped his ale. "She hates me."

"Tough break, sugar," Lynn said. "Hate is a funny thing. At the end of the day, it's not that different than love."

"What do you mean?" Minseo asked.

"Well, you can't really get that angry if you don't care. If you're sure she still hates you, you probably still have a chance."

She was talking to *me*. I knew she was, but she didn't know everything. She didn't know that I'd mourned the loss of Minseo along with the rest of my family. She didn't know that I asked him to stay. She didn't know that he was the only thing I lost that elected to go, and somehow that made it hurt more. I'd had enough. I pulled myself through the doors to the kitchen and stood, earning a puzzled look from Lynn's bar hand. Lynn might have been right about love and hate, but I didn't hate Minseo—I just wanted him to leave and never come back.

A few hours later, Gabriel and I returned to our house with a few Viran guards to escort us. Junho had insisted. Annie, our closest neighbor, opened the door with a smile that faded when she saw Gabriel's bruised face. She was elderly, with soft wrinkled skin and a neat braid I'd watched turn from gray to white over the last few years. Her eyes were filled with understanding but never surprise.

"Thank you, Annie," I said, handing her a silver coin. "Did she give you any trouble?"

"Nothing aside from the endless stories. That child could talk herself dizzy."

Annie patted Gabriel gently on the back before hobbling out the door and back to her home a few yards away. She wasn't one for questions, which in a sense made her the perfect neighbor.

I was glad to find Morgana asleep. I knew she'd worry when she saw Gabriel in such a state. I kissed her head and triple checked there were no candles lit near her room. When I returned to our bedroom to check on Gabe, he was already asleep.

Not wanting to disturb him, I moved into our living room.

Our house felt a little drafty, so I set a fire. I lay in front of it, feeling the warmth on my face as it grew in size, engulfing logs two at a time. I'd need to add some soon, but before I could, I'd drifted off to sleep.

Gray haze again, the familiar warmth of the fire gone from my face. In an instant, I knew where I was. This was the place *we* met, a world so empty it could only possess one thing: us. "Young!" I called into the emptiness. A gust of wind swirled around me, spinning the mist like a cyclone. "Young!" I called, scanning the empty horizons.

"Charlotte!" I heard him call. I raced toward his voice, my heart beating wildly in my chest. I saw his silhouette in the mist just before he burst through, his hands reaching for mine. My body surged with warmth.

A loud crash burst through the grayness, sending me crashing back to the waking world. Stunned, I shook my head to make sure I was awake. The door crashed loudly. "Charrrrrrrlotte!" Minseo bellowed from outside. Afraid he'd wake Morgana or Gabriel, I leapt from the floor, my blood boiling. I swung open the door. Minseo stumbled back, swaying back and forth. He squinted at me."Charlotte," he slurred, and the prickle of ale filed my nose.

"Lower your voice," I warned. He stumbled forward, almost knocking us both over. Now in my house, I closed the door behind him and crossed my arms over my chest. "You're drunk. Go home."

Minseo fell to his knees and sobbed. "Charlotte," he whispered, "I'm so sorry."

I sat down in front of him. "You don't have to do this. I'm fine. I made it. I didn't need you to stay."

"You don't understand," he said, his voice both strained and quiet. "I lost my brother and you were hurting too."

"Don't," I whispered. I bit down on my bottom lip to stop from shaking.

Tears lined his face. "He was my brother." His breathing skipped. "I couldn't be strong for you. I couldn't be the father of his child."

I knelt in front of him, keeping him at an arm's length. "Stop," I pleaded.

He inched closer. "I died with him and so did you, so when I heard you were alive and that Arthur was hunting you—I knew I had to come."

I lifted his face. “Minseo, what do you want from me?”

“Fall in love with me,” he blurted, his eyes wet.

I dropped my hand. “I can’t. I still love Young. I can’t love anyone else.”

“I know,” he said, an inkling of a smile on his lips. He wiped his face on his sleeve in a way that reminded me of Morgana. “But you can love me. I know it. We can bring each other back from the dead.”

I wasn’t sure which, but one of the emotional daggers he’d tossed tonight had struck me and filled my body with a heaviness that reminded me of exhaustion. “I’ll never be able to love you like I love him.”

He shook his head. “I don’t want that. I want you to love me differently. Let’s build something different. Maybe...” His gaze brushed my cheek. “Maybe love is different every time. It has to be.”

I tucked my hair behind my ear, my throat tightening.

“Please, Charlotte. I’m not Young. I’ll never be him, but I understand better than anyone how it felt to lose him—how it still feels.”

I reached out to touch his face but stopped, clenching my hand into a fist and drawing it to my chest like a barrier. “And I suppose you still want me to go with you to Vires. You want me to throw away everything I’ve built and go back to the royal life that once took everything from me?”

He laughed. “Yes, that would be ideal.”

I smiled. He was as ridiculous as he ever was. He lay his head on my lap and, in a few deep breaths, he was asleep.

I’m sorry, Prince Minseo of Vires—love is over for me.

15

MERLIN

The church filled with awe as the veiled bride walked gracefully down the aisle. Her long, white dress glimmered in the sunshine and a diamond-encrusted crown shone proudly atop her head, but the atmosphere didn't feel jubilant like it looked. My stomach quaked nerves as the bride passed my seat in the pue. Then, as if I'd lost control over my body, I stood, pulling the attention of the room. I held my arms out toward the bride, unsure what my hands would conjure. Would it be wind, mist, or plant? What was I doing? My hands ignited and blue flames shot from them, engulfing the bride. Her excruciating shrieks sent the room into a panic.

I awoke with sweat beaded across my forehead. I looked down at my hands. *Fire*? It was an element I couldn't conjure, so why the dream?

I wasn't able to get back to sleep after that, so I spent the dark bits of the morning training in the forest. Blue fire? Perhaps I was thinking about the dream too literally. The same sense of doom I'd felt in the dream remained throughout the morning and into the early afternoon. Even after I returned to the inn, I felt it under my skin, like a lurking demon waiting to strike.

"Are you alright?" Lance asked, scooping a large bite of porridge into his mouth.

I nodded.

He put down his spoon. "Look, if this is about that thing I said—"

"No," I said sharply. "I had a vision. It was a wedding."

He blanched. "Woah, woah, woah, I said you were beautiful. That doesn't mean that I—"

"I set the bride on fire."

He squinted his hazel eyes. "Fire? That's a new trick."

I stared at my hands, remembering the euphoria I felt as the blue inferno manifested from them.

A knock at the door startled me. Lance smirked at me as he stood to answer it. A young soldier stood at attention outside. "Sir," the soldier said, " you have mail."

"Finally," he said, thanking the man and taking his seat at the table. I felt my stomach tighten as his face gleamed as he opened it. My pulse quickened, blue fire. Blue fire. Blue fire in time with my heart. When his smile faded, I knew the dream had been an omen and that the letter was here to deliver evil into our lives.

I leaned forward, unable to wait. "What is it?"

"Arthur has chosen a wife. He wants us to return to his castle to attend the ceremony."

My stomach sank. "Who do you think it is?"

He shrugged. "Maybe some princess he's trying to make an alliance with."

I reached out and put my hand on his. "Lance, I have a bad feeling about this. Maybe we should skip it and resume our search for Charlotte."

"He may not be acting like it lately, but Arthur's like a brother to me."

"I know, but—"

"No, you don't," he said with such conviction it startled me. "I promised him I'd never tell this story, but I need you to understand why he's more to me than a king. Why I'd do anything to serve him."

I nodded, afraid to speak.

"After my parents died in the war with Be—" His gaze scanned the room and he lowered his voice. "The war at Hiems castle, Arthur convinced his family to take me in. For the next few years, we were raised like brothers. Arthur's father taught us his trade, blacksmithing, but neither Arthur nor I had much interest in it. We did, however, love sparring with the weapons."

I inched my chair forward. Despite Arthur's boyish appearance, it was difficult to think of him as an ordinary kid. Especially one with ties to Lance, though it did explain why someone so inexperienced was given a knighthood quest.

He continued, his gaze locked on his hands. "More than anything, we loved to visit the sword Excalibur. For Arthur, it was a bit of magic in the dreary, unforgiving world, but for me, it was a way to change a man's fate. We made the climb to the sword every month, and it never budged an inch, until one day—"

"Arthur pulled it," I said, the story finally catching up with what I knew.

The silence dragged between us, and Lance's hazel eyes glinted more brown than green, his wide jaw flexed.

"Oh," I said, reading the hesitation on his lips. "He didn't."

He shook his head. "It was like any other trip to the sword, only there was a man there. He was tall and had blonde hair, blue eyes, and a near-permanent smile."

My voice shook. "Prince Emmett of Algony."

"Yes, he stepped to the sword and the sun cut through the overcast, illuminating him like a god. He lifted the sword as if it had always belonged to him."

"That's how Emmett became king."

Lance said, "No. After Arthur explained to him that pulling the sword meant Emmett was the rightful King of Drethen, Emmett tossed the sword aside. He claimed it was a stupid way to earn a crown and found his own sword to be of superior quality. In those days, Drethen had a new king every week, each king dethroned by the next in a series of assassinations. With how often they were killed, it was amazing anyone wanted the job, but Emmett stepped right in, publically challenging anyone who would oppose him."

My heart thudded.

"The sword was our secret. We were too afraid to even speak about it until Emmett died. Drethen needed a king, and it was discovered that the sword was no longer in the stone." He sighed. "With a slew of dead kings, I was too scared to take the sword to the castle and claim the title. But Arthur, with his belief that the magical sword would protect him, came forward—Excalibur in hand. And I vowed to protect him. After all, he had given me everything."

I swallowed my disbelief. "Then why hasn't he made you a knight? He must know that's your dream."

Lance's expression softened, the green in his eyes returning. "Like any good brother, he knows that if I don't earn it, it won't mean anything."

"You mean kind of how Arthur didn't earn the throne?"

"Careful, Merlin," he spat. "That sounds an awful lot like treason."

How could it be true? How could the sword Excalibur have fallen into the hands of children under such bizarre circumstances? It had done its magic in uniting Drethen behind Arthur and helping him transform it into Camelot. But it could have been anyone. Even if Emmett had kept the sword, he might've been the true king. He might've survived his battle. The possibilities and potential outcomes swirled within me, and I found myself unable to accept reality as I knew it.

Lost in thought, and without another word, we packed for Bullhorn, the city once a part of Drethen, where Arthur's castle was the crown jewel of a glittering city.

This was a *mistake*, maybe even dangerous, but the promise of a few stolen nights together with Gwenevere blinded him from trusting my vision. The only other time I'd had such a powerfully negative vision was the night before we found Charlotte.

Back then, I'd dreamt of Charlotte's location, the sign to Canburry, clear as day, only it was overgrown with plants. A dead and forgotten place. When I'd told Lance about it and warned him of the feeling, he disregarded it. He was too eager to catch Charlotte, so he barreled into Canburry, questioning every bypasser at knifepoint. Perhaps that's what tipped her off; when we got to her home, she had cases of supplies loaded to a single horse wagon and her home engulfed in flame.

Lance would have caught her that night if not for the frightening cry of a small child. I searched through the smoke and burning light, and there I saw a small girl covered in black ash, surrounded by flames.

The world slowed and I breathed in cool air into my lungs that didn't come from my surroundings. I felt the flow of blood in my veins. A gust of misty air started in my chest and left through my hands, smothering the fire around the child. I saw the little girl run to safety—picked up by a muscular man—before my vision blurred from overuse of my power. Lance made a choice that night, to save my life rather than pursue Charlotte. Perhaps he regretted it and maybe carried it ever since. One thing was for sure: he would face another decision at the wedding, one that might result in the death of either him or his dream.

16

MINSEO

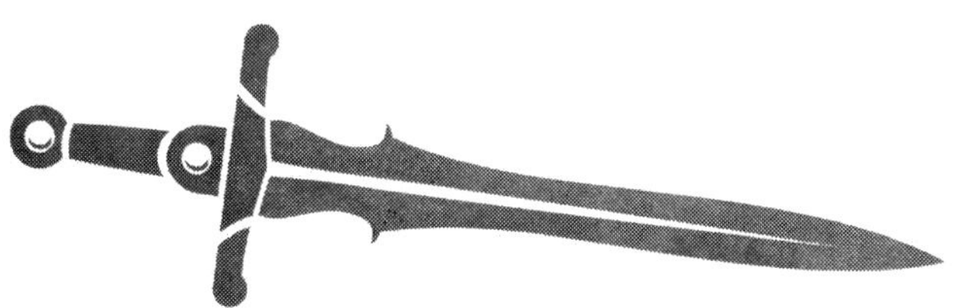

A deep voice boomed from behind me. "Uhm, good morning?"

I awoke, my head still on Charlotte's lap as she slept soundly. I sat up, my shoulder aching where I had my weight on it all night. Gabriel stood over me, his blank expression as unreadable as the rest of him. I braced myself for impact, but he didn't hit me. My gaze drifted down to Charlotte, still asleep on the floor. I quickly stood, scrambling for the words "nothing happened", but the night before rushed back to me with each throb of my pulse... *Except I confessed my love to your wife.*

He stared at me unbothered and said, "Of course not." His easiness bothered me.

Did he not know who I was? How could he not be threatened by me, not even a little? Didn't he care that I'd spent the night with his *wife*? Under his roof?

Suddenly, small footsteps sounded, and a tiny girl sprinted into the room. A touch of pink hit her cheeks as she peeked out at me from behind Gabriel's leg, her mop of curls spanning in all directions like warped rays of the sun. My pulse raced; she looked just like him. Wide-eyed, I leaned forward and, for a moment, I felt like I was looking at my little brother. All the air left my lungs and my eyes pricked. No wonder Charlotte couldn't let go.

"Uh," I said, "I'm Minseo." My gaze moved back to Charlotte who lay still, but she had her eyes open—watching her daughter.

The little girl remained behind Gabriel but said, "Do you like stories?"

"I guess," I said, feeling Gabriel's gaze on my skin.

"Great!" she yelled, a toothless grin on her face. She walked over to me and grabbed my hand—startling me. She led me to a chair. "Sit here," she said. "Once upon a time, there was an evil witch."

Bewildered, I watched her. She was a little person, yet in the glitter of her eyes was the joy of a person who didn't live in the same world as I did. Gabriel took a seat beside me to watch the little girl's performance.

"Shall I make us all breakfast?" Charlotte asked, prompting a scrunched-up scowl from the little girl.

Gabriel leapt from his chair. "I'd better handle that. Why don't you come sit here and listen to Morgana's story."

Morgana. The last time I heard that name, my brother spoke it. I watched Charlotte whisper something to Gabriel as he left, a devious smile on his face. What was that guy trying to prove? That I was no competition at all?

"Listen!" Morgana demanded, her tiny hands on my cheeks.

"Oh. Yes, sorry. I'm listening."

"But the prince didn't care that she was a witch, or about the fire," she continued. "Because he had a terrible secret."

I leaned forward. "What was it?"

Morgana's face dropped. "What was what?" she whispered.

Charlotte reluctantly took a seat beside me.

"What was his secret?" I whispered back.

Morgana sighed. "I can't tell you because it's a secret. A secret means you can't tell the person. You're the person, so I can't tell you," she said.

I laughed, which delighted her to no end. My participation seemed to fuel her performance, and I enjoyed egging her on to see what she'd do next.

I had been right about one thing: there was still a piece of my brother in this world. My focus drifted to Charlotte's hand, and I let myself imagine what this life would feel like. My gaze moved up her arm to her chest—she wasn't a scraggly teenager anymore. She was a woman and a mother. She'd lost the glow of an inexperienced girl facing the world for the first time and instead saw the world as a dragon for her to slay. Her movements were sure and her strength didn't come and go like it did when I knew her, it was earned—hard-fought. Years under the weight of grief had weakened me, but Charlotte wore it well. Heat burned my cheeks. I felt myself soften as she watched Morgana with loving eyes. Without thinking, I reached out for her hand. Before my fingers grazed hers, Gabriel entered, a tray in his hand. I stood quickly. *Should I make a break for the door?*

Charlotte spoke first. "Minseo, are you okay?"

"Y-yes, I have to go and check in with my men."

Charlotte pressed her lips together.

"I'll be back, of course."

Two cold hands wrapped around my fingers. "Promise?" Morgana asked, staring up at me with my brother's eyes.

I knelt. "Of course. I have to find out what happens to Juniper the witch."

She squirmed into my arms. "Junipee," she corrected. My heart warmed; my brother was never this friendly or outgoing. She was my brother in looks but Charlotte in the soul. "How about this?" I said, my gaze briefly meeting Charlotte's. "How about I take you, your mother, and your..." I froze, looking nervously at Gabriel.

"My Gabriel?" she asked. "Yeah, that's right. Your Gabriel. Why don't I take you all to a special dinner?"

Her eyes widened. "TONIGHT?"

"Oh, that's very soon. Perhaps I should give your mother a break."

Gabriel's deep voice filled the room. "How's tomorrow?" he added. Charlotte nudged him. What game was he playing? Whatever it was, I wasn't backing down.

"Tomorrow it is." I headed out into the crisp morning air, feeling free like my drunken confession had lightened my soul. Sure, the way it happened was embarrassing, but she knew how I felt, why I was here, what I wanted, and everything about that felt right.

"You." I turned to see Charlotte closing the door behind her. "You can't just say that stuff last night and walk away like everything is normal." She let her curls fall into her face as if she could hide behind them. "Why now, Minseo? After all this time. Is this your way of coping with Young's death? To try and live the life he left behind?"

I sighed. "I don't think I ever told you this, but I once challenged my brother for you."

Her chin lifted, her mouth dropping open. "I'm going to ignore all the problems I have with that for a second. What?"

I nodded. "It seemed like a good idea at the time."

"What did he say?" she asked, and the question stung.

"He said you were his wife."

She turned away, and I let her stray to give her space. But there were so many things that needed to be said. Things I couldn't bring myself to say when my brother was alive.

I steeled my nerves. "I remember waking up from being

poisoned. Before then, I'd always thought of poison as a humane way to die, like drifting into sleep, but there was nothing humane about the searing pain of poisonous blood while my organs boiled. I would have welcomed a knife to the heart, even done it myself if I had strength enough." I waited for her response, and when it didn't come, I continued. "Back then, I hated every choice Young made. Risking his life for you and your kingdom before you were even married. Jealous, reckless, impulsive. All the things I'd never known my brother to be. I was certain it was insanity."

I ran my hands through my hair. "There I was dying, caught in the crossfire of his insanity, and in you walk. The girl who caused it all. And worse, you just talked all the time. I'm wishing for death and you're describing the color of the trees outside." I laughed, more grounded in my memory than the present. "Day after day, you came back."

"I came back for *him*," she said coldly, "Because of what you meant to Young." I blocked it out. She didn't want to remember; she'd forced herself to forget. "You ran out of seasonal updates after the first few days. You waited until you thought I was sleeping to say anything real, then..."

Her gaze met mine. "You spoke of your father, your desire for a normal life. You told me you felt alone." I held her gaze, her eyes glistening wet. It hurt to look at her, it hurt to continue my story.

I clenched my jaw. "I pretended to sleep for a week straight, waiting for you to fill in the gaps. Then, one day, it slipped. I whispered, 'Why?' You paused and I was certain that was the end. That you'd stop talking or return to updates about the weather. But you surprised me when you answered. We spoke from sunup to sunset every day for months and, before long, I knew you far better than my brother did."

"Stop," she whispered.

"I could tell by the way he spoke about you, like some immortal being. He didn't know how broken you were, or how lost you felt."

"Stop it, Minseo."

"You stop it, Charlotte. We did the best we could. You were a faithful and loving wife to my brother. You ignored my growing feelings for you, even though you knew—but you didn't stop coming to visit."

Her gaze was cold. "I didn't—"

"And soon, I felt jealous, reckless, and impulsive. All the things I'd judged Young for. I was so blinded by it that I raised my sword to my own brother—only snapping out of it long enough to watch him die."

My breath sharpened. "How could I stay with you then? I wasn't the man he was. I was an imposter that had fallen in love with my brother's wife. I didn't deserve a life with you, so I told myself you were dead. I said it to myself so often that I swear I watched you die."

She exhaled, hard enough to make me feel she'd faint if this went on much longer. "It was a long time ago, Minseo. We should let it all go."

"Exactly."

"I mean you and me. A lot has changed. I haven't been waiting for you all this time. I have a life and a family. And the fact that you'd come here to, I don't know, open old wounds, means that you haven't grown or changed at all."

"So what? You're never going to love again? Don't you think we deserve one more chance at happiness? We were teenagers. Still children in many ways, and we went through terrible things. We did the best we could at the time. But our lives are just beginning. You loved him until his last breath despite the marriage being arranged. It's okay to let go. It's okay to be happy again."

"What makes you think I don't love my current husband? Why do you think it has to be you?"

I leaned in. "Because you're still here with me, Charlotte. Just like you were then. You keep showing up. You might've even felt something for me back then, but you had a reason not to let yourself. Now you don't. Fall in love with me, Charlotte."

She rolled her eyes. "Wow, sober and still spouting nonsense."

I took a deep breath and smiled. "To be honest, I don't feel totally sober yet."

Her eyes darkened and, for a second, I thought she'd slap me again, but her anger flickered to sadness and she turned away. I waited for her to speak, but after a long pause, she walked back to her house and vanished inside.

17

LANCELOT

There's no city like Bullhorn. It had been several years since I'd even set foot in it, and in that time it had grown even more luminous and modern. There were more trade routes, merchants, and goods from every corner of the world. The structures were built higher to accommodate the massive population. Arthur's trade deals and alliances brought Camelot from a broken and war-torn land to a kingdom unmatched by power or commerce. He had opportunized taking prisoners and forcing them into labor camps and on their backs, built more than any king before him—and he was only sixteen.

As much as I'd struggled with the notion of how he became king and considered how easily I could have wound up on the throne instead, I had to admit he was a strong leader. Everyone had to.

The castle towered above the city like a great white tower. Arthur had covered the gray stones, that seemed a little out of fashion but made up the structure, with some smooth white clay. The entire city stood in the shadow of his palace.

I was nervous to see him, but this was made worse by Merlin's somber temperament. I wondered if she'd go as far as to mention to Gwen that I'd called her beautiful. I knew how women confided in each other. Would Gwen understand? Perhaps if I told her myself, if I told her I meant it as a friend.

The carriage came to a halt outside the castle. A row of knights stood at attention to greet us and a row of guards behind them. Trumpets sounded as soon as my foot hit the stone path.

It was just like Arthur to make a scene.

Merlin followed closely behind. At the entrance of the white-stone archway, King Arthur stood. His crown gleamed on a head of golden hair, his blue eyes bright with wonder. He looked too small for the fur-lined red cape that trailed behind him, Excalibur radiant even sheathed on his hip.

"Jeremy!" He beamed. I clenched my jaw. "I mean Lancelot," he corrected, winking at me. He was still more boy than man, and perhaps he'd always look that way to me, but when he wrapped his arms around me, I felt the same way I had when we first became brothers seven years ago. It was good to be home.

"Merlin," he said, opening his arms to her. Merlin had to bend down slightly to return his hug. "How's the training coming?"

"Very well, Your Majesty," she said. I found the question odd and wondered if there was a goal they shared that Merlin hadn't told me about, but it didn't matter. I was *home,* and even if it were just for a short time, it would be nice to visit the life I strived so hard to obtain.

The inside of the castle was almost exactly as I'd remembered but with one major difference. Every wall was covered in a great work of art or tapestry, and the floors were covered in fine rugs and furs. It was clear that Camelot was as teeming with wealth as it seemed, and Bullhorn was the center of the universe. All the wealth I'd witnessed on the streets was eclipsed by the gaudy castle interior that brimmed with treasure.

Arthur led Merlin and me to our quarters, and we were allowed to bathe and rest for a few hours before a feast was to commence. But I couldn't rest; I needed to see Gwenevere.

I stalked through the hallway, relying on faded memories to direct me to her room. They led me to the end of the north wing, a hallway with a series of arched double doors that led to rooms belonging to the highest-ranking members of the court. When I reached her room, Merlin's warning flashed through my mind. *Blue fire.* But everything I've ever wanted waited for me on the other side of this door. *Gwenevere*. My mouth dried and I licked my lips, hoping to calm my nerves.

I put my hands against the door and pushed. The door swung open.

The ornately decorated room was empty. Though it still had furniture, the tabletops were as barren as the inn's I now frequented, and what's more, there was no family crest hung on the center wall. All that remained was the dusty outline of where her crest once hung.

Had they moved her room?

"What are you doing here?" My heart leapt, and I spun to see Merlin outfitted in a corseted gown that had been dyed the deepest purple I'd ever seen. "I know you're not worried, but let's stay together just in case."

Why did she always have to talk like that? I sighed. "We're not together, Merlin. I'm looking for Gwen."

Merlin placed a hand on her hip. "She's probably at the feast. We should be too."

She held her hand out, but I slapped it away. "Fine," I said. "Let's go." We headed to the banquet, and an usher led us to a large table set with golden cutlery and porcelain plates. The banquet had several large tables, but Arthur sat at the head of the longest, a boyish grin plastered to his face. The hall was filled with courtiers and foreign visitors, mostly not royal by blood but gifted titles in exchange for their friendship and allegiance to Arthur. Old money was out of fashion. In Camelot, opportunity lay at your feet as long as you were beautiful, useful, or loyal. *Where is Gwenevere?* I scanned each table one by one but couldn't spot her.

"Lance," Merlin whispered, "I have a bad feeling."

"Shut up, Merlin,"

I barked. Arthur sat at the end of the table, eight or nine people between us. He stood, and the guests quieted to listen to his speech.

"Drink some water," Merlin urged.

On edge, I snatched the goblet from her hand and took a large gulp.

"Thank you for joining me on the eve of my wedding," Arthur said. "I feel very fortunate to rule over such a prosperous kingdom, and I'm honored to be chosen by fate and merit rather than blood."

A white haze washed over my eyes.

Arthur continued, "And let us all welcome my lovely wife to be, Gwenevere."

Trumpets sounded, drowning out the thrum of my heart. In walked my Gwenevere in a golden ball gown that glowed in the candlelight, her pink cheeks and hazel eyes as lovely as they'd been four years ago. Rattled with a mixture of dizziness, confusion, and despair, I swerved.

"Cheers!" the crowd shouted. Dread seeped into my skin for one agonizing moment, then Merlin leaned into my ear and whispered, "Sleep."

Everything went black.

18

MINSEO

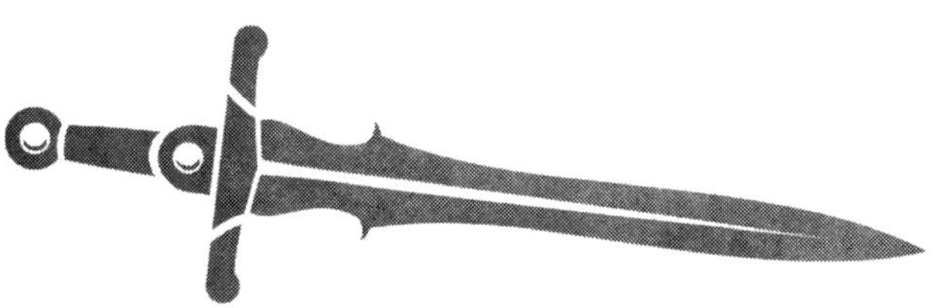

Little brother,

It's been five years since I last saw your face and nearly the same since I've seen your Charlotte. I know this letter is an exercise in futility, but it helps to quell the near constant need I have to speak with you again.

I take comfort in knowing you died without regrets—a death that has taught me much about how to appreciate life and it's fleeting moments. After I lost you, I was as broken as Charlotte and quickly realized that I was not whole enough to console her. I offered her refuge in Vires, and when she refused, I regrettably took my leave without regard for her safety or the cold of the winter that followed.

When I'd finally accepted your passing, I sought her out—though, I must admit, I never expected to find her. I found it difficult to gather information about her whereabouts without revealing her former identity. My travels brought much news. What was once the land of Besmium had been swallowed by Drethen, only to be renamed Camelot and ruled by a teenage tyrant named Arthur. After weeks of fruitless searching, I finally found Charlotte. I was relieved to find she was not the dead-eyed widow I'd abandoned, but a woman of grace and silent strength.

I stopped, unable to complete it. What could I say next? Could I ask his permission to pursue her? Should I mention Gabriel? I sighed and looked out the window as the day crept past at an unbearably slow pace. Why couldn't it be tomorrow? Why did there always have to be another man between Charlotte and me?

I put down my quill and stared up at the ceiling. A few minutes later, Junho entered. "Oh, is that letter for Charlotte?" he asked, his dimples cutting into his cheeks.

"Of course not," I said. "She has a husband."

Junho sat on my bed and stared down at his hands. "You don't know why I intervened in that fight the other day, do you?"

I pushed a hand through my hair. *If you had let him die, I might've had a chance with her...* "Because you're a better man than I," I said, throwing a crumpled piece of parchment at him, but he didn't smile. I sat up in my chair, unnerved.

"It was because of the things those men were calling him." I replayed the incident in my mind, but no specific comment stood out. His voice shook. "They chose to attack him because he likes men."

Relieved, I exhaled. "That's just something that people say—"

His gaze cut me. "No, it isn't."

"B-but that's illegal."

"So is going after someone else's wife." He shook his head. "My point is, if two people love each other, why should that matter to anyone else?"

I stood. "Wait, you don't seriously believe that Charlotte's husband prefers men?"

"I do."

"Why would you even say that?"

"Because I asked him."

I sat beside him. "And he admitted it?"

He nodded.

My mind wandered to a meal I shared with Junho in Vires—with a man who'd watched him closely throughout the meal. My next question slipped out before I was ready to know the answer. "Why would he tell you that?"

Junho didn't answer and, in the silence, the answer hung between us. "Because you told him you prefer men too."

We sat in silence as I processed what this new information meant to me. It felt like something big, something hidden, and as I replayed moments where Junho hadn't lied but hadn't completely told the truth, he waited, a stone-like expression on his face.

"I don't—" I started. I shook my head, organizing my words. "I don't think that changes anything between you and me." His face flushed and we settled into an empty silence. If I recalled correctly, this was exactly the kind of uncertainty Charlotte's world always carried.

"Wait." I sat up. "Does Charlotte know?"

He leaned forward with a huge smile. I must've seemed slow to him. There were so many things happening that I wasn't aware of. His dimples pressed on his face. "That's actually why I'm here. I'm certain she knows. That's probably one of the reasons they decided to team up, so if you're thinking of using Gabriel as a reason not to try and work things out with Charlotte, let me be the first to put a stop to it."

"This is a lot," I said, running my hands through my hair.

He nodded. "So what's the plan?"

"I guess I'll have to prepare something special."

He sucked in air, sharply. "I have a great idea!" He sprinted out the door and returned several minutes later, dragging a large sack with him.

"What is it?"

He reached inside and pulled out a handful of wilted cherry blossoms, the ones Merlin had conjured. Excitement surged through me but quickly faded. I remembered the look in Charlotte's eyes the last time we spoke. I remember the pain our conversation caused her. Gabriel was more of a man than I'd given him credit for. He'd stepped into Charlotte's life, put her back together, and helped her raise her child. All the things I ran from. I cringed. I'd accused Charlotte of moving on too quickly when she never moved on at all. When would I stop messing up?

After going over my past, all hopes of a romantic evening were dead. What was I even thinking? I knew there was no chance of Charlotte falling in love with me and certainly not of coming with me back to Vires. What I was asking her was impossible. What I'd done to her all those years ago was cruel—some of the things I'd said to her more recently were unforgivable, especially in regards to Gabriel. Even now, as I planned this elaborate dinner to win her, it seemed to reduce the gesture to a mere trick. So what then?

I lay back on my bed. Junho laughed. "Don't lose nerve now."

"She already said she can't love me."

Junho sighed. "Fine then, don't prepare this dinner because you want her to love you. Do it because you're sorry."

I stared at the ceiling. "I just... want to be what she needs."

"And what do you think she needs?"

I put my hands in my hair. "That's the thing, I don't think she needs anything."

He lay beside me. "I disagree. I think she needs a friend."

We lay in silence, our minds drifting like a branch in a stream.

"Minseo," Junho said suddenly. "Thank you for, uh, listening. For... understanding."

I closed my eyes. "Thanks for telling me."

As we lay side by side, I wondered where I would have been four years ago if it weren't for Junho. He'd always been there. He'd been carrying around a secret, afraid of what I might do or say. The only reason he dared share with me now was to help me with Charlotte. The more I thought about it, the more friendship seemed worthy to offer Charlotte. I could swallow my feelings for her sake. I'd done it before.

A knock sounded at my door, startling Junho and me. I hurried over and pulled the door open to find Hanbit nervously fingering a letter.

"This came for you," he said, handing it to me. "It's from your father." I took the letter, trying not to read the look in Hanbit's eyes that screamed the same thing my mind did. *It's always bad news.* I ripped open the letter and held my breath as I scanned it, Junho's gaze burning the back of my head.

Son,

The doctor has discovered the reason for Sumin's infertility. He's not well. You need to return to Vires immediately.

Sincerely,
Your father.

Sumin. Strong, brave Sumin isn't well. I could only recall a handful of conversations I'd had with him since Young died. He always seemed cold and disconnected, but I wondered if he'd been sick all along and I was too consumed in my own sorrow to notice. I wasn't sure how bad things were, my father didn't specify, but the fact that he'd signed it *your father* worried me. Was I going to lose another brother?

Junho and Hanbit waited, hardly breathing as I sorted through the news. "My brother is sick. They want me to come home," I said, unable to process the words as I said them.

Junho took me by the arm and led me to the bed. He guided me into a seated position.

"Deep breath," he said.

I tried, but the air stung, caught in my lungs, and stabbed at my head.

"How bad is it?" Hanbit asked, earning a malicious glare from Junho. I held up the letter and Hanbit and Junho leaned together to read it.

Hanbit blinked wildly. "I'll prepare the men for the trip," he said.

"Wait." I held my arm out. "Just wait." I rubbed my palm across my face. "I can't go," I said.

Habit shook his head. "B-but you must. It's an order from the king. You might become the only living heir to the Viran throne."

"He said no," Junho barked. "Now get out."

I reeled in silence and Junho paced in front of the door.

I wasn't going to leave Charlotte again. I didn't care if she'd never forgive me. I didn't care if she never loved me. I was at a crossroads, one similar to the one I'd faced five years ago. But even if I defied my father, even if I wasn't there for Sumin, and no matter the cost of this decision, I knew this time I'd choose Charlotte. I'd choose Charlotte every day for the rest of my life.

19

MERLIN

Lancelot lay serenely on his arm at the banquet table as the feast commenced. Whenever his seemingly lifeless body drew the attention of one of the courtiers, I faked a laugh and offhandedly mentioned, "You know how soldiers are with their wine," an explanation that seemed to instantly quell their worried faces. The room got louder as the party reached its full swing. In fact, I spotted several other people with their heads down on the table from drinking too much—a blonde with curls pinned to her head and a soldier with a vaguely familiar crest. There was no reason for anyone to suspect that I'd drugged Lancelot. But Arthur knew.

The king eyed Lance from the head of the table, no doubt disappointed by his lack of reaction. An hour later, when Lancelot hadn't moved, Arthur's glances at me indicated he knew I'd intervened. It was all too cruel. Gwenevere didn't so much as glance at her former love once throughout the feast. She smiled, like a blushing bride-to-be, while she chatted with her sisters—all as red-haired and lovely as her, but only she would be queen. Arthur could have chosen any of them and spared Lance. This was intentional. I sucked in frustration. They hadn't even warned him. I shuddered to think what hot-blooded thing Lance might have done if I hadn't intervened. Attack the king? Be executed for it? I felt my power surge inside me, and my thoughts returned to the dream. I was angry enough at Gwen to set her on fire, and she certainly deserved it. But fire wielding was not among my abilities.

When the first few courtiers left the party, I knew it was a good time to pull Lance out of there. I supported his weight on my hip and slung his arm over my shoulder. I used precise gusts of wind to help move his legs and lift some of his weight and, in a few minutes, I laid him down in his chamber.

Furious, I hurried back into the hallway and wandered aimlessly through the castle. It seemed so empty outside of the ballroom and the dining hall. All the guards must've been enjoying the party since everyone important was there. Before I knew it, I was pushing open door after door, searching for the lion-centered crest of Gwynevere's house. Six rooms, seven, eight. Finally, I pushed through and froze as I stared up at her crest on the back wall. But this room could have belonged to one of Gwenevere's sisters. I wasn't convinced it was hers.

I pushed open the door to another chamber. The crest again. Another and another. Finally, I pushed open a chamber where the crest was hidden behind a long white ball gown and veil.

I stepped into the room, closing the door behind me. My heart beat a warning—blue fire. Blue fire. I climbed into the closet without an idea of what I was doing there.

I shook, my mind drifting to my mother's face. "She's a *witch,*" she'd said, "kill this ungodly child."

Blue fire. Blue fire. Blue fire. I felt sparks burn the palm of my hands, and a blue glow filled the closet. But my mind was too occupied. *Gwenevere should pay for what she did,* I seethed. With this huff of a candle burning out, a pale blue flame flickered in my palm. I gasped as new energy surged through me. It stung in my blood, like spice in the mouth. One gust of wind against the flame was all it would take to ignite her.

The creek of the door startled me as Gwen's footsteps sounded in the room. I heard the scratch of her gown on the floor and an exasperated sigh. I gazed at the flickering blue flame in my palm. *Witch,* I heard my mother say. But I was not. I took as deep a breath as I could in silence and closed my hand into a fist, snuffing out the flame and stepping out of the closet.

She gasped. "Merlin, you shouldn't be here," she said, a quiver of fear in her voice.

"Gwenevere," I said, unable to make eye contact. "You should have at least warned him."

She sat on her bed, a move of surrender—her gold and white dress a puffy cloud around her. "He was gone—"

"I don't want to hear it," I said, feeling my palm spark. I calmed myself with another deep breath. "Whatever your reason, it's him that you owe the explanation to." I stepped closer. "And you will explain yourself to him."

She straightened her posture. "You dare threaten the future queen of Camelot?"

"I dare threaten the weak and helpless bitch..." I held my hand out with the blue flame hovering just above it, "that could be turned into a pile of ash if I breathe too hard."

She stared into the flame, a mixture of wonder and fear in her eyes, then she turned away. Her gaze got distant as if she'd remembered something. Something that had nothing to do with my threats. She sighed sweetly. "I'll talk to him."

20

CHARLOTTE

M*inseo*. Infuriating. What did he expect? I pulled on my dress, slipping my arms into it and reaching around my back for the ribbons. How could two brothers be so different? How? And there he was lecturing me about how I'd edited my memories. I scoffed. Wasn't he with Milly? Ha, he'd conveniently left that out of his little speech. I laced up my dress, cinching it harder than I usually did.

Sure, Young was hard to know. He hardly spoke at all, but it only took a few minutes to know what kind of man he was. A man of honor brimming with empathy and selflessness. Minseo was the opposite, always running a game.

Even if we'd spoken every day since we'd met, I wouldn't know what his intentions really were. Only that wasn't completely true, was it? When I replayed those memories, I saw something new. I saw how he started to look at me back then. I heard the softness in his voice, felt the heat of his gaze on my face. Had I always known about his feelings? Had I continued to visit him despite them? Maybe I *was* to blame. I sighed as I gazed at my reflection. I was not a princess but a woman who once made decisions without considering others.

I pulled my curls out of my face. Why would they never look the way I wanted? But I was too tired to fix them. I pushed open the door to the living room.

"How's this one?" I said, stepping out of the bedroom.

"Beautiful!" Morgana exclaimed. I twirled.

Gabe flipped a page in his book and, without looking, he said, "It's just as nice as the other seven."

"Wait," I said. "Let me try one more."

"You know," I heard Gabriel say, "if I didn't know any better, I'd say you have a thing for Minseo."

I stepped back into the living room.

"What thing?" Morgana asked, climbing onto Gabriel's lap.

"I don't. I just want to feel good. Strong, you know?"

"So, part of you feels weak around him?"

"Enough."

He closed his book. "Why are you fighting this? Anyone can see that there's something there. You have a chance to be happy."

Morgana scrunched her nose. "What's there?"

"I am happy!" I walked over and threw myself into a chair. "Why doesn't anyone think that I'm happy?"

I felt the tug of tiny hands on my arm. "Like this!" Morgana said, baring her missing teeth like a lion ready to attack.

"See?" Gabriel said smugly. "Like that."

A knock at the door sounded.

"Quick!" I whispered. "Tie this!" Gabriel hurried over and tied the two strings on the back of my dress into a bow.

Morgana threw the door open. "Minseo!" she yelled, throwing her arms around his knees. "Morgana!" He knelt in front of her, handing her a pink flower. "You look beautiful." She twirled. I looked over at Gabriel whose face said it all. No outfit on earth was going to make me strong enough for this. Minseo stood, and his gaze moved to me. He took a deep breath before he spoke. "You look nice too," he said, handing me a pink flower. "Ah," he reached in his pocket and pulled out a letter, handing it to Gabriel, "Junho asked me to give this to you."

Morgana pulled on Minseo's jacket until he took her hand. I forced myself not to smile. Gabe opened the letter, and we stood in uncomfortable silence as his eyes skimmed the page.

Finally, he laughed, looking down at his hands. He turned to Minseo. "He can tell by my hands?" Minseo shrugged, and Gabriel disappeared into the bedroom, emerging a minute later with a wooden lute.

Things felt different today. It might have been Morgana's presence putting us all at ease, or maybe Minseo and I were tired of the battle, but somehow our little group set out together for dinner. It was just a meal, but food had always been synonymous with family —a thought that pushed me back and forth between calm and nervous, like the waves of yellow grains in the wind.

Minseo led us to the forest's edge near a pond, not unlike Gabriel had a few weeks before. I began to suspect a conspiracy. Morgana and Minseo chatted hand in hand as we drew closer. Morgana stopped. "It's magical!" she screamed, and she took off in a sprint towards the pond. The pond and surrounding areas were covered in tiny white flower petals. Candles floated on the pond's surface, the reflection of flickering light peeking through the spaces between the petals. A large quilt was set out and on it an array of carved fruits and pastries that, by the smell, were undeniably made by Lynn.

"Careful," Gabe called after her, hurrying to catch up. Minseo stopped and, in a few steps, we stood side by side. For the first time that night, wc had a few minutes alone.

The sun started to set, illuminating our picnic in gold.

"It's beautiful," I said. "Thank you for doing all this."

"It's my pleasure," he said. We walked toward the pond, the back of his hand mistakenly brushing mine. He stopped. "Charlotte, I just wanted to apologize for everything. For leaving. For that stuff I said the other day. I know a fancy picnic doesn't make up for any of that, but I just want you to enjoy yourself. There's no pressure." He bit his bottom lip. "There are no expectations."

My stomach fluttered as the handsome prince returned. I felt more than nervous— I felt *scared*. Words. I needed words. "Okay," I managed. His face brightened, a gust of wind pushing his hair out of his eyes. He looked a lot like he did when we'd first met confident, handsome, devious. Half in memory, like I'd done that day, I turned to where I'd first seen Young but, of course, I gazed out at the open air.

Minseo smiled down at me. "I can't look at you without thinking about him too."

I shook my head. "I— uh. I'm—"

He touched my face. "It's okay, we both loved him."

He put his arm around my shoulder casually. "Are you going to be tongue-tied all night?" he asked as he led me toward the others.

I smiled away my nerves as we took a seat on the quilt by the others, but the flutter in my stomach remained.

21

LANCELOT

I awoke out of breath, like from a nightmare. I looked around my candlelit room and calmed before the sudden rush of memories crashed down on me. The wedding. *Gwen.*

"Lance," I heard her say. I turned to see her seated on the other side of the bed.

"How could— Why did—" I flailed. My eyes felt heavy and so did my limbs, and it wasn't a minute before I realized I'd been drugged, but the whats and whys of it had to wait. Gwen was here.

She looked down at her hands, her auburn hair amber in the candlelight. "I should have told you."

"How long has this been going on?" I asked, breathlessly.

"It doesn't matter—"

"How long!" I shouted.

"Just this year."

"A year?" I stood and began pacing. Blood drained from my face. "You sent me letters."

"You were gone a long time. I tried to wait."

"Tried?"

"It's not just about that, Lance. He's offering me the throne of the most powerful kingdom in the world."

I turned to her. "Is that it? That's enough for you?"

She inched back on the bed, but I stepped closer. "Do you love him?" She broke eye contact. I lifted her chin and whispered, "Do you still love me?"

Tears touched her pink cheeks. I squatted, wiping them away. "It's okay," I whispered. "It's okay." She shook as she cried into my chest.

"I'm sorry," she sobbed, her voice muffled. Her breath was warm. She lifted her chin to my ear. "I'm sorry."

Slowly, they moved to my neck. She kissed it, sending a frigid chill through my body.

"I'm sorry," she whispered again, her bottom lip dragging across my skin.

"Lance" she breathed, "come here."

I ignored the pain that had shattered every nerve, the thought of her with Arthur. I'd felt my soul leave my body, and only her lips could breathe me back to life. I felt dazed, half of me still waking. The warmth of her breath on my neck thrilled—sending me to the purgatory between awake and asleep. I pushed her back onto the bed and pulled my shirt off, each impulse as thoughtless as the last. She pulled me down to her. I kissed her with a mix of all the anger and love I felt. I needed her to remember—to love me. I tasted her neck like I'd imagined, night after night, for the years we were apart. She arched her back and moaned a sound so rapturous that I stopped to watch. *Yes, Gwenevere. Don't hold back. I want Arthur to hear this.*

. . .

I awoke to an empty room. My body was numb and my eyes were swollen from crying. I recalled the night before.

"Even after that, you're still going to marry him?" I yelled as she scrambled back into her dress.

"You act like I have a choice here. Arthur will never let us be together." Her voice cracked, "He'll kill you."

I grabbed her wrists. "Say you don't love me and I'll let you marry him. Say it." She pulled her hands away. "I won't."

After she left, I cried myself dry, leaving an empty space where love and sorrow once were. I didn't remember falling asleep, only waking to a world where Gwenevere had chosen Arthur.

"Become a knight," she'd whispered. "I heard Arthur say she's in Wellwood." But all I could hear was Arthur's name on her lips. What was the point? Did she mean that we'd continue seeing each other behind closed doors? I shuddered.

A knock sounded at my door and my heart pounded back to life. *Gwen.* I swung open the door to see Merlin, her eyes glittering with worry. "Can I come in?" she asked as my heart sunk with disappointment as her somber expression breathed truth into all the events of last night. It was *real.* Gwen was going to marry Arthur. "You look like hell," she said. I nodded, unable to put together real words.

We sat together on my bed. Her pity nauseated me, or maybe I was sick from the leftover drug. At some point in the course of the morning, I'd put together what happened, what Merlin had done. Either way, there was no denying she'd done me a favor.

"Thank you... for what you did last night," I mumbled.

"Oh, yeah." She pushed a pastel braid behind her ear. "I figured she owed you an explanation."

My thoughts raced. "I meant about drugging me. Did you tell Gwen to come to my room last night?"

She nodded. "At least you have closure. You can move on—"

I stood. "Closure? I know more than ever that she loves me." I sighed. " But she's going to marry Arthur anyway."

She shook her head in disbelief. "Whatever, now you can let her go."

I clenched my jaw as my thoughts turned to Gwen. *Become a knight.*

Merlin hit her palm on the doorframe. "Did something happen?"

I swallowed, and her eyes widened. In an instant, she was out the door. It slammed behind her with such force that I worried the frame would crack.

22

MINSEO

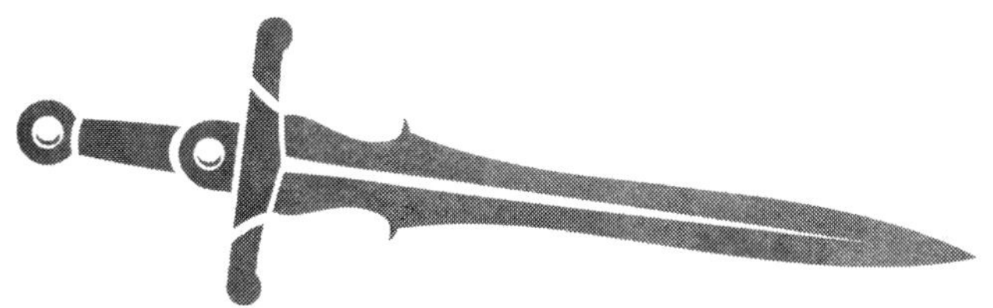

Gabriel strummed a slow tune on the lute that seemed to descend the sun and scale its shining counterpart. Morgana tossed flower petals in the air, casting imaginary spells at the forest's edge. The candlelit pond was the only orange left of the night as the moon poured a silver glow over Wellwood.

I sat beside Charlotte and watched her sway to the melody. She sighed. "This is nice."

"Good," I said. I lay on my back and looked up at the stars—they seemed brighter in Vires, but more beautiful here. Charlotte laid beside me, moving close enough that the top of her head touched mine. My pulse raced from her close proximity. *Friends,* I reminded myself. I wondered if I should tell her about the letter from my father, or if it would add pressure. I didn't want her to worry. I didn't dare interrupt the peace we'd finally found.

"Do you know any constellations?" she asked.

I smiled. "Of course." I pointed to the sky. "Do you see the bright ones, there and there?"

She pointed above her. "This one?"

"No!" I took her hand and traced a shape in the sky. She giggled, and I felt heat rush to my face. "Here," I said, "this is a juicy bowl of banana soup."

She laughed. "You liar."

My cheeks were sore from smiling. I turned my head to see her beaming back at me. Our hands still joined in the air, my smile fading along with hers as our fingers tangled together. My heart thudded against my ribs. Slowly, our hands moved down toward us, intertwined—until locked together on the ground by our side. I swallowed nervously as her chest rose and fell in time with mine. *Friends,* my mind screamed. *Friends.* I inched closer. I felt the warmth of her breath on my lips. I put my forehead to hers, her eyes closed, a touch of a smile at the corner of her mouth. Her mouth... Did I dare? *Stop me, Charlotte.* I slid my free hand to the back of her neck. *Just say no, Charlotte, and I'll stop.* I gazed at her lips. *Stop me, Charlotte,* I thought, but she didn't. Her lips parted, pulling me in. *I'm sorry, Charlotte. I can't just be your friend. I never could.* I leaned in.

A bone-chilling scream sounded from the forest. We sat up, dizzy from a shattered trance. Gabriel sprinted toward the forest, Charlotte and me close behind him.

"Morgana!" Charlotte screamed. The forest beamed with a sudden orange light. Black smoke swirled into the fresh air. Ash rained from the sky like falling stars.

Morgana sprinted from the forest, tears pouring from her eyes. She leapt into Gabriel's arms. "My hands! My hands!" she cried. We caught up to them to find Gabriel pressing her small hands to his face.

"What's wrong, baby?" Charlotte cried, pulling her into her arms. "My hands!" Morgana cried.

Gabriel shook his head. "Her hands are cold. She wasn't burned."

The wind changed direction, pushing smoke into our faces. "How did that fire start?" I said as the flames moved toward us.

Gabriel covered his face. "Maybe she grabbed a candle?"

I shook my head. "A candle can't do this."

He turned to me. "Minseo, run into town. Ring the bell. Get some help. We need to put this out before it spreads."

Six hours later, Morgana slept soundly in her bed. Covered in soot and ash, Charlotte, Gabriel, Junho, Jay Hyun, and I sat in a circle in the living room— exhaustion heavy on our limbs. With the help of almost twenty strangers, we managed to put out the fire, but how had it started?

"I better get back to the inn," Junho said, standing. "I'm glad no one was hurt." Junho cleared his throat, breaking Gabriel from his exhaustive daze.

"Oh, yeah. I'm going to turn in for the night too," Gabriel said.

Gabriel headed into the bedroom, waving goodnight before he left. Taking his cue, Jay Hyun opened the front door, the wind still heavy with the scent of burning wood. "Goodnight," he said as Junho followed him out and closed the door behind him.

I turned to Charlotte. "Listen, about earlier."

"It's a sign," she said solemnly.

I moved next to her. "The fire?"

"Yes." She turned to me with tears in her eyes. "Young doesn't want us to be together."

I took her hands in mine. "So he tried to light his own daughter on fire?"

She covered her face with her hands.

"That doesn't make any sense."

She wiped her face, soot smudging across it. "How could we be happy together when he died for us?" She stood.

"Wait, wait, wait, Charlotte...We'll figure this out. Don't panic."

"I'm sorry," she said. She covered her mouth with her hand and pushed the door to her bedroom open, closing it behind her.

23

MERLIN

I knocked on Arthur's door, his guards watching me closely. As if they could stop me if I decided to kill him.

The doors opened and Arthur grinned at me. "Merlin, to what do I owe this pleasure?"

"I've done it."

He blinked vacantly, combing his blonde hair forward with this fingers. "You did what?" His eyes bulged. "Fire?"

I held my hand out—a blue flame at the center of my palm. He leaned in, looking more like a child than ever. "It's so blue. And your eyes as well. How strange."

The fire snuffed out. "Really?"

"Oh, brown again," he said.

"Your Highness, I wonder if you'd permit me use of the cellar to practice... and a leave of absence from your wedding today."

"Certainly, certainly," he said. "I'm happy to see such progress." He touched his hair again. "Ah, my crown." He looked over his shoulder. "You, bring me my crown." A guard disappeared into the king's quarters. "How is Lancelot's hunt for the girl? He should have found her by now."

I eyed him. "You know where she is."

"How much can I be expected to hand him? I was certain he would have found her by now." He sighed. "What was the key to unlocking this new power?"

I eyed my hands. "I'm not sure exactly, but the feeling is getting stronger. Perhaps my power is somehow linked to Charlotte's. I felt something similar when we'd almost caught her two years ago—though no flame manifested. I'm sure she's connected somehow. When she arrives, I'll be sure to get her up to speed, but it's likely that she'll help me develop my own powers as well. Maybe you should send someone else to get her, someone with a brain between his ears."

"I see the hero worship has finally worn off." He sighed. "Oh, Jeremy," he said, "same thing happened with him and Gwen. Speaking of whom, I better get ready for the ceremony."

Witch, I heard my mother say as I considered outing Gwenevere, but as much as Lancelot had hurt me, I knew I'd never bring myself to hurt him. He'd surely be killed for it when Gwenevere was to blame.

How much time had I spent helping Lance with his quest when I could have been training? How much sooner could I have unlocked this fire?

Lance wasn't the answer. He'd always mistreated me, moping about as he did. Show me a man worthy of me; until then, I'll not lower myself to fit someone less. I'd meant the words, but the sting from the last few days lingered. Perhaps instead of finding love with Lancelot, I could make a sister out of Charlotte. We shared the same gift, the same burden. Perhaps all I ever wanted was for someone to understand.

I headed to the cellar, the place where I'd spent so many hours training before I'd embarked on Lancelot's knighthood quest. A stone spiral staircase led down to the chambers of varying size. I skipped down one flight after the other, deeper underground. The area was lit with wall torches and had broken stone from where the iron cells were pried out. Once used as a dungeon of sorts, the cellar was now as vacant as Lancelot's eyes when I'd last seen him. Arthur loved taking prisoners, but he'd discovered early on that working prisoners built a kingdom, not captive ones. He set up prison camps for manual labor and had all Camelot's prisoners sent there. He even had prisoners carted in from his allies. I heard a rumor that he held a special group of captives somewhere in the castle, but I'd discovered little evidence of that.

For now, the cellar was mine alone. And with gray stone covering every surface, there was a low chance I'd damage anything—but, then again, I wasn't sure exactly how powerful I was now.

I inhaled deeply and felt the warm blue glow on my palm. If I combined it with wind, could I shoot it? I took a deep breath and conjured a short gust. The flame snuffed out. I tried again with varying levels of intensity, but each resulted in a flame weaker or dead. What if I didn't combine them? What if I tried increasing the intensity of the flame itself? I focused on the tingle at the center of my palm. I pushed my life energy to it. It swelled a flash bigger and settled back to its original form.

Ah, that was difficult. How could I maintain enough energy to make it useful? If Arthur saw that weak attempt, he'd likely demote me from battle mage to castle candle lighter.

I tried again, this time pushing every bit of power to my palm. The teal wave blazed, engulfing my hand. It felt like pure energy and tingled in a way that might make a small child giggle with delight. *More power,* I beckoned. The flame flared. Suddenly, the sleeve of my shirt caught, burning red. I screamed as it seared my skin. I shook my hand wildly, too panicked to use another spell to help. I slapped the flame out, and my skin still stung near the edges of the burnt sleeve.

Suddenly, my eyes glazed over, my vision teleporting me to a night two years ago. The orange fire blazed, and the little girl screamed in fear.

Using every ounce of power I had, I pushed the flames away. A man carried the girl to Charlotte, who watched me with troubled eyes. I blinked myself back to the cellar. That night, Charlotte had lost control of her power as well.

I eyed my singed sleeve, a smudge of burn where the fabric lit. *I get it. Blue fire is good and red is bad.*

24

CHARLOTTE

I sat in the empty living room, tempted to check back on Morgana for the tenth time since I woke up. She was sleeping soundly, not a single mark on her hands. *What happened?* I brushed her hair out of her face.

I tilted my head back and breathed deeply.

I was Morgana's mother. I didn't have the luxury of falling in love. Not again. My baby almost got hurt. Even with two adults watching, I let myself drift for one second and almost lost her.

Where was it? Where was the strength I'd been building all these years?

My thoughts drifted to Minseo, a nervous flutter at the pit of my stomach. I'd wanted him to kiss me, and everything about that felt wrong. Why couldn't I push him from my mind? Did I just miss the rush of falling in love?

Minseo had been right about one thing: this was different than what I had with Young. I didn't feel the warmth, calm, or peace I'd felt with him. I didn't feel the heaviness—or the depth. Young's love was all-consuming and endless. Minseo was easy, light. It was full of life in a world where I'd only known death. He sparkled with charm and charisma. It didn't always feel sincere, but it felt good—it felt so good until the guilt set in. Questions rose much quicker than answers. Why couldn't I stop comparing them? Had I always been attracted to Minseo? Did Young know this would happen?

I opened the bedroom door. "I'm headed out for a bit," I said. "Morgana's asleep."

Gabriel rolled over and waved his hand.

I left the house, closing the door quietly behind me. I headed out along the path I'd walked so many times before, but this time I dreaded what I'd feel when I arrived. I entered the clearing—the magnolia tree blooming near the top. Trudging through the overgrown weeds, I put together what I wanted to say.

I put the palm of my hand against the tree. "Hello, love," I said. "Minseo's back." I sighed and took a seat, leaning back against the trunk. "I know... of all the men in the world." The wind picked up, tossing my curls into my face. "He makes me feel like I'm still alive. That there's more life ahead of me. I swear, for a while after I lost you, maybe even until recently, I've been waiting to die. Just barely surviving." I exhaled. "I want to live. I want to fall in love with him."

It was the first time I'd said it out loud, and it startled me. My eyes teared. "Tell me it's okay."

I listened, but all I heard was the rustle of the branches in the gentle breeze. "Please," I whispered. "Tell me it's okay."

The sun rose as I walked along the path to my house, and in the distance, where the path diverged, I could see Junho and Minseo headed up to visit. Minseo's gaze met mine, a soft smile on his face. His eyes glittered with hope. My stomach fluttered, distracting me from the sound of heavy footsteps behind me.

"Charlotte," someone said. Startled, I turned to see a wide-framed soldier, his brown hair shining in the rising sun—his hazel eyes more vibrant than the sky behind him. I knew this man. I pulled my dagger. "Lancelot."

He didn't so much as look at the dagger. "My orders are to take you alive, but that doesn't mean conscious. The choice is yours. Come with me willingly or I'll hurt you."

"What does Arthur want with me? I just want to live the rest of my life in peace."

"You have something he wants."

"Take it."

"It's not something that can be given."

I screamed, "What is it?"

He glared back, stone-faced. "That's between you and the king." Lance's gaze moved beyond me. Minseo's footsteps and heavy breathing came up behind me.

"I know you," Minseo said with a smile. "Lance, right?"

Minseo held his hand out, but Lance slapped it away. "It's Lancelot."

Where was Junho? Didn't I see him with Minseo earlier? Ah. Getting help.

Minseo stretched his hands over his head. "So, uh, where's your girl?"

"She's not my girl."

Minseo nodded. "Ah, you broke up."

Lance drew his sword. "I'm taking Charlotte."

"Look, man, I'm sorry your girl left but—"

"Shut up."

Minseo turned to me, his eyes calm and his demeanor as casual as ever. "Uh, I left my sword at the inn. Can I borrow your dagger?"

I winced at the absurdity; if Minseo pushed Lance any further, we would both die here. I eyed the direction where the Viran guards were sure to come charging in. Any minute now.

"He's trying to take me alive. It's better if I fight him," I said, turning back to Lance.

"Stop stalling," Lance barked, lunging at me. I leapt back, surprised by his force. What was he doing? That could have easily killed me. I swung my dagger at him. He caught my wrist and twisted. I screamed, the dagger flying out of my hand. Before I could pull my hand away, Minseo's fist connected with Lance's cheek and he stumbled back, stunned.

"Owed you that," Minseo said.

Lance wiped at his cheek like he could sweep the pain off. "You I can kill." He swung his sword down.

Minseo slid across the dirt path and scooped up the dagger just as Lance swung down with a second blow. Minseo deflected it with the dagger, but his arms shook. This was bad.

"Stop!" a voice called from behind us. The clang of moving metal filled the air as the Viran soldiers ran to us.

Lance gritted his teeth. "Why this stupid mission?" Lance's arms slacked. As Jay Hyun and the other guards reached us, they leapt in front of Minseo while Junho handed him his missing sword.

25

MINSEO

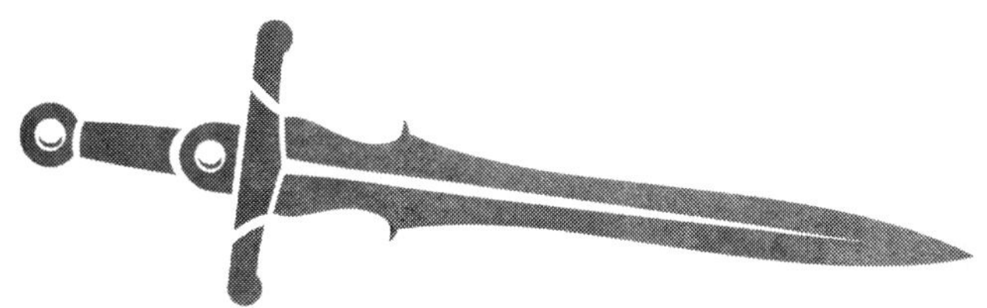

Rusty and weak. How long had it been since I'd adequately trained? Those daily drinking binges and wallowing in Vires had taken their toll on me. Granted, having a sword could have evened the odds a bit, but I wasn't confident that I could actually take that guy.

What's worse is Charlotte saw everything: the sucker punch and my looming defeat. If my guards hadn't arrived, I could have lost Charlotte.

We were lucky he was alone this time. With Merlin, he would have crushed us, guards included.

Lance threw his arms out in surrender. "So what's it going to be?" he said, glaring at me. "I get a few more guys and come kill you and your ridiculous friends?"

I took a deep breath. "Sir Lancelot, was it?"

"Lancelot."

"So this *is* your knighthood quest." I nodded to myself. " Capture Charlotte."

Lance sheathed his sword. "You understand why it's essential that I take her then."

"I understand that you're supposed to complete a knighthood mission alone, thus why knights are superior to soldiers here in Camelot."

Lance bristled.

"I'm not sure why your king let you take your girlfriend along, but in any case, she's gone. Charlotte is under the protection of Vires now. You can either fight all eleven of us by yourself or get a new dream."

"Fine," Lance said.

"Fine, what?"

He stepped forward. "I'll fight all eleven of you. One on one."

I giggled. "That *would* be the honorable way to do it, wouldn't it?" I smiled. "You know, my brother Young was an honorable man. That's the kind of deal he would have made." I tilted my face up at the sun. "Unfortunately for you, I'm not honorable. And I'm certainly not the kind of man he was."

Lance shook and, for a moment, I wasn't sure if he would attack me or cry. The bulky swordsman he'd been a minute prior dissolved into a teenager mid-tantrum. I breathed relief when he turned and walked off in the direction from which he came.

"Prince Minseo of Vires," he said, looking over his shoulder. "I'll kill you someday."

"Later, then," I said.

I turned to Charlotte. "Are you hurt?" She shook her head. I nodded. "He was lucky we've been out of practice. We'll get him next time," I said.

"You think he'll be back?"

"Without a doubt."

Charlotte turned to my men. "Thanks for coming. I'll make everyone breakfast."

We walked back to Charlotte's house with the energy of a triumphant victory while a lonely soldier returned defeated to Bullhorn. I'd known that kind of defeat—I'd lived it for a long time. I should have thought about what could be born from that level of despair; I should have taken responsibility for my part in feeding the beast.

Junho, Jay Hyun, and the other soldiers entered Charlotte's house before us, but she stopped me before I went in.

"Minseo," she grinned, "want to see my garden?"

If that's some kind of innuendo, yes. "Of course," I said and she led me around the house to the back.

A large kitchen garden sat tucked away behind the house. It had rows of leafy stocks and flowers beginning to bud. It was preened, and the way Charlotte beamed told me that she'd done it herself. "These are hydrangeas. They'll be big and blue in a month's time." She knelt next to a leafy row, pulled a large carrot from the soil, and handed it to me. "Lovely!" I teased, dusting the dirt from it.

"I know!" she said too loudly.

"Those are called buttercups. They're yellow. I found them by the river and replanted them here."

"And what did you name these?" I said, pointing to a green patch.

She rolled her eyes. "That's lettuce. Pick one, will you?"

We picked several of her spring vegetables and carried them into the house. It was the kind of work I'd never done. I hadn't even watched anyone do it, but I'd never imagined it could bring someone such joy. Perhaps Charlotte was happy about our defeat of Lancelot, or maybe she was happy for another reason.

The soldiers didn't fit well in the house, but they sat cheerfully around the room as Morgana treated them like her personal toys. I laughed at how she looked ordering them about and how they listened. She was a princess of Vires through and through.

Charlotte cooked and, before long, she hummed a familiar melody that I couldn't place.

"So you're just going to toss them all in and boil it?"

She shrugged. "How else?"

I pulled out some bowls and plates, anything we could use to feed everyone. They were all different sizes, mostly made from wood. Many of them seemed like they'd never been used, or hadn't been used in quite some time. I rinsed the usable ones, all the while Charlotte hummed.

I like to think I brought a little peace to her that day, and that there was a chance that she'd change her mind someday and return with me to Vires. But it was too soon to ask her. Still, I relished seeing her that way. *Welcome back, Charlotte.*

Back at my inn that night, I picked up the letter I'd been writing to Young and read over my last sentence.

I was relieved to find that she was not the dead-eyed widow I'd abandoned but a woman of grace and silent strength.

What else? How could I describe her?

She sang while she cooked and spent long stretches of time in her garden. She picked wildflowers and gazed up at the stars.
When she speaks of you, she smiles to herself then looks off into the distance, as if she's waiting for her time to come so that she can be reunited with you in the next life. Through all the loss she suffered, she somehow became more.

Ah! And Morgana.

Your young daughter, Morgana, glitters with all the charisma and poise of royalty and all the mischievousness that you and I possessed in youth. When Charlotte's gaze fell upon her, I saw in her eyes the glimmer of love that I'd only ever seen when she looked upon you.

But something changed. Today, I saw it when she looked at me.

Though Charlotte prefers to remain tied to the simple life she's accustomed to—

I will try to win her love. I'll raise Morgana as my own in Vires. We'll be a family. I was a horrible brother and a liar. Why couldn't I write the truth?

I will return to visit your daughter as often as time allows. And if Charlotte permits me, I'll bring her lavish gifts and toys from Vires.

I sighed, disgusted by my lie. I'd rather die than return to Vires without them. Was this guilt? He'd asked me to take care of her. *Ugh.* He couldn't have meant this. Come on, Minseo, write *something* true.

Though she was born untitled, she'll remain a princess in my eyes. Morgana is true joy embodied, and it seems her most treasured moments are spent telling magical tales.
Can you believe it—she has your smile.

With all my love,
Minseo

I'm a fraud. I threw my face into my arms.

"Oooooh, is this for Charlotte?" Junho said, pulling the letter from under me. I grabbed for it, but he spun. The smile and dimples dimmed from his face. I clenched my jaw. I hadn't heard him come in. "After all this, you plan to leave her?"

"Of course not."

His gaze was sharp. "Is it because of Sumin? Because he's sick? There's nothing you can do to help him."

"That's not it," I assured him. I felt lucky to have a friend who cared, a friend who wanted what was best for me.

"Then what's this, Minseo?" he asked, shaking the parchment in the air.

I dropped my head. "He'd never understand. If the roles were reversed, I'd never forgive him." I didn't need to explain which *he* I meant.

Junho sighed. "Have you considered, perhaps, that he was a better man than you?"

I laughed, wiping the wet from my eyes. "Every day of my life."

26

LANCELOT

I spent years searching for Charlotte, and this was the second time I had to walk away without her. Would I die a nameless soldier? My sole purpose had been to become one of Arthur's knights. Rich enough to marry whomever I chose, respected at Arthur's right hand—but what was it all for? Arthur had taken the only thing I'd ever wanted, reduced my life to stolen moments and secrecy. I'd be nothing but his pawn. He was no brother of mine, was he?

The bell tower at the Wellwood city center struck noon. They'd be getting married right about now. My face burned. Did he even love her?

My mind flashed to the night I'd spent with Gwen—the blush of her cheeks, the clasp of her fingers.

I hoped he loved her because somehow I'd capture Charlotte, I'd become a knight, and whenever his back was turned, I'd have his wife.

The problem was Charlotte was untouchable. How was I supposed to capture her when she had ten Viran guards around at all times? Arthur wouldn't grant me a single one of Camelot's soldiers for this mission. He'd even refused to let Merlin accompany me until she'd begged, and even she'd abandoned me.

What was her problem anyway? Regardless of how she felt about me, I never misled her. I was always going to return back to Gwenevere. The least she could have done was see the mission through to the end. Years of partnership tossed aside in an instant, for a crush. I'd never admit it to her, but I needed her more than ever. Her power, sure. But more than that, I was hurt and alone. Isn't this when friends or family are supposed to step in and lift me? But it had never been that way, had it? No. When I found a way to be knighted and made something of myself, they'd all come, basking in my success like they'd guided it.

I recalled the icy glare Merlin gave me when I last saw her. No, enlisting her help wasn't an option even if I did swallow my pride enough to apologize.

Which left Arthur. I'd have to convince him to allow me some assistance—appeal to the part of him that might still consider us brothers. Yes, I'd ask for his help in order to ultimately betray him. Just like he'd done to me after I basically handed him the throne on a silver platter. It had agreeable symmetry. With a haphazard plan in place, I felt reinvigorated. I didn't need foolproof, I needed possible.

I spent my trip home in reflection. So much of my time I'd been searching, but I wasn't sure that I'd been looking for Charlotte. I wanted what everyone did: strength, sense of self, and a place to belong. Had I purposely delayed my return? These lackluster searches and drawn-out training sessions—did I really need to train to catch some girl? Every path I forged in my mind led me to the same conclusion. I hadn't been before, but now I was ready. Ready to be a knight, ready to give myself the title, and *that* was worth more than what Arthur could bestow.

I returned to Bullhorn not as a disgraced failure but as a man ready to embrace my new path. I strode proudly into the castle, let my gaze linger too long on Gwenevere in broad daylight, and demanded an audience with Arthur.

Based on the number of guards and the caliber of the knights that attended our meeting, Arthur understood how dangerous he'd made me. Knighted with a title, I'd be all the more deadly. But I wasn't there for his life. I was there for his help.

He paced. "Vires, you say?"

"Yes, sir. Ten of them. I'd need half as many to defeat them. Please bend your conditions and allow me to—"

"What an interesting opportunity," he said. "Perhaps this is the perfect moment to use my ace and expand Camelot's reach."

"Sir?"

"Jeremy, do you trust me?"

Not as far as I can throw you. "Yes, Your Majesty."

"Permit me a few weeks. Stay in Bullhorn and I'll see to it that your next meeting with Charlotte will result in your knighthood."

"Thank you, sir," I said as I turned to exit.

"Will you be joining me for dinner?" he asked, his voice returning to that of a teenage boy.

I shook my head. "I'm tired."

He sighed. "Gwen as well. Perhaps Merlin will join me?"

I turned away before the smile cut into my face.

27

MINSEO

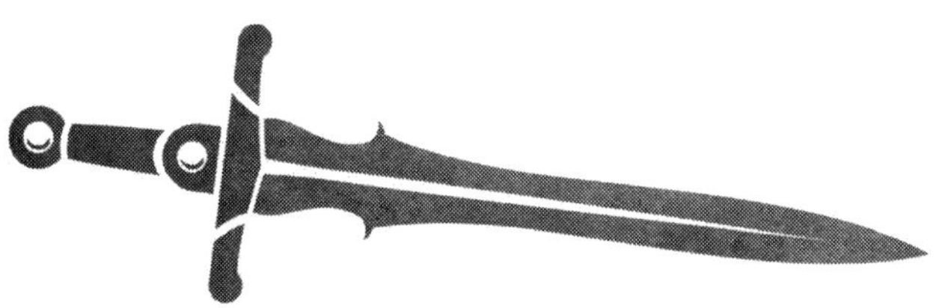

A knock sounded on my door, and before I could open it, it flew open and Morgana ran in. "Minnoooooow!" she yelled. It had been over a week since a slip of the tongue had given birth to this heinous nickname, and I still wasn't used to it. She leapt onto my bed and jumped herself out of breath. Gabriel peeked in. "Hey, man, do you have a minute?"

"Sure, come in," I said.

He rubbed his hands together. "So, Morgana has never spent a single night at this inn. Did you know that?" His voice was exclamatory.

I mirrored it. "Is that so? And does my little princess want to stay here with me?" I reached for her and she jumped into my arms, wrapping her little legs around me, a large heap of her curls bouncing into my mouth and up my nose. I shook them away.

"Actually," Gabriel said, his voice flattening, "I was thinking maybe we could…" He shook his head. "Trade?"

I blinked blankly back at him.

"Morgana and I will take this room and you can stay in my room."

"Your room?" I gulped. "You mean with Charlotte?"

His eyes darted to Morgana. "It'll be like a game."

"Game!" Morgana shouted.

"Ah," I said, biting back a smile. "And, um, does Charlotte know about this game?"

Gabriel's eyes shifted. "We thought you could surprise her."

I exhaled a stomach full of nerves. "We meaning you and Junho."

Morgana squealed. "And me."

I tickled her. "And you, of course."

I nodded, a calm exterior hiding the hurricane of chaos inside. It was too soon. Things had been going so well. The last few weeks were a dream. Charlotte and I spent every second together that we could, and I could feel it changing. We'd never gotten close again, not like that night by the pond, but we started talking again, the way we used to.

The day Charlotte, Morgana, and I spent by the river, she'd laughed so hard she cried. And a few days later, when she dared speak of the past, her eyes sparkled at the realization that even for a short time, I knew her father, her mother, her friend, the cook, Leon, many council members, and mutual acquaintances. I'd known her, before all the loss, and suddenly the happy memories she'd shut out with the bad ones were there for us to enjoy together. But I still couldn't bring myself to mention Sumin—or my father's order to come home, the one I disobeyed with every passing day.

Each day I spent with her, I worried that another letter would arrive—a letter informing me of my brother's death.

I appreciated what Gabriel and Junho were trying to do, but if they'd given us another month or two, maybe something might happen on its own.

But time was against us, both because of Sumin's condition and because no one would say it but everyone feared what Lancelot would try next. We were already on borrowed time. We had to return to Vires, while we still could.

It just all felt too contrived. Was I just *scared*? Maybe, but once that line was crossed, there would be no going back.

Before I knew it, I'd handed Morgana to Gabriel, oblivious of the cheesy smile stuck to his face and mine.

"Goodnight," he called, but I was already out the door.

I was out of breath when I knocked on Charlotte's door. Had I run there? What was I doing? I wasn't seriously thinking of going through with this, was I?

A moment later, the door swung open. Charlotte stood in the doorway, a bright smile on her face. I froze. "My brother is sick," I blurted. "Sumin. My father asked me to come home weeks ago."

Her mouth fell open. "Oh, you're going then?" she said.

"No," I breathed. "I'm not." The thrum of my heart drowned out any attempt at explanation.

Her gaze barreled into me, and I felt myself grow weaker with every breath she took. She looked behind me. "Are Morgana and Gabriel with you?" she asked.

I shook my head. "We traded rooms," I said matter-of-factly.

"What?" she whispered as I eased her back and shut the door behind me.

I pulled her body to mine and felt the heave of her chest against me. My body pulsed. "Minseo," she whispered to my lips. My heart slammed against my chest. I stared into her eyes and felt her body shake beneath my fingers. I wrapped both my arms around her and held her, hoping her wild heartbeat might calm mine. A hug? What the hell was I doing? Did I just blow that? Was I waiting for her to protest? Yes. Of course. She wasn't as foolish as I was. Only one way to know.

After this, if I lost her again, I'd die. Shit. I was panicking. She took my face in her hands, her eyes stripping bare each emotion. Fear and doubt burned into ash by adrenaline and desire.

"Minseo," she said, her fingers sending chills down the back of my neck. "Fall in love with me."

I stepped back, dizzy, the top of my fist over my mouth. "Mmmm," I moaned. It was as if, once again, she'd struck me. I took her hand and guided her to her bedroom.

I sat on the bed and pulled her onto my lap. I exhaled, my forehead against hers. "Damn, Charlotte, please say it again."

Her face brightened into a smile. "Fall in lo—"

But it was too late, my mouth was on hers—and the line I'd been so hesitant to cross dissolved to nothing.

28

CHARLOTTE

Time blurred as I let myself be devoured by this new feeling. Minseo had been right; loving him was different. Young had been a glowing gold but Minseo was deep, crimson red. Here, where we floated, there were no regrets, there was no fear, nothing held back. It was the time to surrender—a time to let everything melt away but him. *More,* I felt my heart beg, or was it my body? They'd become one and the same, and so had Minseo and I. A timid knock sounded at the door, thrusting me back into the world.

"My dress," I whispered. "Where is it?" Minseo leapt up, searching the room for his things. We dressed in a hurry, and Minseo came up behind me to tie my dress. "Good, okay," I said and rushed to the door.

"Wait," he said.

Disoriented, I turned. "What?"

He grabbed and lifted me, pushing me against the wall. He kissed me from my collarbone up my neck to my jaw. I dizzied as he moved to my lips. Why had we even left the bedroom?

A knock sounded again at the door, startling us. Minseo and I swallowed a laugh, and I quickly adjusted my dress before I pulled the door open.

Gabriel and Junho stood at the door, Morgana asleep on Junho's hip. They bit back their smiles as they appraised us. "Did you forget about us?" Gabriel said.

I shook my head. "No—of course not."

He laughed. "It's been two days."

"What?" Minseo said.

Gabriel said, "Well, we tried to come back…"

"A few times," Junho added.

My face burned scarlet.

Gabriel smiled at me. "Glad you're alive."

Oh. My. God.

"Should we come back?" Junho said.

Yes. One more day, please. "No, come in," I said, stepping aside. As they entered, I felt Minseo's hands on my waist. My heart thudded. If I didn't make myself used to him somehow, I'd go mad.

I was worried that things with our group would be different since things had changed with Minseo and me, but as I watched Gabriel, Junho, and Minseo laugh by the fire, Morgana asleep in his lap, I saw something that knocked the breath from my lungs. *A family.* After all I'd lost and everything I was afraid of, Minseo had brought the feeling of home back. I looked at the men in my living room and I knew they'd be around for Morgana's whole life. Families were built with love, and any kind of love would do.

Dinner boiled over the fire and I crept to the door to the living room and listened.

"... and maybe you could show me," Minseo said.

Junho's voice sounded through the door. "Aww."

Gabriel said, "From what I can see, you're going to be a great parent. But don't worry, I'll be there the whole time. Junho said he can show me some markets where I can…"

I heard the sizzle of my pot overflowing behind me. I turned, grabbing my cooking mit and moving the pot farther away from the fire.

Vires, I thought. I knew I couldn't keep Minseo here any longer. His brother was sick, and it was selfish to keep him. Of course, he'd ask to go. I'd never been as far as Vires, but if my family would be there together, I knew we'd be fine.

The next day, Minseo, Morgana, and I visited Young's grave. Morgana ran to the tree and turned to Minseo. "My father died in the war," she said, patting the tree. "We come here to visit him."

Minseo smiled. "You know, Morgana, I knew your father."

Morgana's eyes widened. "You did?"

Minseo took her hand. "He was my little brother."

"Well," she pulled at her hair, "what did he look like?" I couldn't help but laugh at the question. She'd never asked me that before.

"He looked just like you," Minseo said.

Morgana spun, delighted. She beamed. She pointed to the tree. "Look at the pretty flowers."

I took my usual seat at the base of the tree, Listening to their banter.

"In my kingdom, Vires, all the trees turn pink this time of year."

"Don't lie," Morgana said.

"It's true. Your dad and I used to shake them and pretend the flower petals were snow."

Morgana squealed.

Minseo took a seat beside me, Morgana skipping around the tree.

"So," I said, "say hypothetically we went with you to Vires, what would our lives be like there?"

He pulled me onto his lap, a confident smirk on his face that reminded me of how he looked when I'd first met him. "Well, first —hypothetically—you'd become my wife." He paused, waiting for me to object, but when I didn't he kissed the top of my head and tightened his grip around me.

"What about me?" Morgana interjected.

"You'd become a princess. You'd go to school to learn to speak Viran."

"Teach me now!" she demanded.

Minseo laughed, pulling Morgana onto us both. "Alright," he said. "When we get to Vires, you can call me Appa."

"Appa! Appa!" Morgana leapt up, her small knees digging into my ribs before she broke away. "Appa!" She danced. "Appa."

Each time she spoke the word, Minseo smiled so warmly that I'd answered the question before it left my lips.

"What's that mean?"

He leaned in, pausing just before his lips touched mine. "Father," he said. He kissed me so deeply that I hardly felt the cold band slide onto my finger. He pulled away, his hand still on my chin. "Charlotte, will you marry me?"

Marriage. My heart raced. How had I found myself here again? It was a reckless decision—a scandal, really. Former princess marries fallen husband's brother and regains royal status. I could feel my mother's eyes roll from beyond the grave. I'd never wanted a royal life and knew I didn't want that for Morgana—but Minseo I wanted. Was it wrong to want him? How quickly I'd forgiven him and allowed him to topple my walls. How cruelly I had pushed aside my guilt or allegiance to Young for the chance to love again. No matter how brutally life passed, I was still the same thoughtless girl I'd always been— only now, I didn't care. Minseo was offering much more than his love. He was offering to become Morgana's father and, with Camelot grabbing allies left and right, Vires seemed like the safest place on this side of the world. Minseo and I could raise Morgana together, and without fear. There I was trying to convince myself that I was carefully weighing the options, but I wasn't—I was always going to choose Minseo. Which is why, when he asked me to marry him, I said yes without a moment's hesitation. Prince Minseo of Vires, I belong to you now, and you to me.

29

MINSEO

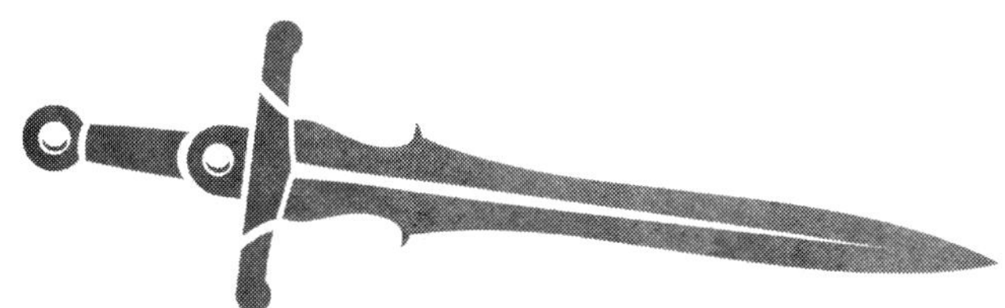

It was a whirlwind of planning, nerves, and bliss that I'd never imagined I was capable of feeling. *Appa,* Morgana had said. It was the only role that had taken me by surprise more than Charlotte agreeing to become my wife. I kept waiting for the light to leave her eyes, for her to turn away, but she didn't. Winter was over and spring had brought a new life for us. Maybe life wasn't this cruel and meaningless sequence of events but rather a collection of extraordinary moments. What if everyone lived this way and extraordinary was, in fact, ordinary? I took a disbelieving breath. Why were moments with Charlotte the only ones that made any sense to me?

I'd been lost for so long, convinced myself that Charlotte died with my brother who, even in death, had guided me to be a better man.

I would step into the life he left behind and hopefully become a man worthy of it. *Appa*. I smiled. What a concept, me a father. Charlotte, Morgana, and I safe and sound in Vires. My heart beat so fast as the plans came together. We'd leave tomorrow. Gabriel had agreed to come along. He hadn't even required a bit of convincing before he heartily embraced all of it. Me in Morgana's life. A co-parent. Knowing he'd be there too gave me more courage. There was only one moment when I felt guilt slip in. It was when Charlotte said goodbye to her friend Lynn. Charlotte described the encounter with great detail, the excitement in Lynn's eyes, to hear of our engagement, and the tears in them when Charlotte said her goodbyes. Good friends were hard to come by, and I felt an ache inside me when I thought of taking Charlotte away from that. Still, her and Morgana's safety was paramount.

Junho packed our things at the inn— humming along like he'd orchestrated all the events that led here. Perhaps he did. Maybe he was my guardian angel all this time, or just one hell of a friend.

A knock sounded at my door. The apocalypse? Some tragic twist of events? No. Charlotte. My future wife, Charlotte, with a gentle smile and mischievous look in her eye, that I'd learned meant she wanted some time alone with me. A look that hammered my chest so hard it could bring me back from the dead. This was my life now. I shut the door behind her.

This was my life. This was my life. This was *my* life.

The next morning, the guards finished loading the carriage. Hanbit had given up his seat in the carriage for horseback to allow Morgana and Charlotte to have a seat inside. Morgana pet her favorite two horses, who she named Jelly and Lulu, before stepping up into the carriage.

I squeezed Charlotte's hand as the horses pulled through the Wellwood city gate. We were on our way. This was my life. *Almost.* A few minutes later, the carriage stopped.

No. My heartbeat. Unwelcome as the grim reaper coming to claim my soul—I knew it was over. I had no reason to suspect the delay wasn't a herd of cattle, or a wide-framed carriage passing by

—except for this was my life and, in my life, happiness was temporary.

"Stay here," I said to Charlotte and stepped out of the carriage. At the center of the road were a horse and a man. *Lancelot.*

I drew my sword, but he didn't reach for his, the calm look on his face raising my pulse with each beat of my quaking heart.

"I have a letter for Mr. Hanbit of Vires," he said.

Shaken, Jay Hyun, his soldiers, Junho, Gabriel, and I turned to the sniveling man who paled so quickly I might've thought him dead. He stepped forward on shaking legs and Lancelot handed him a letter that I hadn't noticed in his hand until that moment.

Silence chipped at my faith as Hanbit's eyes moved across the letter.

"It has the king's seal," he said finally.

I ran a nervous hand through my hair. "Arthur?"

He shook his head. "The King of Vires. It's from your father."

I swallowed hard, the air too thin to sustain me.

He turned to the guards. "He has asked us to deliver Charlotte to King Arthur as a mandatory term of the Vires and Camelot alliance."

"That's impossible," I said, my voice shaking. "There must be some kind of mistake. My father would never agree to ally with Camelot." There was no way. I *knew* my father. I trusted him. He'd never sell his kingdom out, let alone to a man like Arthur. I turned to Lancelot. "You think we'd fall for such a pathetic trick?"

Lancelot stepped forward. "She won't be harmed."

There was nothing but pity in his eyes. Why did he look so certain? It was a lie, and not even a good one. I ripped the letter from Hanbit's hands.

"There's no doubt," he said. "It's written by our king. It's in Viran. It has his seal. It's an order and we must obey."

I stared at it, reading it again and again. It was unmistakably written by my father. My legs weakened as the truth set in. *No.* I wasn't going to lose her like this.

I turned to Jay Hyun. "You're not seriously going to obey."

He shook his head. "I-I'm not sure." He looked at the ground. "It's a direct order from our king." He turned to the other guards. "It's time to make a choice."

One by one, the guards voted. *Obey. Obey. Obey.*

I shook with disbelief, rage surging through me.

"Disobey," Jay Hyun said, standing beside me.

I walked up to each guard and looked them in the eye one by one. They had been with us this whole time. They'd gotten to know Charlotte. How could they follow an order like this? When they didn't waver, I drew my sword. "You'll have to kill a prince of Vires first. See if your king welcomes you back—"

I felt a soft hand on my shoulder and turned to see Charlotte. "No," I breathed. "Get back in the carriage. I won't let them take you."

She touched my face, her voice a gentle whisper in the wind. "I need you to take your daughter away from here. Take her to Vires. Find out what's happening."

"No, Charlotte."

"Morgana could be next. Get her away from here."

Tears streamed down my face, all my hope draining from my body. "I'll find you. Stay alive. I'll find you, I swear." I fell apart, a sobbing wreck as my dream slipped away without so much as a fight.

She kissed me softly and stepped back. When she looked back up at me, I saw the light in her eyes had gone out. This was *goodbye.*

My nine soldiers walked alongside Charlotte and Lancelot, lifted her, and placed her on Lance's horse. Hanbit hesitated a moment, debating which path to take before he stood beside our carriage.

"Jay Hyun," I said, "go with Charlotte. Make sure nothing happens to her."

"Yes, sir," he said.

"Promise me."

"I promise." He hurried after them, taking his place beside Charlotte.

This couldn't be happening. Through sobs, I spoke, "You think this makes you a knight, Lancelot? Having your king do everything for you." I gasped. "You think you're an honorable man?" I drew my sword, desperation flooding my body. "I'll fight you right now for her."

Lance turned to me somberly. "I am not an honorable man," he said. "Not anymore." His words seemed meant to wound himself rather than me.

"Please," I begged, dropping my head.

"Mommy?" Morgana's soft voice sounded from behind me. Fear swelled. She ran to me, peeking at her mother from behind me. I picked her up and carried her back toward the carriage. Afraid that, Lancelot heard or saw her. I couldn't let her be taken. "I'll get her back," I whispered." Wiping my wet eyes, I glanced back at Charlotte—her eyes a storm of whispers. *Save her. Get out of here.*

I put Morgana into the carriage, nodding to Gabriel and Junho.

Charlotte would have to wait, but my father would pay for this. The whole world would. We were going to Vires—I had to dethrone a king.

30

LANCELOT

A hollow victory. At least he had the decency to make a show of it. *You think this makes you a real knight, Lancelot?* I wish he hadn't said that. That question revolved in my mind again and again as we began our trip to Bullhorn.

It didn't matter how it happened, right? I got the girl. It was a stupid knighthood mission to begin with. Why couldn't I have gotten one like Pansley—climb the highest peak in Camelot? Or one like Owens—win twelve fencing tournaments. No, I had to kidnap some girl and, even so, needed Arthur's help to do it.

The guards spoke in Viran and I couldn't tell if it was to hide their thoughts from Charlotte or from me. Eventually, to drown them out, Charlotte spoke. "So you'll be a knight now?" she said casually, her dark curls moving with each gust of the wind or step of the horse.

"Yeah," I said weakly.

"What's different from being a regular soldier? Because I hear soldiers in Camelot make three times those of anywhere else."

"More money, plus the title."

"So you did all this for a pay raise? In that case, I'll pay you more if you let me go."

"You're not a queen anymore." I looked at her tattered dress. "I doubt you have enough to fill your table."

"I am to become a princess of Vires."

So Merlin was right. "Aren't you advantageous? And I suppose you're doing this for money and a title?"

"For love," she said. She'd spoken it so earnestly that I stopped walking.

"Me too," I said involuntarily.

"Is it that girl, Merlin? I saw the way you rushed to save her the night you found us two years ago."

I didn't answer. I didn't need some girl poking around in my head. I pulled the reins of the horse forward.

"You know," she said, "somehow that makes me respect you more."

"What do you mean?"

"You're a hero in your story. On a quest for the sake of love. Sounds like a hero to me."

I turned, only to feel the sharpness of steel cut into my cheek as a flash of red swept by. My cheek stung, and on the ground beside me was a red, dragon-hilted dagger stuck in the ground. If I had kept walking, she could have killed me. I turned to her, waiting for her to shrink in fear, but she didn't. "I'm the hero of my own story. I have my own love to return to."

I bound her hands and gagged her. I wouldn't be fooled by her again. I'd consider the dagger a trophy from my quest, but something bothered me. Why use a dagger when she had Merlin's power in her blood? Was she showing mercy? I didn't ask. One of the reasons Arthur had used Viran troops to capture her was to deter her from killing any of Camelot's troops with magic, but this had been smooth. Too smooth. The only possibility I could think of was that Merlin had been wrong. If it was love Charlotte was fighting to get back to, she would have used every ounce of power she possessed. It was unlikely that she had any power at all, but I wasn't about to tell Arthur that. Not before he knighted me.

Although she'd drawn my blood, something she said quelled my fears. No matter the circumstances of the quest, everything I'd done was for love, and that was a heroic cause.

Even Arthur had acquired his position through questionable means; maybe that's why he'd shown me mercy. But it didn't make him less of a king. It didn't take away from the fact that in five short years he'd transformed empty, broken Drethen into thriving, wealthy Camelot.

If it weren't for his pursuit of Gwen, I might've been proud of him.

Quest or not, I was going home. I'd have Gwen. I was a knight, and I'd earn that title as Arthur earned his.

31

MERLIN

Fire wielding was a slow process. It was easy to lose control of the flames, and I'd suffered several minor burns in the process. As soon as the flames flickered red, my chest seized with fear. The basement was an easy place to avoid burning anything important, but it still filled with heat and smoke.

When the stones in one room blackened, I'd rotate to the next. I could burn almost two rooms in one day at my current level. I raised my hand, the blue glow cutting through the back smoke like rays of sun through the clouds. I inhaled deeply to muster my energy only to choke on lungs full of burning stone.

I gasped for fresh air, this time crouching below the smoke, but it was no use; once I started choking, I couldn't recover. I burst through the open door as the smoke was pulled deeper into the cellar by an invisible force. Left, that was the way out. The way toward fresh air, I was certain, but why then did the smoke drift right?

I followed it through the row of empty rooms, one after another. I hadn't ventured this far; there was no reason to. Each room was exactly the same in size and contents, without exception. However, the staircase I'd come in by was, as far as I knew, the only way down here, too far below the ground for windows. So what was pulling the smoke this way?

Further and further I strode, until the last row of lit torches. The darkness stretched out in front of me, pulling the smoke in like hell's gates, summoning a ghostly figure. I swallowed a lump of nervousness I hadn't realized I'd felt, lit a timid blue flame, and entered the dark unknown.

The bleak blue light of my flame drenched the corridor in a wintery glow. I resisted the urge to check each cell I passed for anomalies and instead stayed my course and followed the smoke.

A ghostly whistle stopped me in my tracks, and I felt the wisp of cold air run through. It was odd, but what had I to fear? Even drained of most of my power, I could incapacitate any foe I uncovered, but something here was sinister, evil, dangerous. My intuition urged me to turn back.

The dark corridor seemed endless, and my growing anxiety spiked as I stepped forward into clean air. I raised my hand, the blue light catching the black smoke as it sucked into one not-so-special cell. The corridor continued on in darkness, but the smoke was my guide. I turned into the cell, the back of my mind still curious about how far the corridor went on. I made a mental note to continue exploring until the end... another day.

Each step brought me closer to the eerie whistle. I approached the back wall of the empty room. The smoke hummed as it sucked into a gap between two stones. What was this? Extinguishing my flame, I blinked through the total darkness as I placed my hands flat against the frigid stone. I pushed, and when it didn't budge, I lowered my shoulder and rammed it into the wall. My stomach dropped as the stone door slid forward and the cold whoosh of open air hit my face. I stumbled through, lighting my hand with the shaken panic of a child afraid of the dark. *A secret passage?*

Inside was a room half the size of the cell I'd come from. It was empty except for a black rug that glowed blue in my light. I saw the flicker of the flame mirrored in an object at the center of the rug. There was an archway, at the far end of the room, that looked like a staircase.

Excitement thudded at my chest as I knelt and examined the silvery stone. It looked like a precious metal. Round, an oval in shape—but it was too smooth to have come from below the earth. I reached out and rubbed it with my free hand, surprised by its warm surface. *What is this?* It was the source of evil that had led me here, and in it, I saw my glowing blue eyes for the first time reflected back at me. I stared in awe of them, my mind brushing over my mother's last word to me: *witch*. I tried lifting the stone, but it was heavy and I needed two hands. I wasn't ready to extinguish my light, and end my exploration, not when I'd finally found something.

Leaving the stone, I walked beneath the archway and held my hand up to see stairs that led up. The smoke rose the staircase and I followed. My adrenaline pulled me up, flight after flight, but drained as I huffed breathlessly with no end in view. Determined, I continued. My legs burned, growing heavier with each step up the endless staircase. Finally, I saw a bright green window at the top. Recharged, I climbed the rest of the way, my gaze glued to the glowing square.

At the top of the stairs was a large door with an arched window at its center. The opening was covered on the outside by green, leafy vines, but I could still hear the whip of the fresh air beyond. I yanked at the handle and pushed at the door, trying to get it open, but it didn't move. Where did this let out? If I'd been brave enough, I would have burned the door down, or sliced the hinges with a precise gust of wind, but I wasn't sure where it led or if I'd draw attention to the door. I wanted to get the unusual stone out of here, to examine it in my room where I had natural light. Surely it was worth something and, if it was, it belonged to Arthur. I needed to get it out of here before it was discovered by someone else. I turned and descended the stairs, vowing that I'd inspect every inch of the castle's exterior until I found the door again, from the outside.

32

MINSEO

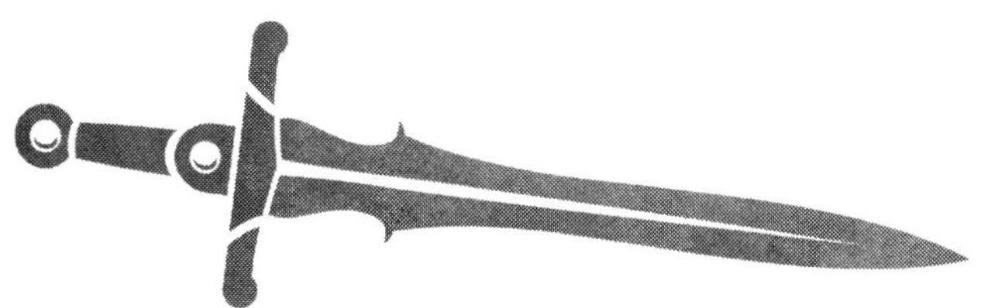

When Morgana realized that Charlotte wasn't joining us, she was inconsolable. I held her little body to mine; it was so hot that I feared she'd burst into flame. Her arms were wrapped tightly around me as if she feared letting go, and I ached when I looked at her. Her screams and cries were an echo of how I felt inside. I held her in my arms. It was my fault her mother was taken. Finally, it was more than I could take, and I let myself fall apart once more.

My tears drew her attention, and she cupped my face in her hands like a concerned parent. When she looked into my eyes, I swear I saw my little brother looking back at me. She took my hand and sat silently beside me as if she understood. I was not her enemy, I too wanted Charlotte back. She wiped my face with her sleeve, and we fell back into a weighted silence.

She didn't cry again after that, as if she feared I'd cry too. Children cry, overwhelmed by the world around them, certain that adults have the answers. To witness that illusion break must've unsettled her.

I wasn't ready to lose Charlotte this way, but neither was Morgana. I couldn't be the man I was when I left Vires. I could not drink Charlotte away this time. I couldn't rely on the crutch of numbness to pull me through. I needed to become the kind of man my brother was—strong enough to pull Morgana out of harm's way and return to Camelot to get Charlotte. Strength was the key to making everything right. I thought of Morgana's hands on my cheeks—she was scared. She needed comfort, to know everything would be okay, and instead she was forced to comfort me at age four.

Then it hit me; this was probably how Charlotte felt when Young died. Lost, overwhelmed, scared. It was in a moment of gloom on this level, or worse, that I'd left her in.

I took a deep breath and Morgana mimicked me. I smiled. It wasn't for nothing. Despite this pain, I felt more alive than ever. Charlotte brought me back; she trusted me to look after Morgana.

I was still alive. I could fix everything.

I took Morgana's hands between mine and rubbed them warm. She smiled, but maybe just for me.

An hour later, I was relieved that Morgana fell into a deep sleep, her head bouncing with every jerk of the carriage until the coach came to a stop. My first instinct was to panic. Was it Lancelot again? Was he here for Morgana? My nerves eased when Gabriel climbed in, his wide frame jostling the carriage until he rested on the seat.

"How's she holding up?" he asked.

"She's alright," I said.

"And you?" I looked up at him, his dark eyes scanning my face. "I figured as much," he said, "But you're not in this alone."

I nodded, unable to find my voice.

"I've never seen Morgana take to anyone so quickly."

I sniffed. "I'm really happy you agreed to come with us. You've been a great teammate throughout this whole ordeal. I promise, once I know Morgana is safe in Vires, I'll get Charlotte back."

"I know."

I blanched, "What? How?"

He smiled and leaned back in his seat. "Because love always wins."

I sighed, disappointed that he didn't have a more concrete answer. "Tell that to my brother."

"Minseo," he said, biting his lower lip, "there's something else. I didn't want to say anything to Charlotte because I wasn't sure, but now I wish I had."

I leaned forward, making sure not to wake Morgana. "What is it?"

"I don't think Charlotte has what Lancelot and Merlin are looking for. But if she's figured this out, she'll probably pretend she does."

"What are you saying?" I asked.

Gabriel eyed Morgana, her breath still steady. "Perhaps we should talk about this outside the carriage."

33

CHARLOTTE

I'd never been to Bullhorn. Five years ago, it was tucked safely behind Drethen borders two armies between their great kingdom and mine. It was all Camelot now, as far as I'd ever traveled. What wasn't Camelot by name, was in alliance. Even Vires had somehow fallen into Arthur's hands. Still, I trusted Minseo—he'd sort it out, he'd protect Morgana, and for now it was as far as I could send her away from Arthur's castle.

Once again, I'd lost everything I cared about—Morgana, Minseo, Gabriel, Junho—all for the sake of a title I thought had perished years ago.

The Viran soldiers I'd come to know hardly spoke a word to me. They marched me in like the prisoner I was. Was it shame that silenced them? Sadness? Regret? No matter, I felt the isolation seep in with each step we took away from my loved ones. I didn't know what a man like Arthur wanted with me, but I knew from experience it wouldn't be good.

As we traveled overnight, I had to stop my mind from cosseting the burgeoning doubt inside. Of course, it was over. I dared to love again. I'd already learned what the consequences of that were. I thought of tilting my head back, calling out to Young for help as I'd done so many times over the last few years, but he wasn't there. Not out there in the endlessness of space and time, nor inside me. I bit back my urge to cry, and Lancelot reached for his sword. Half out of breath, he glared at me. What did he think I would do? I was outnumbered eleven to one, but the look in his clear green-brown eyes was fear. I recoiled, scrunching my brows together. Based on his mirrored expression he seemed equally puzzled. After a few dragging moments, he sheathed his sword and we continued. *What don't I know?*

I saw Bullhorn in the distance, a towering city that swallowed the horizon. Trading carts clogged the streets, people rushing in all directions, roads spitting out in every direction like waves from an island. The castle perched above all, from its podium at the center, like a white crown floating above the chaos. *Impossible.* That kind of growth took hundreds of years. How? How in such a short time did Arthur turn the depleted Drethen empire into this—the center of humanity?

I should have known it was something spectacular, something more tangible than the alliances that rallied so many behind a teenage boy. One thing was certain: Arthur wasn't just anyone—he was born to be a king.

The castle was half-embedded into the mountain, the white walls only on the half that reached toward the sky. The rest could only be seen up close, with windows carved into the stone of solid rock peeking out at the city below. Attacking Bullhorn Castle would be as useless as knocking down a mountain. It would never fall, and for the first time in five years, I allowed myself to surrender to hopelessness.

Lancelot hesitated before helping me off the horse. I stepped down, feeling slightly dizzy and unbalanced from the long journey.

Up close, I could feel the immense size of the mountain castle, like being swallowed by the earth. I tore my eyes away and scanned for Arthur. Who was the boy capable of all this?

My gaze stopped on a striking girl with green braids. I'd seen her before; she'd saved Morgana from the fire two years ago. Her black eyes were gentle and sympathetic but changed when she turned to Lancelot.

"Merlin," Lance breathed. "Where is Arthur?"

Merlin spoke, her voice low and beautiful, like the start of a song. "He thought it best that I settle the girl in myself." She smirked, lighting up her whole face. "I'm actually surprised you made it here in one piece," she said, and her gaze flitted to me.

Once again, what did they expect me to do?

Merlin turned to the soldiers. "You're dismissed," she said.

Jay Hyun stepped forward. "With all due respect, I've been ordered to stay with Charlotte."

Merlin walked up to Jay Hyun, his posture stiffening. "Did Prince Minseo say so?" My heart thudded as a silent moment lingered between them. Jay Hyun remained frozen.

My voice sounded, "Please," I said. She turned to me, holding my gaze before turning back to Jay Hyun. She sighed. "Fine, we'll accommodate you."

She turned to me, her face softening. "Charlotte, please come with me."

I turned to Lancelot. "My dagger, please," I said.

Lancelot looked befuddled but handed me the dagger without so much as a word. I eyed the shallow cut on his cheek as I sheathed it.

The dark-fleshed woman turned to Lancelot. "Lance," she spat, "take care of the others."

"Take care?" I asked as we walked toward the entrance of the Bullhorn Castle.

"Water and a place to rest until they're ready to return to Vires," she said.

I wasn't sure, but from the short interaction between them, it almost seemed like Merlin preferred me to her partner Lancelot, and I wondered where her allegiances lied.

34

MERLIN

As I led Charlotte into the caste, I felt the sudden overwhelming sense of belonging that I hadn't expected. Since leaving Lance, I went days at a time without speaking to anyone. It dawned on me that I'd never met a person who could understand what this power felt like—what it meant—the way Charlotte could. She was a stranger but also all I had. What words would she use to describe the sensation? How did her powers differ from my own?

I resisted the urge to bombard her immediately with questions and instead felt myself reaching for her energy. I wondered all the while if I'd be able to feel the tingle of that which was beyond the ordinary. I pushed the smallest bit of my own energy to mix with hers. An ordinary person wouldn't notice that I'd done it, they'd feel a wave of light-headedness or ask for some cold water, but they never suspected I'd had an effect on their energy. But Charlotte wasn't ordinary. She was a witch like me. A future battle mage, a sister. If she felt it, she didn't show it. So I pulled my energy back with a bit of hers, but all I felt was loss and unwavering despair.

The guards closed the doors behind us, Charlotte's eyes tallying them as we walked.

Impatient, I said, "You're not in any danger."

Her gaze met mine. It was not unkind but cold. "Why did Vires ally with Camelot?" she asked. "What does your king have on them?"

I pushed a braid behind my ear. "The king doesn't share such details with me."

"Then who are you to him?"

My chest warmed. "I'm his battle mage."

"Mage? As in magic?" She stepped back. "So what they say is true. You're Merlin of Camelot."

I paused, waiting for her to connect it all, but her eyes didn't light with understanding.

"What does he want with me?" she asked, her curls bouncing around her head like Medusa's coiled snakes.

I almost laughed, right there in her face. Was she joking? Did she think I was a fool?

It wasn't possible that she didn't know. By the time I was thirteen, I'd caused enough property damage and sent enough innocent people to the hospital to be burned at the stake—and I would've been if not for Arthur. There was only one possibility: Charlotte was lying. I had two options, earn her trust or force it out of her. I preferred the former. There was no reason to make an enemy of her, but it was possible that Arthur had already done that by bringing her here alone. She was dangerous. With such powerful emotions and a score to settle, she was a threat to the king. He was wise to keep her in my charge until we were certain what she could do.

We stepped into our shared quarters, her bedroom beside

mine. The design was meant for new mothers with young children, the second bedroom a private place for the nurses to care for the babies without being too far away from the mother, but it worked for our purposes as well. Charlotte appeared unimpressed with the castle. Was her sadness masking all other emotions or was it her royal upbringing that numbed her to such grandeur? I wanted to ask, but I wasn't sure how to word it without insulting her. She hardly spoke another word to me as she compliantly lay on her bed, so I returned to my room. Just as I was about to drift off to sleep, my stomach tightened as the gentle sniffle and muffled breaths of a broken heart sounded on the other side of the door.

The next morning, I woke to the dazzling red of a jeweled hilt, the blade an inch above my chest.

"I'm leaving this castle," Charlotte said. "Either you help me or you die." *Why use a dagger?* A quick gust of wind sent her flying off the bed, the dagger narrowly missing her leg.

She gasped, out of breath. "Right. Magic." She dropped her head. "I have a family," she said, "I know you're a good person because you saved us once."

My mind flashed to the night I first saw her. The handsome medium-skinned man and the little Viran baby. Was that who she meant?

I eyed her as she pulled herself from the floor and sat down beside me. "Why won't you tell me the truth?" I asked.

"What truth?" she burst.

Frustrated, I leaned closer. "That you can do things!"

She scrunched her brow. "You mean magic? I can't. I'm not. I'm not what you think I am," she stammered. "Is that why Arthur wants me here?"

"Ye,." I pleaded. "You're like me. Think about it—when you're scared or worried. Things growing. Sudden wind or unexplained fire."

Her face softened, her eyes widening at the word *fire*.

Her hand rose to her mouth, her chest heaving with understanding.

"Yes," I whispered. "It's fire, isn't it? That night when Lance nearly caught you, you started that fire."

She turned away from me as if she worried I'd read her mind, but I'd already seen the truth. She'd conjured fire. She was a witch, like me.

She spoke, her voice cracking, "Yes. *Fire*."

I leapt from the bed, filled with such a surge of excitement I could have turned the bed to dust. I wasn't alone. She shook—but I understood. I too used to fear that confession. But she was safe. I'd show her that she was safe here, that she could trust me. But how? My thoughts brimmed with possibilities. I'd share one of my secrets. I hurried to my closet and pulled out the silvery rock I'd smuggled from the basement cellar.

Energy spiraled through me, sending a swirl of unintended wind around me as I carried the strange stone to Charlotte. When she looked up, her eyes were wet.

"It's okay, Charlotte. You're not alone," I said. Her gaze was fixed on the stone. "I thought I could share one of my secrets with you." I shifted my weight nervously, "You know, as a show of faith."

A soft smile touched the corner of her lips, and she wiped her eyes and stood. "What is it?" she asked.

"I don't know," I said. "I found it the other day." I held it out for her to touch.

She reached for it. A sickly snap followed by an array of small crunches sounded from the stone as a crack zigzagged up the side.

35

CHARLOTTE

I was not a queen, I was not a princess, and I certainly wasn't a mage, but the more I thought about it, the more I realized that my daughter Morgana may have become all of those things.

Merlin was mistaken. She wanted it to be true, she wanted me to be like her, she wanted not to be alone. She wasn't alone. My daughter understood. My daughter had stories to tell and, while I'd always listened, I never understood. *Magic* and *fire*, the starring role in all her stories. How had I missed it? Was it because, before all of this, there had been no magic in the world, or had I ignored the signs, desperate for my child to live the ordinary life I craved? I knew they'd go after her. I knew my lie wouldn't hold for long, but maybe I could buy her a little time.

I reached out to touch the mirror-like ball, certain it was a royal ornament, but before my fingers could brush the smooth surface, the stone split. My first thought was that Merlin had done something to it with magic, but her face flashed with bewilderment. She yanked back her hands and I instinctively bent and caught it.

In an instant, I regretted it. The stone was warm. It moved from the inside, something jabbing at my hands like an irregular heartbeat. The pulse increased, cracking the stone with each thrash. I worried it would slip through my fingers as the weight shifted inside. Through a crevice, I saw a glossy yellow eye—like a cat's but twice the size. Paralyzed with fear, I stared down at it. It calmed and poked a pointy green-scaled nose through the crack. It flashed a red, two-pointed tongue and sucked it back before it stretched, breaking the last of the silvery shell, sending pieces crackling to the floor. Talon-ribbed wings outstretched, it peered at me.

Merlin gaped, "A dragon."

The creature climbed out of its shell, perching on my wrist, its body heat warming my chest and face. Its body was lizard-like but sharp-fanged and nimble. Its scales were soft to the touch and as shiny as the egg it hatched from. I froze with fear. "Merlin… take it. Take your dragon."

The creature's neck shot back, and a soft blue glow emanated from its throat.

"Merlin," I said, nervous to spook it. It spewed blue flame at my arm and, without hesitation, I yanked my hand back and tossed it into the air.

"Kill it!" I screamed as the creature flew clumsily around the room, knocking into walls and tangling itself in the chandelier. We ducked as it swooped down at us. I grabbed a candlestick. "Kill it, Merlin!" I screamed.

She shook her head. "I-I… I don't know what to do."

I swatted at it with the candlestick and it screeched with delight. "It's your dragon. Do *something*!"

Merlin threw her head back and burst into laughter, clutching her stomach and gasping for air. I swatted mindlessly at the flying lizard before I collapsed on her, and we roared with laughter. Tears streamed down our faces as we struggled to pull our sanity together, ducking at the occasional crash of broken objects around the room that prompted more laughter. "Control—" I sobbed, my cheeks sore from laughing. "Control your dragon." I sighed. "And this is my life now. You know, nothing surprises me anymore."

"Speak for yourself," Merlin said, finally able to bring herself to words. "I had no idea that was a dragon egg—or that dragons were actually real."

"So I guess you're opposed to shooting it down? I think it burned my ar—" I stopped, looking down at my wrist, but instead of blotchy red skin, I found a silvery bracelet clasped tightly around it. It was the same smoothness and sheen as the dragon egg had been. "What's this?" I said, shaking it at Merlin.

I tried pulling at it, but it was too tight to slip off my hand. The dragon slammed back into the chandelier with a loud crash. We took cover, Merlin taking my wrist. Her hand lit with an aqua flame that she held to the bracelet. After several seconds, she took my wrist out of the flame and held it to her cheek.

Her eyes flicked to me. "Still cool."

I sighed as the dragon thrashed about, caught in the chandelier. The ceiling creaked, threatening to give out.

"For god's sake, dragon, just sit down."

The green beast calmed, stretched its wings, and glided down. It sat in front of me, the tip of its nose raising and lowering with curiosity.

36

LANCELOT

It was the day of the ceremony, my final moments as the street urchin I was. Knighthood meant my family would live among the nobility forever—my bloodline permanently stained blue.

There was only one loose end left: Merlin. I hadn't seen her or Charlotte since we arrived at the castle. I knew they must be busy training, but Merlin was now a threat; she knew my secret. That was the kind of secret that got a newly knighted soldier beheaded around here. Of course, Arthur hated getting his hands dirty and much preferred to imprison those who opposed him, but every so often, someone would cross a line and lose their head. This was my moment, and I didn't want to kneel before Arthur and wonder if he would knight me or lop my head off then and there.

I took a deep breath outside Merlin's chamber. How would I handle this? Would I try to appeal to her feelings for me? It wasn't a long-term plan. Eventually, she'd realize I was bound to only Gwenevere and she'd have just the leverage to get revenge. I could leverage our friendship, though. Four years on the road together.

Sparring partners, drinking companions. A crash sounded from the inside of the chamber and I felt relieved that she was in there. The ceremony was set to begin in an hour, and I was grateful not to have to search for her.

I knocked and held my breath until the door swung open and Merlin's slender body stepped into the frame. "Lance," she said, glancing back over her shoulder.

I cleared my throat. "Can I come in?"

"No," she said quickly. The clang of crunching metal blasted from behind her. "Charlotte is training."

"Look, Merlin, we've been friends for a long time. I wanted to know if— Well… if you were going to say anything to Arthur about—"

A heavy thud rattled the chandelier behind her. I tried to look but she stepped into my line of sight. "So you're still not planning on stopping?" She sighed. "We're friends, you say?" she asked with a smile. "And I suppose you want me to protect you?"

For a split second, my nerves soothed.

"I love how we're always friends when it's convenient for you." Her bedroom rattled behind her. "Gwenevere is married to Arthur."

I fought my urge to turn away and check the area for listening ears.

"I say we let it all out at your little ceremony today and we'll just let you get what you deserve."

"I don't know why you're being like this."

"Me?"

"I never lied to you. I always told you how I felt about her. Whatever you built up inside your head is on you."

"And whatever acts of treason you commit are on you. Glad we have that settled." She stepped back and began to shut the door. I stuck my foot between the door and the frame. I stopped and, with one furious push, the door was open.

A green mass flew at my face and I ducked. I turned to see a hound-sized lizard scrambling towards me, it's wings retracting flat against its back.

"Is this a—"

"Get out, Lance."

My heart rammed into my chest as I tried to blink away the illusion in front of me. *It couldn't be.* With a familiar, unearthly gust of wind, I slid backward out of the chamber.

"Fine," Merlin said, "your secret for mine.." Her eyes blazed blue and a swirl of blue light appeared in her hand. "But this does not mean we're friends or allies. I don't need to describe the level of hell that will rain down on you if anyone finds out about this."

The door slammed shut in my face so hard as my mind raced from one strange phenomenon to the other. Blue eyes. Blue... fire? Dragon? When had Merlin unlocked that ability? How did she come to discover such a beast or get it into the castle unseen? As usual, my meeting with Merlin had led me to more questions than answers, but at least my secret about Gwen was safe for now.

An hour later, trumpets sounded as the ceremony commenced. I knelt before Arthur, an equal mix of brotherly admiration and the hatred of a rival swirling inside me. He was still more boy than man. His golden locks peeked out from a crown that slid too far down on his head. He looked like a child in a play, but there wasn't a man or woman in Camelot who would snicker at the expense of their king. The kingdom was dripping with wealth, allies, and trade, and there wasn't a citizen of Camelot who didn't benefit in some way. The extraordinary events surrounding the sword, Excalibur, might have been looked at as a silly contest for the throne but was now viewed as divine purpose. And Arthur was the god of this new religion. Each time the story of how he pulled the stone was told, it was stretched into an even holier version. Arthur stood tall, confident that he'd won the hearts of everyone in his kingdom.

But why had he chosen to marry Gwen of all people? Was she just the forbidden fruit? Was it a show of power? A test of allegiance? Arthur never did anything without a purpose. I needed to know, but neither a soldier nor a knight could question a king. He looked down at me and, for the first time since I embarked on my quest, I saw the loving brother I'd once known. There was something he wasn't telling me, a reason for marrying Gwen I hadn't guessed at. Something Gwen also failed to mention. And while a knight couldn't ask a king for his motives, certainly a brother could ask a brother.

Arthur raised Excalibur, the golden-hilted broadsword, drawing in the sun's light through the stained-glass windows only to reflect it into the eyes of all in attendance. His arm shook as if it would give in from the weight, but Arthur didn't lower it. He spoke, "By the power vested in me, by the divine through the mighty sword Excalibur, and by all the witnesses here, I dub thee Sir Lancelot."

He sheathed Excalibur as the crowd's cheers thundered through the throne room.

37

MINSEO

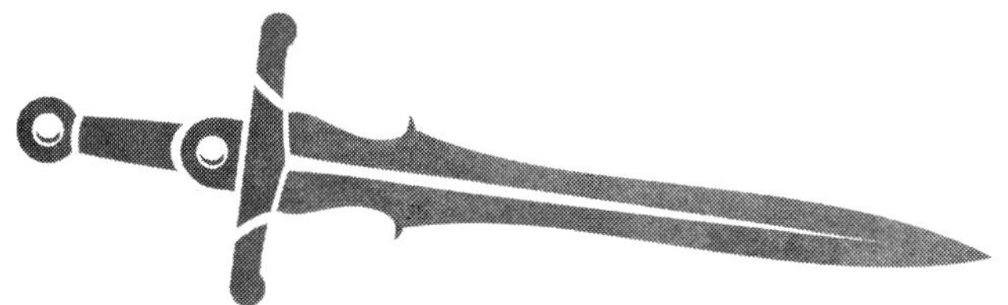

We moved along the winding roads of Vires, through the mountain ranges that ran through the land. Morgana had been restless ever since we'd gotten off the ship and back into the carriage that waited for us on the other side of the sea. I could tell she'd never traveled so far and longed to stretch her legs. Luckily for me, she was better company than Young or Junho and had a nearly endless supply of games to entertain and distract us along the way.

Even I was surprised when the carriage halted outside the Viran palace. It was dark, but I wasn't sure how late it actually was. I saw the glow of the red lanterns outside the throne rooms flicker. My father was still awake.

We stepped outside the carriage, and Morgana gasped at the sight of the castle. She may have seen a castle or two before, but I was certain she'd never seen anything like this. I'd forgotten how lovely it was, until I watched her dance with delight, bowing to each structure as if each was a prince beckoning her out to the dance floor. She sang a song with no learnable melody and threw her hands into the air. Her world seemed much more beautiful than mine. But I couldn't stay here and play like I wanted to. I had to fix my world and rescue Vires from a senile old fool.

I turned to Junho. "Stay here."

"You're not going to do anything reckless, are you?" he asked.

"No," I said, but I knew it was a lie. I didn't know if he believed me, but I was visibly shaking and I hoped he wouldn't notice. I knelt to Morgana. "Morgana, see that green tree over there?" She nodded. "Once a year, that tree turns pink. Why don't you go check it out with Gabriel and Junho while I go say hi to my father."

Vires was just a puppet of Camelot now. Sold to the highest bidder by my father. He was a fraud. My mind raced through all he'd taught my brothers and me. Honor, duty, respect. Tradition, family, history. What had it all meant to end like this? A few months ago, it wouldn't have mattered. It felt like I had nothing worth protecting, but now I did. I had Morgana. I'd wanted more than anything to raise her in Vires where I knew she'd be safe. But now the world belonged to Arthur, including Charlotte—the only thing that made any of this worthless throne madness worth it—and my father was to blame.

Charlotte, I'm so sorry I left you.

I pushed open the double doors of the throne room, my father seated calmly on the throne. Sumin was seated to his left, dark circles around his sunken eyes. How did Sumin get this sick? Other than him not conceiving a child, what were the signs? Was this illness the cause of my father's decision? I shook away the thought and turned my attention to the king. No. He'd sold his entire kingdom. There was no excuse.

My heart beat, *Charlotte, I will find you.*

"You bastard!" I yelled, drawing my sword. I charged forward. The guards reached for their weapons.

Charlotte, we'll be together.

I gritted my teeth. "You sold Vires to that snake?" I gasped, tears flowing down my cheeks.

Charlotte, we'll be a family.

"It's your fault he took her," I cried.

His face was as emotionless and frozen as a stone sculpture. He sat poised like he'd been waiting for me.

"You don't deserve to call yourself King."

My father stood, waving off the guards. He walked down the stairs that led to the throne and stood in front of me.

I'm sorry, Charlotte. I love you, I thought, as if she could feel it.

"You will die by my hand for selling Vires. Hundreds of years of history gone. What did he offer you? How much gold does your dignity cost?"

I raised my sword, my father frozen beneath it.

And nothing, nothing will ever come between us.

"Brother," a voice sounded from beside the throne. *Who dare interfere? Sumin? No.*

I turned, struck with paralysis as Young walked toward me. Mouth agape, I reached my hand out to the phantom, but with bone and flesh, he took it. I dropped my sword, the clang of it jolting me awake. *Young*. I reached out and wiped his cheek with my thumb, the wetness of it still warm. "You're alive?"

I shook a miraculous moment drug into an endless loop. Face to face with my fallen brother. *How?* He'd been dead for five years. It was impossible. I'd heard him die. Hadn't I? Yet, like a phoenix from the ashes, he stood before me unharmed—years older as if the dimension he passed through bore the same time rules as this. Was it magic? Was it divine intervention?

"It's my fault," Young said, his voice a sound I feared I'd never hear again. Dazed and overwhelmed, I turned to my father, his emotion cracking through. The hurt of my words no different from what he must've said to himself a thousand times. There in his wounded eyes were all the answers and, at once, I understood.

I turned back to Young, the boyish curves of his face, straight and pointed, and the kindness in his eyes still present. He was an inch taller, his muscles strong and defined as mine had been years ago. His hair was grown out past his ears, his eyes mirroring the awe within me. I clutched his shirt as if at any moment he'd slip through my fingers.

My father had made a difficult choice, and I'd judged him too quickly. I should have thrown myself to the kind king's feet and apologized, but I couldn't let go of my brother. With my free arm, I reached for my father and pulled him in for a hug. We all cried a mix of tearful sorrow and laughter. Our kingdom belonged to Arthur now, but he'd traded something more precious than gold. Arthur's hidden currency: love. I wiped my face, but the tears kept falling. "Father," I croaked, "I would have made that deal." I sobbed. "I'm sorry."

I meant it, but all hope of avoiding war with Camelot came to an abrupt halt the second the deal was made. Vires wouldn't go quietly. Sumin watched from his seat at the side of the throne. He smiled weakly, an endearing glow I hadn't seen in him in many years.

Young lifted his chin, looking me in the eyes. I wondered if I'd ever get used to seeing him like this. "We'll get her back," he said. The word *her* on his lips lit a fire in my chest, leaving me with more questions than answers.

"Appa," a small voice called, drawing the attention of all of us. Morgana trotted past the soldiers, wormed her way between my father, Young, and me, and wrapped her arms around my legs. I picked her up. "Appa," she said. "Why are you crying?"

I looked up at Young, his eyes a tempest—the odd ends of the human emotional spectrum mixing. Dangerous. Combustible but serene.

War with Camelot and its allied kingdoms was imminent, and Charlotte was locked away in Arthur's castle, but I felt something far worse was on the horizon—a war for something more precious than a kingdom. Life is cruelly balanced. Young was alive and, in his place, something had to die.

It's not until the sun is setting that I remember how brief a time we have. In a matter of moments, the glorious rays of light are swallowed by the horizon and we're all plunged into darkness once again.

AUTHOR'S NOTE

I hope you enjoyed Kingdom Soul. While it's still fresh in your mind I'd love to hear your thoughts.

You can review Kingdom Soul HERE.

Thank you!

Enjoy the final book, in the Kingdom Cold Trilogy.

One must lose.

KINGDOM UNTOLD

A KINGDOM COLD NOVEL

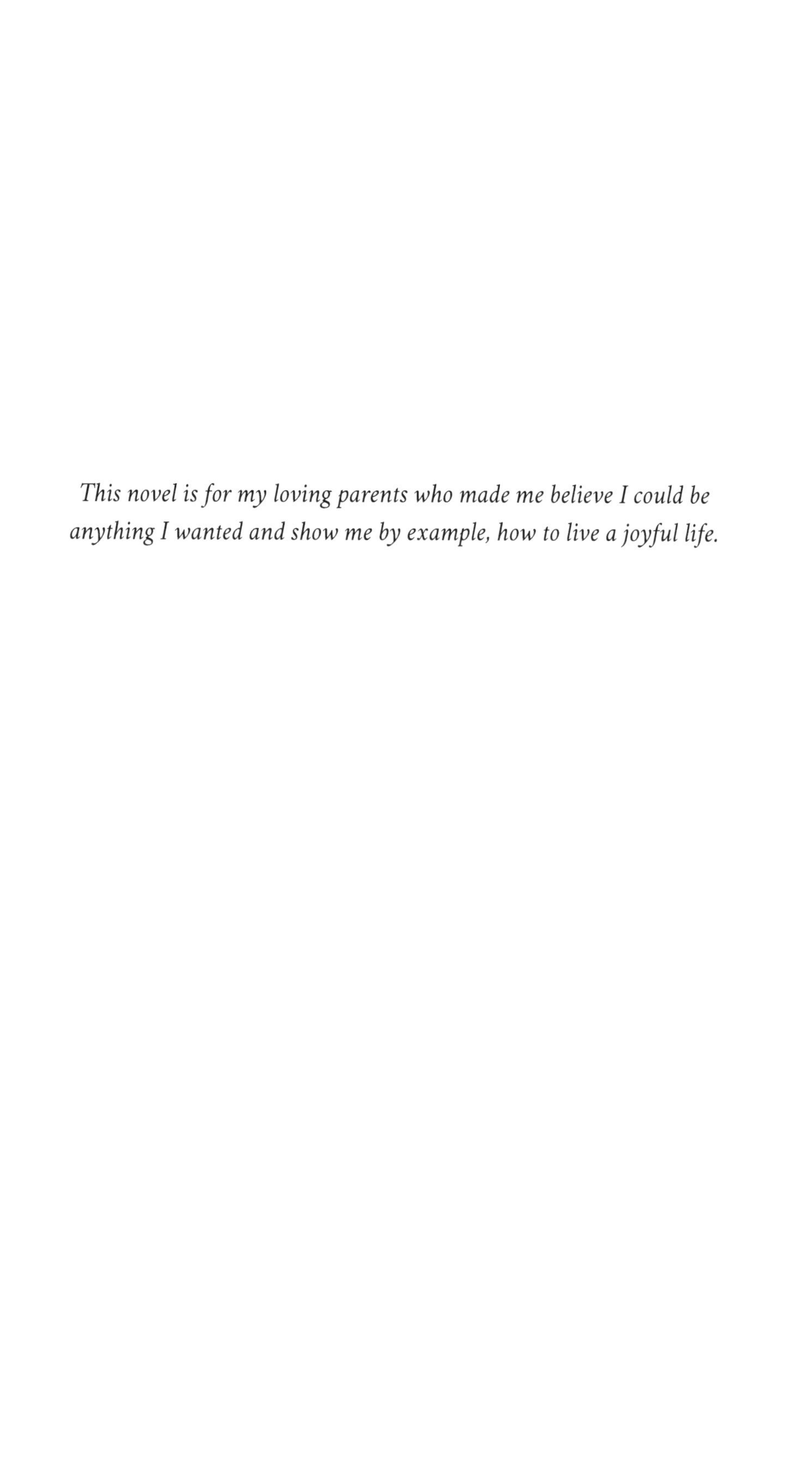

This novel is for my loving parents who made me believe I could be anything I wanted and show me by example, how to live a joyful life.

CONTENTS

1. Charlotte 413
2. Minseo 419
3. Charlotte 422
4. Young 426
5. Charlotte 429
6. Minseo 432
7. Charlotte 437
8. Young 442
9. Charlotte 447
10. Minseo 452
11. Arthur 458
12. Charlotte 463
13. Lancelot 467
14. Minseo 470
15. Charlotte 474
16. Young 479
17. Charlotte 482
18. Arthur 488
19. Minseo 492
20. Charlotte 496
21. Arthur 500
22. Young 505
23. Charlotte 509
24. Merlin 513
25. Charlotte 515
26. Minseo 520
27. Young 527
28. Charlotte 532
29. Lancelot 537
30. Charlotte 539
31. Merlin 542
32. Minseo 545

33. Charlotte 551
34. Young 556
35. Merlin 560
36. Charlotte 564
37. Minseo 571
38. Lancelot 575
39. Charlotte 579
40. Merlin 584
41. Young 590
42. Arthur 594
43. Charlotte 598
44. Merlin 603
45. Young 607
46. Arthur 611
47. Charlotte 614
48. Minseo 619
49. Arthur 623
50. Charlotte 628
51. Minseo 635
52. Young 640
53. Charlotte 644

Acknowledgments 647

1

CHARLOTTE

The only thing darker than that moonless night was my betrayal of Merlin.

Two months earlier, I stood beside the west stables, Merlin's gaze clawing at my face. "You're not focusing," she pushed, her seafoam braids tied in a bun on her head.

I stared at my empty palm with full knowledge that a flame would never light in it. It had been a month since I'd been imprisoned in Arthur's castle and there was no doubt Merlin had become suspicious that I wasn't the mage I'd implied. I'd been able to barter a place in the castle for Jay Hyun to keep watch over me, but I hadn't seen him since I entered Arthur's castle. I heard they sent him away just three days after we arrived. My fate was left to Merlin, yet her faith in me and hope that we were the same compelled me to put up a show of effort.

What I hadn't expected was how quickly we'd form a bond, one incomparable to any I'd experienced. Our ties were made from openness, which was a stark contrast to any other relationship I'd formed. I was always hiding something; from my family, for the sake of propriety, from Gabriel for the sake of secrecy, and from Minseo for the sake of the sadness that some topics brought. Merlin was open, soft, and uplifting. We talked about everything: our hopes and dreams, love, the meaning of life, topics that reminded me just how connected all of humanity was. We quickly considered each other kindred, which is why she seemed determined to bring any trace of magic out of me.

But we were bound more than by our conversations. The dragon we'd discovered, Garix, had grown to the size of a large dog, too big to remain hidden away in Merlin's quarters.

With some crafty magic by Merlin and Garix's obedience inexplicably tied to the metallic band on my wrist, we'd snuck him to an empty stable.

"Come on," Merlin said. "Feel your body." I kept my eyes shut with concentration, but instead of feeling magic swell inside me, the way Merlin described, I felt Garix's blood pulse through him. I felt the beat of his growing heart. He remained hidden in the stable a few yards away, yet in my subconscious, I could feel him.

As Garix's appetite grew, more quickly than Merlin and I could keep up with on our own, we had to enlist help from two of Arthur's servants but, with each new person in our circle, the higher the risk became that Arthur would find out.

"Focus," Merlin said, her frustration fully unmasked.

I channeled my emotions, pushing them to my hand. Picturing the flame as I'd seen on Merlin's palm. I willed the flame to light.

A screech sounded and I spun to see the stables burst into red hot flames.

"What happened?" I screamed, running toward the smoke.

"Garix!" Merlin cried, her long legs carrying her past me. With a wave of her hand, she lifted the water from the troughs, pushing the liquid mass together like a great airborne river. The water was clear enough to see through but distorted the burning stable behind it, thrashing about like a living being. I slowed to marvel as Merlin whipped the flames with the magical stream and doused the fire.

I shook the unusual sight from my head and sprinted into the stable. Garix's dewy scales sparkled with the droplets of water from Merlin's spell. He gleefully snapped at the ashes of the burned debris as they drifted past him. The tension in my body drained. He was unharmed. My heart warmed as I watched him play. He reminded me more and more of Morgana as he grew. How I missed her bright spirit. I missed her little hands and endless stories. I even missed the sound of her name, for it was the one truth from my past I dare not mention to Merlin.

The leftover warmth was promptly sucked out the open stable doors and windows.

Merlin exhaled with relief before the chaos of what happened finally sunk in.

I turned to Merlin. "Did he just breathe fire?"

She lifted a weary hand to her head. "Maybe he did it because of your spell?"

Reaching out for Garix, I ran my fingers along his cool scales. Relieved to find him unharmed, I surveyed the blackened walls of the barn. "But why hasn't he breathed fire before?"

Merlin's eyes shot open. "Shit, the smoke!"

"Quick, blow it away!" I shouted, but Merlin's glossy, unfocused gaze and slumped posture meant she was through. Water was the element that drained her most, which is why I'd only seen her wield it twice. I sprinted out of the smoky stable while Merlin stayed inside to combat as much of the smoke as possible.

Sure enough, when I scanned the side of the courtyard, nearest to the castle, three soldiers rode towards us. *No.* Not soldiers, knights.

I squinted at them, hoping Lancelot was among them. He had

kept our secret thus far, so perhaps Merlin and I could signal him to reroute the other two.

My hopes dissolved as the figures of Lamorak, Galahad, and Percival came clearly into view. *Not these three.*

Lamorak and Percival were twin brothers, freckle cheeked with red-orange hair. They were never more than three feet apart and I would have believed them attached at the hip if not for them riding toward me on separate horses. Their starkly different personalities were so unbalanced, and their actions intertwined, that they seemed to be two halves of one man. Percival would do nearly anything for a laugh and Lamorak could never be found without a sour pout. It resembled a party trick more than a way of being, and they were quick to draw attention. The same traits that made them bothersome to behold were what made them deadly on the battlefield, a fact that Galahad, a square-jawed man with raven black hair often spouted the moment anyone let on their irritation with the twins.

"You there!" Galahad called. Though we'd been introduced, I'd never heard him call me by name. Perhaps I wasn't important enough to remember.

His dark eyes bore into my soul with a twisted smile that could unnerve the steeliest of men. But those things were secondary. One look at Galahad, or rather his sword, sent a hellish surge of rage and sorrow through me that never failed to knock the wind from my lungs. The dragon-hilted sword I'd given to Young on the eve of our wedding now rested in the scabbard of a wicked man. The sword, the one that matched my own dagger, was a reminder of all that was taken from me, and Galahad flaunted it any chance he could, even threatened me with it on occasion, while his knowing eyes scoured my face for a reaction.

"Hello, Sir Galahad. No need to worry, it was just a little training accident. It's under control," I said.

His horse came to an abrupt halt in front of me, blocking out the sun and haloing his head in light. The redheaded twins followed closely behind. Lamorak's furrowed brow expressed his growing concern as his blue eyes drifted past me toward the shed while Percival picked at his nails with disinterest.

"Where's Merlin?" Lamorak asked, his voice far more musical than his unapproachable demeanor.

Garix, don't move. Stay quiet.

"Merlin!" I called with a gritted smile that was so forced my jaw twinged with pain.

Galahad's posture relaxed when Merlin stepped into view, and I understood that they'd been worried I hurt her.

Percival groaned, "Can we get lunch now?"

Lamorak snapped, "It's not yet noon, you oaf."

Galahad rolled his eyes but didn't engage. His gaze lingered on me. "How about a demonstration," his voice boomed.

No.

"I apologize, Sir Galahad. I'm all out of stamina for today."

He nodded toward Merlin. "She looks out of stamina."

"You look like you don't possess an ounce of magical ability."

I turned to Merlin. She'd been covering for me for the last month, but she was in no state to fool them today. Galahad had suspicions about me from the very start. I turned back to him. "I'm sorry, sir."

His face darkened. "Are you refusing?" He dismounted his horse, stepping closer to me. "You know, Arthur has been asking for a volunteer among his knights to pay a little visit to Vires..."

My stomach tightened.

"Collect taxes, punish traitors." He smiled. "That sort of thing. I've been cooped up in Bullhorn too long anyway."

I seethed at the implication. My heart racing, my blood boiling as it coursed through my body.

"Isn't your husband there?"

"Enough," Lamorak interjected. Galahad looked as bewildered by the interruption as I felt. Lamorak's gaze met Galahad's, the hard line across Lamorak's forehead a cipher Galahad quickly decoded.

He sighed, the tension in his shoulders relaxing, and the moment passed like the ashes of the stable in the wind.

But I didn't appreciate the threat on Minseo's life. I shook and felt a twinge of fear at the dark thoughts that crept in.

Without warning, Garix let out a bone-rattling cry, pulling everyone's attention. He burst from the stable in a crash of unbalanced flight, thrown off by the wild bouts of fire that poured out his widespread jaw.

Galahad drew his sword, "A dragon." He gaped. "Percival, go alert the king. We found it."

2

MINSEO

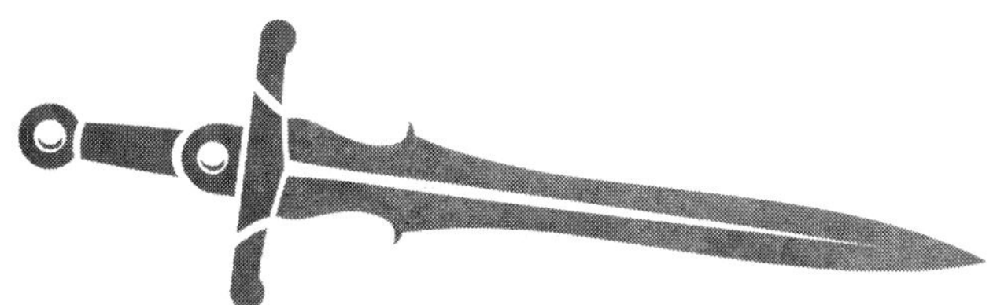

I stalked through the moonlit night, Vires cloaked in a silver glow that felt ghostly and unsettling. I made my way to my little brother's quarters with the single purpose of checking on him. The tiled roofs shone, casting dark shadows along the walls beneath them. I was unnerved by how often I made this journey in the middle of the night. I'd wait outside his room, ear pressed to his door, straining to hear the sound of him tossing in his sleep or even just a snore, anything to calm the throng of my nervous heart.

While Young had returned unharmed, it didn't stop the nightmares from crippling my sleep. It didn't quell the worry that I'd wake up, once again, in a world without him.

"Minseo," a soft voice whispered in the breeze. I turned to see my father, the King of Vires, his eyes tired and heavily lined with age. His gaze was knowing and tranquil. He carried a lantern, the flame flickering with life inside, vanquishing the silver moonlight with a fierce orange glow that lit his face.

"Father, I was just going for a walk," I said. "I didn't mean to wake you."

He nodded, his gaze flickering toward Young's quarters. "You are a good brother," he said.

"Sometimes what the mind knows to be true and what the heart fears cannot align."

I nodded, feeling transparent.

"But fear is not the emotion through which you should live."

"Yes, father," I said, but as I reached inside myself for a weapon stronger than fear, I found none. I bowed and turned back toward my room.

My father sighed behind me. "Just be quick about it," he said. "I need you well rested. We need to discuss something important in the morning."

I bowed. "Yes, father."

I heard the shuffle of my father's footsteps behind me, moving toward his bedroom as I headed for Young's room. I evened my breathing as I neared it but stopped as I noticed a flicker of light inside the hanji walls.

I moved to the door and steadied my nerves before I whispered, "Young?"

"Minseo? Come in," he said. My posture slacked with relief as I slid his door open to find him sitting at his desk with a quill in his hand. "Couldn't sleep?" he asked.

I took a seat in front of him, my curiosity drawn to the blank parchment in front of him. "Yeah, you either?"

He nodded. I drank in his features, still jarred by the five-year difference. He was certainly an adult now. His dark eyes were familiar and unknown to me. His jawline was sharp, his cheekbones angular, and the last wisps of boyhood buried by the hard lines of his mouth.

I resisted the urge to reach out and touch his cheek, still in constant need of reassurance. My brain tolled again and again that he was here. That he wasn't dead. But my heart remained broken by his loss.

He sucked in a breath, jolting me awake to the fact that the silence that hung in the room was filled with uneasiness and tension. This level of discomfort was new. It had sprung to life with his return, but our inability to communicate was a lifelong trait of brotherhood. Still, it felt worse somehow. Maybe it was because there were so many new things we dared not discuss. Maybe we still needed time to fit back into each other's lives. But my darkest thoughts warned that it was possible he harbored feelings of hatred for me. After all, I'd pursued Charlotte; I'd fallen in love with her, I convinced her to fall in love with me, and I'd taken on the role of Morgana's father. And all of this was revealed to him with one small word: "Appa."

Although it was weeks ago, it was a cloud that hung over our interactions. If I had the nerve, I'd tell him how sorry I was. I'd tell him I'd never come between him and Charlotte again. I'd tell him I planned to help him rescue Charlotte and step aside to allow them the life together they deserved. I wanted to tell him that she never would've given in to me if we weren't certain he was dead. But I dreaded his response. I feared I'd lose him again and, like my father implied, fear was my unwavering companion.

I found my voice. "What are you writing?" I asked.

He looked down at the blank parchment. "I'm not sure."

Again, the thick veil of uneasiness cloaked the room and my stomach tightened at the memory of how I used to feel beside my brother. I alone was to blame.

3

CHARLOTTE

I knelt before King Arthur, the sharp of Galahad's blade or, rather, Young's blade, pressing menacingly between two of the bones in my spine. I kept my eyes fixed on the stony marble floor. Its white surface was drenched in deep purples and reds as the light poured through a narrow stained glass window above the throne room, casting a multicolored pattern of light across the floor that looked like a narrow carpet leading to the throne. The room was bizarrely shaped, molded to fit the shape of the mountain it was erected inside. The room steeped, the ceiling highest just above Arthur's golden throne.

Arthur's throne was more than gold, encrusted with red and orange jewels and lined with purple silks and satin cushions. Such a throne could blend comfortably into the castle of Olympus, but here, it swallowed the tiny stature of the boy with the golden crown, who looked almost like a child when he sat atop it. His feet dangled off the edge, and though he was finally of age, he was still was unable to discard the vale of youth that shrouded him.

Merlin stood tall beside me, unwilling to leave me to my fate. I was a prisoner and her a highly regarded member of Arthur's army, yet she remained at my side, her power-filled body between Arthur's and my own.

"So you're to blame for the missing dragon egg," Arthur said, his voice inappropriately playful. "You wouldn't believe me if I told you what such an object cost."

"Please, Your Majesty," Merlin interrupted, her voice shaking with fear. It dawned on me, as I felt her looming over me, that her fear was not for her life but for mine.

"As luck would have it," Arthur said, "I planned to give the egg to you and your apprentice to see if you could use your magic to hatch it."

Merlin bowed, tossing her mint-green braids into a wave before us. "So, there is no harm done."

I steeled my nerves and risked a glance up at the young king. There were five or six stone steps that led to Arthur's throne, which sat proudly atop a marble slab. The base of the slab was where Arthur's knights usually stood. But today there was only Percival, Lamorak, and Gawain, a middle-aged man I'd never heard utter a single syllable. With Galahad behind me, the three knights and Arthur hardly seemed a formidable force. But I knew better than to underestimate an enemy based on physical appearance alone.

There were two aspects of Arthur that did feel kingly and dangerous: the cruelty of his icy gaze and the malevolence in his crooked smile. As my gaze lifted to his face, he wore such an expression that made my stomach tighten. I returned my attention to the floor in front of me.

"Perhaps," Arthur said, his voice carrying around the room like he was a large man, "I guess it all depends on where your loyalties lie."

Merlin said, "Of course with you, Your Majesty."

"And that of your apprentice?" Arthur said. I felt the heat of his gaze on my forehead but dare not look back up.

"Rise," he said.

I stood, determined to keep my gaze from Arthur. His frosty blue eyes reminded me of the man who murdered my father. My knees were sore from kneeling and I felt grateful to put some distance between myself and Galahad's sword.

"Come," he said.

I turned to Merlin, her gaze a torrent of worry, her posture still sagged with exhaustion. If things took a turn for the worse, there wouldn't be much she could do.

I started up the stairs and felt Arthur rise from his throne as I neared the top. Even with his crown, I was an inch or two taller. He drew my gaze to his with the silent whisper of his will and looked into my eyes like he was searching for something in them.

"Where do your loyalties lie?" he said, but this time, his voice was so faint it didn't carry enough to echo.

My mind flashed to Minseo as he played with Morgana. It had been four weeks since Lancelot brought me here. It felt like a lifetime ago, yet the wound was still fresh. I relished in the pain, for the memory of them hadn't yet lost its bite, like the memories of my childhood now had. My heart ached, a motivating pain that reminded me not to lose hope, that soon I'd find a way to escape captivity and join them in Vires. "With my family," I said. His eyes flickered as he nodded then chewed on his bottom lip like my response had irritated him.

"Your Majesty," Merlin intervened. "Her abilities are not as strong as I predicted. I vow to you that I will burn her alive should she seek to betray you."

Arthur's gaze dropped to where Merlin stood, but he didn't move to look around me. Instead, he stared at my collarbone as if he could see through me to her. "If not gifted with magical blood, what use is she to us?"

I felt the prickle of sweat on the back of my neck, fearful of what Merlin might reveal. We'd tried in vain to remove the metallic bracelet from my wrist, especially when it first appeared, but the bracelet and the obedience of Garix were tied to me alone. If Arthur knew the details of that, he wouldn't hesitate to lop off my arm for the chance to obtain such a gift. At my core, I trusted Merlin. Not only for the kind and compassionate person I'd come to know, but as a thoughtful woman who considered her actions like a chess master mid-game. She was the only guardian of my secret. My sister, not in blood but in bond.

"She's proven to be a gifted dragon trainer," Merlin said. "We can use her to get Garix ready for battle."

Arthur stepped to the side, the blue slits of his eyes glaring down at her with distrust. "Garix," he scoffed.

"Your enemies will cower before you," Merlin said, feeding his need for significance. Her voice was loud enough to reverberate off every misshapen corner of the throne room.

Arthur's eyes glossed over as if he watched the possibilities play out in his mind's eye before he took a seat back on his throne. "Galahad," he said, finally. "From now on you will watch over the dragon's training and report to me."

Galahad sheathed his sword. "Yes, Your Majesty," he said, his armor gleaming with the blood-red light of the stained glass.

"And Galahad," Arthur said, "that dragon egg was supposed to be delivered to this castle weeks ago, meaning it's been gone without your notice all this time."

Galahad's usually proud smile faded, his face going stark white.

Arthur continued, "Don't disappoint me again."

4

YOUNG

The sun woke me, an uplifting reminder I was no longer a prisoner at Bullhorn. But as quickly as my revery found me, it was crushed beneath the sadness and guilt of knowing Charlotte had taken my place.

One moment I knelt in the atrium at Castle Cadere, certain I was breathing my last breaths, and the next I was being carried away in chains and carted off to Bullhorn. Those first few weeks in the dark, I prayed for the death I was promised, but it never came.

"Brother," Minseo called from outside my room. I sat up, pushing my blanket off. I sighed. Even when we were small, Minseo was never this attentive. "Coming," I called, my voice cracking with disuse. It was as if I were injured, or as if Minseo worried I'd be captured again. During my captivity, I'd imagined he was okay, living in Vires like he always wanted, so this new reality wasn't difficult for me to adjust to. I could sympathize with how challenging the last five years must've been for him, believing I was dead. But, if I was honest, in the back of my mind I couldn't shake the anger I felt.

I slid open my door and headed into the morning air, which was already hot though the sun had just risen.

"How are you this morning?" Minseo said. His hair was barely above his ears and a little more tousled than I remembered. His eyes were circled with the darkness of insomnia, and he wore a stubbly mustache and goatee that looked like a shorter version of Father's.

"I'm fine," I said. "You?"

He ignored my question. "Did I wake you?"

I shook my head and clenched my jaw to restrain a frustrated sigh. *My sentimental brother.* I'd played it over in my head a thousand times. It was the perfect combination of events that led to this stomach-churning outcome.

It was as if Minseo could sense my distaste, my rage. It muffled every interaction as if he could mend it with these exhausting pleasantries. Deep down, I knew there was no one to blame but Arthur.

"Are you alright?" Minseo said.

"Yes," I said as I grabbed my scabbard and sheathed my sword, but my tone was biting, and he wasn't going to let it go.

He sighed. "Look, if this is about Charlotte—"

"It's not," I said quickly.

His face drained of color.

I turned away and headed for the lake that surrounded the throne room. That wasn't a conversation I was ready to have or even a situation I wanted to unpack.

Minseo grabbed my arm. "Wait. Please," he said, his voice heavy with regret. "Tell me then."

"Tell you what?" I said, slapping his hand away.

"What's wrong? I want to fix it." He ran a hand through his hair. "I can't keep tiptoeing around you."

I huffed. "Then stop." I turned away, unable to stomach the hurt look in his eyes. Minseo's weight came crashing down on my shoulders, sending us toppling onto the gravel path. My elbow scraped against the tiny stones and rang out with pain.

"No," Minseo said, rolling off my back. "I won't stop. We're brothers."

Before I gave my body permission, my fist collided with his jaw. Minseo cradled his chin with his right hand, his left still supporting the rest of his weight along with his knees, but the pain in his eyes had already vanished and, in its place, the corners of his lips peaked up with relief. I knelt beside him. "How could you let this happen?"

He swung suddenly. I threw my weight back to dodge. We scrambled to our feet. "I'm sorry," he said. He charged me, gripping my head under one arm. I punched at his stomach but he didn't release his grip.

I heaved breathlessly. "You— You let our father sell our kingdom to Camelot!" I shouted. "One life in exchange for the whole kingdom," I yelled through gritted teeth.

Minseo eased his grip in surprise. "Is that what this is about?"

I swept his legs and he landed with a crash face up on the gravel and a wide grin on his face. I hesitated, lost in the sudden memory of our relationship as boys. How I used to let him talk me into all sorts of mischief with no reward but that same smile.

I shook the memory and kicked him in the ribs. He doubled over, blocking his ribs with his arms. "It's nice to have you back," he said, spitting blood from his cut lip.

But that was exactly my point. How could I enjoy this return when so many lives would suffer because of it. I kicked him one final time and turned away before his smile softened me. "So…" he choked, "this is a *little* about Charlotte then."

I shook my head as I walked toward the throne room, calling back over my shoulder, "No, I'll need my sword for that one."

5

CHARLOTTE

Galahad was a pill, but it didn't take long to show him I did have the ability to train Garix. I occasionally said something with my mouth and ordered Garix to do something else in my heart, to avert the suspicion I wasn't so much training Garix but controlling him. It was much easier to explore his potential when we weren't in hiding and, after a few short weeks of training, I noticed a new presence inside myself.

It started at the end of a long training day. Garix soared through the rays of a pink sunset, snapping at the clouds in the distance like puffs of candy on the wind. Merlin and I watched like proud parents, astonished by how quickly Garix had grown. Gone were the days of the lizard-like baby or the puppy-sized teen he once was. He was now the size of a full-grown bear, with an appetite to match. With his wings outstretched, he could block out the sun and plunge us into darkness with his menacing shadow.

Merlin, who was once my mentor, was now forced to wield water just to keep the fire damage at bay. Still, many of the tactics she shared to control her elemental magic applied to successfully commanding Garix, and I wondered if I could use those same nuggets of knowledge to help Morgana control her elemental magic when she was older.

Suddenly, at the pit of my stomach came something new. An exhaustion that threatened to knock me off my feet. I put my hand to my head and focused on the new sensation which somehow reminded me of the color yellow.

I felt Merlin's cold hands grip my arm. "Are you alright? Charlotte, what's wrong?"

I shook my head. "I'm exhausted." She looked at me quizzically. We'd been standing around watching Garix all day; It was hardly strenuous. Especially compared to others we'd had.

Her eyebrows pinched together with concern. "Physically or mentally?"

"It's—" I almost stopped myself from blurting the silliness that I felt, but I trusted Merlin to understand. "It's my wings," I said.

She blinked twice, then her eyes widened with understanding the same moment it clicked with me. Our gaze shot to the sky and I willed Garix to return quickly and rest. Relief swept over me as he flew into view. He lowered down to us clumsily, landing too hard and shaking us off balance. The garden blackened under a haze of dust, and Merlin and I squealed with excitement from the revelation of our new ability.

Galahad cleared his throat and we turned to him, his dark empty eyes dripping with suspicion. "We, uh..." Merlin stammered, "we thought we lost him for a minute."

I walked over to Garix, running my fingers along the scales on his face and willing him to know how proud I was of him. I let him know I'd felt his emotion and that I would be waiting for him to share another. Without a moment's hesitation, I felt it in the pit of my stomach. Like a link of empathy had been opened between us. It hit in the same low point in my stomach. Barely distinguishable from my own emotions, I understood. While the first emotion hit and felt oddly like the color yellow, this one was red. Garix was hungry.

An hour later, Garix shredded a goat between his teeth, blood spurting out as the poor creature's corpse was tossed about between bites. It had been a horrifying scene the first time I witnessed it, even if it had only been with a mouse, but his meals had become more gruesome as he grew and fed on larger prey. I got into the habit of zoning out and picturing something more palatable, usually Garix soaring among the clouds. I had to be careful not to feel an order to him as I did so, a mistake I made often at the start of training. It was during one such thought when the idea came to me. Garix was not the small, helpless creature that hatched from the egg but a powerful being that grew with each day. Was it possible for Garix to carry me out of here? *No.* Was it possible for him to carry me to Vires?

6

MINSEO

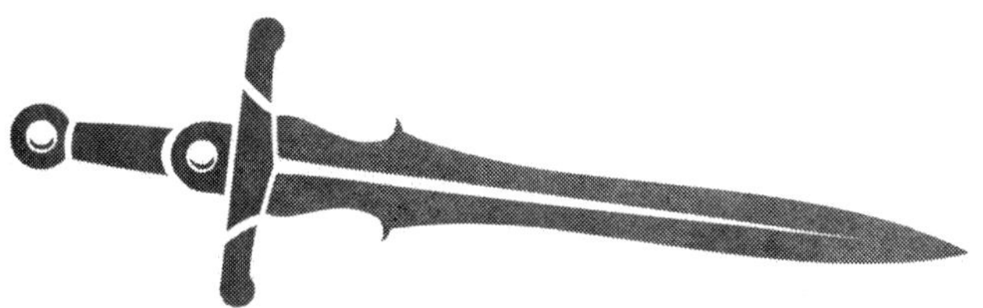

Of course Young was angry about the alliance with Vires. We were only a few months away from having to pay our first taxes to his knights. Only Arthur could be happy about such an arrangement, one that would bankrupt our kingdom in a few short years. I imagined that all the weight between Young and me came from whatever conclusions he'd drawn that night in the throne room when Morgana called me "Appa." Maybe some of it was, but if I knew my brother, remembered who he truly was and not how I'd idealized him all these years, duty was a much bigger influence on him than it ever was on me. My jaw still throbbed from where he'd struck me. Finally, he'd addressed some of his feelings, though I had to instigate it with a fight. I pushed my jaw from side to side, appraising the damage. He certainly wasn't the runt he was when I lost him.

His willingness to fight somehow meant we were still brothers. I lay back on the gravel beside the palace lake, relief washing over me like a wave on the shore. The morning sun felt warm on my face and I exhaled a breath I felt I'd been holding since Young returned. Exhaustion settled in and, just when I thought I might fall asleep, I heard a voice that startled me.

"Is he dead?" Morgana asked, her cold hands already poking at my face.

"Hi, honey," I said, sitting up.

Gabriel stood over me with a wary smile. "No, Morg, it looks like Minseo had too much to drink last night."

I stood, lifting Morgana and resting her on my hip. "Where's Junho?" I asked.

Gabriel's gaze slipped to the left. "How should I know?"

"Oh. Sorry. You're just usually together," I said, putting Morgana down and taking her by the hand.

"We're just friends," Gabe said. He leaned closer. "Why, did he say anything?"

I smirked and he winced in response. "I have a council meeting," I said, taking pity on him. "Can I swing by after to play with my little princess?"

"Sure," Gabriel said. "We were thinking of spending the day at the river."

"Perfect. I'll meet up with you both later." I spun Morgana and knelt in front of her.

"I'll see you soon."

"I'll miss you," she said, scrunching her face.

"Oh yeah? How much?"

She stretched her arms out to the side, nearly throwing herself off balance.

"Well, I'll miss you this much." I mimicked her, my arms reaching far beyond hers. She beamed and I tousled her curls before standing. I headed toward the throne room but turned to wave to Morgana one last time.

"Minseo," Gabe said.

The way he slumped alarmed me.

"Uh... never mind," he said.

"No, no. What is it?"

His gaze lifted to my face. "Maybe you can convince your brother to come this time. Y-you know, for Morgana."

I felt the knife slide painfully from the wound. "Oh, sure, of course."

I walked across the lake on the stone bridge, my thoughts still lingering on what Gabriel said. I knew Morgana wasn't my daughter, and the fact that I wasn't going to be "Appa" for her anymore stung. I also couldn't ignore that Young hadn't shown much interest in that role.

I knew he had a thousand things to adjust to, and our little scuffle revealed he carried guilt for the poor political situation in Vires. A smile pinched at my sore jaw as the pain, for the first time, made me feel that Young was truly home. I walked into the throne room, a long table routinely laid out in the area to the right of the throne. Twenty or so chairs were set up around it, but aside from Young and me, there were only two members who had come this early: Hanbit, the mousy advisor who I hadn't spoken to since we returned to Vires after losing Charlotte, and the red-cheeked man who wore an orange sash. Young sat at the head of the table, in Sumin's seat.

With so much happening with Camelot, Sumin's condition never seemed to be a topic of discussion. It was difficult to invite the possibility that I could lose another brother. It was beginning to be a concern of the council as well, just like his infertility had been, only this time no one spoke about it overtly but in whispers or taverns.

My relationship with Sumin was complicated at best, enough to rival that of Young and me. I had been consciously avoiding going to see him and I gave myself a multitude of excuses. I didn't want to bother him, I didn't like seeing him that way, but if I was honest with myself, I was terrified of what he might say.

"Minseo," my father said. His voice behind me startled me. "Take your seat."

I sat down beside him. It was the same place I'd been sitting when I had a breakdown. It was the same place I begged the council to go to war with Camelot, time and time again. I was prepared to do the same. It was no longer out of revenge for my brother but for my… I stopped, mentally stumbling over the slip... but for Charlotte.

I couldn't see Young from where we sat on either side of my father, but I didn't need to see him to know the serene look that practically lived on his stone-like face. It reminded me of my father. Part of me envied Young's self-control. He certainly garnered the respect of the council members, where I was always disregarded as a hot-blooded and unreliable mess. At times like this, I wondered if he cared for Charlotte at all. If so, how did he manage to stay so calm at these meetings? I wasn't sure what I wanted, maybe for him to scream and cry for her so I knew I wasn't letting her go for nothing.

We needed to save her, and every day without her was a terrible loss. However calm Young seemed, I was counting on his influence to finally convince Vires to consent to war.

Later that evening, I sat with Junho at our favorite tavern, a bottle of makkoli between us.

Junho raised a cup of the milky liquid and bumped it with mine. He sighed, "So, that's it then. You're going to let him be with her?"

I swallowed a mouthful. "She's his wife."

Junho poured us both another cup of rice wine. "Is it because he kicked your ass?"

"I got in a few shots," I said.

"I'll pretend I believe you."

I sat back in my chair. "The guy has done nothing but workout for the last five years."

"And you've done nothing but drink." He raised his glass. "Geonbae."

I grinned, toasting with him. "What about you? How's Gabriel?"

"Good."

I put my elbows on the table. "That's it?"

He pressed his lips together. "I'm giving him time to settle in."

"You mean you're too scared to make a move."

"We'll see who's scared to make a move once you guys rescue Charlotte. I can't wait to watch this play out."

"Pick a team," I spat.

"Yours, obviously. I'm just saying… It's complicated."

7

CHARLOTTE

I got into the routine of waking up early, before sunrise. For the first few days, Galahad begrudgingly followed, keeping watch on my new and inconspicuous routine for grooming Garix. As expected, after a few days, he stopped supervising. The courtyard where we trained was walled in by steep mountain faces on two sides and the man-made fortresses that made up the castle on the others. Of course, it could be easily escaped by Garix, but there was little anyone could do to convince a dragon to stay if he wanted to leave, except me. I wasn't sure why no one brought up the possibility of dragon riding. Perhaps because Garix was such an anomaly already. But since the thought burrowed into my brain, I couldn't think of anything else. Morgana needed me to come home.

I knew I wouldn't get many chances at this. If someone spotted me on Garix, they'd know what I was planning. I couldn't reasonably make a break for it without testing it.

I didn't know if I'd be able to hold on or how far Garix could carry me without tiring. Vires was a long way. A journey that took weeks to complete, with a brutal bit of it at sea. I didn't have any idea how long that might take by air.

But, before sunrise, Garix and I had the skies to ourselves. Merlin slept late and it was too dark for anyone in the castle to spot me, the perfect time for some short practice sessions. They might have been able to spot the dark shadow of Garix in the sky but not the silhouette of a rider on his back. Not even if they were looking for me.

I ran my fingers along the scales on Garix's pointed snout, the hot rush of his breath steadily pushing through his curved nostrils. "Ready to try this, Gar?"

A wet snout nuzzled into my palm. It was now or never. I scanned the darkened courtyard, but as expected, we were alone. I put my palms on the top of Garix, ready to pull myself up when the reality and danger of what I was about to attempt finally set in. I could feel his warm and steady pulse beneath my fingers. I felt the raw power of his muscles flex. He was immense. No longer the wild hatchling I must've still considered him internally.

A flush of emotion from Garix cut through my fear—an emotion that felt a lot like the color orange. I steadied myself with a memory, one of Morgana learning to walk. How she'd stumbled and fell countless times and fearlessly rose to try again. How I envied the bravery of children. With all my strength, I leapt up and pulled myself clumsily onto Garix's back. I scrambled to find a spot where it felt natural to sit, but sitting on a dragon was anything but natural. I shimmied up to a relatively flat area, where his neck met his shoulders, and wrapped my arms around him. With every breath and twitch, I felt I'd be tossed from my place. No grip felt tight enough to keep me saddled to the smooth creature.

The sensation reminded me of my first few horseback lessons. The way my body naturally fought each movement. How fragile I felt atop the giant.

Walk slowly, I thought to Garix. I held my breath as he stepped forward. His right shoulder jutted up, tossing me toward the left, my body tossing back to the right with his next step. I tightened my grip, my arms already sore.

I gritted my teeth and thought, *Fly*. The moment Garix's wings spread, I regretted my decision. Between each flap of his wings, my stomach dropped. Just a few yards off the ground, I felt the prickle of tears in my eyes. I wasn't sure if it was from fear, exhilaration, or just wind. One jerked movement from being tossed off, I decided to tell Garix to land.

When we were safely on the ground, I slid off, my legs like noodles beneath me. I collapsed onto the ground and looked up to the sky. My heart raced. "It's a start." I needed a better way to hold on, that was for sure.

Several hours passed as I lay weakly in the grass, considering the options. Rope maybe, or if I can get some long fabric and sew the ends together I could put it around Garix's neck without hurting him, and encircle myself with the other end, making an eight of sorts.

"There you are," Merlin said, blocking the sun as she leaned over me. "What happened?" she asked, tossing her mint green braids out of her face. "Did you wake up early only to sleep out here?"

I smiled and sat up, rubbing the sleep from my eyes. My body still felt the effects from my early morning adventure, but I'd recovered a little. As I scanned the courtyard to get my bearings, I was reminded that I wasn't in my garden on the edge of Wellwood like I had dreamed but in King Arthur's courtyard. I sighed. Even the walled-in courtyard felt like a prison. "Merlin, what's the deal with Arthur?" I asked.

She sat beside me. "What do you mean?"

"Why does he need so much land? I mean, what's his ultimate goal?"

She sighed. "It's always about ego with men like him."

I looked at her face, her dark ember skin a sudden reminder of my father. "Why do you serve him? You could..." I lowered my voice and eyed the empty courtyard suspiciously. "You could take the throne easily."

She smiled so brightly that my heart warmed. "Only fools want the throne," she said. I couldn't help but laugh. She was right. How long had I loathed my royal upbringing only to be proven right? During my reign as queen, I'd lost more important people than at any other time. I knew I liked Merlin, I trusted her judgment. She'd learned that valuable lesson without ruling a kingdom of her own. Perhaps her magical abilities taught her the same about the burden of power.

Her gaze softened as if she could read my thoughts. She tilted her head like an older sister about to impart advice. "Actually, Arthur was one of the first people to show me kindness. He has his flaws, but who I am, and how I see myself, was much different before I met him. He's more than a king, he's a—" Her gaze drifted beyond me, so I turned to follow it.

Sir Lancelot stepped into the sun, his armor gleaming in the light. His hair had grown a bit since I'd last seen him, dark brown and almost to his shoulders. His normally hazel eyes were bright green beside the green stretch of the courtyard.

Merlin turned away, the certainty and power of her movements dulled as if the sun that beamed from within her had been shrouded in storm clouds and torrential rain. It always happened when he was close by, or even when she thought of him. It didn't take long to spot the tells. Part of me liked seeing her this way, so human, but I couldn't help but feel the sting of spite for the man who stole the light from her.

8

YOUNG

She's just a girl, I mulled. A harmless little girl. But every time I saw her, I felt overcome with dread. Morgana was beautiful, and her little curls made my stomach ache with memories of Charlotte, yet my heart warmed when I saw just how alike we looked. She'd gotten so many of my traits: eyes, cheeks, lips. There was no mistaking she was my child. But we were strangers, different in every other way. What could I possibly talk about with a five-year-old?

"You ready?" Minseo said, sensing my hesitation.

"Of course," I lied. Minseo had convinced me to meet up with Gabriel and Morgana by the river, but I was doubting my choice. Who *was* Gabriel? How had he come to be Morgana's caregiver? These were questions I had the night they all arrived in Vires but I couldn't bring myself to ask. For five years I longed to know the truth of how everyone fared and, now that I could, I didn't have the nerve. If Minseo, chatty as he was, didn't feel compelled to tell me, chances were I didn't want to know, but my mind filled in the gaps with horrors that it conjured.

As Minseo and I walked through the forest, I wondered why he hadn't chosen a closer river. But I realized when we arrived that our destination was more of a stream. It was slow moving and shallow and I concluded it was specifically chosen for its child-safe calm. The sides of it were rocky with scattered ferns and long fronds scattered between. A few yards back from the river on each side was an overgrowth of grass and a line of trees that made me think the river had once been much bigger.

It was late afternoon. My heart sank as we neared the bank of the river and Morgana spotted us. Waist deep in water, her smile beamed as she scrambled toward the shore, her gaze locked on MInseo. "Minnnowwwwww!" she screeched.

It was a beautiful reunion, the kind that would make a bystander smile. Except I was the bystander, and watching that beautiful little girl brim with joy over my brother reminded me a lot of how Charlotte looked at him when they'd first met.

I wondered if Charlotte's heart still belonged to me, but as I watched Minseo's bond with Morgana, the less likely it seemed.

Morgana reached the edge of the river, her dark hair slicked to her head. She leapt into Minseo's arms, splashing water all over us and drenching Minseo in one squirming hug. Minseo lifted her and put her on his hip, turning to me.

"Hi, Appa," Morgana said to me, her dark eyelashes sprinkled with water droplets. I knew the word was for me, but it seemed more appropriate for the man whose arms she was in. "Hello," I said.

What do I say? What do kids even talk about? Maybe her favorite color? A sudden gust of wind made her teeth chatter, her lips already tinted with a touch of purple. My gaze drifted to the river where Gabriel stood. He had no shirt, despite the water coming just past his knees. His skin was dark and his body wide and muscular. He waved a gesture that felt inexplicably foreign.

"Good afternoon," he called.

Minseo replied, "Beautiful weather."

Gabriel replied by throwing his arms out and falling back into the water. Minseo turned back to Morgana. "Go jump in before you get too cold."

"Are you coming too?" she asked.

Minseo eyed me. Even as a kid, I never wanted in while Minseo would jump into any bit of water he could find. A preview of today flashed in front of my eyes—Minseo playing with Morgana while I sat on the sidelines. But I knew I'd underestimated my brother, and his intentions, when he spoke again. "We'll watch you from here."

We took a seat on the river's rocky edge.

Morgana pouted.

"Can you go underwater?" Minseo asked.

Morgana's eyes lit and she instantly forgot her sadness. She pinched her nose and puffed her cheeks before plunging below the surface.

A second later she emerged, a prideful grin plastered to her face.

"Wow, that was great!" Minseo said.

"Watch this," Morgana said, floating on her back.

Gabriel took a seat beside us, and I could feel the cold of the river radiating from his skin.

He scanned the ground until he spotted a flat stone. He picked it up, turned it over in his palm, wound up, and skipped it downriver. It skipped several times. As if it were beyond our control, Minseo and I searched for flat rocks of our own.

I found one first and stood, facing downriver. I wound up and threw it, noting that it skipped farther than Gabriel's.

Minseo's shortly followed, but it didn't catch right on the water and sunk after the first bounce. The three of us erupted into laughter as we scrambled for more stones.

"Seven!" Gabriel yelled as I wound up for my fourth throw.

Minseo said, "My last one was at least eight."

The side of the riverbank grew barren of flat rocks and our competition started to lose steam. "Wow," I said, chucking my last rock. "She's lucky, isn't she?" I said, my gaze drifting to Morgana who searched the river shore for a rock.

Gabriel sat. "She certainly is."

A flaming stone shot by, spewing steam from it as it skipped along the river, several yards past where our farthest throws sunk. My gaze snapped to its origin, to Morgana. My eyes widened.

"Are you okay?" Minseo said, already ankle deep in water.

"What was that?" I yelled.

Morgana stared at her hand before her eyes flitted up to Minseo. "It was an accident," she said.

He dunked her hand in the water before looking at it closely. "It's okay, princess," he said. "As long as you're not hurt."

Minseo's gaze moved to Gabriel and Gabriel nodded slightly. *Ah.* They knew exactly what that was.

Unsure if this was something I could ask about in front of Morgana, I walked over to Gabriel, keeping my voice low. "What *was* that?"

He eyed Minseo and Morgana to make sure they were out of earshot. "She has some kind of fire ability," he whispered. "We've had a few incidents."

"What do you mean 'fire ability'?"

"She can…" his brow furrowed as he searched for the right words, "make fire."

"Out of what?" I said, looking around. "Nothing?"

He nodded. My skin prickled at the insinuation. My mind raced with the improbability of it. It was undoubtedly impossible, but I'd just witnessed it. His words were more of a confirmation of the conclusion I had already formed. My eyes drifted to Morgana, her gaze searching me for signs of concern. I stuck out my tongue to ease her and felt a flutter of delight when she returned it across the way.

"So," I whispered to Gabriel, "it's magic?"

9

CHARLOTTE

I was a prisoner. Captive, ripped away from Minseo and Morgana. I played these truths in my head again and again but couldn't stop the guilt from clawing at my stomach. It had been almost a month since my first flight on the back of Garix. He was getting stronger and my makeshift saddle felt adequate enough. I'd become accustomed to the feeling of flying, even longed for the sweet weightlessness and freedom that waited for me in the damp clouds. We had flown as far as I dared before returning, just before the silver glow of dawn broke the horizon. We'd made it to the edge of Bullhorn, a far cry from Vires, but there was only so much training we could do before the risk of getting caught grew too great. If I was going to escape, it was now or never.

Only I couldn't. Merlin was an unexpected obstacle. After all we'd been through, after the bond we'd forged and how voraciously she'd protected me, how could I leave her without an explanation?

I ached when I imagined the hurt she'd feel as she'd unknowingly walk to the courtyard to find me and Garix gone to the wind. My eyes pricked as my mind's eye watched her standing alone wondering why I hadn't trusted her enough to tell her.

But, worse than that, if I left she surely would be punished for it. There was the possibility that, due to our close bond, Arthur might suspect she helped me—an act of treason that could result in her death.

That thought compelled my body forward. I sat up, blinking through the darkness of the early morning. I had no choice but to tell her. I strode through my bedroom and pushed open the door that joined our rooms.

My heart raced in my chest. If this went badly, my whole plan would be destroyed and my family would once again fall out of reach.

But Merlin loved me, and I loved and trusted her. If she wouldn't come with me, she'd surely let me go.

I stepped up to her bedside and sat on the edge. She looked so serene. She didn't stir or twitch, not even when I sat down beside her. I would have thought her dead if not for the slow and silent rise and fall of her chest. My memory flashed to my first night in Arthur's castle, when I'd tried attacking her with my dagger. How different my intentions were now. I took her hand and, without waking, her long fingers embraced mine.

"Merlin," I whispered. She blinked awake, the intensity of her features springing to life with her eyes.

"What's wrong?" she said, her body still strewn across her bed.

"Let's run away," I said. "You and me."

She smiled. "Here we go."

"I'm serious," I urged, but my voice cracked.

"I know you want to see your family, but Arthur is a fair king.

If you prove your worth to him, I'm certain he'll allow you to see your family again."

I bit down on my bottom lip, holding back my disappointment. I was also afraid to reveal any more than I already had. Still, I had to try again, for Merlin.

"Why do you stay here? With your magic, you can go anywhere."

She smiled and cupped my cheek with her hand. "This is my home." The gleam in her kind eyes pleaded with me to understand, and I unfortunately did. I was a prisoner of Bullhorn, Merlin was not.

I looked down at my hands, unable to find my words.

"Just give it more time," she said, "Trust me."

I had trusted her. But, while this was her home, it wasn't mine. I had a family to get back to. If Arthur was as loyal to her as she seemed to be to him, her life would be spared. Wouldn't it?

I didn't know for sure. It was a gamble. Her hand dropped from my face and slipped into my hand. "Trust me," she repeated.

I steeled my nerves as I felt myself settle on the decision to leave her. "Merlin," I said, "I have to tell you something."

I turned away from her nervous gaze and stared down at our joined hands. "I can't wield magic."

When she didn't respond, I caved to the urge to check her expression, but it was expressionless and statuesque. A moment later, her eyes widened. "The little girl…" she said, her eyes moving quickly between mine.

I nodded as fear surged through me. Had telling her been a mistake? Did I just put Morgana at risk? She slipped her hand from mine and I felt my stomach churn.

She sat up so quickly that I flinched. She wrapped her arms around me and whispered in my ear. "Thank you for trusting me. I see why you're so eager to get home," she said into my hair. "Give it some time."

She pulled away and I immediately felt the loss of her embrace. I wondered if that was the last moment I'd ever see her. I wanted to hold her again and thank her for taking care of me, but either of those would alert her that I was up to something.

"Goodnight," I said, memorizing the curves of her face to call upon when I missed her. I certainly would. She was as close to a sibling as I'd ever had, and I was leaving her behind. She laid back and settled into her bed, a soft smile on her lips, before her eyes blinked shut. By the time the sun rose to wake her, I'd be soaring out of Bullhorn on the back of Garix.

The repercussions of my decision would fall to her alone. I wasn't sure if she'd ever forgive me, or if I'd see her again, but I hoped that over time, and with the knowledge of my daughter, she'd come to understand.

I lay awake in my bed for a full hour before I dared to move. I slipped easily out of Merlin's chamber and into the hallway. It was a bit earlier than I usually started my secret training with Garix but not too early to explain if I was caught on my way out. My heart slammed into my ribcage, adrenaline surging through every vessel in my body as I made my way to the courtyard in the moonless night. My forehead beaded with sweat as I walked towards Garix. *This is it.*

I hadn't planned this around the lack of moonlight, but I was grateful for the extra protection. The uncommonly dark sky urged me forward with its infinite possibilities. Freedom awaited.

Garix's split tongue shot out and lapped at the scales atop his nose. His crest had grown into small rigid spikes over the last few weeks and I'd learned the hard way to avoid them. I wrapped the fabric around him, noting that it had become a bit snug. I hadn't accounted for his rapid growth. But I had to make it work. I wasn't going to be a prisoner for another minute. I was not a damsel but a dragon. *I'm coming, Morgana.*

I mounted Garix, my decision to leave Merlin the last of what weighed heavily on me as we rose into the dark sky. I couldn't shake the feeling that, by leaving Merlin to suffer the consequences, I'd betrayed her.

10

MINSEO

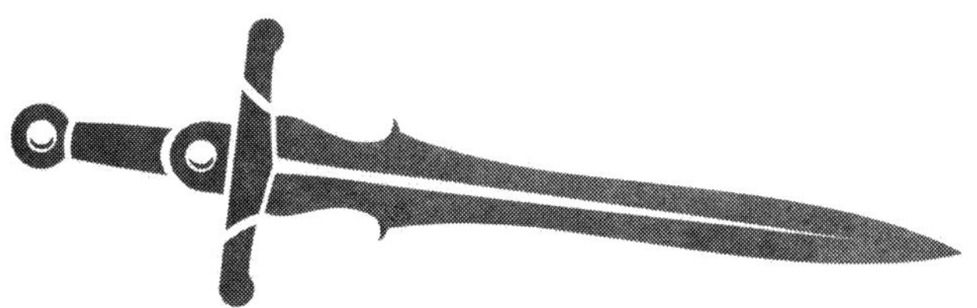

My mind was preoccupied with thoughts of the war meeting. No one wanted to pay Camelot's new alliance tax, but there was no fathomable scenario where we went to war with Camelot and won. Young had fought bravely in the meeting, drawing upon the history and tradition of Vires and how it was our duty to die protecting it, but he was just a boy when the council last knew him. The council went to great lengths to discredit him. One member even made a ridiculous accusation that, in those five years, Arthur had turned Young into his spy. As if Young was capable; the man breathed honor and duty. The idea was quickly dismissed as ludicrous, but the claim seemed to sweep the wind out of his argument's sails and replace it with stale air.

I just wanted Charlotte. Every passionate plea to attack Camelot dripped with my love for her, despite the efforts I made to conceal it. With every uncomfortable shift Young made from his side of the table, I felt myself hold back my arguments until I was unable to put together anything the least bit convincing.

We needed to convince my father and the council that we had a chance at winning, but in all truthfulness, we didn't have one.

I felt the irrational part of me form a plan to break into the castle at Bullhorn alone and rescue Charlotte myself. I knew this feeling well. I was spiraling and only one thing ever made me feel better: Morgana. As I walked to Gabriel's to see her, an odd thought occurred to me. I used Morgana to ease the sting of being away from Charlotte, much in the same way I'd used her to ease my loss of Young. I wondered if I afforded her the same comfort.

I hoped Morgana was in good spirits today. She usually was, but even my little ray of sunshine had her days. I hadn't known her for long, but I thought about her all the time. I laughed to myself when I thought of her calling me Minnow. Oh, how that little nickname had grown on me—just as that little angel did. I hadn't been the only one she'd won over either. I was grateful she was never short of attention, but even with three father figures to look after her, she missed her mother, and so did I.

Gabriel had elected to live outside the castle walls. His home was small but at the center of town where he could be closest to the market. He had gone on hiatus from his job as a merchant until his Viran language skills were adequate enough to thrive. The clay-tiled roofs, stone fences, and hanji paper walls were fairly uniform, but Gabriel began to cultivate a large garden in the typically barren space between the gate and the home. I wondered if it was due to the boredom of unemployment or for Morgana's sake. I knocked on the door. It slid open and Junho stood in its frame, a grin on his face.

I took a quick look around, wondering if I'd come to the wrong place. "Junho," I said. "Long time no see."

"Good to see you," he said, waving me in. "Gabriel is making some tea. Should I tell him to add a cup?"

"I'm actually here to see Morgana," I said, eyeing the dimly lit room.

"Oh, she went out with her—" He stopped, his jaw clenching for a moment before he continued. "Young."

Her *father*. "It's nice to see them finally warming up to each other," I said, but Junho's brow furrowed like he thought me disingenuous.

"So," he said, "shall we get you some tea?"

"Hello, Minseo," Gabriel said as he entered the room with a tray of chattering porcelain. "Morgana isn't here."

"I know, she's with Young," I said, hoping the subject would be dropped quickly.

Gabriel set his tray down. "Is this something we need to talk through?"

Still halfway out the door, I turned to go. "No. I'm fine," I said, making my escape.

"Wait," Gabriel called. I turned back. He crossed his huge arms over his chest, his black eyelashes flitting with judgment.

"I know, I know... " I said. "I have issues with my brother."

He shook his head. "Brothers." He lifted an eyebrow and looked mischievously at me before going back into his house, sliding the door shut behind him.

My heart sank. *Sumin*. I'd made a conscious decision to avoid him. Over the years, many people, our mother, in particular, commented on our mutual distaste for one another, but they didn't understand. It was the nature of our relationship, one both Sumin and I were comfortable with. The last thing I wanted was to go see him and have things be suddenly different because he was sick.

I wondered if he was feeling any better. If he did, he might have enough influence to convince the council to go to war. I headed toward his room on the palace compound but found myself mindlessly kicking a rock as I went. Out of the corner of my eye, a figure drew my attention. My mother, seemingly headed from Sumin's room. Her movements were slow, her eyes thoughtful and distracted. I couldn't blame her; I'd hardly recovered from almost losing Young and now my older brother was in danger. I couldn't imagine how difficult it must've been to lose a child. Since Sumin took ill, she'd been taking turns tending to him with his wife. She glanced at me and nodded slightly as she passed before turning away without a word.

It was obvious Sumin's condition took its toll on her, but it wasn't until I reached his door that I felt my nerve leave me. I didn't want to bother him. Maybe I should just let him rest.

"Even your breathing annoys me," Sumin's voice shot through the walls of his room. Relief flooded my body and a bright smile rushed to my face. Of course, he would be the same. I slid the door open, and my smile dropped the moment I saw him. Sumin was pale, his face sunken in. Dark circles around his eyes made his face look skeletal. His skin was as thin as rice paper, and old, like the life and youth had been drained from him. I froze.

"You honestly don't look much better," he said. I forced a slight smile, but the truth I'd been avoiding was staring me in the face. My brother wasn't sick, he was *dying*.

I gulped, looking around the empty room. "Where's your wife?"

"Why?" he said, his lips chalky and white. "Are you planning on stealing her when I'm gone?" He looked musingly down at his hands. "That is your *thing*, isn't it?"

My mother wouldn't've understood, but it was a show of kindness. Brotherly love in our way. I sat down on the foot of his bed. "Exactly," I said, "Why else do you think I'm here?"

He smiled weakly and we fell into a silence that made me suddenly aware of his labored breaths. It was a scratchy wheeze that unnerved me.

To break the silence I said, “Actually, I thought I’d come to ask you how I can convince the council to go to war.”

“You want to save Charlotte,” he said thoughtfully. His eyes changed back to their mocking glare. “What will you do once you retrieve her?”

It was an honest question. Direct. Maybe he was running out of time. I wondered how different our relationship would have been if we’d always spoken with candor. “She’s his wife.” I turned away. “I just want her to be safe.”

“I know you better than that,” he said.

A flicker of rage surged through me, blacking out the sight of his illness. “No, you don’t.”

I turned back to him, surprised to find a kind smile on his face. “Convince them Vires can win.”

It took a moment for me to realize that he’d reverted to my previous question. “How?”

He turned to the window, the light lingering on his face, strong enough to hide the sickness, and for a moment he looked like my older brother again.

“Think like a king. You may be one yet.”

My father had mentioned the possibility of me becoming king, but I’d always assumed Sumin would recover. Looking at him now, I wasn’t sure. I certainly didn’t like him implying that. It was like he was giving up. I clenched my fists. “How about you just don’t die.”

If he hadn’t smiled so wide, I would have thought he hadn’t heard me because he continued his sentence like I’d never spoken. “Think beyond yourself. Think beyond Vires.”

“Okay, wise, dying sage. Why not just tell me how?”

We erupted into laughter, the bed shaking as we gasped for air. I clutched my stomach and toppled forward. Sumin’s laugh rang in my ears and I felt him pat me on the back. I lifted my head off the bed, my cheeks stinging from overactivity. A light breeze flowed in from the window and chilled my cheeks. I wiped them with my hands. When had they gotten wet? It wasn't funny, Sumin was dying. I needed him to be strong. It wasn't until Sumin pulled me into his arms that I realized I wasn't laughing at all, I was sobbing.

11

ARTHUR

"Traitor!" I screamed from my throne. I looked down on Merlin, the voice in the back of my head reminding me not to provoke her. She was, after all, very powerful, and that irked me now that I could no longer consider her a reliable tool.

"After all I've done for you, you betray me, your king!"

She bowed her head in shame, keeping her gaze locked on the floor. "I didn't know what she was planning," she muttered.

"Do you think I'm a fool? You wish me to believe that she just left you here without a word?"

Her eyes flitted up to me and I could see that they were wet. Taken aback, my first thought was that it was another deception, but I'd never seen her show anything but power and strength in all the time I'd known her, even when I pulled her from the abuse of her former life.

With such power, she didn't need to debase herself with such a deplorable tactic.

I huffed, releasing more frustration than I wanted to. "Do you have any idea what that egg cost me? How dangerous it is now that it's in the hands of our enemy?"

My gaze moved to Lancelot whose impartial gaze lay upon Merlin. I never thought clearly when angry and, unfortunately, Merlin gave me few options for punishment. With her abilities, she could easily break out of my prison camps. And I doubt she'd accept her execution. The last thing I needed was someone undermining my authority. It had been so hard-fought just to force this kingdom to overlook my age.

"Get her out of my sight," I said. "Clear out this room! Except for you, Lancelot."

Lance's eyebrows rose and he looked up at me expectantly. Oh, how I liked it when he looked up. I liked it when they all did. I was undeniably the king. The greatest king the world had ever seen, despite the way I came to it. Still, even after more than five years on the throne, nothing satisfied my urge to prove it.

When the room emptied, Lance stood at the base of the stairs, in the middle of the red light that poured in from the stained glass. I started down the stairs but stopped two from the bottom to keep Lance below eye level. His lips were pressed into a hard line, his eyes vacant and unafraid.

I waited for the creak of the throne room door to sound and for the thud of it coming to a close.

Then I spoke, liking the pitch of my voice as it sounded off the hallowed walls. "Jeremy," I said, trying to shake him. "Merlin has become a problem. I'm short a dragon and someone must be punished."

"You're afraid of her," he said, but it wasn't a question.

"I am the king. I fear nothing." I felt my skin prick with irritation.

His face threatened to crack but slid back into its neutral state. He was a perfect soldier—following orders on command, but the look in his eyes was defiant. I'd assumed it was because he was there when I'd earned my spot, but I was starting to believe he had another reason. Some time ago, I'd lost his love. I never had his respect. Now all I wanted was for him to fear me.

"Where do your loyalties lie, Jeremy?"

"With you, Your Majesty," he said, but the way the word skipped from his lips felt like an insult.

I grinned. "Then you shall kill her."

His neutrality broke, his eyes widening. "I'll never get close enough. She... she's too powerful."

Power and fear were a currency I'd used to my advantage throughout my reign, and I still had a card or two to play on Lancelot. "I heard a rumor," I said, a smile sinking into my cheeks as the fear grew in his eyes, "that my wife has a lover."

He sucked a breath so sharp I thought it might cut his tongue. *I had him.* "I hear he lives in this very castle."

Finally, he shook beneath my gaze. His face returned to its neutral state, but his eyes flooded with worry and fear. "You think I didn't know what was going on in my own castle?"

His gaze dropped to the floor. "Why not just have me executed? Why make Merlin do it? Do you get some kind of sick pleasure from these games?" he spat.

Amused, I tilted my head. His body shifted from the red into the purple light.

"You look so small," I said, losing my train of thought. His arms were crossed over his chest as if they would protect him from what was coming next. "I have a story for you," I said.

"I'd prefer if you'd skip to your point."

"Oh, believe me, you'll want to hear this one. It's the story of how you stand before me now, with your head intact." His gaze lifted to mine.

"Several months ago, I thought dragons were a myth until a

high-ranking man I knew well from court approached me with a family secret. An heirloom passed down ten generations. It was a treasure worth more than gold—a dragon egg. Of course, I didn't believe him, so I went to his home to inspect the artifact. What I found was a most peculiar object I couldn't explain. Still, what the man asked in return was extraordinary. After all, in hundreds of years, the egg never moved. It was practically a relic. It wasn't until I got it in my head that Merlin's magic might be able to hatch it that I felt any real interest at all."

Lance's eyes jotted from one of my eyes to the other as he connected the dots. I continued, "It was a gamble but one that could prove worth it." I turned my face toward the stained glass window. "So I made the deal. His daughter's hand in marriage and right to the throne for the egg."

"Cornwall," Lance muttered under his breath.

"That's right. Gwenevere's father."

"So..." His mouth fell open as he gulped in air. "You never loved her."

His response surprised me. It was such an unusual thing to say. But when I looked down on him, I saw love. Not for Gwen, but for me. The same brotherly affection I'd once associated with his face. Taken aback, my mind raced to connect what I'd said to garner his reaction.

Sensing my bewilderment, he said, "You didn't want her."

"Of course not," I said like it was obvious, but it wasn't, and now that I'd so passionately objected, it hung awkwardly in the air. "I… uh. What I mean to say is—"

Lance stepped up and wrapped his arms around me, tears springing to his eyes. I flinched, but he hugged me. What was happening?

A heartbeat passed as I froze, in shock. Finally, I pulled my wits together and pushed him off with one straight arm held out between us.

He stumbled off the step and smiled. He wiped his tears and then stood back at attention. His face was neutral, but the corners of his mouth ticked upright. *What is he doing? Why is he happy?*

My cheeks seared hot with discomfort. "Which brings me to my plan to get Merlin to lower her guard," I said, trying to snap him out of whatever mood he'd crossed into. "You will marry her."

"Yes, Your Majesty," he said without hesitation, and for the first time I didn't see love, respect, or fear in his eyes. I saw all three.

12

CHARLOTTE

My stomach fluttered when I imagined reuniting with Minseo—his playfulness, his vibrant emotions, his smoldering gaze, and his tousled hair. How long had it been? Three months? Maybe a little more? I missed the hum of his voice, the taste of his lips. Even the thought of him made me dizzy. He was the home I was running to. Perhaps Arthur would still be my lethal shadow, but we were stronger together, maybe even strong enough to kill a king.

I had never been to Vires. A fact that became clearer to me as I attempted to navigate Garix to it, using only a vague knowledge of which direction was east. I wondered if I'd ever find it—ever make it home to him. Those were the thoughts that pushed me to keep going when I felt hungry, cold, or tired. I'd gone nearly five hours before I got the nerve to land and let Garix rest. And almost a full day of foraging for anything I could get my hands on before I got the idea to order Garix to hunt. After that, we'd settled into a nice routine. Garix would catch something, flame it for a bit, and we'd eat. We spent as much time in the air as we could and I spent every second terrified we'd be discovered and caught by Arthur and his knights.

We made sure not to pass over any cities and flew at night when we could. But sleeping during the day could be more dangerous.

No matter how much I reasoned with them, I couldn't make my nerves settle. What had I to fear? I had Garix. What really scared me was my history. I crawled through, cowering, because I knew the more powerful something was, the harder it fell in the end. Life was one cruel lesson after another, aimed pointedly toward those with the most to lose. Now that I was free, I had a lot to lose, so I focused on my destination, desperate for a win.

The sensation of true freedom took hold as the signs of Arthur's kingdom waned to rolling hills and empty forests. I spotted the occasional miller mulling around their business, with no need to look to the skies. I was free. No longer tied to a castle or a kingdom. It was the kind of life I'd always dreamed of, though the dragon was a surprise.

I began to wonder if Garix would ever know such freedom. He was a slave to my every whim, wasn't he? I couldn't remove the metallic bracelet that bound to my wrist just after he hatched, nor did it appear that he could disobey an order. During our journey, I tried to consider his feelings. I landed when he was tired and let him hunt when he was hungry, but was that really the same as being free? If I willed him to disobey, would it really be his choice? I contemplated such an existence, unsettled by the thoughts that emerged, and it didn't feel that different from my memories of my royal upbringing.

If a dragon's will was always tied to a human's, it was no wonder that before Garix I'd believed them to be nothing more than a popular myth. Who could wield such a power and also protect it? Since the beginning of time, the daughter of power was corruption. I'd only had a taste of it and already betrayed Merlin.

Garix lifted me above the earth and, with my hair entwined with the clouds and my skin kissed with sunshine, I could feel my heart churning away the torrent of revenge as my thoughts released the scores I had yet to settle. Perhaps Arthur would let me go too.

Garix and I had a long rest when we met the coast of the Jin Sea, as the cobalt blue waves licked at the rocky shore. The salty air stuck to my skin and my hair thrashed in the wind like it did when Garix and I flew together. It smelled more like fish than salt, and I noted the difference between my childhood memories of the sea and what I now experienced.

It was a few minutes before dawn and the water held all the darkness of night as well as the leftover glimmer of the stars which were no longer visible in the light blue sky. Each time a wave slammed down on the shore and pulled, the smooth gray stones that covered the shoreline rattled together with a sound that resembled heavy rain. It made the ocean seem less like a sleeping giant and more like a hungry predator waiting to devour its next meal. Garix didn't seem to feel the same way as he stamped around the stones, his ears twitching at the scrape of polished rock beneath his clawed feet.

The horizon was still and empty. It promised nothing, no haven or sanctuary. There were no boats in view, no distant coast to welcome us. There was no sunrise to whisper encouragement and promise, just the blank slate of the endless unknown. I wasn't sure how long it would take to fly across, or if Garix could make it the whole way without resting, but knowing that Vires was on the other side, knowing that my family was just one obstacle away, was enough to take the risk.

I hadn't pushed Garix any longer than six hours at once and I figured we might be able to go seven or eight hours before we absolutely had to land. I hoped that this journey wouldn't take longer. I was grateful that we had a clear day instead of the alternative, though when I closed my eyes, the sound of the stones deceived me to believe otherwise, especially as I drifted in and out of sleep beside Garix.

The sun was at its peak when I felt Garix was rested enough to make the attempt. I knew we were far ahead of Arthur and any attempts he could make to pursue us, but I didn't like the idea of waiting around in the open, especially when everything I've ever wanted waited on the other side of this sea.

Are you ready? I thought to Garix. He let out a screech that greatly resembled the birds that drifted in the harsh winds above the sea, and without any time to second guess my decision, we ascended into the unknown, hoping the shore we believed would show itself before we fell from the sky was worth the risk.

13

LANCELOT

I knew there *was* a reason. I knew Arthur wouldn't marry Gwen just to prove he was king. Not even Gwen knew his true intentions. I'd spent so many months hating him that I felt a weight lift off of me. Above all, I wanted to make up for doubting him. *Marry Merlin and murder her while she slept*. Even if it was a risky mission, I had to try. Our wedding night might be enough to make Merlin lower her guard, but getting her to agree to marry me would be a nearly impossible task in itself. If he'd given me this task a year ago, I would have easily been able to convince her, but those days were long gone. She no longer brimmed with joy in my presence. Now, we treated each other like strangers, passing by like we hadn't spent four years together—like we hadn't known each other as well as lovers.

I'd made no effort to reach out to her either. Not since she abandoned me just before I'd succeeded in my knighthood quest.

If I started courting her out of the blue, she could get suspicious and use her seeing ability to figure out my motive. If that happened, she could kill us all.

But there was hope. She'd been wandering around the castle looking aimless and lost ever since Charlotte took off with the dragon.

Charlotte was a chink in her otherwise impenetrable armor.

One afternoon, I snuck down to the dungeon where Merlin practiced. On the best of days, the dungeon was a dark and foul-smelling place with creatures that skidded through the dark crevices. Devoid of windows, it invited the feeling of being buried alive, scarcely luring anyone from the castle to its torchlit corridors, but ever since Merlin began training there, it had become even less alluring. Smoky, hot, and blackened with soot and ash, it became synonymous with my image of hell. After five short minutes, I was sweaty and oxygen-starved. I couldn't imagine spending days on end down there, especially of my own will.

I walked past several blackened cells before I heard the sounds of Merlin training a few cells ahead. I shuddered at the sight of the cells she'd destroyed with her new power. Fire wasn't an element she could conjure back when I knew her well. From what I remembered, she was gifted and precise with air magic, decent with plants, and horrible with water. And then the annoying mix of air and plants that somehow came out as a sort of purple fog. Let's not forget her random and inconvenient visions that rendered her useless in a battle.

As I neared the source of the noise, I slowed my pace, making sure to keep my footsteps and breaths as quiet as possible.

She shouted a fearsome battle cry and the hallway flushed with heat, a blue glow emanating from her practice cell. I ducked around the corner to compose myself before approaching. I visualized greeting her but each mental attempt felt less genuine than the last.

She shouted again, flooding the hallway with a blue glow.

Okay Lance, let's go. I hesitated. What was I afraid of?

I crept into the hallway, but before I could step into her cell, I heard a sound that stopped me in my tracks. A sniffle and a sob. My body tensed. Was she hurt? She must've been. Merlin didn't cry over emotional things, did she?

I stood frozen just outside of her view and listened. My stomach tightened as I heard the smallest wisp of words as she mumbled them through sobs. "Why am I always alone?"

14

MINSEO

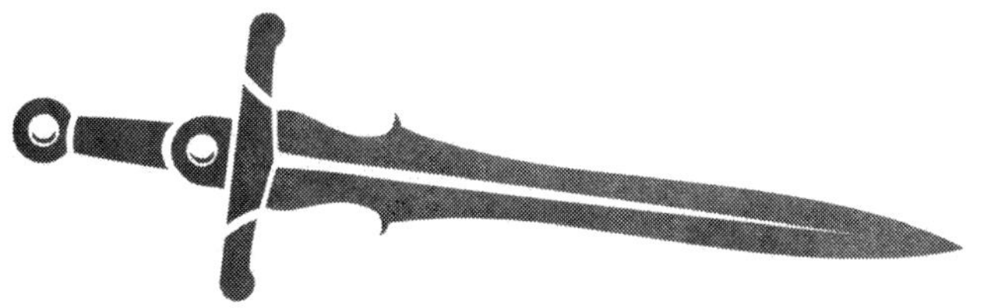

"Your Majesty!" a husky voice bellowed in the throne room. Though he addressed my father, the suddenness of the intrusion pushed Young and me instinctively to our feet. The man ran through the large hall toward us. I recognized him as Jay Hyun, a loyal soldier who helped me find Charlotte in Camelot. His expression of bewilderment sent my thoughts to months ago when Merlin, the enchantress who once shook my understanding of reality, had put that same disoriented gaze on my face.

"We're under attack. At the edge of the city," he said, his voice wavering. My father stood. My heart leapt into my throat as the impossibility of the situation sunk in. If Arthur was attacking, we would have known he was coming the moment he started loading troops onto ships at the Jin Sea. We had soldiers posted everywhere and a very efficient warning system. We also lived in a mountainous region that would make marching troops to Vires extremely unwise and dangerous. But the look in Jay's eyes left no doubt that this was Merlin, this was magic. Had she somehow cloaked their arrival?

My body surged with energy laced with nostalgia. I'd felt it before, the mixture of hopelessness, uncertainty, and survival that had come alive within me just before Besmium fell. I'd been pushing for war and training legions of soldiers, but we were out of position. The enemy was here.

"How many soldiers?" my father said, the sweat on his brow betraying his calm exterior.

"It's..." Jay swallowed a mouthful of doubt before he tried again. "It's a dragon. No soldiers. Just a dragon."

I chewed my bottom lip to stop from laughing. What a day this was turning out to be. My father sat back on his throne, his shoulders sagging with relief. Young's gaze moved to me, unlocking the last bit of self-control I'd mustered. I threw my head back in a stomach-tightening laugh that filled every crevice of the throne room. Young smiled, his gaze locked on me as I drowned in one fit of laughter after the next. Young turned to Jay Hyun. "Are you okay?" he said.

A second soldier ran into the throne room. "Dragon!" he screamed. "Rally the troops!"

Stunned, my laughter faded rapidly into concern. One overworked soldier spouting nonsense was hilarious, two were improbable. Was there really a dragon? Before logic could take hold of me, I was halfway down the stairs from the platform.

My heartbeat thrummed as my body swelled with so much excitement that it had no room for any other emotion. Magic? Dragons? This was a world I wanted to belong to and I didn't care one bit about the consequences.

"Wait," Young called from behind me. I froze. Ah, there *was* a consequence I couldn't bear. I turned to see him beaming, the thrill of such an outlandish threat not lost on him. My gaze skipped past Young to my father. As if we were linked, I recognized what I felt in the solemn gaze and haunting glisten of his eyes. I took a deep breath, knowing this would drive a bigger wedge between Young and me, but before I got the words out, my father took them from me.

"Young," he said. "I need you to stay here and look after Sumin."

Young recoiled like he'd been struck. "N-no. I'm going."

"You will not," my father said. Recognizing that our father had ended the conversation, he turned to me, his eyes lit with hope.

I turned my face away.

"Minseo!" he yelled, so forcefully it startled me. "Tell him to let me go."

I looked at him, the boy with a face I once knew. The boy I'd never recovered from losing. My father and I shared that and, now that he was home safe, we intended to keep him that way. As his brother, I knew it would surely kill him in another way, but I'd rather have him upset and alive than happy and dead.

"Please," he whispered, and I felt my resolve crack.

"I'm sorry," I said as I turned and hurried toward the door, *but nothing could convince me to risk losing you again.*

"I'm not some fragile child! You don't have to protect me," he called as the door closed between us.

I'd make it up to him, somehow.

I waited at the gate to the dusky city with the two soldiers at my side. As soon as we mounted our horses and headed through the heart of Vires, we passed small groups of soldiers headed to the outskirts as well. All it took was a rumor of a dragon and the calvary came running. Like me, I knew it was mostly for curiosity and not heroics. Ten, fourteen, eighteen, twenty-five. By the time we reached the edge of the city, more than fifty soldiers were huddled together.

It took nearly a half-hour to reach the spot. There was only a sliver of light left on the horizon that set behind the silhouette of a hideous monster.

Our horses thrashed with defiance as we stepped forward until it was clear we would not be able to coax them closer. The dragon was eerily still and gargoyle-like. I would have thought it was some kind of prank if not for the obvious rise and fall of its shoulders as it breathed.

Unbelievable. Mesmerized, I moved closer with no regard for my well being. Chances were if that monstrous creature wanted to burn Vires to the ground, and me along with it, there would be little we could do about it. From the size alone, I doubted my sword could injure it. I needed a closer look. I wanted to see more than a darkened silhouette.

On foot, I walked closer, motioning to the other soldiers to stay back. The dragon seemed relatively still and I didn't want to risk startling it. It was starting to get dark, so it was possible it couldn't see me moving closer. I considered sneaking up on it, but it seemed to be positioned in my direction and I had the feeling it was watching me. Slowly, I made my way to the beast, hearing the nervous chatter of the crowd behind me give way to the suck and blow of air through the giant lungs of the beast.

For the first time, the immensity of its large frame, the size of a small home, corroded at my nerves and I wondered what compelled me to continue to close the gap between us. A flash of movement shot my hand to my sword. My body surged with intensity as the question arose. Run or fight? Then I heard a voice that stopped my heart. "Minseo?" she said. And the sword slid from my grip.

15

CHARLOTTE

"Minseo?" I said, the word involuntarily slipping from my lips. I slid off Garix, my body aching from prolonged time spent in one position, but it didn't matter. Through the darkness walked the figure I'd journeyed so far to see. "Minseo!" I shouted as the last of the sun's rays brushed his stunned cheeks. I ran to him and threw myself into his chest. He wrapped me so tightly in his arms that the breath left me, and I didn't care. I buried my face in his neck. I felt my eyes prick but my heart beat too fast and too joyously to cry. That was until I felt the wet of Minseo's tears on my shoulder. I pulled back a bit so I could see his face and cupped it in my hands. His eyes were dark, even with the glint of his tears glossing them over. His hair had grown a bit. The sharp lines of his cheekbones glistened with tears and I wiped them with my thumbs.

He laughed, though fresh tears still fell. "Why do you have a dragon?" he said, half laughing. "Did you," his gaze moved to Garix, "ride it here?"

"Oh. That's a long story."

"Is he going to eat us?" he said, pushing my curls out of my face.

"Probably not."

He held me and drank me in, his gaze reflecting all the love I felt. Then his eyes dropped down to my lips, and my face seared with heat. My heart thudded into my chest. A tear, either from him or me, dropped down like ice on my burning collarbone as my breaths became labored. I'd seen that look before, the one that whispered, *I'll devour you*. A haze dropped over me as I leaned into him. He snapped his eyes shut like he'd been struck, clenched his jaw, and turned away, dropping his arms from me. His brow pushed together and he brought a hand to cover his face.

Stunned, I reached out. "Minseo, what's wrong?"

His hesitation combined with the heave of his chest as it rose and fell in the darkness unnerved me. "What's wrong?" I asked again, but the fear that tore through me was so intense it came out as barely a whisper.

"Charlotte," he breathed. "I have to tell you something." He turned to look at the row of soldiers that were no doubt gathered due to Garix, but they were now heading back to the city. I hadn't seen Minseo order them away, but I was glad no one but Garix was here to witness my unexpected rejection.

My mind raced through one horror after the other, the biggest coming to my lips first. "Morgana?"

"She's perfectly fine."

I swallowed a gulp of relief. His quick response, merciful.

"Then whatever it is, we can get through it." I reached for his hand but he pulled it away. "Minseo, you're scaring me." I looked into his eyes but didn't see the glow of love or joy that had been present a moment ago. I saw only sadness and, when I looked a little closer, I saw I was wrong. It was not sadness but pain.

"I want you to know," he said, "that I meant everything I've ever said to you." He walked towards me, his gaze lifting to mine. My heart collapsed as each word was one dagger after another. My head screamed, *Why*? I *knew* he loved me. I knew a few months apart wouldn't change anything. But something had.

Minseo's voice snapped my attention back to him. "But I won't hold you to anything that you said or did."

I shook my head. "Wh-what are you saying? I meant it, Minseo." I choked, but his gaze had gone cold. *Come back to me.* "I love—"

"Don't," he said. A fire lit in his eyes as he turned them on me.

Anger tore through me. "*You* don't. There's nothing you could say that could—"

"Young is alive."

Silence dragged as a sudden gust of wind whipped around us. Minseo studied me as those three miraculous words forged an invisible barrier between us, one we could never break. Locked in stasis between confused, overjoyed, and heartbroken, I stared blankly back at him, my rapid heartbeat a stark contrast to my frozen body.

Young is alive. His words echoed inside me. It was impossible yet I had no reason to doubt him. It was the one and only possible explanation for Minseo's change of heart. He stood in front of me, as immobile as I was, but his eyes betrayed him as a windfall of emotions flickered in them. He was moments from unraveling. My heart yearned to reach out and touch his face, to pull him in my arms and tell him that nothing had changed. But something had. My first love, the father of my child, my husband, the man who filled every inch of the world with gold, was alive.

"Where is he?" I asked, my voice cracking with the emotion I desperately fought to suppress.

Minseo's exhale skipped. He tried again but that too caught in his throat. When his voice sounded again, it was as if it was spoken by someone else. “He’s at the castle. I’ll take you there.”

I had so many questions. How had Young survived? Where had he been all this time? Did he know what I’d done? Had he changed? Did he know about Morgana?

But those questions would all be lances at Minseo. Minseo who had brought me back to life, Minseo who, a moment ago, had been my home.

Hungry. Garix whined an emotion that felt like the color yellow at the pit of my stomach.

“Garix needs to eat. Do you have any livestock? He likes goats.”

Minseo turned to look at Garix, his eyes widening as if he’d forgotten there was a dragon. I could hardly imagine there’d be a moment in my life when my presence would eclipse that of a dragon, but there we were.

“Let’s take him to a farm for the night. He’ll be able to get a meal and rest without...” he scratched at the back of his head, “burning Vires to the ground.”

I smiled, but it only reminded me of how sad I felt. Minseo must’ve noticed because after that he hardly looked at me. We’d gone to the closest farm and Minseo explained the dragon to its owner in Viran. The man seemed apprehensive to take Garix as any sane person would be, but Minseo was a prince of Vires and, therefore, pulled rank. I was surprised to see Minseo speak Viran. I liked the way his mouth moved when he spoke it. His voice seemed different somehow, but I was tired. I might’ve imagined it.

When Garix was settled in with a trough of water and a fresh goat, we finally entered the city. Soldiers waited at the city line to welcome Minseo and finally solve the mystery of the dragon’s sudden appearance. Minseo waved them off and promised them answers in the morning. He ushered me into a carriage before I could get a decent glimpse of the Viran capital. My limbs and eyelids were heavy from both physical and emotional exhaustion. I wanted to call out to Minseo and ask how long the ride was to the castle, but I felt myself slip into a heavy sleep, my mind racing with thoughts of Young and my heart still beating for Minseo.

16

YOUNG

Considering there was a dragon attack happening, the city was unbearably quiet. I kept listening for something—anything. Any clue of what was happening outside the city. I paced the grounds of the castle, furious that I was forced to hide here, like a child, but my sense of duty wouldn't allow me to disobey my father.

The new age lines on my father's face were beyond the five years I'd been held captive. My stomach tightened at the thought that I'd hurt him, that he'd suffered in my absence. But Minseo's agreement threw me. I knew he cared, but once upon a time he understood and believed in me. I had to battle with my selfish thoughts as I waited for my moment to join the fight.

I let out an exasperated sigh as I stomped toward my room. I couldn't bear the silence for another moment. I slid open the door to my bedroom and lay down, my body stiffened with anticipation. A dragon? How had everything gotten so confusing?

There was a time when the world made perfect sense. I longed for the days in my childhood when life was beautifully divided into black and white. Logic was the basis of everything, all with a reason and explanation. Now I was drowning in gray. It was no wonder humanity turned to the sky, to some distant god or power for the answers. It was unbearable to think that all of this was random. The world had changed to one where there were battle mages and dragons, but those things weren't what confused me most. Adulthood was not, as I'd expected, a time of great wisdom and understanding. Adulthood was staring at your greatest fears day after day until you became numb to them.

I sighed, exhaling my greatest fear—Charlotte falling in love with Minseo. I didn't know the details of what happened during my capture, but as I'd come to fear the truth, I knew it would find me eventually. It was another dragon I couldn't slay.

"Young," Minseo said from outside my door.

I jackhammered up to a seated position. "Minseo? Are you okay?" I scrambled for the door.

"It's Charlotte," he said.

My pulse quickened. My voice barely a whisper as I slid open the door. "Is she oka—" I froze.

Charlotte stood in front of me. Her curls a wild crown around her head. Her skin was sun-kissed, a few shades darker than it was when she lived in the castle, giving it a healthy glow complete with pink cheeks. My heart thrashed inside me as my gaze dragged down her new body and rose back to her face. Her bottom lip shook, and I noticed she was breathing more air out than what was coming in. Her eyes glossed over and she reached for me the same way Minseo had when I'd seen him for the first time after my capture. Afraid she'd faint, I pulled her to my body, supporting most of her weight as she wrapped her arms around me, her tears already seeping through my shirt. With my opposite hand, I reached for my door and began to slide it closed behind us. Just before the panes locked together, I caught a glimpse of Minseo, pain peering out through clenched teeth and wet eyes.

I didn't take any pleasure in witnessing the cracked and broken man outside my room. I didn't have time to think about what the intensity of his gaze meant or how Charlotte must've been feeling. There was nothing I wouldn't do for the brother I loved so much, except for one thing. I wouldn't let him have her. *Charlotte was mine.*

17

CHARLOTTE

Young carried me to his bed. My heart raced at the intimacy of the moment as I carefully considered the man in front of me. He was a stranger, my mind unable to age him the five years he was gone. But his eyes held the same kindness and sincerity I'd missed. His hair was cut short, his muscles swollen and defined. I gulped. They certainly hadn't been that way before. He lay down in front of me, the space and discomfort between us a sudden reminder of our wedding night.

He brushed my cheek, his touch more gentle than I was used to. I swallowed a mouthful of nerves and guilt when I realized I was used to Minseo. My memory flashed to Minseo's sadness and I found myself worried about what he might think about tonight.

Young's gaze dropped and I wondered if he knew what I was thinking about, or rather who.

"You're alive," I said, trying to get a read.

He nodded. I felt my heart melt as the memories of him flooded back. The silence between us familiar but lost. *Gold*. My heart beat.

There, I felt it. It was buried, but Young was still there, hidden away in my heart.

"W-we have a daughter," I said.

The brightness of his smile said he'd met her. It made my body weak. Those smiles were earned. Another pang of guilt cut through my stomach. My eyes pricked and a tear slid down the side of my face and onto my pillow.

Young watched me carefully for a moment. I'd already started to adjust to the quiet that came with him when he surprised me and spoke. "You feel guilty about whatever happened when you thought..." His gaze lowered. "When you thought I was dead."

It wasn't a question. My jaw was a dam, holding back the flood of emotions ready to spill out. I pressed my lips together and nodded.

He took a deep breath and noticed it was to steady his own nerves. I was surprised to find I was better at reading him than I'd been when we were teenagers.

He took my hand in his, pulling it to his chest. "You shouldn't feel any guilt. But I have to ask..."

His voice was low, a little different than I remembered. I shook, dread seeping in as I shuffled through the questions he might ask. Had Minseo and I slept together? Was I in love with him? He didn't want to hear the true answers to those questions. But I had forgotten the kind of man he was, so I couldn't anticipate what he'd say next.

"Do you want me to let you go?"

My heart raced. *Never.* Of course not. But the words didn't make it to my lips.

"Please. Charlotte," he said. "If there's no hope—"

"There is."

He bit down on his bottom lip and my memory fluttered past a moment when I bit down on that lip. My face burned red and his followed. His eyebrows raised and the corners of his mouth peaked as if he easily accessed my thoughts from my expressions. I held my breath to pass the moment, and when I couldn't any longer, I pushed it slowly through my teeth.

He faked a laugh to break the tension. That was a new trick for him. "So, we'll take it slow then and see if I can't win you back."

Now I was the silent one. There was so much to say, so much to ask, but for the first time since I met him, we had time.

"Get some rest," he said. "We'll talk tomorrow."

I closed my eyes and realized just how hard I'd been fighting my exhaustion. Still, my mind was a blur. How had Young forgiven me so quickly? How had I forgotten what he felt like? He planned to fight for my heart which meant two things: I needed to let myself fall back in love with him and I needed to stay the hell away from Minseo.

I awoke without having remembered falling asleep. I turned to see Young sleeping soundly. His face was serene without his open eyes to give him away. I thought about waking him but it seemed cruel. I looked around the room, finding it peaceful with the simple clean lines and furnishings. The bed was much closer to the ground than I was used to, as was a small table with several mats laid neatly around it. It was such a stark contrast to the style of the western world. Curiosity about the rest of the castle clawed at me. I'd missed most of the view in the confines of the carriage and barely got a glance around before Minseo plopped me in front of Young's room. He was a good man for that. A great man, but I was committed to Young and getting back what we had. I tried wrangling my hair into a hair tie, but it was no use without a mirror. Finally, when it was out of my face, I slid the door open and stepped out, carefully sliding the door closed as to not wake Young. I turned back to the morning and gasped at the painted wooden structures and elaborate curved gables, the clay-tiled roofs and brightly colored carvings that wove up each column and statue. Yellows, greens, blues, and reds in perfectly balanced harmony. The castle compound did not reflect it's simple interior in the least. I stepped forward but tripped over a large mass on the ground.

I wrenched my body to pull my feet under me before I hit the ground and spun to see a stunned Minseo sitting on the step. *What the?* The dark circles around his eyes answered each question as they popped into my head. *Oh. Minseo...* I exhaled my disbelief. "You slept here?"

He stood and looked into my eyes. It was our usual distance but, suddenly, it felt too close. I stepped back, still waiting for a response.

"I... uh... wanted to make sure you were okay."

I was irritated, not by his absurd actions but mostly by his handsome face and how much I wanted to touch him. "Minseo..."

"Did something happen?" he blurted. His eyes widened. He bowed a frantic apology, a gesture that struck me and I wasn't sure if it was one that came from Vires or from royalty. I wasn't used to either.

"I'm so sorry," he said. "Don't answer that." He huffed. "I'll do better. I just," he ran his hand through his hair, sending chills through my whole body, "I just need a second to get used to it."

I swallowed my tongue. *Yes. Get used to it, leave me alone, please, because I'll never be able to resist you on my own.* But I said, "Maybe we should talk through things."

He shook his head. "Better not."

Silence hung between us, but unlike with Young, it wasn't comfortable. It wasn't a warm, peaceful feeling of home but torment.

Minseo cleared his throat. "I thought you'd like to see Morgana and then maybe go see your dragon before he eats everyone in town."

"Yes! Perfect," I said, excitement surging through me.

He looked down at his feet. "Maybe you could," he shrugged, "not tell Young about the whole sleeping outside thing."

I shook my head. "Huh?"

He lifted his shoulders. "Just don't tell him."

Right on cue, I felt the door behind me slide open and Young step to my side. Panic flooded my veins. I wanted to blurt that it wasn't what he thought, but something bigger took precedence. It was the first time the three of us were together in five years and I wasn't sure how it was going to go. If Young made a show of this, I'm not sure how well Minseo would handle it. *Please don't kiss me. Please don't be possessive.*

Minseo spoke first. "Uh, I was going to take Charlotte to Morgana and then her dragon. Are you ready to go?"

Young stepped off the platform. "I need to set up a meeting with the council. If Charlotte escaped Camelot, they might come after her. And if this dragon of hers is as Jay Hyun described last night, we might have the chance we've been waiting for."

His gaze moved to me and he offered a one-sided smile. "Minseo will show you around. I'll meet up with you later." He turned but quickly turned back. "Ah, you forgot this." He reached in his scabbard and pulled out my dagger, the red stones aflame in the sunlight. I took it, hoping that our hands would touch but they didn't and he walked away. In a few steps and without a glance back, he disappeared behind a room identical to his a few yards away.

I wasn't sure who was more stunned, me or Minseo.

That wasn't possessive at all. That was borderline indifferent. I mean, he could've acted a little like he liked me. Still, his confidence was attractive, an obvious contrast to that possessive alpha male act I was getting from Minseo. I had to admit, he was a little too cavalier about the situation. I made a mental note to ask him about it later and was ready to let it go when Minseo spoke again.

"What the hell was that?"

"What?" I said, not exactly sure where his anger was coming from.

"He doesn't even consider me a threat."

I spat laughter.

"No, seriously. Doesn't he know what could happen if we're alone?"

I rolled my eyes. "Nothing will happen Minseo."

Ignoring me, he said, "Does he know what I want to do to you? What I *have* done to you?"

"Okay, so we do need to talk about this," I said. "Look, this wasn't the plan, but Young is back and I owe it to him to give this a real chance."

"Wow, that sounds romantic," he said, his words dripping with sarcasm.

"Minseo," I said. "I don't know what else to do. This is hard and confusing already." My voice caught. "Please just..."

The teasing smile dropped from his cheeks and he nodded. "Of course. I'm sorry. I'm off my game today."

I felt it coming, so I looked away and only caught him run his hand through his hair, out of the corner of my eye. Unfortunately, it was just as effective.

He looked me up and down and I suddenly became aware that I was wearing my crusty five-day-old training suit. It was caked in dirt and grime, each brown particle magnetized to the animal hide garment that hugged me like a second skin.

"Shall we get you cleaned up?"

I nodded and promised myself I'd see Morgana the moment I was clean.

18

ARTHUR

"Prepare for war," I said, feeling the pulse of exhilaration as the words echoed through my throne room.

"Yes, Your Majesty," Galahad said with a bow. He turned and hurried out, but the thrill of what I'd just set into motion remained.

Up until now, I'd expanded Camelot's borders considerably, and through my alliances, we'd gone from a war-torn mess to a formidable and wealthy kingdom. But the mark of a true king lies in his actions in war and Charlotte's little escape along with my dragon gave me the perfect reason to attack. This was my chance. When I wiped out Vires, executed Charlotte, and took back my dragon, I'd gain the respect and finally wipe out what was left of my reputation as a child king. I would be a fearsome conqueror. A legend. The man who ruled Camelot with Excalibur for a thousand years.

I made my way through my castle soaking in the riches displayed about. Fine tapestries, displayed jewels, rare furs. It was a museum of my success. I had half a mind to head to the armory to commission a fine set of armor, the one I'd envisioned myself in when I daydreamed victory. Gold trimmed and encrusted with jewels. But I knew the castle smiths, along with every other, were busy preparing armor for the war ahead. As the king, I could order them to prioritize my armor, but I needed something exceptional and I had a specific smith in mind.

I pushed through the doors of my castle, and the sudden rush of wind on my face made me realize it had been a significant amount of time since I'd been outside. Weeks, maybe. I ordered a guard to fetch my horse and, while I waited, I checked the wall for knights to accompany me as protection. At the base of the giant doors stood the knights Lamorak and Percival, who seemed to be too engaged in a heated discussion to notice me. *Anyone else?* I thought as I scanned the wall. I guess they'd have to do.

I walked over, intentionally dragging my steps to alert them to my presence.

"A bow by itself is way more effective than an arrow," Percival said.

Lamarck threw his hands up. "You're a bloody idiot. An arrow has a pointed end."

Percival huffed. "It would snap like a—"

"Ahem," I said.

They dropped to a knee. "Your Majesty," they said in unison. Both were so tall and broad that they even looked like giants when they kneeled.

"I need you to guard me on a small errand."

Lamorak opened his mouth to speak but I cut him off.

"Neither of you will speak a word until I have safely returned to this castle. Understood?"

They nodded, their gaze low to the ground.

"I said, understood?"

Lamorak looked up at me, his eyes dimly blinking with confusion. I didn't know what he was thinking until the thoughts blurted from his brother's mouth.

"But you told us not to say anything."

I'd already decided to slice their heads off, then and there, when a soldier arrived with my horse. I let out a sigh and mounted, eager to get a close look at my kingdom. Percival and Lamorak stood and fell in step behind me, walking on foot beside my horse.

When we breached the walls of the castle, the kingdom beyond didn't disappoint. The streets were packed with people adorned in fine silks. The businesses and homes were multi-level and lavish with flowers and elegant design. After just a few minutes, I decided I needed to raise the taxes, both domestically and abroad. There was plenty of wealth in Camelot to go around. However, considering I was the reason the citizens enjoyed such spoils, they certainly paid me no mind. I passed without much of a glance from anyone, and even with a golden crown on my head and a magic blade sheathed to my belt, the eyes of the people passed me and found the striking red-headed brothers that guided my horse.

When I was a war hero, everything would change, and I felt determined to earn their love and admiration.

It wasn't more than fifteen minutes before we arrived at a small unlabeled building that was hardly able to warrant the description shack. It was a hovel, built pre-Camelot and much smaller than I'd remembered. It's strange how places you know well in childhood can change along with your perception of the world.

Turning to the twins, I said, "Wait here."

Percival said, "Yes, Your Maje—" Lamorak's elbow slammed into Percival's side, cutting his words.

I rolled my eyes, suddenly unable to remember why I'd given them a title.

Without knocking, I pushed open the door to the small shop

and stepped inside. The room was cluttered with half-finished swords, tools, and various metal plates that were bent but unrecognizable as any specific object. The room was heavy with the smell of smoke even as the open windows on each side pushed a draft of air through. The left side of the room had a small kitchen, and the right was almost completely taken up by a staircase. There was a fire pit at the back that had gone out, but from the smoky smell of the room, not long ago. The gavel had an unfinished sword on it, half bent and beaten, the hammer laying flat on top instead of in its proper place, like the smith had left in a rush. But I knew he hadn't, because by the window was a rocking chair where a late-middle-aged man slept soundly. The skin around his eyes were wrinkled in the corner, where bags of skin hung down like the soft folds of a newborn puppy. His mouth was agape and, despite the obvious wear on his body, he was still muscular from the strenuous work he endured day in and day out. His gray hair was stuck to his forehead with sweat, and I thought he looked very much like my father. But this man wasn't the gentle soul my father had been, despite their shared genes. He was a grouchy old coot. I took a look at the unfinished, unpolished weapons lying about, wondering if he'd lost his touch or if reuniting with him was worth getting the armor I'd imagined.

I sighed, determined to make my dream a reality, no matter the cost. "Uncle Roger," I said, and his eyes snapped open.

19

MINSEO

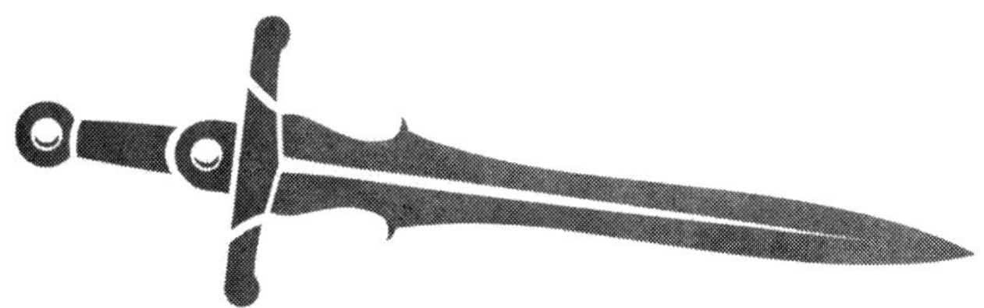

I needed to get it together. I knew that. The moment I discovered Young was alive, I knew it meant letting Charlotte go. They were married and the thing we'd bonded over, Young's death, wasn't valid anymore. But there we were, reunited, and every action and word that fell from my mouth was a desperate plea for her to choose me. There was no choice, Minseo. There was no possible future where she'd be mine again. But the problem was I was *hers*.

My thoughts flashed back to Young's cool departure earlier that morning. He didn't seem to have any trouble remembering there was no choice. His unwillingness to compete infuriated me. The old Minseo would have taken it as a sign that he didn't love her. After all, he practically pushed us together, but the old Minseo lost his brother. I wouldn't make the same mistake, not even for Charlotte.

Still, what I knew and what I felt were two different things. My body couldn't ignore the woman who broke out of Camelot on the back of a dragon. As if I needed another reason to find her attractive. I scoffed. Why didn't Young just grab a dragon and get out of there? I chuckled at the absurd thought and tried to ignore the heat radiating from my hand that hung inches away from Charlotte's as we walked the palace grounds.

"What's so funny?" Charlotte asked. Her cheeks were a deep pink and I wondered if they were sunburned.

Oh. She said something. "What?" I asked.

"You laughed."

"Yeah. I uh, I was wondering why Young didn't just grab a dragon and come home."

She laughed, a beautiful open-mouthed chuckle that brought me directly back to every moment I'd heard it before. It was a joy to witness, pulling me into a smile with her infectious glow. *Enough.*

I stopped in front of the bathhouse. The bottom was made with carefully stacked stones with pockets that the servants filled with coals to heat the various stone baths. Above the base were wooden pillars and walls painted white and red. The roof came together with two curved wooden panels that were tiled and protruded off the edge so we could hang lanterns.

I turned to Charlotte who gaped at the structure. I eyed it, but I was so used to seeing it, I hardly noticed it anymore. I tried to imagine it through her eyes, and when I looked again, I saw it for what it truly was. It was the finest Vires had to offer. Combine that with a style of architecture she'd never seen, and I could see the cause of her awe.

"So there are attendants inside," I said. "They'll put you in different baths with different temperatures and then scrub you."

She bit her bottom lip. "Can't I scrub myself?"

"You can, but they'll get all the dirt off, plus the dead skin. It's actually nice."

She nodded.

"I'm going to go check in with Young and the council. Will you be okay?"

She pressed her lips together.

I tilted my head. "What's wrong?"

"What if I need you to translate something?" she said with a pout.

I pushed my palms together. "You... want me to supervise your bath?"

"Oh, uhm no. I'll be fine. I'll see you in a bit." She turned and walked into the bathhouse alone, leaving me with the image.

It was several minutes before I moved from my spot outside, finally scrubbing a slew of lewd scenarios from my head. I headed for the throne room, the furthest point from the bathhouse inside the castle compound. In fact, there were so many buildings between, I couldn't even see the lake from that side. By the time I made it, my body and mind had calmed.

I walked across the stone bridge and entered the throne room to find the council deep in discussion, with Young standing at the head of the table. My father watched intently from his throne.

"One dragon does not win a war," a council member said, his gravelly voice rife with frustration.

"You're thinking too small," Young said, his voice commanding. "We leverage the dragon."

Silence hung in the air as the council waited for the rest of Young's plan. "We'll inform the other allies of its existence and use it to convince them to join us against Camelot." His eyes lingered on each council member before moving to the next. "They just have to believe we have a chance. None of them are happy with the conditions of this alliance."

"You mean fly the dragon out of Vires?"

"No," another member interjected. "We can't risk our only advantage. It stays in Vires."

The discussion shot across the room from one council member to another.

"How will we convince them that the dragon exists?"

"We can intercept their kingdoms' traders for testimony."

"That just might work."

"Your Highness," Hanbit said. "Do you plan to take on this mission?"

"Yes," he said, his lack of hesitation surprising me.

"No," I interjected. "I will."

Suddenly noticing my presence, the council turned to me.

Young turned to the table. "Please, excuse me for a moment," he said. He marched over to me, the furrow of his brow reminiscent of eight-year-old him after I once broke his sword.

"What are you doing? This is my mission," he said.

"What are you doing? Charlotte needs you here, and so does Morgana."

"That's exactly why I'm doing this. I want them to be safe. I want Vires to get out of this situation. I'm the reason we're in it."

I put a hand on his shoulder, "I get that. But I can complete this mission, for you and for Vires, and you can get your life back." He looked down at the ground thoughtfully.

I spoke more gently. "You're pushing her away." *And into my arms.*

He nodded. "You're right. I need you to take on this mission. Thank you, brother. There's no time to waste. Go to the market, find someone from one of Camelot's allied kingdoms who is ready to depart. Show them the dragon and ride with them." He stopped and looked me over. "Are you alright? You look tired."

"I'm fine," I assured him. "I'll leave immediately."

20

CHARLOTTE

I stood naked at the center of the bathhouse as a woman on the crest between middle-aged and elderly peeled the last of my training gear from my skin. I squirmed to cover my body, crossing my legs and using my arms as a shield, but it was futile. I was as naked as the day I was born. I scanned the room, struck by the set of stone baths that were scattered throughout the wooden room. The stones were dark gray and reminded me of the ones that lay along the shore of the Jin Sea to the east, in both color and smoothness.

The pools spat clouds of steam that fogged the room with a pleasant floral scent that was both familiar and unplaceable. But my bare skin exposed in such an open space alarmed me, even with the movements of the old woman so nurturing and sure.

Without a word, she led me over to the first pool. Her gaze bore into me, the creases around her eyes telling me my hesitation perplexed her. I'd had servants wash me before, but it had been quite some time since I'd been a part of that world.

As I stepped into the pool, my breath caught. It was much

hotter than I imagined it would be. I jerked my foot back. The woman gestured back to the pool, her white hair neatly pulled back into a bun at the nape of her neck.

"It's hot," I said.

She gestured back to the pool. I sighed and stepped in, my foot tingling as I felt around for the next drop. My feet reached an edge, and I stepped down on the gray stones that were black under the water. Once at the pool's center, I lowered my body until the warmth covered my shoulders. A freezing chill slid down my spine before my whole body pricked with overheat. My body adjusted slightly, but each micro-movement sent a new flush of heat to that area. But then the heat sunk deeper into my flesh and soothed my sore muscles. I closed my eyes to savor the sensation.

Just as I started to relax, the woman of the bathhouse plucked me from the water. Her strength was mismatched with her small frame, her tired, crescent eyes contrasted by the speed with which she moved.

This time, she placed me in a lukewarm pool that felt cold against my heated skin. It was refreshing, like the first morning of winter. After a few minutes, the woman appeared behind me. I scrambled out of the pool as not to burden her with lifting me and she gestured to a third pool. As expected, this one felt hotter than the first. Luckily, she didn't leave me there for long and shortly after led me to a gray stone slab at the back of the room.

Without hesitation, she sat me down on the slab, lay me back, and positioned me in the middle of the stone. I was struck by how surely she touched me, like a mother dressing her child, only rougher and we were strangers. I found myself clenching my eyes shut, ready to surrender to whatever unusual custom came next. I heard the shuffle of her feet grow fainter but return a minute later. Her hands came down on my stomach and my eyes snapped open. Her hands were gloved in a strange material with a rough surface.

I clenched my teeth as her hands began to scrub. Once again, her strength surprised me. The scratch of the material feeling good on some parts and agonizing on more sensitive ones. The worst parts were the areas that tickled. I fought the urge to squirm off the stone slab as she moved to my inner thigh. Next, the woman grabbed my arm and lifted it above my head as she scrubbed my underarm.

I had a sudden urge to both laugh and cry. I shut my eyes as the small woman stroked and scrubbed every bare inch of me. I felt the flick of something hit the stone in front of me and opened my eyes to find it covered in rolled flakes of dead skin. Stunned and mortified, I fought the instinct to flee. The woman lifted a bucket and poured a mass of water onto me and the slab. Most of the skin washed away, but I felt some particles gather underneath me.

Then, in one smooth motion, she flipped me over with force and scrubbed me again, without a sign that the dead skin would cease. She occasionally poured hot water onto me, which was welcomed as I started to shiver with cold, even in the steamy room.

When she finished, my skin was raw, red, and softer than I'd ever felt it. She washed my hair and dried me before standing me in front of a mirror. She came up behind me and examined my naked body in the reflection, a half-smile as the only indication she was pleased with her work.

The embarrassment I'd felt when we started had washed away with my dead skin and I took a moment to embrace my curves and stretch marks, earned from birthing Morgana. The woman brought me clean undergarments to change into. When I put them on, she returned with a long spool of pink fabric. *What is this? Is she going to make something? Now?*

Instead, she put the fabric across my chest and my hand on top to hold it as she wrapped it tightly around me. My breasts pooled over the top, but each time I tried to adjust it, she slapped my hand away. She tied a thin strand of fabric, in the same color, a hand above my waist and tied it tightly.

I gawked at the gorgeous floor-length dress in the mirror. It hadn't been a spool after all, but something beautifully Viran. I looked much like a princess, but it had been quite some time since I felt like one. I still felt the top was too exposed. Even back in Besmium with courtiers always trying to outdo each other, it never came to this. Relief filled me as the woman returned with a short jacket that just barely covered the area of my concern. It was white and crisscrossed in the front. Once secured, the woman pulled over a stool, stood on it. She wrangled my already frizzing hair into one braid down my back, tying a ribbon to its end.

I couldn't take my eyes off the dress. It was beautiful and elegant. I moved my hips, in love with the sway of it as the smooth material held its cone-like shape.

"Hanbok," she said, pointing to the dress.

"Hmm?"

She repeated herself.

"Hanbok," I said back to her, and the word was as foreign on my lips as the gown on my body.

21

ARTHUR

"Uncle Roger! It's me!" I yelled as the bulky man rushed toward me with an object cocked over his head. "It's me, Arthur!"

The blaze of intensity in his eyes extinguished and his face returned to his default scowl.

He grumbled. "Then you should know better than to sneak up on a man while he's sleeping."

Instead of paying me any more mind, he turned to the fireplace and began to stack coals in the pit.

"Uncle Roger, I need you to make me some armor, a full set. With gold accents and jeweled—"

He spat on the floor. "What on earth do you need armor for, boy?"

My memories of Roger rushed back. He'd always been cranky, but now he just seemed senile. I hated the way he made me feel small. "I-I'm the king. We're going to war with Vires. I need to be prepared."

"I'm not a fool, boy. I'm asking why *you* need armor."

My face flushed with heat. I spoke again, annunciating each word to highlight my frustration. "I am the king. I will lead my men into battle."

"I thought you appointed those knights of yours so you never had to get your hands dirty."

Clenching my jaw, I drew Excalibur, putting it's point to his back. "How dare you disrespect me. I am your king."

He sighed, and when he spoke his words were so calm that they alarmed me. "You are just a boy."

I swung Excalibur into a table and several unfinished weapons clanged as they hit the ground. I stared my Uncle Roger down, satisfied by the loud noise.

He stood slowly and walked over to me. "Pick it up."

I shivered beneath his blue-eyed gaze. There were no official titles in this room. He was my father's brother, there when I was born, when I took my first steps and spoke my first words. I needed him to understand, most of all, that I had changed. Why couldn't he see it? I bent and collected the fallen items, clumsily placing them back on the table where Excalibur still stuck. I worried I'd look even more helpless if I tried to wrench it out and was unsuccessful.

Like the sword belonged to him, Roger slid it out of the table with ease and examined it. "Do you want to know why I think you're just a boy?"

I gulped back my response like a reprimanded child.

He continued, "Because you come here, asking for armor with frills and decoration when you've never spilled a single drop of blood. You don't know what it means to take a life. You don't know the burden and can't comprehend the cost."

I felt my eyes prick, and I clenched my jaw so tightly it burned to kccp from crying.

"I'll tell you what." He scratched the dirty stubble on his chin.

"If you succeed in one simple task for me, I'll build you a set of armor with such exquisite craftsmanship, Excalibur will look tarnished beside it."

"What's the task?" I asked, but my voice broke. I held my breath, hoping he didn't notice.

He turned with Excalibur in hand and headed to a door at the back of the kitchen area.

The door was so covered in grime and soot that I hadn't noticed it when I arrived. I followed him out and wondered whether it was a mistake not to alert Percival and Lamorak of where I was.

We stepped out into a narrow animal pen that had gates on each side of a grassy plain and a barn of sorts at the far end. The neighboring buildings had the same setup, though their barns were more elaborate and the pens wider than the small patch that belonged to my uncle. It was an unusual sight, not visible from the main roads. A chicken pecked around my foot and I fought the urge to shoo it away.

"Stay here," Roger barked and then entered the barn. I stood nervously by the door, my mind racing with the possible tasks this might yield. Was I going to be made to do farm chores, feed his chickens? What could the point possibly be?

He opened the barn door and a flash of pink flew towards me. A piglet darted wildly around the pen, shuffling around as it tried quickly changing directions. It squealed with delight in the sun as it raced in circles, making the most of the tight space.

I watched as it played, a smile stinging my cheeks. It was the kind of pure joy I hadn't felt since I was a kid. I watched so intently, I didn't notice Roger cross the pen to stand beside me. He handed me Excalibur and I felt a wave of relief to have it back.

"So what's this task?" I said, my attention still on the small pig as it munched on a clump of grass.

“I want you to kill that pig.”

My heart raced as understanding settled onto me like grains of sand embedded into my skin at the end of a beach day. I took a deep breath. “That’s it?” I asked, turning to his frosty blue gaze.

He smiled, a foreign expression to his face. “That’s it.”

“Easy,” I said. I walked over to the piglet, my confidence waning with each step. It lapped at its snout with delight as I approached. Its little mouth hung open and lifted at the corners as if it were smiling. When I was right over it, I could hear the little snorting sound it made each time it moved. It was cute, adorable even, but I had something to prove and nothing could prevent me from proving it. I drew Excalibur and raised it above my head. My heart slammed into my ribs and I felt my breath leave my body. The pig craned his neck up as if expecting a treat. Instead, I lowered the blade and sliced into the tiny animal, it’s shrill bird-like scream rattling my bones. My sword slid through like butter, the pig’s red juices pouring through the wound. I turned away, covering my mouth with my hand in alarm.

“Look at it!” Roger barked from beside me. I turned back to the splattered animal as it made it’s final twitch, the glisten of life dulling in its beady eyes.

I felt a lump in my throat. My nose prickled. The lump traveled down to my chest and I felt myself gag. Suddenly, all at once, vomit spewed from my body.

Roger rubbed my back and, for a moment in my disorientation, I thought he was my father.

He spoke. “War is an ugly business. It’s not about golden armor or glory. It’s about pain and death.” His hand left my back, and the next time he spoke, his voice was further away. “If you’re serious about going to war, I suggest you grow up and understand what you're getting into—what you're getting your soldiers into.

Because killing a man is a hell of a lot harder than what you just did."

22

YOUNG

I stood outside the bathhouse where Minseo told me to wait for Charlotte. A flutter of nerves raced around my stomach, irritating me. I would not compete with Minseo. If Charlotte still wanted me, she'd return. As I waited, it dawned on me how little I knew about this dragon-riding, dagger-carrying woman in leather. We hadn't had the chance to share our lost years with each other. I had to admit she hardly resembled the girl I'd dreamt of all those days in captivity. She certainly wasn't the delicate princess I married. I swallowed the thought as she stepped out of the bathhouse. She wore a pink and white Hanbok, her western features mismatched with her Viran attire, making a traditional garment hundreds of years old new again.

My heart raced. Maybe I'd compete a *little*.

She handed me her dagger. "I uh, don't have anywhere to put it."

I eyed her skirt, the memory of her pulling a sword from her skirt striking me. "It won't fit in there?" I said. My mind pleaded for her to remember. She flashed me a devious smile that assured me she did.

"Where's Minseo?" she asked, and all the joy from seeing her melted away. I wrestled my expression to be neutral. Still, her mouth dropped open as if stunned by her own question.

"I mean," she stammered, "I was meant to meet him here. Are we waiting for him?"

"He's preparing to leave Vires. He's going on a mission to turn Camelot's allies against them. He leaves today."

Her gaze dropped and she looked lost in thought for a moment before a bright smile lit her face. "Shall we go see Morgana?"

I took her arm to lead the way but couldn't pull my gaze away from her. We were together in Vires at last. I'd never get used to seeing her dressed like this, and I wasn't the only one. Despite the fact that every noblewoman in the castle grounds wore some variation of a Hanbok, Charlotte drew the unabashed gaze of every person we passed. She fixed her gaze ahead, seemingly unconscious of the attention. Perhaps she was used to it, or maybe her thoughts lay elsewhere.

As we left the castle grounds and moved into the city, Charlotte's lips parted, her eyes moving from one structure to the next as she took in the city. Viran people filled the streets, all going about their business until they caught a glimpse of the foreign princess, the one who I'm sure had already garnered a reputation as a dragon rider.

I watched as Charlotte's years as a princess took effect. She smiled and waved, giving special attention to the children who seemed most struck by her presence. I heard what they called her in whispers on the street before crowds of peasants got bold enough to chant it: Dragon Gongju.

She turned to me, her eyes glittering with curiosity. She asked, "What does it mean?"

I took delight in translating. "Dragon Princess." She smiled thoughtfully, fiddling with her hands, and I wondered if, had her hair been loose, she would have twirled her finger in a curl like she used to.

I felt nervous for her as we neared Gabriel's home. I knew I was walking into a heavy and emotional moment and was already itching to escape. Even to me, it seemed heartless not to want to share it with her and Morgana, but the truth was, ever since the commotion the previous night, all I could think about was getting a glimpse of that dragon.

We arrived outside Gabriel's home and I stopped short. "It's this one here. I'll be back in a few hours to get you," I said. Her gaze locked on the door and she moved to it like a woman possessed, blocking me out along with everything else. I had no doubt she was imagining the little girl who was on the other side, and I was relieved she didn't ask me to stay.

She knocked and I waited only until I heard the door slide open, then I turned back to the city, unsure if I should meet up with Minseo and make sure everything was going well at the market or give in to my curiosity and seek out Charlotte's dragon.

As if there hadn't been a choice at all, I headed straight for the edge of town where the dragon was being kept.

It was a decision I was grateful for the moment I arrived.

The dragon's neck was outstretched, the scales of its face splattered with blood as it tore through an animal I could no longer identify and devoured it. It's sharp teeth gleamed red, reminding me a bit of Charlotte's dagger and it's matching counterpart. The dragon's size was just as I'd imagined, yet shocking to look at just the same. His glossy eye moved to me and a chill fell down my back. Something so deadly and unpredictable couldn't possibly exist, yet there it was. What I hadn't expected was it's reflective scales that couldn't be assigned a single color, but if I had to choose just one to describe it, I'd say silver. This was more than what I'd promised the council. I found relief in that fact, though I didn't know it was a concern that subconsciously dug at me until I was released of it.

I laughed, overcome with the possibilities. We could do it. We could pry Vires from Camelot's grasp. This dragon was our trump card, a warrior strong enough to turn the tide of a battle. But I had a secret—I'd come to discover a second warrior who I could make formidable in time for the battle. At that very moment, she reunited with the Dragon Princess.

23

CHARLOTTE

I swung the door open to find the soft, loving eyes of Gabriel staring wide-eyed at me. His dark lashes as ever flitted with disbelief. I'd been so focused on getting back to Morgana that I somehow skidded over thoughts of *our* reunion. Breathless, I pulled him in for a hug. His muscular arms wrapped around me like a soft blanket, making me feel small and child-like.

"It's true," he breathed into my hair. " You're here." He started to pull away but I stopped him, squeezing him tightly.

When he spoke again, I could hear the smile in his voice. "How did you escape?" he asked, but I could tell by the sly tone that he already knew and just asked for confirmation. Of course, even with the language barrier, he found a way to stay privy to the kingdom-wide gossip. "Dragon," I said simply, rubbing my face on his chest.

I dropped my arms and looked up at him, my heart warming from seeing my long lost partner. "Where is she?" I asked as we stepped into the house. I looked up and across the room stood a stunned little girl. Her Hanbok was the same color as mine, her curls pulled back into a single braid. Her lips parted, giving me a glimpse of a growing tooth that hadn't been there when we got separated. I held my arms out, but instead of the smile I'd imagined, her brow furrowed and she shattered into a mess of tears. We ran together and I lifted her into my arms. Her small frame jostled as she struggled for breaths between sobs. My heart broke just to see her that way, and I understood because I felt the same. I held her tightly to my body, but not as tightly as her tiny arms and legs wrapped around me. She was a touch heavier, maybe a bit taller too. My heart crunched when I realized that, for the first time, I'd missed her birthday.

"It's okay, baby," I said, rubbing her back. "We're together now."

I took a seat on Gabriel's couch and cradled Morgana onto my lap. I was taken aback by how quiet she was. This wasn't the Morgana I knew. The girl I knew was a talker, a storyteller. What I wouldn't have given to see her perk up and tell one of her tales at that very moment. After a few short minutes, her sniffles slowed and I felt her breathing deepen into a restful sleep. I stared down at her, grateful I'd somehow made it back to her. I never wanted to spend another day away. The sudden rush of all the worries I'd suppressed lifted off me and I had to bite back more tears from bursting forth. I pulled her to my face. "I love you, Morgana," I whispered.

Gabriel, who had been watching quietly from across the room, took a seat beside me. "Have you seen him?" he asked.

Did he mean Young? I nodded, fearful that the question might push me to reveal too much about my current thoughts on the subject.

He leaned closer as if to ask for more information, but I had nothing more to offer. I hadn't come close to processing any of it myself.

"It must've been a strange night for you. When I heard you'd arrived, and *how* you arrived," he held a hand up, "we'll come back to *that* later. I knew you'd come by at some point today." A glint of mischievous intent flickered in his eyes. "How *was* your night?"

I turned my face away, hoping to block him from reading anything from my eyes or face, then answered as indifferently as I could muster. "I uh, was tired. I stayed with Young and—"

He gasped. "What did Minseo say?"

I chewed on my lip. "He slept outside the door."

Gabriel's face lit so brightly that you would've thought he'd been crowned king. "So what are you going to do?"

I tossed around his question for a moment before answering. "There's nothing to do. I'm married to Young."

His dark eyes widened, putting his thick lashes on full display. His eyebrows rose and his mouth fell open. "But—"

"But what?"

He slid his palms down across his face. "Say it."

I shook my head in confusion as if this small action could jolt my brain back into the conversation. "Say what?"

"You still love Minseo."

I rubbed Morgana's arm for comfort and to make sure she was still asleep. My heartbeat suddenly drew my attention. Finally, the denial of Gabriel's claim came to my lips, but I didn't speak it.

A jewel of an idea slipped into my head and I flipped my gaze back to Gabe. "How are things with Junho?" I asked.

It happened in a flash, but I could swear I saw a touch of pink on his cheeks. "What? Nothing. What do you mean? We're friends."

It was too many answers in too short a time to be innocent.

"So you guys haven't...?"

His gaze drifted to the top left of his field of vision, a tell I'd come to know was for memory. "No, of course not. Have you seen him yet? Did he say something?"

Guilty. I'd struck a nerve, just as he had with me. In surrender, we changed the subject to Morgana, but even that led back to the same place. "Minseo visits nearly every day," Gabriel explained. "But lately Young has been taking her hiking. A couple of times this week and once last week. I think they're starting to bond. Morgana seems excited to go."

I smiled weakly, alerting him to the fact that we once again strayed into volatile territory. My heart already knew Gabriel was right. Just like my reunion with Gabe, I'd felt the greatest sense of peace and joy when I saw Young again. But nothing could touch the burn I felt for Minseo. My only option was to deny the truth until I found a way to douse the flames.

The ties of love that pulled me had become a convoluted web. I started to miss the simplicity of war.

24

MERLIN

I must've searched the whole castle a hundred times before I let myself believe that Charlotte left me. I ran through our last conversation, again and again, wondering how I'd missed it. Why would she confide in me her greatest secret and then leave me here to die? A guilty conscience? Some skewed perception of reality?

I was bleeding out and I'd noticed my magic had become as volatile as it was when I was a child. Even Arthur's wintery gaze, heavy with disappointment and disgust, reminded me of my mother who had disowned me. She just *left*. I wasn't sure which emotion was most prominent. Anger, sadness, loss, disappointment. How could she just leave like that? How could she take Garix with her? Didn't she know how much he'd meant to me? Didn't she know what would happen to me if she left me behind? How much she put my life at risk? All the questions had me spiraling, and now that Charlotte had ruined the courtyard for me, the only place I felt somewhat normal was the castle dungeon.

I didn't know I'd get one, but I needed a win immediately. I needed to prove to Arthur that I was still on his side and that I could make up for my mistake.

I could help him get the dragon back. He'd already announced his decision to go to war with Vires. If I helped him prepare the troops and made myself useful to him, maybe, just maybe, I could win back his favor. I needed to do something. Every step in the castle felt hostile. Not just from Arthur either. The other knights, soldiers, and courtiers looked at me the same way, as a traitor, like I'd helped Charlotte escape. Like she hadn't left me here to die.

And Lance, Lance was a different story altogether. He looked at me like I was wounded, exchanging half-smiles and clearing the room when I entered. Once I thought I saw him scold some soldiers for glaring at me, but I must've been mistaken. I felt utterly isolated. If Lance was taking pity on me, things were worse than I'd imagined.

No matter how many times I put myself on the line to be close to someone, I kept coming back to the same truth. I couldn't count on anyone but myself. Humans, in general, had always proved themselves huge disappointments. For once, I didn't want to belong to them. I stormed through the hallways, headed for the peaceful solitude of my training dungeons. I stopped short when Lance stood outside the staircase that led down. Was he waiting for me?

He looked as puzzled to see me as I was to see him.

"Hey, Merlin," he said, turning away shyly.

"Move," I barked, and with a wave of my hand, I pushed him face-first into the stone wall and held him there until I passed. *Ugh.* Sharks always circled when they smelled blood in the water.

25

CHARLOTTE

I was glad to make it back to Gabriel's house before Morgana woke up.

I didn't want to leave Morgana during her nap. She'd suffered enough. I was assured by Gabriel that she'd been her same story-telling self and he was confident she'd return to form once she adjusted to seeing me again. I longed to see her that way, the care-free little girl I loved. Then I'd know for sure she was okay. I wanted to stay and hold her all day, but I didn't have a chance to check on Garix and I was beginning to worry that, without instruction, he could become dangerous.

I slipped out, and when I got to the farm at the edge of town, I knew I'd worried for nothing. Instead of the fire-breathing, human-eating creature he looked like, I arrived to find him play-fully chasing the livestock. True, the animals he played with would likely become his lunch later, but he was as soft-hearted as Merlin, the woman who raised him.

My stomach tightened as I thought of her. Her beauty, her silent strength. I hoped she was doing well and missed the feeling of having her around. "Please, forgive me," I whispered to the air as I watched Garix.

I stepped over the fence, a frail set of wooden poles that Garix could have leveled with a sneeze, and he turned to me. He wiggled his nose in recognition but quickly turned his attention to a goat who appeared so frazzled he could've laid an egg.

A chuckle sounded from behind me and I turned to see Young outside the pen. Had he been there the whole time? Leaving Garix to play, I turned and walked to Young.

"For some reason, he reminds me of you," Young said, his hands crossed behind his back.

The ground was uneven, but I was struck by how tall he seemed to me. Had he grown while he was away? "I only terrorize goats on special occasions," I said.

He half-smiled, but his gaze was intense and searching. I wondered if I was as difficult to read as he was. I scanned his face and felt a chill run through me. My mind still struggled to comprehend having him back. All this time he had been an invisible force I tapped into to get through life's difficult moments, a kind of religion.

He'd been so far for so long and, even in the best of times, Young wasn't much for sharing his thoughts or feelings. Most of what I knew of him came from his actions five years ago and the stories I told myself in order to explain them.

He was more of a stranger to me than when I'd first met him, and something about that hurt me when we were together.

"Young?" I said.

He turned his gaze back to Garix as if he knew and feared what I was going to ask next.

"Will you tell me about what happened?"

"You mean after you escaped?"

"Yes."

He shrugged. "I was captured and brought to Camelot."

"That's it?"

"What else do you want to know?"

"Everything. I want to know you—"

"I have to go," he said suddenly.

"Where?"

He shook his head.

I continued, "Where are you running to? Why do you keep running away from me?"

"Because it hurts to be around you."

I felt my heartbeat in my throat and I swallowed my sudden desire to let him walk away.

"Let's talk it through. Let's build something again."

"Build what? Everything's broken!" he shouted.

I froze, stunned by the rare display of emotion.

"You belong to Minseo now and Vires belongs to Camelot."

I felt my body numb. Where was this coming from? "We all thought you were dead. Any of us would have done whatever we could to get you back alive."

"And if I was dead, everyone and everything would be better off."

I took a step toward him. "That's not true. We can fix all of this. We can beat Camelot. You and I can start over."

"How can we start over?"

"We can talk everything through."

"Okay," he said, walking up to me. He glared down at me. "Tell me, Charlotte, are you in love with Minseo?"

I held his gaze. "Yes."

He turned to walk away and I was grateful not to see the hurt in his eyes.

"Stop. Don't go," I called.

He turned back. "Why shouldn't I?"

"Because we can find a way to overcome this."

"What do you want? You want me to win you?"

"I want you to stay and fight for us. Make an effort. Work with me to fix this."

He shook his head. "I shouldn't have to fight for the love of my own wife."

He walked away and headed towards the farmer's house, instead of his own.

Instead of going after him, or even watching him go, I turned my gaze to Garix and fought the urge to cry. I understood Young's anger. It was an impossible situation. My feelings for Minseo had grown from bonding over Young's death, but that gave little comfort to this situation. I was glad, at least, that Young had expressed his frustration. It was a step forward, but the trouble with moving forward is that, while you move toward something, you move away from something else.

I was consumed by guilt and uneasiness. I hadn't intended on hurting anyone, especially Young. All three of us suffered and there was no easy remedy.

Garix cocked his neck back and screeched into the sky, startling me. As the shrill sound traveled through the mountains of Vires, I recognized it as my own sadness, a mournful shade of dark blue. Garix blinked again blankly and then returned to chasing the terrified livestock. But the sound echoed inside me.

My thoughts drifted to Minseo. The levity of his presence, his warmth, and I wished I could've said goodbye. I wished I could crawl into his arms where I felt invincible and strong.

Garix shot into the air, landing in front of me with a gust of wind. He lowered himself to the ground, the way he always did before we flew.

The decision to chase after Minseo wasn't mine; it was more of Garix's suggestion. At least, that's what I told myself, even if I was acutely aware that his emotions and actions were bound to mine. Minseo was an impulse, one I couldn't let go.

Any feelings I had for him were wrong, weren't they? And, though I still intended to work through things with Young, he certainly wasn't making it easy. In the last few minutes, something major had changed. I'd confessed to Young that I loved Minseo. It was no longer hidden, not from Young and certainly not from myself. Minseo was likely the only one who didn't know. I traced my fingertips along Garix's wings. Perhaps it wouldn't hurt to say a quick goodbye.

26

MINSEO

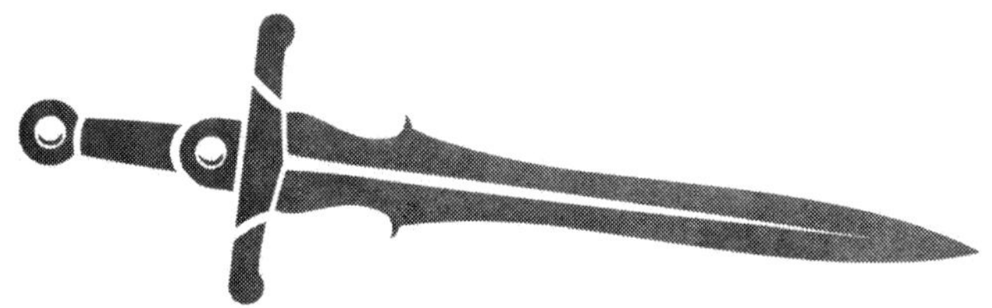

The market buzzed with life, the air heavy with unique smells and bright colors as merchants shouted at passersby waving their assorted goods. Some had tables draped with fine cloth and elegantly displayed fruit, weaponry, or jewels. Others had their vegetables or carvings laid out on woven mats in front of them. There was so much to touch and look at, it was easy to lose time there, but I had no time to waste. I needed to find a foreign merchant quickly.

I made my way through the rows of stalls, the merchants there as diverse and colorful as the goods they sold. I closed my eyes and tilted my head back, catching the sun's rays on my face. I took a deep breath and listened for any language that wasn't Viran.

"That's a good way to get robbed, Your Majesty," a gruff voice barked.

I opened my eyes to see a man in his late fifties with a long beard and a lumpy purple hat that had a black feather in it. *English.* His clothes were a bit odd for Vires, but I couldn't place his kingdom just by looking at him.

"What's a good way to get robbed?"

"Close your eyes in this market. There are pickpockets everywhere."

I cocked my head to the side. "Where?" I asked, wondering if I was out of touch, naive, or if this man was simply paranoid.

He pointed his scarred hand at a group of little boys playing near a fruit stall.

Oh, great. This guy was never going to be credible enough to convince his king that we had a dragon. Before I could answer, he started shouting at the group.

"Hey, you!" he yelled. "Kid! Give the prince his sword back."

I reached for my sword and, sure enough, felt the empty sheath. *No possible way.*

The kid turned to run and the man shouted, "He'll have you beheaded."

The boys huddled into a group before pushing forward the smallest among them. He couldn't have been much older than Morgana. He bowed his head with shame as he held my bare sword out in front of him. It was alarming to see a child that small holding a sword, let alone imagine that he'd stolen it without me noticing. I carefully lifted the sword from his small hands, but he didn't look up to see my forgiving smile.

"You," I whispered in Viran, "be a good boy."

He nodded to me without looking up and backed away until his group grabbed him and they vanished behind the mass of people.

When I spun back to the old man who warned me, he'd already disappeared into the crowd. Luckily, his hat was distinct enough for me to track him down. "Sir," I called, weaving through a swarm of people. "Thank you for your help. I'm Prince Minseo."

"Levario," he said. I was a little struck that he didn't bow. He didn't reach to shake my hand either.

"May I ask where you're from?"

"Faresa," he said.

I knew it. It was on our side of the Jin Sea and only recently pulled into the alliance. He was a perfect candidate for my mission. "Are you leaving today?" I asked, hoping I'd already found a suitable partner.

"Are you kidding? Do you see this crowd? I can't leave today. It's a gold mine."

I scanned the crowded street and nodded. "Ah, yes, I see."

"This is a once in a lifetime haul. They're stalking up on luxuries before the alliance tax hits."

Ah. I hadn't accounted for that. Still, Faresa was a perfect place to start as it was closer to Vires than Camelot, which would be ideal in a battle. If this was a good trade day, I'd likely run into the same problem with anyone else.

"You know what else is a once in a lifetime experience?" I said. "Seeing a dragon."

His eyes lit but his face remained neutral. "So the rumors are true."

I had him. "Don't you think this information would be worth more to your king than an extra few sales at the market?" His gaze skidded across the crowd. I cleared my throat to regain his attention. "Listen, I'll take you to see the dragon, and in exchange you leave for Faresa today and allow me to accompany you on your trip."

He sighed in defeat. "Fine, fine. Let me gather my things. But if I find out you're lying—" I raised an eyebrow. It certainly was a strange way to address royalty, but it amused me.

Noticing my surprise, he pressed his lips together. He turned away and waved me to follow.

A few minutes later, we'd escaped the cluster of people in the market and found ourselves wandering through a nearly deserted Vires. It really had been a great market day. Levario was quiet as we neared the farm on the edge of town. I was surprised to see Young standing at the edge of the farm, his gaze locked on the shimmering beast. I realized that Levario had stopped walking a few steps back. I turned to urge him forward but saw a softened man with tear-filled eyes. Perhaps that was the correct reaction to witnessing such a creature, a miracle. He wiped his eyes, unashamed and unbothered by my gaze.

We walked toward the dragon, a bit slower than the pace we used to get there, and while Levario drank in the sight of the dragon, I searched for the girl who flew him to Vires. When we reached Young, he turned to me with a neutral expression. His face lit when he saw Levario beside me. "Oh, is this your merchant? Which kingdom are you going to first?" he asked.

"Faresa," Levario said bluntly.

I giggled, becoming more amused with him every moment.

"Oh, that's perfect," Young said, ignoring Levario's rough greeting.

Young turned back to the dragon. "She named it Garix."

I looked at the beast as it playfully chased the livestock around the fenced-in land. Did *she*? Where was *she*? I wondered, but I knew better than to ask. Still, why was Young so hesitant to spend time with Charlotte? If she was my wife— I stopped. I took a deep breath of surrender and turned my attention to Levario. "Shall we go?"

He nodded but kept his gaze locked on the dragon, unwilling to turn away.

That afternoon, as we neared Vires' southern border, Levario, his trade cart, and I were plunged into darkness as a gust of wind whipped us. Three seconds of unsettling confusion passed before I realized the shadow blocking the sun was a dragon that stalked us, and that the true danger was on its back.

Levario comforted the horses who bucked with alarm as Charlotte landed her dragon a few yards away. I walked over to meet her, my heartbeat wild as I neared. The dragon was not still and statuesque like it had been the first time I saw it. It craned its neck, curiously absorbing its surroundings. Charlotte, however, had her gaze fixed on me and she didn't look happy. She stood with her arms crossed as I approached. She was back in her leather suit, but her hair was pulled into a single braid though several of her curls had been pulled free from it by the wind.

When I reached her, her gaze traveled down my body and back up in appraisal. "You weren't going to say goodbye?"

My cheeks burned. I could've sworn this woman enjoyed making me crazy. "I thought it best if I just slipped out. You know, give you some time to figure things out."

She chewed her bottom lip for a moment then spoke, "How long will you be gone?"

The guilt hit my stomach before I made the move, my eyes jutting to Levario to check if we were being watched, but the gray-bearded merchant's attention was consumed by Garix and I wasn't sure if it was for the sake of privacy for me and Charlotte or curiosity about the dragon.

When I turned back to Charlotte, I could see a distinct blush across her cheeks as if she knew what I was checking for, but, except for the free tendrils of her hair dancing in the wind, she remained motionless. If she wanted a difficult goodbye, I'd give her one. I stepped toward her and pulled her body to mine with greater force than I'd intended. I felt her knees buckle and I was certain that if I let her go, she'd drop to the ground. Instead, I rubbed her cheek with my thumb like she had done to me when she first arrived in Vires, and I leaned in close. I gazed into her dark eyes and saw the answers to the questions that had been plaguing me for months. Yes, she still loved me. No, she didn't want me to let go. Nothing had changed. Her bottom lip quivered as I threatened to lean closer and kiss her, but the whole reason I'd volunteered for this trip was to give her time to sort through her feelings. She was still Young's wife. I felt the push of her chest as she breathed heavily and her heart raced. My body responded. If I didn't let go now, I wouldn't be able to.

"Minseo," she said, "can I ask you something?"

"Yes," I said, my thoughts in tune with every movement of her body beneath my fingers.

"Do you think a man should have to fight for the love of his wife?" she asked, her eyes a little dewy.

The word "love" on her lips took me back to the months we'd spent together. I thought of the nights she'd whispered to me in the darkness, and the joy I'd felt when she agreed to marry me. I felt myself smile, half lost in the memory and said, "Every day of his life."

Levario cleared his throat, pulling our attention. I quickly pressed my lips to her ear. "Goodbye Charlotte," I whispered, pulling her body tight to mine one last time before I released her.

As soon as we parted, my blood ran cold. Was my decision to leave going to break this love of ours? Was I pushing her to Young, like I'd accused him of doing to me? Fear tore through me and I felt my sure steps toward the cart slow. I looked back over my shoulder at Charlotte, and my fears vanished. I saw everything there, on her face. The dazed dream-like expression, the gentle smile. The red of her collarbone. She understood that this was not goodbye and that there was nowhere I could travel where she wouldn't be with me.

Out of respect for my brother, I would leave for this mission. I'd give him a chance to reconnect with her and give Charlotte enough time to know for sure how she felt. I trusted that what Charlotte and I had was strong enough to endure this test. I trusted her to make the choice that was best for her and planned to accept it, even if after everything she chose Young. However, if I came back and her heart still belonged to me, I was going to take her and never let her go again.

As I mounted my horse, I felt like myself again. The version of me that I thought had died with my brother. But if Young could be resurrected, why couldn't I?

27

YOUNG

My face was hot and I felt myself cringe every time the memory of my argument with Charlotte slipped back in. After lunch at the farm, I noticed Charlotte had taken Garix out, so I slunk to the throne room to distract myself with the council.

I was relieved that I arrived to find them passionately debating the war. A perfectly suited distraction. While they'd agreed to send Minseo to try to draw allies to our cause, his was a mission of subtlety. The council was still undecided on the war.

Everyone agreed we should prepare in case Arthur came for Charlotte's dragon, or if he heard of our plans to gather allies. Only a few members were convinced the war was a wise decision.

After everything I'd seen, there was no risk too great to reclaim Vires' independence. But until Minseo returned with confirmed allies, I had nothing to convince them. Hours of the same arguments going back and forth dragged on.

Suddenly my heart sank as Charlotte walked into the throne room and over to the table where the council met. I, along with the other council members, gaped at her, none of us certain on how to react to her presence. She didn't know anything about the customs and proceedings of our system, and if she did, she'd know she wasn't welcome to speak there. And worse, I'd just yelled at her and was attempting to use this meeting as a much-needed escape. What could she possibly have to say?

My stomach churned with anticipation. She turned her gaze at my father. *No.* She wasn't actually going to address the king?

"Your Majesty," she said.

My heart raced and I vehemently debated intervening.

"I wish to thank you for your hospitality."

The room fell silent and several of the council members turned away in discomfort.

"You are most welcome," he said, and the room collectively let out a sigh of relief.

"I wish to discuss my dragon and his place in Vires."

The king nodded.

Charlotte divided her attention among the members of the council evenly. "I would like to swear my and Garix's allegiances to Vires. I realize that my presence here has put Vires in danger. In exchange for our sanctuary, we will fight on your behalf should a war break out."

She spoke like a queen, her voice full and sure, her posture straight, her gaze piercing as it moved from one person to the next.

"The dragon follows my commands alone as a consequence of my participation in its birth. He is still very young but grows rapidly in size, power, and endurance. With help, we could train him to be a valuable asset in battle. He may even be able to outmatch Arthur's battle mage, Merlin."

She pulled a wisp of hair out of her face, and her gaze fell to me for a moment that left me too breathless to anticipate her next words.

"I know it's not my place, but I believe, given enough time, we can win a war with Camelot."

The king eyed her, cautiously planning his reply. "Do you not understand what is at stake?" he asked.

"Yes, Your Majesty, I do. I understand better than anyone else in this room as I've suffered the loss of my family and my kingdom."

Silence hung in the air.

"You may lose those again," the king said.

"Not this time."

My father stroked his chin. "And what of your daughter? What of your husband? Are their lives worth the risk?"

She took a deep breath through her nose and her gaze once again fell to me. "I can tell you that the guilt from feeling responsible, when your kingdom falls, is a burden greater than death."

I tore my gaze away from her. She may have been here on my behalf, but I wasn't ready to forgive her.

Sensing her case had been made, she bowed and hurried out of the hall, leaving the rest of us in contemplative silence.

Even with her compelling speech, the council bickered throughout the week, unable to commit to the war. I made sure to take Morgana out for what we were calling hiking, but I still needed more time away from Charlotte. It wasn't her fault, my mind screamed, but even if it wasn't, it still hurt. It hurt to look at her. It hurt to want her. But, more than anything, I was afraid. What would happen if I did fight for her and still lost her to Minseo?

The person who plagued my every thought night after night while trapped in Bullhorn was gone. Five years apart had changed her. It changed us both. What if we found out we didn't fit together anymore? I could understand why it happened, but even so, I didn't want her to be with Minseo.

If I didn't find a way to think about something else, I would drive myself to the brink of insanity. So I focused on the political situation in Vires as it was only slightly less hopeless than my problems with Charlotte.

For the moment, my main concern was convincing the council to go to war, and it seemed like they'd never commit to attacking Camelot unless forced, until a vile stranger arrived on the shores of the Jin Sea. Sir Galahad of Camelot.

The moment Galahad reached the the Jin sea, reports from our borders started coming in. Sir Galahad and twenty of his soldiers had boarded a ship bound for Vires, claiming to be on a tax collecting mission.

The council had gone into a frenzy. Did we plan to pay their tax? Should we send Charlotte and her dragon away? Should we meet him at the coast with the money to stop him from sniffing out any information? Should we take him as a prisoner to aid us in the potential war?

My father raised his hand to hush the chaos. "We will send Charlotte and her dragon to meet up with Minseo in Faresa immediately."

My breath caught.

He continued, "We will triple the presence of our soldiers in the capital city. Enough for a show of strength, but not enough to lead him to believe we are preparing for war."

Hanbit asked, "Do we plan to pay the tax?"

The king spoke again, his voice commanding attention with its subtlety. "Yes, but this will be the final time we pay. We will treat him and his soldiers with hospitality and begin full war preparations after he departs."

The room buzzed with preparations. Despite having a sizable military force, Vires always favored diplomatic solutions. Even now, my father had the option of paying the tax and walking away without a life lost, but after Charlotte's speech, and the unannounced and thinly veiled scouting mission by Galahad, Arthur had pushed my father too far. Our soldiers were skilled but lacked battle experience. They'd been thoroughly trained, but most never dealt a fatal blow. Camelot was a ruthless force, even before they earned the name and left Drethen behind. They were experienced, brutal, and had far greater numbers and resources than us. However, just as we wanted out of the alliance, I was certain other kingdoms did too. They would be our only hope in defeating Arthur. And it seemed like Minseo was our only hope.

My stomach was in knots. This was what I'd been waiting for. We'd finally begin a full mobilization of our troops for war—but once again Charlotte would be reunited with Minseo. It was like some invisible force pulled them together. Even when Charlotte and I had good times, I'd always felt that same force tearing us apart; our wedding had been canceled, Emmett tried to steal her, her family was killed, her kingdom fell, and then I was captured and imprisoned while she believed I was dead. Somehow all of those things served to bring her and Minseo together. I'd finally had enough. Charlotte was *my* wife. I didn't care if God himself was against it. If she was leaving to see Minseo tomorrow, I only had tonight to remind her who the better man was.

I stood, drawing the attention of the chattering council members. "I'll inform and prepare Charlotte for her journey," I said. If Charlotte wanted a fight, I'd give her one.

28

CHARLOTTE

I tilted my face to the sun as Morgana recounted the mostly true story about our time apart.

"And then," she said, "I told Minnow not to be sad and put a happy spell on him."

I grinned, feeling warmth in every facet of the word. "Oh. He was very lucky to have you around." My thoughts moved to Young. I'd been told he took Morgana hiking, but she hadn't mentioned it. "What about Young? You've been spending time together too, right?"

She nodded. "Hiking."

That's it? I waited for her to continue, to regale me with a tale about how they discovered a unicorn or defeated a Minotaur. One word answers were uncharacteristic for her. I fiddled with her curls and decided to gently press about it. "Oh, and how is that?"

She turned away and looked at the sky. "Mommy, do you really have a dragon?"

I sat up quickly. "Yes, would you like to see him?"

Her eyes bulged. "B-but you told me they weren't real!"

"I was wrong. His name is Garix and his scales shine and he's very kind."

Her gaze on my face was so focused as she contemplated each word that I wanted to keep talking forever. I could see her mind racing from the flit of her eyelashes to the far-away gleam in her eyes. My heart swelled. I'd missed her so much. I had no idea how I even survived without her for so long.

"That's how I got back to you. I climbed on his back and flew all the way here."

She lowered her head, looking up at me with a deliberate gaze. "I need to meet him."

Inching forward, I tapped on the tip of her nose. "Let's go."

Morgana leapt from the blanket and grabbed my hand, pulling me along before I could gather my belongings. "Wait, honey! We have to get our things."

"Mom!" she said, her eyes bulging. "There's a dragon. I need to meet him."

I bit back laughter as I grabbed our blanket and water pail, scrambling to put them into my bag as Morgana bounced around like the delay brought her physical pain.

I slung my bag over my shoulder and followed Morgana as she skipped through the forest on the outskirts of town.

"Charlotte!" a voice called.

Through the trees, I saw Young walking towards us. Even through the greenery, I could see he had an energy about him I hadn't seen since his return. My body pulsed; we hadn't spoken since our fight the night before. Morgana ran to him.

"Careful, Morgana," Young and I said in unison. Young squatted down and Morgana leapt onto his back, a sort of dance that appeared to be well-rehearsed. Amused, I hurried to join them.

"We were just headed to visit Garix," I said when I was close enough to be heard easily. "Would you like to join us."

Young smiled, giving my stomach a quick jolt of surprise. "Absolutely. Actually, Charlotte, I have something important to talk to you about later."

Morgana squirmed.

Young laughed. "It can wait, though. Dragon first."

I pressed my lips together to suppress the sudden rush of nerves. Young's smile affected me just as Minseo running his hand through his hair often did. I was starting to think that, not only did they know that, they were using it to their advantage.

"Dragon first," I repeated.

We walked along the outskirts of town, a grassy path outside the walls overrun with wildflowers. Morgana chatted incessantly, and I found myself clutching to this memory as we made it. It was odd, but even though we were a family on paper, it felt too new to be familiar. Our threesome didn't possess the familiarity it had with Gabe or the ease of Minseo, but it felt nice. It was the kind of afternoon I'd fantasized about for five years. Although I no longer felt the same about him, I wanted nothing more than for us to play this part—a fantasy glimpse of what might've been. Each time his gaze fell to me and he smiled, I felt a flare of heat that unlocked a truth I had buried away. It was entirely possible for me to fall back in love with Young. I'd done it once, and the power he'd once held over my every emotion remained. Wouldn't it be better for everyone if I did? For everyone except Minseo.

As if he could hear my thoughts, Young's hand brushed mine. *I remember you.*

When we arrived at the farm, Morgana squirmed off Young's back and thrust herself over the fence. I was alarmed at how fearlessly she charged up to Garix. *Be still,* I willed to Garix.

In the light of the afternoon sun, Garix's scales shone brightly. I could imagine how magical he looked, standing alone in the grassy field, his gaze fixed on the small child frantically charging him.

Morgana threw her arms around Garix's neck. I felt a twinge at the bottom of my stomach, violet. My heart fluttered at the sensation. Garix liked her. Young and I hurried to catch up, me because I was curious about what she was saying to him and Young because he felt nervous about her being so close to such a large and unpredictable creature. But for me, Garix *was* predictable. He remained still as a doll as Morgana patted his lizard-like head.

"Show me your wings," Morgana said.

My stomach dropped when Garix ignored my command for Morgana's and stretched his wings out in front of her.

I gasped, running over to Morgana's wrist to check for the same metal band that allowed me to control Garix, but her tiny wrist was unmarred.

"What's wrong?" Young asked, his gaze moving between the dragon and me.

I lowered my voice so Morgana couldn't hear us. "He disobeyed me."

"Should we get her out of there?"

I traced a finger over the metal band on my wrist, the one born from the dragon egg. "I think she's safe. But I don't know why he did what she said. I… I didn't think that was possible."

"Do you think it's because of her magic?"

Stunned, I turned to him. "You know about that? Has there been another incident?"

"I wouldn't say incident. She's getting a bit more used to it, I think. Minseo and Gabriel have been keeping a close eye on it."

"I was going to tell you. Do you think it's from your side or mine?"

He shrugged. "Do you have magical people in your family?"

I shook my head. "Do you?"

We laughed together at the absurdity. Until I took a deep breath, resting my hands on my hips. Young took me by the waist and kissed me. My heart raced. In a panic, I stepped back, my shock reflected in his expression. The click of the kiss rang in my ears, the softness of it still tingling on my lips.

We stared at each other as I made my best effort to pin down a single emotion, as each one flew through me, driving me wild until I grabbed hold of one. *Curiosity*. Was loving Young the same as I'd remembered? What would that feel like, if we tried it again?

His voice broke my train of thought. "We need you to travel to Faresa tomorrow with Garix."

"Oh. Is something—"

"We just don't want Garix to be here when the knights come to collect the taxes."

I nodded. "You can tell your father I'll be ready."

I noticed Young's cheeks flush before he spoke again. "I was thinking that, since I won't see you for a little while, maybe you could stay with me tonight."

"Oh."

He bit his bottom lip. "I mean, you don't have to if—"

"No," I said, pressing my hands to my stomach to ease the rush I felt there.

"No?" his eyes bulged.

"No, I mean yes. I—"

He smiled, causing me to melt and for the overwhelming sensation of curiosity to take hold. I mean, I knew what might happen if I went, even if I promised myself I wouldn't let it go that far, but I'd asked him to give us a real chance. How could I deny him now?

I felt my body shake and it reminded me a lot of how I'd felt on our wedding night all those years ago. My mind drifted to the man who slept outside Young's room on my first night in Vires. Wasn't this why he left, so I could explore my feelings for Young? I swallowed my frustration, determined to hide it from Young. Someone was going to get hurt; there was no way around it.

29

LANCELOT

Merlin was going to be the death of me. I had no idea how to go about trying to woo her, let alone if that would make her drop her guard long enough to kill her. All women had their scary moments, even my soft-tempered Gwenevere, but Merlin could roast me alive with a single wave of her finger. I needed a plan.

I lay back in my bed, closed my eyes, and replayed my memories of her, particularly the ones where she was fond of me. Back when we were close. Had I done or said something to make myself more desirable? The one time I'd called her beautiful, she reacted negatively. So what was it?

My eyes opened as the answer slipped in. *Gwen.* I'd been pining for Gwen for the entire four years Merlin and I were on the road. Maybe what she liked most about me was the competition with Gwen.

I sat up. If my relationship with Gwen drew her interest in me to begin with, it could do it again. My thoughts tripped over a potential snag. If I let Gwen in on my plan, she might get jealous and sabotage it. I needed her to play the part of a jealous girlfriend, but in a very specific way. No, she'd have to be left in the dark, and after I murdered Merlin, I'd be able to explain everything.

My stomach was wracked with nerves as I waited for night to come and my plan to commence. As usual, after midnight, Gwen slipped into my room.

I gulped with anticipation as she kissed my neck, knowing that what I was about to do to Gwen was just as dangerous as driving my sword into Merlin's heart.

She climbed on top of me and, taking control until my room filled with the steady thrum of my bedpost hitting my bedroom wall, my body surged with heat and adrenaline as I waited for my moment. Gwen's eyes rolled back, her pace suddenly erratic. *Now.* "Yeah, Merlin," I moaned. "Yes, Merlin." I yelled this time louder to make sure she heard me. Gwen froze. Her eyes wide, the color drained from her face. She leapt off of me, pulling the blanket up to cover her exposed breasts. Her mouth dropped open and she blinked silently at me with disbelief. "Wh-what did you say?"

I sat up, my body covered with sweat and Gwen's juices. "I'm sorry. I meant to say Gwen."

"You said it twice," she said, but she was no longer talking to me. She was already off the bed and half-dressed, as if the room was on fire. I felt a twinge of sadness, but if I was being honest, also a hint of satisfaction for hurting her. Something inside me had never forgiven her for marrying Arthur. She stormed out of my bedroom, slamming the door behind her. Everything had gone according to plan, but the pit of my stomach ached with the thought that I might've done something that couldn't be undone.

30

CHARLOTTE

Even with a full afternoon of Morgana running through the field with Garix, it took her longer to fall asleep than I expected. I'd loved seeing them play together, like siblings. It was as if they'd known each other all their lives. Perhaps it was Morgana's adrenaline from meeting Garix or her suspicion that he could understand her. She'd also given me quite a battle when I told her I needed to take Garix away for a couple of days, but eventually the exhaustion took her and she lay back on her pillow, fighting sleep. I wished I would be around the next day to put Morgana's influence on Garix to the test. As it was, I felt rather unsettled about it. I couldn't think of anything more terrifying than a five-year-old with control of a dragon. Even a five-year-old as sweet as Morgana could level a kingdom with a small tantrum.

"Storytime," Morgana whispered, clapping her hands with the last of her energy. Her head was half-sunken into the pillow, her curls snaking from her head like medusa. I wondered what it might be like to have a child who wished for me to tell her stories instead of the other way around. I smiled down at her. "Go ahead."

"The evil witch saved the day but then blood spit out of her!"

"Morgana!"

She looked up at me wide-eyed. "What?"

I shook my head in disbelief. "Can't we ever have a *nice* story?"

She fluttered her eyelashes at me. "Do you like the color red?"

Unfazed by her change of subject, I said, "Yes, it's very beautiful."

"Then blood is beautiful, which means my story *is* nice."

I pulled the blanket up to her shoulders. "Alright, time for bed, before you give me nightmares." She giggled. My gaze drifted to the window where the sun had long since gone down. Young was waiting, a thought that pushed fear into me. It wasn't that I didn't trust him. I didn't trust me.

I lay beside Morgana until she fell asleep, and when she finally did, I hesitated to move. My mind ran through every possible outcome of the night. I didn't like any of them.

My stomach was fluttered with nerves by the time I turned to leave, made worse by Gabriel's giddy response when I told him where I'd be. He'd even pressed me for answers about what I thought might happen. The truth was, I wasn't sure. I didn't even know *if* I wanted anything to happen.

I'd be lying if I said I hadn't felt anything for Young as we spent the day together. Part of me knew I always would. Still, it felt like a betrayal of Minseo and I wasn't sure why it wasn't the other way around. Logically, Young was my husband and I owed it to him to make things work, but when I closed my eyes and placed my hands over my heart to feel it beat, it was always for Minseo. All I could truly offer Young was an open mind. I should have felt excited; we were reunited and finally connecting, but the tension and flutters I felt weren't from excitement but from anxiety. Someone was going to be hurt tonight... and it would most likely be me.

As I kissed Morgana's forehead one last time and waved guiltily to Gabe, I suppressed the alarm bells ringing in my mind. After all, what was wrong with me spending the night with my husband? But it was a foolish question. I knew what was wrong. My heart belonged to Minseo and every step toward Young was a step away from him. It was a risk I wasn't willing to take, yet, a few minutes later, I stood outside of Young's room.

31

MERLIN

I paced the halls of the castle in the dead of night cycling through the emotions that hadn't allowed me a moment of sleep since Charlotte left. Rage because she'd left me to Arthur's wrath. A danger that I felt hovering over me, like the gavel waiting to drop. Betrayal because she didn't tell me what she was planning. I wrung my hands. Above all sadness. Regardless of her reasons, I'd lost a sister and I was alone once more. And Garix, my sole focus for the three months we had him, was another irreplaceable gap in my life. It was almost enough to wish for my own death, to welcome Arthur's punishment when he finally decided to implement it.

A soft sniffle sounded through the empty halls and, for a moment, my hopeful heart convinced itself it was Charlotte, come to beg my forgiveness. I followed the sound and saw a wisp of a girl turn the corner. I followed, lighting a small flame in my hand.

I turned the corner and heard a loud knock.

"Fuck, fuck, fuck," Gwen said, shaking her locked door. I froze in place as she slid down the door, her nightgown hanging off her left shoulder. She sunk into herself and sobbed, her sharp breaths echoing in the dark hallway. *Walk away, Merlin.* But I didn't. I knelt in front of the fragile and broken queen and reached to push a strand of her hair out of her face.

She lifted her face, her red, swollen eyes wide and bulging. She slapped my hand away.

"Gwen, what happened?" I asked.

"Y-you bitch," she yelled. Her voice traveled dangerously through the arched, church-like corridor. "How long?" she said through sobs. "How long have you been sleeping with Lance behind my back?"

I couldn't stop a laugh from splitting through my lips. "What? Never. We haven't."

"Don't lie to me!" she spat, her blotchy red face ablaze with anger.

Distant footsteps sounded in the hallway, and my body tightened with fear.

Gwen didn't seem to hear the approaching steps because she continued. "He," she gulped, "said your name when he..." She screamed into her hands.

I yell-whispered, "Look, I'm not interested in you or Lance or your melodrama." I grabbed her by her arm and pulled her to her feet. "And I'm not about to get executed because your delusions are trying to pull me into your little love triangle."

Snot oozed from her nose.

I sighed. "Please don't take offense, Your Highness, but you're kind of disgracing our gender. You're the queen of Camelot. Get it together."

She wiped her face, but it remained twisted into an animalistic snarl.

A voice sounded behind me. "You ladies need to get to your chamber— Oh, Your Highness," Galahad said in recognition. His eyes wandered to me with suspicion when he saw her in such a state.

"I-I," my words caught. "I was just leaving."

The queen's rage melted into sobs and I felt my mind wonder about what had caused her such distress. It had to be a lie or mistake. But as the queen choked on her own pain, I didn't sense the deception within her.

I took a deep breath. Why did I have to investigate? I couldn't just let a sleepless night be only that.

Galahad lingered as if waiting for Gwen to give the order to have me executed for her distress. It wasn't beyond her. It wasn't even a bad plan, but ever since I'd threatened her with fire, she'd acted differently around me, as they always did when they realized the magnitude of my abilities. I'm sure she worried about what I might do, or worse, what I might reveal about her and Lance's nighttime routine.

"I have to go," I said guiltily, taking a few slow steps back. I turned to leave and heard Galahad question the queen to find out what I'd done to her, but the queen's life depended on her maintaining the lie.

After I returned to my quarters and lay back in bed, I contemplated the improbability of what she said. Lance said my name during *that*? It made me nauseous to think about. I appreciated that Lance mostly no longer made an effort to connect with me. We'd decided to go our separate ways and could pass as indifferent acquaintances. But Lance making that kind of mistake was weird.

A year ago I would have counted it as a sign that Lance had feelings for me, not that I believed that to be the case but because I desperately wanted it to be true. I was not so naive now, nor was I still in love with him. He'd burned me before, and when I found out what he was up to with all this Gwen drama, I'd burn him back.

32

MINSEO

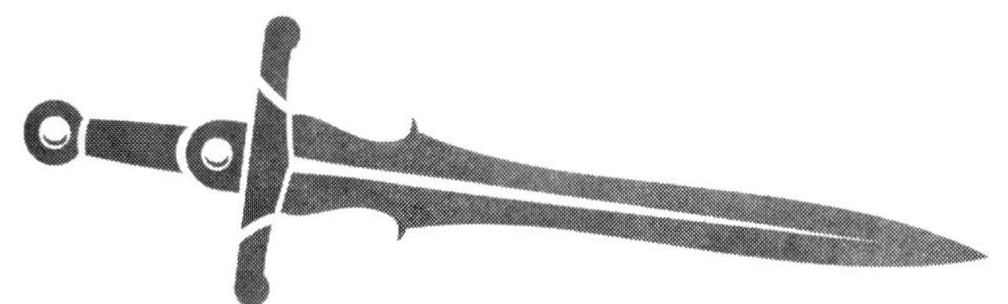

King Ruban's throne shook the beaded flourishes that clacked together as he roared with laughter. Even from within the castle, I could hear the chirp of the cicadas ringing in the night as if echoing the king's brash sentiment.

"A dragon," he bellowed. "You're bloody mad." His deeply dimpled cheeks were stretched by his grin. The small strands of silver in his sleek hair and beard were the only indications he was over twenty, as his bronze skin glowed with youth and he moved around with energy and vigor. It was uncommon to come across a king so young. He was an exception, as my brother had been in Besmium, and similarly, he took the throne as a result of several tragic events.

"I assure you, Your Majesty, it's quite true."

The king scratched at his thick, peppered beard, his smile fading. He turned his gaze on Levario. "And you saw this dragon as well?"

"Y-yes, Your Majesty. It was huge!"

The king stroked his chin thoughtfully. "Can you describe it in greater detail?"

Levario began, "It's a shiny silver color and its wings are—"

"Enough," I said, frustration welling.

Levario's eyebrows shot up as he turned to me.

"He doesn't believe you. He's mocking us," I said.

As soon as Levario's gaze found the king, the youthful king erupted into the fit of laughter he'd been suppressing. I sighed. *We need a new tactic.*

"If I bring the dragon to your kingdom and you see it with your own eyes, will you join us?"

He huffed, the slick shine of his hair pulling my attention to the red jewels in his domed crown. "War with Camelot means certain death. Pay your taxes and accept that life for you and your kingdom will always be a little bit worse."

I ran a hand through my hair. "How can you accept that? Especially now that we have an actual chance?"

"By remembering the kind of suffering that made me sign that alliance to begin with," he said.

I dropped my head and eyed the shiny white tiles that covered his throne room.

King Ruban's voice softened, reminding me of my father's. "Don't chase fairies, son. Protect the people you love."

I balled my fist. "You think Arthur's going to stop here? He can raise that tax whenever he wants until your people starve."

He stood, sending a shiver through my body. "How *dare* you speak to me in such a way. You endanger this entire kingdom just by being here."

A breathless guard rushed in, giving me a brief moment to compose myself.

"Your Majesty," the guard said. "A bird just arrived from Vires. The message said that they wish to send a… a…"

"Spit it out," the king said.

"A dragon." The guard looked around the room, unassuredly. "It's from the king."

King Ruban's gaze didn't leave my face, a fire blazing behind his eyes. He tilted his chin up and crossed his arms over his chest. "Out of curiosity, I'll allow you to summon the beast to Faresa, but I will not, and never will, go against our alliance with Camelot. I suggest you reconsider if you value your life and the lives of everyone in your kingdom."

"Can I at least count on your discretion?"

He paused, considering the potential consequences before saying, "You can."

With a nod, he dismissed me.

I hurried out of the room, gutted. I couldn't go home without Faresa's support. I wasn't sure when that dragon would arrive here, but I'd need to somehow sway the king in my favor so the dragon could do its work when it arrived. Young trusted me to succeed in this mission. If he was here, he wouldn't take no for an answer. Still, you could only be so pushy with a king.

"You!" a voice called from behind me.

I turned to see Levario, red-faced and snarling. Instinctively, I held my hands out in front of me. "You made me look like a fool in front of my king," he said.

"You know there's a dragon. You've seen it. I was certain he'd take the word of his own."

He stepped close enough to feel the heat of his breath. "Are you implying that this is somehow *my* fault?"

I laid a hand on his shoulder. "In a matter of days, perhaps even tomorrow, the dragon will arrive and your name will be cleared."

He turned and walked toward the castle doors. "Are you coming?" he called back.

"Where?" I asked, looking around the white-tiled hallway.

"The tavern is the best place to check the temperature of the kingdom."

I followed. "You're still going to help?"

He made a grumbling sound in response.

We arrived at a tavern that was eerily close to the castle and was a beacon of light on a dark night. It was lively, packed full with local women, and mixed with guards and castle workers that seemed to be trying to catch each other's eyes. The tavern could have been any eastern tavern, plain with mostly wooden furnishings, but what made it unique was the style of the women packed in there. They had their hair wrapped in brightly patterned silk twisted atop their heads, filling the room with a festival-like atmosphere and energy.

I followed Levario closely, like a puppy, feeling oddly out of place in the bustle of Faresa's lively local scene.

The majority of the crowd was concentrated around one particular table. At its center, a man sat on top of it, his arms stretched out in explanation of something I couldn't hear, but I could tell he was telling the story rather well and that his audience was enthralled.

"Two ales," Levario said to the man behind the counter.

I craned to see the man telling the story as I heard Levario mutter, "Oh no, he'll be paying for them both."

I winced and dropped some silver into the man's hand and then pushed my way through the crowd to listen. When I reached the front, I was shocked to see King Ruban of Faresa at its center.

My mind flooded with questions until I heard the gruff voice of Levario beside me. "I know what you're thinking, but no, that's not him." He handed me a cup of ale.

"That's Finn. He's a trader by day and a bard at night. Got in trouble a while back for portraying the king in a play."

I scanned the man, searching for differences, but the resemblance was uncanny. The only differences were the commonplace clothes, pleasant demeanor, and the incredible charisma of the bard.

"And *that*," Finn said, standing on the table, "is the tale of the Dragon Princess."

Stunned, I took a gulp of my ale while the crowd erupted into cheers. Did he mean Charlotte?

"That's the stupidest thing I've ever heard!" a man yelled from the crowd, quieting them.

Without the slightest hint of surprise or insult, Finn grinned as if he'd received a great compliment.

Struck by his kingly poise, I looked for an opening to pull him aside to ask him to retell the story.

The angry man shouted, clearly thrown by the fact he hadn't rattled the popular performer. "You said it was a true story."

"I assure you it's quite true," Finn said, taking a seat on the bar table. "You can go to Vires to confirm it or…" He suddenly turned his gaze to me, gesturing with the dramatic flair of a magician. "You can ask the Prince of Vires yourself."

The room fell quiet as the gazes of every person in the tavern turned to me, trying to riddle out which parts of the bard's claims were true and which were only meant to entertain.

Clearly disappointed in my lack of response, Finn egged me on. "How *is* Princess Charlotte doing?"

It was the opening I needed. If more of the kingdom believed Charlotte and her dragon existed, the easier it would be to make my case.

"In fact," I said, trying to mimic his tone, "Charlotte and her dragon will arrive in Faresa within the next couple days."

"You heard it here first!" Finn shouted, sending the room into a wild torrent of cheers. Silver and bronze coins dropped in his empty lute case, though I noted no trace of a lute. He hopped off the table and walked over to me, leaning in so closely it alarmed me. “Thanks for the assist, mate,” he said, “How can I repay you? A refill on that ale, perhaps?”

Looking down at my nearly empty ale, I said, “How about you tell the story of the Dragon Princess instead?”

He raised an eyebrow and shot me a mischievous smile, “From what I hear, you know that story quite well.”

“Humor me.”

33

CHARLOTTE

We were just going to talk. That was all this was. I gulped. I stood outside Young's bedroom, my rattled nerves tearing through me. I willed myself to turn away and go back to Gabe's house where I knew I couldn't get myself into trouble, but the same curiosity that had compelled me to agree in the first place was tugging at me now.

"Young?" I said, but my voice was hardly a whisper. I reached my quivering hand to slide open the door and peeked inside. The room was covered in flower petals and flickering candles. Nope. I wasn't going in *there*. I wasn't an idiot and no woman could resist that kind of— My thoughts were cut short when I noticed Young, asleep on his bed, shirtless. The curves of his muscles glowed in the candlelight. Where did *that* body come from? He didn't look like that when I married him. His face was relaxed, his arms strewn above his head as his toned chest rose and fell with each silent breath. Heat burned my cheeks as I stood frozen in the doorway between what I should do and what I wanted to do. I pressed my lips together and held my breath as I slipped inside the room and slid the door shut behind me.

The air smelled sweet and I wasn't sure if it was from the candles or the flowers, but they'd been so thoughtfully placed around the room that my memories of being royalty flooded back.

Fearful that I'd keep ogling him, I cleared my throat. "Ahem. Young," I said. What was I even *doing*? He moved a little and then sat up slowly, rubbing the sleep from his face with his unmistakably muscular arms. He smiled at me and I melted, the back of my knees weakening.

His eyes widened suddenly. "Sorry!" he said, scrambling for his shirt. "I didn't want my shirt to get wrinkled and I must've fallen asleep."

"It's okay," I said, pleading with my body not to blush.

He pulled his shirt on and tapped the bed beside him. I wasn't sure if I one hundred percent believed he hadn't planned that stunt with the shirt, but I'd known him to be honest and I was still trying to convince myself that nothing was going to happen.

Oh god. Oh no. *Relax*, Charlotte. I was just having a seat... on his bed.

I sat and I felt his gaze on my face.

My breathing grew deeper.

"Are you okay?" he asked.

"Yes. I just, no. Well—"

He laughed, pulling my attention to his bright smile. *Oh no.*

"Nothing can happen," I blurted.

He smirked, unconvinced.

The words spilled out. "I'm still trying to figure everything out." I meant it but noticed a sharp pang of disappointment when he nodded in agreement.

"Then let's play a game," he said. He hopped up and walked over to his desk, pulling out a wooden box.

I tried to catch my breath as he took a seat on the floor. He waved me over. So I followed and took a seat across from him. He opened the box and pulled out a handful of wooden sticks each with markings on them, and a red circular cloth that he laid out between us.

He looked me in the eye and my heart leapt as I saw Morgana's features reflected in him, as well as her kindness. She was ours and he was the man who gave me her. *No,* I reminded myself. None of *that*.

"So, this is called Yut Nori," he said. My gaze drifted to his lips and another wave of curiosity swept through me.

"We take turns throwing these sticks and, depending on what it lands on, we move the pieces." He gestured to two smooth stones that sat between us on the patterned cloth. He grinned and pointed to one of the stones. "That's yours," he said.

"Ah." I picked up the sticks, examining them closely to keep from gawking at his smile. I didn't remember him smiling so much five years ago. It was like he'd somehow figured out my weakness. "How can I tell how many spaces to move from this?" I said, looking at the symbols marked on each one.

"I'll tell you," he said.

"How do I know you're telling the truth?"

His smile faded. "I always tell the truth."

"Tell the truth then," I said, raising my eyebrows and crossing my arms.

He pushed his lips out. "Really? Now?"

"Isn't that why we're doing this?"

He put his hand to his face as if hiding and sighed deeply. "I'm nervous," he said, "You've grown into such a beautiful and enticing woman and I'm having a hard time not thinking about how much I want you."

I dropped my arms to my side.

"I'm honestly trying to think of anything else so please," he continued, "let's just play this game so I don't lose my goddamn mind."

Who *was* this person? I bit my bottom lip to keep the shaken feeling inside my chest from showing on my body. I reached out and grabbed the sticks. "Like this?" I said, tossing them between us. My gaze met his, the sticks landing with several fresh clunking sounds. But we didn't look down. Energy surged between us. My pulse raced as my body screamed to be touched. Without looking away, he leaned forward, moving his legs slowly.

I froze, afraid he might kiss me, but instead he rocked back onto his knees.

Smile. Do it, please. His gaze traveled down to my lips, then my neck. It lingered on my collarbone and slipped down to my chest. His gaze shot back to mine, his eyes wide with guilt.

A gorgeous smile stretched across his face. *Oh no*. I was going to give in. He laughed. "Sorry! Sorry! That was an accident."

In response, I crossed my arms, giving my breasts a purposeful lift. His smile stopped and he stared down at the game as if it was the final move in a tournament. Curiosity tore through me, but I waited for him to resume the game.

He looked over the symbols on the wooden stick. "Fuck it," he said finally, and with one sweep of his arm, he obliterated the game, scattering the pieces across the room. He reached for me, yanking my body to his, his lips hot on mine. He was a taste I didn't know, an intensity I hadn't expected. His tongue brushed mine. He pulled away only long enough to bite into my neck, and with four swift pulls, he unlaced my corset and slipped it over my head.

He took his shirt off, pushing me back to the floor and ran his fingers over my undergarments, the last thin barrier between us. My back arched with delight. All at once I remembered. The same feeling had been hidden in the deepest recesses of my memory, brought forth by every soft kiss to my neck. He wiggled out of the last of his clothing before leaning back over me, brushing my curls out of my face.

Please, don't stop.

He leaned in just as a loud bell sounded from outside, resonating through the room.

34

YOUNG

I froze. No. Not this. The bell rang and I lifted my head to listen. Not now. Charlotte breathed heavily beneath me, otherwise as frozen as I was. The bell tolled again. Please, not three. Please, not three. When the third bell rang out, my heart sunk. I rolled off Charlotte and she sat up, her eyes wide with panic.

Any suspicions I had that the world didn't want me to be with Charlotte were now confirmed.

"What is it? What does it mean?" she asked.

I hurried into my clothes, Charlotte struggling into hers as well. "It means a royal has died."

"What?"

"I think my…" I fought my voice from cracking. "I think Sumin is dead."

I headed for the door and turned to Charlotte who was unsuccessfully reaching for the strings on her corset. I walked behind her, tightening the strings quickly and tying it. "I'm sorry. I have to—"

"No, it's okay. Go. Do you want me to stay here?" she asked.

"I—" I clenched my jaw, feeling a sliver of grief slip through my shock and confusion. Shaking my head, I slid the door open and stepped out. I ran all the way to the throne room and knew my suspicions had been right when I found my father waiting there.

I swallowed, not allowing myself to ask what had happened. My father simply nodded. I doubled over and felt myself sway. I took a deep, steadying breath when I heard the sob of a woman outside the room but didn't allow myself to look. I knew it was Sumin's wife. As the sound of her crying floated through the throne room, I thought of how little I knew her. I'd made some effort to spend time with Sumin since I'd been home, but never when his wife was present. Hearing her pain made me think of Charlotte and how she looked when we separated five years ago. My mother's calming voice swept through the room from outside, mollifying Sumin's widow.

In a blur, several council members rushed in, the wordless confirmation passing around the room as each new member entered. We stood in silence, each preoccupied with different thoughts on the same tragedy. My father's first son, the most kingly of all his children, taken away too young for no godly reason. Not a war, not in defense of a loved one, merely an illness that swept through and stole his life.

I felt broken, not only for losing a brother but for my father's pain, Sumin's wife, my mother, and above all Minseo. While Sumin and my age gap prevented us from being close, we had a fairly standard relationship, but as far as I knew, Minseo was never able to fix the shattered pieces of their turbulent past. I was certain he'd be hurt the most by the news and I wanted to be there for him when he found out.

My father's weary voice filled the throne room. "I need to speak to Young alone," he said, drawing the mournful gazes of the council members. They bowed deeply before taking their leave and left me alone to face my father.

"You are to go to Faresa with Charlotte and deliver Minseo home immediately."

"But father—"

"Enough!" he shouted. The sheer volume and body of his voice startled me. It was unlike my father to raise his voice. Even given the sad circumstances, it was unusual for him to shed his calm demeanor. "Not today," he said. Silence filled the room and, when he spoke again, his voice was gentle, but his words cut nonetheless. "He is the future King of Vires."

My skin pricked. "I'm aware of how succession works."

His eyebrows lifted. "Are you?"

I swallowed a lump in my throat. "May I have permission to stay in Faresa until they agree to join our fight?"

"I want you both home."

I gritted my teeth. "War is coming. We need this alliance."

"And I need my sons to stop dying," he said.

"With all due respect, Sumin died in his bed. In Vires. And if we don't secure at least this alliance, or one from another kingdom before Camelot's army arrives, many more people will die."

He wiped his lips. "I am first and foremost a father. I need to protect my children first."

"No, you need to protect Vires above all," I said.

My father stood and walked slowly down the stairs at the base of the throne. "You are not a king," he said.

"But I am a father."

"And you would risk Morgana's life to win a war?"

My breath skipped in my throat. "I would do whatever I needed to protect every person in this kingdom. They are all equally important."

He sighed, his gaze skimming over my face. "Then you are not a king and you are not a father."

I turned away to hide my face from him and clenched my jaw as I headed for the door. My face was hot with anger and I reeled with every step, resentment forming for my father and for Minseo. Neither of them had the ideals of a true king, nor what it took to save Vires from falling. Did they think it was impossible? I'd witnessed a kingdom fall and so did Minseo. Why was I the only one trying to save Vires? It was their choices that put us into this alliance. The walk back to my room was a blur, and I'd forgotten about the girl waiting for me there.

Exhausted, I slid open the door to my bedroom. It was dark, all the candles burned out or blown out by Charlotte when she'd left. But then I noticed her sitting at the edge of the bed. She turned to me, her eyes and cheeks red.

She got to her feet, rushed to me, and threw her arms around me. "I'm so sorry, Young," she said. I buried my face into her curls and cried until Charlotte took me by the hand and beckoned me to lay in bed. She lay beside me and rubbed my back, the soothing circles my only comfort in the world until I cried myself dry and sleep finally claimed me.

35

MERLIN

I was determined to get back in Arthur's good graces and had gathered a unit of soldiers to run some training drills. My plan was to make them enough of an asset that Arthur would forgive me for letting Charlotte get the best of me. However, I knew the moment I stepped into the courtyard that my plan wasn't going to work.

"Why should we do what you say?" a slender soldier said.

A few of the men snickered. "You're a woman in the army. I ain't taking orders from the likes of you."

My palm lit with blue flame, but the group of men growing rowdy didn't seem to notice my threat.

A pock-marked man chimed in, "Yeah, it was you who let the dragon go in the first place. I hear you're going to be executed for treason."

I sighed. *I was hoping not to roast anyone today.* My eyes moved up to the clear blue sky. It was too nice of a day. It seemed a shame that the smoke of their ashes would smog it. But I also worried Arthur might think I was intentionally weakening his forces.

The fifty soldiers I selected nodded in agreement, chatting indistinctly about my accused treason.

"You like treason?" a voice said.

The slender soldier's face paled and I turned to see Lancelot.

"Merlin is the king's battle mage," he said. "She vastly outranks you, and you will obey her or I'll look the other way as she uses you all for target practice."

Lance's gaze moved to me, his hazel eyes a forest green, as they typically were in the courtyard. His face was severe and lacked any trace of amusement as he took a seat on a small stone statue and gestured for me to continue.

"Line up!" I shouted, ready to begin, and the men obliged but all through the training my mind was captured by Lancelot. Who did he think he was? I wasn't some damsel who needed rescuing. First that bizarre incident with Gwen and now him rushing in to help me. Something was definitely going on, and I wasn't going to rest until I found out what it was.

Later that night, I sat quietly at the banquet table watching Lancelot eat, without a word to anyone else. Gwen was in full form, wearing a tightly corseted gown that showed far too much of her chest, and was drunkenly laughing at everything Arthur said, a clear attempt to draw in Lance's attention, but it appeared unsuccessful. The moment Lance finished eating, he stood and exited the hall without offering Gwen so much as a glance.

I saw my opening and followed him out, despite the fact I hadn't really finished eating. He turned the corner and headed to his chamber and I followed closely behind, using spurts of well-placed wind to silence my steps, an ability I'd been working on during my late night strolls through the castle.

When we were out of the common area, I hurried to catch up. He reached for the door and I spun him, slamming him against it.

"What is your deal?" I spat. "What are you doing?"

He sighed, as if he'd expected me and said, "I'm trying to go to bed."

I pulled a stray braid behind my ear. "Don't play dumb." I waved my finger in his face. "What are you *doing*?"

He smiled softly, startling me. His eyes were no longer green but a rich honey brown.

He crossed his arms. "Oh, how I've missed this. Look, there *is* something, but let's go in my room. I don't want anyone to hear this."

I stepped back in defeat and followed him into his room.

He sat on his bed, and I stopped just on the other side of the door, feeling suddenly out of place.

He patted the bed beside him, so I crossed the room and took a seat.

He looked down at his hands. "I know what you're doing," he said.

"What *I'm* doing? We're here to talk about whatever *you're* doing."

"You're trying to win over Arthur."

I chewed the inside of my cheek. He looked up at me, waiting for me to deny it, but he was right. I felt a flutter in my stomach from a past life.

"I think we can help each other."

I turned away. "I don't need your help."

He stood. "Okay," he said, gesturing to the door. "I'll see you around."

I shook my head in confusion. "You—you were supposed to tell me what you're up to."

His eyebrows rose. "Well, the truth is, it's pretty embarrassing. You're right, you don't need my help. It was a dumb idea anyway."

Embarrassing? Was he going to bring up the incident Gwen was upset about?

"I'm sure it was. But please do tell."

He gulped, somehow making me nervous.

"Arthur asked me to pick a bride. You and Gwen are the only women I really know, and she's like already—"

"I'm going to stop you right there." I leapt from the bed. "You can act as weird as you want. I don't care what you're up to. It's clearly your business."

He grabbed my wrist. "Stop," he said. "It could get you back on Arthur's good side."

I scoffed, ripping my hand free. "I'm not going to marry you, Lance. Are you insane?"

I stormed out of the room, slamming the door behind me so hard I heard the hinges rattle. *The nerve of that guy.* Has he lost his damn mind? I marched angrily back to my room, a rush of heat and emotions surging so strong, I thought I felt the flicker of a new power. But when I lay in my bed, I realized that not all the emotions I felt were negative. The guy I'd once pined over just kind of *proposed* to me, and the more I thought about it, the less I could find the anger, or fight back my smile.

36

CHARLOTTE

"Charlotte," Young said, waking me. I blinked through the light of the morning, disoriented and unsure where or even when I was.

He spoke again. "Can Garix carry more than one of us?"

I shook my head. "I don't know, I never tried."

He nodded. "We have to try. I'm going with you."

I sat up. Suddenly, the memory of the night before rushed back. I felt my cheeks burn red. I'd nearly slept with Young. I most certainly would have gone through with it if those bells hadn't interrupted, but I felt differently upon waking. There was no candlelight or flowers to cloud my judgment, nor was the ache of curiosity coursing through me. The flame had gone out just before it went too far. I was grateful I hadn't made a mistake I couldn't take back.

"We're going to meet up with Minseo in Faresa. We have to tell him about Sumin and bring him back."

"Has Faresa agreed to help us?"

He shook his head. "I don't know. Let's hope Minseo was able to convince them, and if he wasn't, we'll have to make our case quickly."

"What's the rush?"

"Galahad's tax collection is likely more of a scouting mission. I'm sure Camelot is months away from marching on us. And..." He took a deep breath and his gaze dropped to the floor. "And Minseo is now next in line to rule Vires."

He lifted his gaze to me, and I could see in the glisten of his curved eyes that this was a fresh wound.

I nodded, hopping to my feet. "Let's get ready and go. I'd like to say a quick goodbye to Morgana before we head out."

As it turned out, Young did not think we had enough time to say goodbye, and I couldn't help but notice a sudden change in his temperament. I'd seen grief and its effects before and knew that it was my turn to be there for him, as he'd once been for me.

The promise of a full-grown cow was enough to convince Garix to fly us both. But finding a comfortable way for both of us to saddle onto Garix's back was a major problem. The talons on his back had grown, even in the short time I'd been in Vires. After several attempts, and with some cloth and rope, we managed to get off the ground, but it was clearly a temporary solution.

Young and I were surprised when a few uncomfortable hours later we began seeing signs of Faresa below. We'd underestimated how quickly we could travel on the back of a dragon. A few scattered homes soon gave way to crowded streets and a castle with seven pointed towers.

We circled the city center several times before coming to the conclusion that we would not be able to land near the castle. We found a small patch of open land a few blocks away, but after we landed, a large crowd formed around us, causing Garix to twitch nervously.

I brushed my hand along his head and willed a soothing periwinkle toward him.

Young stretched his back before turning to me with his plan. "You stay here with Garix, I'll go to the castle to find Minseo and see if we can get an audience with the king."

I nodded but felt regretful as soon as he disappeared into the crowd. It was difficult to find comfort with so many eyes on Garix and me. I heard the whisper of a familiar term, *Dragon Princess*. I wanted to call out to them, to tell them that, although I had a dragon, I was no princess. As I looked around, the complexion of the crowd was less varied than Besmium or Camelot. It was generally a deep brown with red undertones that reminded me a little of Gabriel. The thought of Gabriel comforted me and I leaned against Garix, who purred softly.

I couldn't have been waiting for more than twenty minutes, but the sun was starting to set and both Garix and I were getting restless.

Suddenly, I saw a face push through the crowd that raised my pulse. *Minseo*. He stepped through, leaping over the stone wall that the others dared not cross.

"Hello, beautiful," he said.

"Minseo," I breathed, and a wave of sadness hit me as I recalled the sad turn of events from the previous night. Though the bells brought Young and me the news of Sumin's death, it looked like I would have to deliver it to Minseo.

He leaned in, taking me by the hand. "What's wrong?"

I knew it was better just to say it. "Young and I are here to bring you back to Vires. It's Sumin, he..."

Minseo's energy drained. He exhaled, his gaze on me but his mind elsewhere.

I took his hand and pulled it to my chest. "I'm sorry, Minseo."

He forced a half-smile for my benefit then pulled his hand away. "Where's Young?"

"He went to find you and get a meeting with King Ruban."

He nodded, then his gaze moved to Garix. "Let's find a place for Garix to rest for the night, then go look for Young. The king won't see anyone until morning. We'll have to stay at the inn and meet with him tomorrow."

It was dark before we'd found a suitable place for Garix, a farm similar to his home in Vires only with a more eager farmer. After I was sure he was settled, Minseo and I returned to the center of the city. I was worried we'd have trouble finding Young in the dark, but Minseo was confident he'd find his way to a tavern just beyond the castle walls. Minseo strode through town with his usual confidence, but he was uncharacteristically quiet, so I knew the news about Sumin was weighing on him.

I knew I shouldn't bring it up, but I needed to know. "Are you okay?" I asked.

He stopped in his tracks and turned to me, his face shone with silver moonlight. He slipped his hand to the back of my neck and pulled me in for a kiss. My knees buckled and I leaned into the warmth of the kiss. My body surged with heat, but Minseo pulled away too soon, the corners of his mouth slightly turned up.

"Now," he breathed, "I'm okay."

Kiss me again. Kiss me again. But he turned away. I caught his wrist and pulled him back. I wrapped my arms around him and brought his lips to mine, this time deepening the kiss. In a rush, I fisted his hair. I was out of breath when we finally pulled apart. I ran my fingers along his jawline. My heartbeat raced against his.

That was how it was supposed to feel. It was the kiss I'd been craving since I was taken prisoner in Bullhorn.

"Wow," I mouthed.

He ran a hand through his black hair. "Yeah, I know," he said with a smile.

He let me go and the coolness of the night rushed my body. "We're almost there," he said as he began to walk again. He slipped the hand closest to me into his pocket. Of course, we couldn't hold hands. Young was somewhere around here and I hadn't had the chance to tell him that the previous night had been a mistake.

A pang of guilt hit my stomach as the memory of my night with Young rushed forward. I had to tell Minseo.

Before the words made it to my lips, Minseo spoke, "This is it."

If I had been paying any attention at all, I would have seen it coming from down the road. There was a large crowd of people congregated outside the brightly lit tavern. Music, light, and laughter poured out of every window. We pushed through the crowd, making our way into the massive tavern.

At the center of the room, a lively man with a bright smile stood on a table. "Minseo!" he called. And many of the drunken tavern goers turned to appraise us. "Look who I found," he said, and he pulled Young onto the table beside him. Relief pushed through me as we made our way through the tavern to Young.

"Is this the Dragon Princess?" the man asked, taking my hand and kissing it.

I winced.

The man asked, "And where is your dragon? I've been told he's somewhere around here."

"Yes, we found a farm for him to rest tonight," I said.

"I'm Finn," he said. "Young has promised me a round of drinks with you lot," he said, and his eyes twinkled mischievously as his gaze drifted between Young, Minseo, and me.

A couple of hours and several rounds later, I felt the sway of ale hitting my system. With every round, Young touched me more, putting his arm around me and kissing the side of my head. Minseo had done well to hide any distaste for it, but in the last few minutes, it had begun to show.

We'd been playing a game that Finn suggested where we take turns asking each other if we believed something was possible. It was fun at first, as Finn had a story proving just about everything to be true. We'd learned there was a man in Algony who could lift three full-grown men over his head, and a woman in Nilith who could hypnotize men by singing a special song.

Finn leaned back in his chair, shaking his empty cup in the air. He waved it at Young. "I believe it's your turn," he said. Young stood, pulled my hand to his lips and kissed it before he headed to the bar.

I ran my finger over the rim of my cup to avoid Minseo's reaction.

Finn said, "Your turn, Minseo."

"Charlotte," Minseo said suddenly, "do you think it's possible to be in love with more than one person at once?"

I held his gaze, feeling my pulse race and my stomach tighten, filled with a mixture of ale and adrenaline. I owed two men a conversation, two men who'd just lost their brother. The guilt of stringing them along had caught up to me. But now wasn't the time or place to talk about it. I wanted more than anything to comfort Minseo. I wanted him to know I'd chosen him. I hoped that with a simple response, he'd understand. So, I said, simply, "No."

Without breaking eye contact, he took a large gulp of the last of his ale and a deep breath that relaxed his shoulders.

Without acknowledging the weight of the exchange, Finn

turned to Minseo, continuing the game. "Do you believe it's possible to wield magic?"

"Absolutely. I've seen it."

Wait. He wasn't going to tell him about Morgana, was he? I scrambled to kick Minseo under the table.

"Merlin, Camelot's battle mage, once blocked my carriage by growing a tree before my very eyes."

The bard's eyes glittered. "Oh, a wonderful story to add to my collection."

Young walked over to the table with the ales in hand, taking a seat beside me.

Finn patted him on the back. "It's your turn, my boy."

Young turned to Minseo and draped his arm over my shoulder. "Do you think a king should put his kingdom above everything?"

Minseo pressed his lips together as he thought carefully. Then he said, "Depends on the king."

Finn slammed his hand down on the table. "Boring! Let's play a new game."

We nodded in agreement, three of us unsurprised that in lieu of the last few days, the game had taken a dark turn.

37

MINSEO

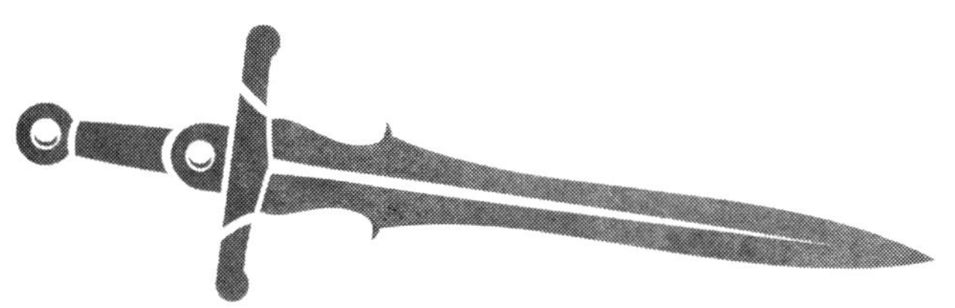

Three separate rooms at the inn, of course. Young's room was next to mine and Charlotte's just across the hall. The ale had made me drowsy, and I had to admit I didn't like seeing Young with his hands all over her at the tavern. The sudden change in his interactions with her told me something had happened between them, which caused me to doubt everything. Even with Charlotte answering my question, the way she did, I wasn't a hundred percent sure she meant she only loved me. After the kiss we shared, I was certain her heart was mine, but imagining her with Young was a dagger to any possibility of sleeping. I needed to hear it from her. I needed to know the truth. I knew the moment we were given our rooms that I would sneak across the hall. I just wanted to make sure Young was asleep first.

I heard the creek of Young's door and jutted to a seated position on the bed. I heard three steps then a light knock. I raced to my door on my tiptoes, to make as little noise as possible, and pressed my hand over my mouth to quiet my breath. I heard Charlotte open her door.

"Young," she said.

My heart raced.

He said, "Uhm, I was thinking that maybe we could…"

Don't say it.

"Finish what we started last night."

My stomach clenched and I tore myself away from the door. I sunk into my bed and pressed my face into my pillow. It was as if someone punched me in the gut. I heard a door close, but I didn't know whose. A moment later, another door opened and closed, and my busy mind riddled that Young had gone back to his room. Whether he was alone, I didn't know. I didn't *want* to know. I lifted my head to slip my pillow out and instead placed it on top of my head. God almighty. I swear if I hear a single sound, I'm going to burn this entire inn to the ground.

I began counting the seconds as they passed, thinking it might calm me down, but it was infinitely worse, so I pulled myself out of bed and walked out into the hallway with the intention of going for a walk. As soon as my door closed behind me, I stood silently in the hallway, listening for the slightest sound. Minutes passed in silence and I suddenly regretted not listening longer at my door.

I eyed Charlotte's door, picking at my fingernails. My body moved toward it without my consent until I gently tapped on it.

A moment later, the door swung open as if she'd been waiting behind it, and Charlotte stood before me in a sheer nightgown that made me grind my teeth. "Oh, Minseo," she said. "What are you doing here?"

Embarrassment flushed through me and I suddenly felt silly for being there, and very unwelcome. "I uh... had a question."

"Well, I'm really tired," she said. "Can it wait until tomorrow?"

I swallowed a lump of shock and disappointment that tasted like spoiled stew. "Oh, yes. I'm sorry. Goodnight." I turned, ready to hide in my room for the next hundred years when she grabbed me by the wrist. When I looked back at her, she held a finger to her lips, her gaze moving between me and Young's door.

Oh. She'd thought this through more than I had. She pulled me into her room and closed the door behind us. Forgetting the trauma that had brought me there in the first place, I followed her like the undead, mindless and hungry.

"Minseo," she whispered. "I have to tell you something."

My mind snapped back into focus. *This was it*. If she brought me in here to tell me she was with Young now, why was she practically naked? Women were cruel. It was unbearable, and my next words slipped out. "I don't want to know," I said, but what I meant was, *Please, don't hurt me*.

"Last night," she started.

I turned away and paced.

"Something happened between me and Young."

I buried my face in my hands. "I don't care, Charlotte."

She shook her head, her loose curls bouncing. "Please, just let me say this. I feel horrible—"

I walked towards her and took her face in my hands. "I don't care. I just want to know if you're leaving me or not." I felt my eyes prick. "I just want to know if this is over."

"No," she said.

I exhaled.

"But I need to tell you what happened."

"Don't," I spat, taking a seat on her bed.

"Then let me just say this." She took a seat beside me. "I'm sorry it took so long for me to get here. I thought I owed it to Young to give us a chance, after everything. I felt curious more than anything after so many years of wishing for him. I thought if I slept with him—"

I took a sharp breath in. "I understand."

I felt her lean closer. "We didn't."

I looked up at her, sadness hanging on each of her features.

She continued, "But I would've. The bells last night kind of…" She sighed. "But then this morning, I felt horrible because I knew that it would have been a mistake. Mostly because, before I let anything happen, I already knew I was in love with you. I already knew my heart couldn't be changed. It's not fair to him that you and I happened, but it did and we can't go back. Mostly because now I know the truth."

My mind raced, my palms suddenly sweaty. A tear slid down her cheek and she said, "That love *is* different every time."

I leaned in and kissed her gently, resting my forehead against hers. I exhaled, warmth filling me. "I love you, Charlotte."

She whispered, "Good," then stood suddenly. "Now out." She gestured to the door.

"What? No! You're wearing that!" I said, scanning her blurred silhouette through her nightgown.

"I haven't had the chance to talk to Young about us yet. I'd like us to... pause things until then."

I shook my head, heading for the door. "So you just wore that to make me go easy on you."

She smirked. I ran my hand through my hair and a small, *mmm* sound escaped her lips. I tilted my head to the side. What was *that*? *Was this a thing*? I strode towards her, pushing my hand through my hair a second time.

Her face and neck went red, her eyes glassy, and her lips parting to invite my kiss. I leaned in, her lips parting more. I stopped just before our lips touched and whispered, "Interesting." I turned and headed for the door, calling back over my shoulder, "I was just checking something. Goodnight."

38

LANCELOT

It wasn't like I thought Merlin would say yes, but even with this whole proposal bit as part of Arthur's plan to kill her, I found myself perplexingly disappointed. I mean, Merlin used to look at me with admiration. She wanted me despite me making no effort to impress her. Gwen was so different, always asking me to prove my love for her with gifts, vows, or demonstrations.

I lay back in bed and stared at the ceiling. At least Merlin didn't attack me. That had to mean something, right? She could've killed me on the spot. She could kill anyone on the spot, including Arthur, and that was why he made this plan. But I couldn't stop thinking about Merlin trying to win Arthur's trust back. She'd trained those men. She stayed at the castle, despite knowing her life was at risk. It was more than not having somewhere else to go; she wanted to serve Arthur. She was loyal to him, and that meant Arthur was tossing aside one of his best assets for nothing. And, if for no other reason, Merlin and I were friends once.

Sure, she'd left my knighthood quest before its completion,

after I told her I was going to stay with Gwen, but she kept my secret. Maybe I'd been looking at it wrong all along. Maybe she wasn't getting revenge on me by leaving; maybe she was protecting herself.

It seemed like she'd gotten over any feelings she had for me, but it didn't matter. I had to see if I could save her. Arthur was making a mistake.

I sat up and headed for my door with the intention of finding Arthur.

I swung open my door to find Merlin with a fist raised. I'd caught her just before she decided to knock. She pushed past me and strewn herself across my bed like it was her bedroom.

"Ugh," she huffed. "Can you really help me win Arthur back over?"

Stunned, I closed the door behind me. "Are you serious? Are you saying you'll marry me?"

She sat up, "No." She shook her head, setting her green braids into a wave at her lower back. "I'm just trying to open up the conversation." She grinned playfully. "How about you convince Arthur to trust me and I *don't* marry you?"

"And what's in it for me?" I asked with a smile. I hadn't realized how much I missed our banter or how easily we fell back into it. She was right in front of me, as she'd always been, but I still missed her.

"Let's see," she said. "How about I don't roast you?"

I put my hands up in mock surrender. "You know how hard life is... Roast away."

She shoved me. "Lance!"

Laughing, I put my hand on her leg. She swatted it off immediately but her smile didn't fade.

"What?" I asked. "I figure we're going to be married, why not get to the fun stuff now?"

Her eyes bulged. "I never said we're getting married." She sighed. "Get over yourself."

She crossed her legs and turned to me, threading her fingers together. "So tell me, what does Gwen think about all of this?"

A pang of uneasiness settled at the pit of my stomach. I hadn't seen her since I, *ahem,* set my plan in motion. If I was being honest, I felt a little relieved to put some distance between us. Four years on the road had changed me. I grew, physically and emotionally. I was starting to suspect I'd grown closer to Merlin than I knew when we'd returned to Bullhorn.

My tunnel vision on Gwen blinded me to the fact that she was the same dramatic, attention-seeking girl she was years ago, and that might not fit with me so well anymore.

"Oh, uh, we got in a fight."

Her gaze moved to the door. "Yeah, she told me."

Typical.

I felt Merlin's gaze move to me, searching for information, but I knew better than to offer any. What I'd done was cruel, and though it appeared to have served its purpose, it was nothing to be proud of.

"Let me get something straight," Merlin said, the volume of her voice startling me. "We're getting married. *As friends*. There will be none of, whatever." She stuck a finger in my face. "Understand?"

I grinned. "You must really want to impress Arthur."

Her gaze dropped to her hands. "Yeah, well, after Charlotte..." She tucked a braid behind her ear and took a breath before continuing. "Well, before... Arthur was the first to see my worth."

I threw my hands up. "What? I saw your worth first."

Her eyelashes fluttered. "That's a lie. You *still* don't see my worth."

"I just asked you to marry me."

"I just agreed," she smiled, "to a friendship marriage."

I huffed. "You women always think you have so much willpower. You're fine with being friends until you aren't. We'll see how long it lasts."

"You're the worst."

Laughter cut through me, splitting my stomach. "You didn't deny it."

She tossed a braid over her shoulder. "That's because it's foolish."

"Prove it," I said.

She stood. "I'm sure that kind of thing works on the Gwens of the world." She turned to me, putting a hand on her hip. "But I don't think you've met a woman of my caliber before."

"You know Gwen's the queen, right?"

She chuckled. "Queen?" She shook her head. "I don't think so."

With that, she left my chamber, leaving me to wonder two things: whether I should talk to Arthur or Gwen first and what winning the heart of a woman of her caliber would actually be like.

39

CHARLOTTE

I awoke the next morning feeling lighter. The decision had been made and all that was left was to tell Young and accept the consequences.

Minseo was impulsive, jealous, and sometimes childish, but I loved him for those things. He wore his heart on his sleeve and always tried to do what was best by me. I craved his levity and the fun our imagined future held.

Young was my husband, Morgana's father, and I wanted to give us a chance, but even as his wife, he was hard to be close to. He rarely shared his feelings and I had to expel a great deal of effort just to know him. Sometimes it felt like shooting arrows in the dark, at an invisible target. He'd give me one-word answers until I hit my mark. Even after all this time together, he had hardly spoken a word about his time in Bullhorn. I wanted someone I could share my life with—someone I was certain wanted to share his life with me.

With Young, I was never certain, and when we were together I still longed for the effortless nature of my relationship with

Minseo. Was it so wrong to want something a little easier? Someone I didn't have to teach how to love me?

Young was loyal, strong, and fair—a born leader and a far better royal that I'd ever been, but Minseo had my heart, and I knew it would stay with him.

As I dressed for the day, I considered when a good time was to tell Young that I'd chosen Minseo. I certainly couldn't blurt it over breakfast. Both guys had just lost their brother and the funeral was waiting for our return. I sighed as I pinned my hair up, my thoughts moving to Young as he cried in my arms the other night. I didn't want to hurt him. Maybe it was better to postpone it for a little while.

A knock sounded at my door, startling me. I slipped one last hairpin in my curls before pulling open the door. Young and Minseo stood side by side, Young with his intense, princely stare and Minseo with a charming smile. I bit my bottom lip to keep from laughing and pushed away the daze that smacked me from the sight of them. *The Viran princes.*

Minseo spoke first. "Ready to meet King Ruban?"

I nodded and, after a painfully quiet breakfast, we headed out into the streets of Faresa. I was surprised to find that there weren't many people out for such a lovely and temperate morning. And even more strange were the few people who passed us rushed by, all headed toward the castle. As we neared, we saw a large crowd congregated around the small patch of land where we flew in the night before.

My stomach dropped. *Garix*. I could see his reptilian frame at the center of the crowd. It was impossible. We'd left him at the farm. I'd told him to stay there until we returned. Had he disobeyed? Had he hurt someone? My heart pounded in my chest as I instinctively ran toward him, shoving strangers with both arms to get through. Garix wouldn't disobey… Unless. I understood a second before I burst through the last line of people.

I gasped as Morgana reached her hands to me. I snatched her into my arms. "Morgana, how did you get here?" I said breathlessly.

"Garix came to get me," she said, burying her face in my neck. Minseo and Young stepped out of the crowd and rushed over to us. "What happened? How'd she get here?" Young asked.

Minseo rubbed her back. "Are you okay?"

"You left without saying goodbye," Morgana said, her eyes tearful.

"How did she call Garix?" Young asked as he turned to me. "How far away do you have to be to communicate with Garix?" I shook my head, my mind reeling to put together how Morgana got here. "I never tested it before."

Minseo clenched his jaw, his gaze moving to Garix. "Why didn't he listen to you, Charlotte?"

I took a breath. "We think," I said, my gaze moving to Young, "Morgana can overpower my orders."

Minseo exhaled loudly. "So she what? Called Garix all the way from Vires and said, 'Take me to Mommy'? My god, they must've flown through the night. She could've—"

Young interrupted. "She's very brave."

The sound of trumpets rang out, pulling our attention to the castle which was partially blocked from our view by a lofty church on the corner of the block. The crowd chattered with excitement. "It's the king," I heard someone say. "He's come to see the dragon."

I had more questions than answers. How had Morgana gotten away from Gabriel? How did Garix feel her command from that far? How did she hold on for so long? But the mystery of Morgana would have to wait. The king was approaching and we needed to convince him that we not only had full control over Garix but that, with his support, we could win a war against Camelot.

Young leaned closer. "Let's not talk about this in front of—"

"We got it," Minseo said, and a cold glare I didn't understand passed between them.

Garix, spread your wings, I willed.

Tired, hungry, he said in a slew of oranges and yellows at the pit of my stomach.

Soon.

I reeled, trying to keep as much of my panic from my face until I found a royal mask inside me I hadn't worn since Besmium fell.

The onlookers parted and, sure enough, the king strode fearlessly into the grassy plot. Forgetting my manners completely, I gawked at the king. I wasn't struck by his power or obvious wealth but by his uncanny resemblance to the tavern bard.

In fact, where *was* Finn?

"Your Majesty," Young said, and my attention snapped back. I curtseyed as best as I could with Morgana in my arms. The king scratched at his beard as he examined Garix. Garix was, as far as I knew, the only living dragon in the world, but the king lacked the standard disbelief, excitement, and terror that usually came with seeing Garix for the first time and instead appraised him like a collector.

After only seconds in his presence, I was no longer suspicious that this was the same man from the tavern. The two couldn't have been more dissimilar in temperament and personality.

King Ruban spoke. "Who does he answer to?" he asked.

Minseo, Young, and I swapped loaded gazes, silently agreeing. "He answers to me, Your Majesty," I said.

He eyed me. "May I?" he said, reaching his hand out to Garix.

"Yes, of course," I said, stepping out of his way. The onlooking crowd was silent with anticipation, as if expecting some tragic event to occur, and it rightfully fit the uneasiness of the meeting.

King Ruban put his palm on Garix's shoulder and closed his eyes as if recalling a fond memory. After several uncomfortable moments of everyone in attendance waiting, he took a deep breath and his eyes opened once more, turning his attention to Minseo. "Let's head to the castle to discuss our business. The girl can stay with the dragon."

Minseo and Young looked like they'd been struck, and I choked back a laugh. I shook my head to signal the boys to let the king's behavior slide. "Yes, Your Majesty," I said.

We needed Faresa on our side no matter what, but if I was being honest, I had no interest in their meeting, especially with Morgana half asleep in my arms.

40

MERLIN

I strode through the moonlight of the courtyard, where Charlotte and I had once trained Garix, the empty stable a continuous reminder of the choice she made to be with her family—her *real* family. Now it was my turn to think about family. Because of her, my hard-fought respect had crumbled. I lost the faith of Arthur and, along with him, it took Lance to convince the other soldiers to train with me. As if I'd accomplished nothing in my life, I was alone in the world again—except for Lance. I wasn't sure if he was someone I could trust, but in my darkest hour, he offered an alliance. A *marriage*. I could feel this part of me soften, the part I never showed to anyone. The part I hid behind threats and magic. I wanted someone to stand by me. Anyone. And if they did, I would earn it. I would die for them. I would— My head split with pain as a vision slammed into view, blocking my sight.

I was looking down at Arthur's throne room from the view of his window, the room uncommonly quiet and empty with only two figures below. Lance stood in the light of the stain-glass window and Arthur looked down on him. The daylight splayed about the room told me the vision wasn't happening in the present, but Lance and Arthur looked no older or younger than they were today.

Arthur's voice filled the room. "Merlin has become a problem. I'm short a dragon and someone must be punished."

Matter-of-factly, Lance said, "You're afraid of her."

"I am the king," Arthur bellowed. " I fear nothing."

But the way he stood a step higher than Lance gave him away.

"Where do your loyalties lie, Jeremy?"

"With you, Your Majesty," Lance said obediently.

Arthur grinned. "Then you shall kill her."

I blinked back into the courtyard. "*No,*" I said, straining back to the vision, but it was gone and I was once again alone in the empty courtyard.

I clenched my hand into a fist. *I knew it*. I felt my throat tighten and choke of tears threatening to rise. *No*. I refused to be hurt by these heartless demons. I pushed my body into numbness as I planned my next move. I'd tried to make peace. I'd been a loyal soldier and friend. To Charlotte, to Arthur, and to Lance. They would all pay for making a fool out of me. I wanted nothing more than to watch them burn one by one. I looked up at the moon to be sure I remembered what it looked like the night they turned me into the witch they feared. The moon was just as beautiful as the sun, without hurting the person who looked, yet it was unappreciated and unloved by the day-worshipping masses. It would all stop tonight, and Lance would be the first to die.

With a flick of my wrist and a wave of concentrated air, I thrust myself toward the castle at the pace of a sprint. Even with my focus, I couldn't keep myself in the air without using a few steps on the ground to regain my momentum. I slid through the hallway, my powerful gusts ripping the tapestries off the walls as I passed. I slowed just as I was about to turn the corner to Lance's hallway. I took a deep breath, hoping to find a touch of humanity inside, but the last of it had been slain with a single vision, the death of my last hope.

The sound of footsteps put my hair on end. I pushed myself against the wall, listening to the steps around the corner as they drew near. I had every right to walk the castle at night, but I felt the words murderer, witch, and traitor carved into the flesh on my forehead and I didn't want them to be seen until my deeds were done.

As the person passed, seemingly unaware of my presence on the other side of the wall, I peeked to see who would dare roam the dark halls in the castle with a murderous witch on the loose. My heartbeat skidded to a stop when I saw it was Lance. *This was my chance.* He was nothing, just flesh, bone, and evil. Everything he'd ever said to me was a lie, a set up to kill me.

If anything, this was self-defense. Yet, as he moved farther away, my body remained frozen behind the wall, until finally I stepped out, stalking my prey through the dark corridors.

He stopped outside a familiar room, the private room of Queen *Gwenevere. Typical.* This was going to be two for one. I crept toward the door and put my ear to it, waiting for my moment to attack.

"I know you're still mad about what happened," Lance said. "But I'm not here to make up. I'm here to end things officially."

"What are you talking about?" Gwen said, her voice hard and icy.

"I'm going to marry Merlin."

She gasped. "Wh-what is this? Is this some kind of joke? Are you and Arthur plotting against her or something?"

My palm burned blue and I turned the doorknob.

"It started that way," Lance said, "but I don't know... Something's changed. I care about her."

I slowly let go of the doorknob. Was this another trick? Did he know I was here?

"Arthur wants her killed," Gwen said. "They'll call you a traitor too. You'll go down with her."

He sighed. "I already spoke with Arthur. I staked my life on her loyalty. He's ready to forgive her."

"Why are you here, Lance?"

"I want you to leave us alone," Lance said. "You made your choice."

"You'll get bored with her too," she said, her shrill voice piercing through the door.

Lance said, "You don't get bored with a woman of her caliber."

My heart swelled and I pulled myself away from the door and down the hallway, ducking around the corner to avoid being seen when Lance left. It had to be a trick, right? Or had Lance really changed his mind some point after my vision?

The words that he used were so tied to our last conversation.

It was several panicked, sweaty minutes before I heard Lance leave Gwen's room, but he didn't go in the direction I'd expected, back to his room. Was he headed to *my* room?

In a panic, I flew down the hall, the long way to my room, in hopes I'd make it there before him. I peeked around the corner, but I was too late. He was already standing outside my door. He took a deep breath before he knocked, fixing his hair in rushed, nervous swipes.

Aww. I bit my bottom lip, standing up straight and walking around the corner.

"Lance?" I said. "What are you doing here?"

His green eyes widened when he saw me walk into view. "I uh, I need to tell you something. Is this a bad time?"

I pushed open my door and waved him in, curiosity clawing at me.

I crossed my arms defensively. "What is it?"

He sighed and said, "A while back, Arthur asked me to kill you."

Bold. I stared back, unflinching.

He clenched his jaw. "Oh. You knew. Of course. Why did you agree to marry me then?"

I shrugged. "Curiosity."

"I'm so sorry. I quickly realized how bad of a mistake it was to agree, and I've been trying to fix it." He walked toward me and I instinctively took a step back.

"I told Arthur I wouldn't go through with it and that he can trust you."

I put my hands on my hips.

"I just started to think about what it would actually be like if we did get married, and the more I thought about it, the more I liked the idea."

I nodded. "So I'm just supposed to forget that your entire proposal was a plan to murder me?"

"No, no. By the time I proposed to you, I meant it."

I looked around my bedroom, hoping to rid myself of the weakness I felt growing inside.

He reached out and touched my arm. "I'm not expecting you to forgive me, but I want you to know that I don't want you to accept my previous proposal."

I threw my hands out. "Okay, great."

He stepped forward, staring into my eyes, an intensity pulsing between us. "I don't want a friend marriage. I want us to try the real thing."

I gulped back a wave of nerves that tore through my body.

He leaned in, and I feared he was going to kiss me, but instead he knelt in front of me, reaching for his pocket.

I stood frozen, feeling the tickled rush of something new between us.

He opened a small box and at its center was a ring which held a glittering emerald. “Merlin, I promise I’ll be by your side forever. Will you marry me?”

Breathless, I looked down on him, carefully weighing my emotions against the clash of my thoughts. For the first time in my life, I was truly afraid.

“Yes,” I said, unknowingly sealing my fate and his.

41

YOUNG

King Ruban's words ran through my mind in an endless loop for the next few months. "Our spies tell us that Camelot is well into their war preparations. Even with your baby dragon, you cannot win this war. Your kingdom will fall and everyone in it killed if you do not surrender."

The warning was meant as a kindness, but it was a vale of doom that hung over Sumin's funeral, making it feel less of a celebration of his life and more like a waste of precious time. I was grateful that Charlotte had kept her distance since we arrived home. The war was fast approaching and all my time and effort needed to be devoted to that. Minseo, too, was always in war preparations while Charlotte split her time between training Garix and spending time with Morgana.

During those few months, we'd taken Garix to four other kingdoms to attempt to win an alliance, and each time we were turned away.

But after a few months, we saw significant progress in our own war preparations. They were extremely successful with both

Minseo and me, overseeing the training and recruitment. If it had been an ordinary war, Vires would have been a formidable force, but this was Camelot, and even with our successful recruitment, they had us outnumbered as well as the seemingly indestructible Merlin fighting on their side.

Our one glimmer of hope was Morgana. If Charlotte and I were to blame for getting Vires into this, our daughter could save us. Almost five days per week, under the guise of hiking, I took her to train. Because of her young age, I disguised it as a game, and she delighted in the fun of the destruction and obvious improvement, but I knew something no one else knew; she was a prodigy. A near-endless pool of magical energy. I was certain she could roast hundreds of men before her stamina waned, and she may even be the key to defeating Merlin.

I knew that if I trained her well enough and could demonstrate just how incredible her skills were, my father would find a way to utilize her safely.

One afternoon, I took Morgana to the mountains to the west of Vires' capital city. They were a steep, rocky set of mountains that didn't get much foot traffic and was barren of greenery that could catch fire.

"Here?" Morgana asked, bouncing on the balls of her feet.

"Let's go a little farther."

"Ugh," she said, putting her hands on her hips. "Why so far?"

I refrained from laughing as she looked so much like Charlotte. "So no one will see your fire," I said, waving her over.

She dragged her feet as she came and turned away from me, knowing exactly why I'd summoned her. I gathered her hair into a high ponytail and wrapped a tight ribbon around it. "We don't want your hair to catch," I said routinely.

"Why can't we show anyone?" she asked with a pout.

I took her hand. "I told you, it's going to be a big surprise."

"For the war?" she asked.

I squatted in front of her to even our heights. "You know about the war?"

She grinned with her whole face. "I know everything."

I chuckled. "Yes. Well, your power is important. You're strong and maybe you'll help us win." I brushed a stray curl out of her eyes. "You can protect the people you love, like your mommy or Gabriel."

"Or Minnow?" she said. I poked her nose. "Exactly. Now, let's hike to the other side of this ridge and we'll get started."

An hour later, we stood at the center of a rocky area that was leveled on one side. There were black streaks of burnt stone that fanned out in stripes in every direction, one stripe still burning red from Morgana's last attack.

I watched proudly as she lifted her hand for another.

"This time, I want you to pretend you're very very angry."

She took a deep breath and focused her eyes on a strip of gray stones that hadn't yet been marred by fire. She pushed her little face into a pout.

"Good. Now angrier."

She breathed harder, working up the emotion until she screamed, a bright red burst of fire shooting from her right hand. The burst scorched the stones in one concentrated line, like the fireball of a trebuchet.

She jumped up and down and clapped. "Did you see how far that one was?"

A voice sounded behind me. "What is this?"

I spun to see Minseo with gritted teeth.

"I was just helping Morgana with self-defense," I muttered. Guilt poured into me, but I couldn't place why.

"Surprise!" Morgana shouted as she ran to Minseo.

He picked her up. "That's amazing, Morgana, but I think you're too young to do something so dangerous. How about we go get some candy in town?"

Her eyes bulged. "The pink kind?" she said.

"Of course," Minseo said.

"Wait, I—" Minseo shot me a glare that froze me where I stood.

He turned and carried Morgana away without another word.

42

ARTHUR

I held the breastplate of my new armor in my hands, running my fingers across the ridges of the gold pattern embedded with colored jewels. It reminded me of my stained-glass window, and it was the finest piece of armor I'd ever seen. Despite my embarrassing victory, my Uncle Roger had kept his word and completed the set in time. I'd resisted the urge over the last few months to check its progress so I could better appreciate the finished result, and it didn't disappoint. He'd even had time to grant me an additional request, a sword modeled after Excalibur—a wedding present for my most trusted knight, Lancelot.

I was hesitant at first when Jeremy told me he no longer intended to kill Merlin, but over the last few months, she'd been instrumental in preparing our troops for war. I'd looked in her eyes as she reswore her allegiance. I believed her, but even more, I saw the love in her eyes when she looked at Lancelot. He'd mended the burned bridge between Merlin and me and consequently cemented our victory. With my prized battle mage protecting me, I could join the front lines without the fear of death.

The only concern we had was the dragon. Not a person alive had the experience of battling one, and we weren't sure how difficult the task would prove to be. But our strategy was to kill Charlotte first, to break her control over it before it could attack. I was going to be the one to do it. A hero. A legend in the making.

My castle was draped in white fabric as the staff prepared for the wedding. It was a bit thrown together as most of our resources were devoted to preparing for the battle our troops would embark on in the morning, but it was common for kings to throw a celebration before a battle. It motivated and rewarded those in attendance, started the battle off on a positive foot. It was even believed to bring luck.

The cheerful nature of the event seemed to have a positive effect on everyone. The energy was much different than my own wedding, as if the guests as they arrived could detect the genuine love of the couple, a love that had not been present in either party on my wedding day.

But I couldn't tell if I was giddy because I was happy for Lance or if I was excited to take my place in history in Vires as the greatest king who ever lived.

As the guests filed into the throne room, I admired their opulence. The women were jeweled with full gowns and expensive wigs in curled towers on their heads, the men in fine silk robes and feathered hats. All of this was highlighted by the sheer white fabric draped around the room and the crystal chandeliers that I'd ordered specifically for the event.

I'd certainly made an impact on Bullhorn, and all who lived here enjoyed the prosperity of my reign.

Lance entered the throne room, his nerves on full display. He chewed his cheek and shifted his weight from one foot to the other, like a small child in need of liquid relief.

Out of the corner of my eye, a man drew my attention, my Uncle Roger. He stuck out of the crowd with his untrimmed beard and a worn suit that had its edges frayed. It was a sandy brown color that had likely gone out of fashion before my birth. In my excitement to receive my armor in time, I'd extended him an invitation to the wedding, but I never imagined he'd accept. I was glad he could see up close the wealth that, as king, I was responsible for, but I felt guilty I hadn't thought to invite him to my own wedding.

Roger stood and waved a dirty hand in the air to get Lance's attention. Lance's jaw dropped at the sight of him, drawing the attention of the other attendees. Lance turned and looked up at me, suspecting I'd orchestrated his arrival as a wedding gift. I waved proudly as if I had, but my real gift was the sword that waited for him in his chamber, the one he'd carry into battle when we arrived in Vires. The orchestra who sat at the base of the throne began to play an ethereal but muddled mess of notes, distorted by the strong echo. The doors swung open and Merlin stepped through, sending an audible gasp through the room.

She was a vision, in a simple uncorseted white dress that flowed freely as she walked. Her green braids were curled and half pinned up. She looked angelic, a goddess among mortals. But, as if her appearance alone wasn't enough to strike awe into everyone in the room, several flickering candles floated weightlessly around her, moving forward down the aisle with each sandaled step she took. The softness of her peaceful expression clashed delightfully with the obvious display of otherworldly power, and no one could look away. That is, until the sniffles of Lancelot sounded, throwing many of the onlooking guests into tearful revery. Friends and strangers alike broke under the emotional weight of the ceremony.

For the first time, I wondered what it might be like to care for someone that way and why I hadn't wanted it before.

43

CHARLOTTE

The fall leaves had yielded a radiant display of oranges, reds, and yellows and had already begun to surrender to the wind. It was the season between life and death, and we were as prepared as we could be for the looming war. With Sumin's death a few months behind us, I knew it was time to tell Young about my decision to be with Minseo, but he always seemed too busy. He had volunteered to take Morgana hiking nearly every day and, when he wasn't with her, he was prepping more troops for the war. He had taken her that morning and I had to commend him on how much effort he put in to be a good father. Morgana always returned with a confidence and strength that I liked to see in her.

The crackle of thunder echoed through the mountains, the dark gray clouds threatening to give way to rain. I wrapped myself in my jacket outside of Gabriel's house and looked out towards the west, where Young said he was hiking with Morgana, hoping they'd make it back before the rain. I rubbed my hands together to warm them but soon retreated to the warmth of Gabriel's home.

The fireplace crackled and Gabriel hummed a familiar tune as he sipped his tea. We'd settled easily into living together again, with Morgana, over the last few months. It felt natural—a slice of normal in our otherwise foreign surroundings.

"So," I said, as I took a warm gulp of tea. "You haven't mentioned Junho in a few weeks. What's going on there?" I asked. The tea slid to my chest, giving me goosebumps.

He raised an eyebrow. "I don't want to jinx anything."

"Does that mean you guys are a thing now?"

He sipped his tea, the playful glint in his eyes framed by his dark eyelashes. He teased, "Are you and Minseo a thing?"

I ran my finger around the rim of my teacup and shook my head.

"What's stopping you? Did you change your mind?"

"Of course not," I said. "I just don't know what I'm going to say to Young."

"How about, 'Sorry, Young, your brother is hotter and more fun than you.'"

I nearly spat out my tea but instead forcefully swallowed and nearly choked. Gabriel's bright smile eased me. "Gabe?" I said, pulling his gaze from the fireplace. "Thank you for coming with me and Morgana. Thank you for always being here."

"We're family," he said.

I nodded. "If something happens to me in the battle, I want you to be Morgana's guardian."

He reached out and touched my arm. "Promise me nothing will happen. She needs us both."

I turned my gaze to the fire, taking a mouthful of tea before I spoke again. "Just in case."

The door swung open and a rain-soaked Minseo stepped in with Morgana in his arms. Young followed closely behind.

Gabriel stood. "Looks like you didn't make it back in time."

"Minseo," I said, feeling a flutter in my stomach. I hadn't expected to see him today, let alone with my daughter in hand. "What are you doing here?" I said.

"Mommmmmm!" Morgana yelled, dripping water onto the floor as she ran to me. Minseo's cold gaze cut into Young. "Outside," he said, pushing the door open. He followed Young out without another word, closing the door behind them.

Gabriel's mouth was agape, his eyebrows raised. He'd clearly heard the venom in Minseo's simple command. "I," I mouthed, pointing to the door.

"Yeah, I think you should," he said, then he turned to Morgana. "Let's get you out of these wet clothes."

I hurried over to the door, pushed it open, and stepped into the icy rain.

Minseo swung, his fist colliding with Young's face. "Tell her. Tell her now."

Young swung at Minseo and missed. He turned and kicked Minseo in the stomach, knocking him onto the ground. "Is this your plan to win her over?" Young asked.

I ran toward them and shouted, "What are you doing?"

Minseo barked, "Tell her. She deserves to know."

Young drew his sword as Minseo got to his feet. My heart raced as I sprinted toward them.

"Stop!" I screamed.

"Draw your sword," Young spat, holding his sword to Minseo.

Minseo held his hands up. "I won't."

Young yelled, "You coward! You owe me this much." Blood slid down his nose. "You went after Charlotte. She's *my* wife. Draw your sword, you coward!"

"I won't," Minseo said softly.

I threw myself between the tip of Young's sword and Minseo as the rain slapped against my skin. "Stop!"

Young froze in place and I heard Minseo's voice behind me. "Tell her."

Lightning cracked through the sky shortly followed by a clap of thunder that shook the earth. It sounded like a rockslide, stone scraping stone growing fainter until the next large blast. Young breathed heavily in silence, his gaze past me to Minseo as he slowly lowered his sword.

"Charlotte," he said, "I can explain."

I shook my head. "I don't understand."

Minseo said, "He's been training Morgana for the war. He's going to toss his own daughter into battle."

I blinked in disbelief. "What?" I stared into Young's eyes, waiting for him to contradict Minseo, but he remained silent. I spoke again. "No. He wouldn't. She's only five years old. It's—"

"He did," Minseo said. "Tell her! Tell her that hiking is your code for war training. Tell her that you asked Morgana to lie."

Young took a deep breath. "I can explain."

Minseo said, "Charlotte."

My heart raced.

Minseo's voice blurred with a crack of thunder. "Charlotte, what are you—"

I gripped my dagger.

"No!"

I leapt toward Young, slashing at him with my dagger. He slipped each cut, moving backward out of my range. "You monster!" I screamed with a new wave of attacks. A high kick clipped his chin, briefly disorienting him. "I'll kill you!!" With a sweep of my leg, I brought him to the ground, his sword landing on the stones with a clang. I knelt on top of him and he didn't resist. I held the dagger over my head, ready to strike, Young's expressionless eyes peering into mine. "I should have killed you from the start."

I brought the dagger down. My wrist stopped short as Minseo took hold of it, knocking the dagger from my hand.

Minseo's arms wrapped around me, pulling me off Young and holding me to his warm body.

My knees buckled and I felt the warmth of fresh tears on my cheeks as I buried my face in Minseo's chest.

44

MERLIN

I felt the shake of Lance's hands in mine as I spoke, "I promise to protect you all the days of my life."

His hazel eyes were more brown than green in the light of my candles, and they were wet with joy. He smiled genially as he blinked away the tears. I was sure no one had ever looked at me that way before, with such pleasurable satisfaction. With pure love.

"I promise," he said, "to be your family always, and to never leave your side."

I squeezed his hands in mine as my thoughts raced. We'd been friends since I'd convinced Arthur to allow me to join Lance on his quest. We'd been lovers since his second proposal, and although tonight would not be our first time together, it would be our first night as husband and wife. We were bound, forever. His capacity to love as strong as I'd always known, and finally for me.

I felt fear ring inside me, reminding me he'd wake up one day with a new heart and leave me behind the way he'd done with Gwen, but fear had made a liar of me all my life and I wanted nothing more than to leave it behind with the girl who was certain she'd be alone forever. The same girl who believed magic was the reason she'd lost her family and that it was the currency she'd use to buy a new one.

But Lance, like always, paid my magic no mind. It was not a gift or a hindrance, just part of me, like my body or my spirit. I made a conscious choice not to let fear attend this ceremony so, with all the power I had stored inside, I wished it away, leaving only gratitude in its wake.

I adjusted the strap on my nightgown as I sat quietly on Lance's bed, mindlessly picking at my fingernails. He'd been called into a meeting with Arthur just after the ceremony and hadn't returned for nearly an hour.

I was surprised to find a lavish golden sword laid out in the chamber when I arrived. Arthur had spared no expense to commemorate the occasion, and I was excited to see what Lance would say about it. But as the night dragged on and he still hadn't appeared, I let fear creep back in.

I sprang to my feet as the door jostled and Lance stepped through. His face was hardened and tense, with bulges on each cheek where his jaw was tensed. His eyes softened when he looked at me, but only for a moment.

"What's wrong?" I asked.

His gaze swept the room, landing on Arthur's wedding gift. His face brightened. "What's this? It looks just like Excalibur."

"Arthur had it made for you," I said.

He walked over, running his fingers along the jeweled hilt. He lifted the sword and checked its balance by placing it on two fingers just below the bottom of the hilt. Perfectly balanced and excellently crafted, it was difficult to imagine it was made by human hands.

"Lance," I said, interrupting. "What's wrong?"

His shoulder sagged as he put down the sword and turned to me.

"Arthur is sending Galahad, Percival, and Lamorak to lead the charge."

It was not an unexpected choice; they were the most battle-tested. I doubted Lance would've been thrown by it, so I waited to hear the news that had been enough to alter his euphoric mood.

"We'll go with Arthur to…" he took a deep breath, "to take down Charlotte. Once she's down, no one will have control of Garix, and it'll be an easy win."

My pulse quickened. Charlotte hurt me. Part of me really hated her for what she did. I was still angry, but she was a prisoner trying to make it back to her family. I desperately wished she would have told me she was leaving. I wish I could've said goodbye or even convinced her to stay. But none of those things could condemn her, and there was no way I could take her life.

My mind raced as I sorted through the possible scenarios. Not only would I be unable to kill Charlotte when it came down to it, but I might also have the impulse to save her. That could not only put our entire battle at risk but, more importantly, it could get Lance or Arthur killed.

Sensing my distress, Lance walked over and rubbed the cold from my arms. He pulled my face into his chest and ran his hand up and down my spine. I wanted to disappear, feeling a home-like comfort I could scarcely remember from my early childhood. Now that I had Lance's unconditional love, I couldn't remember why I liked to fight to begin with. I had nothing more to prove and no enemies to slay. Lance spoke softly into the top of my head. "I know she's important to you. If I were king, I would stop this. You know, even if we weren't going to fight her directly, she's part of the enemy kingdom. Someone has to lose. It isn't personal. It's war."

I nodded, the warmth of his chest easing me.

"She's fighting for her family." He pulled back, cupping my face in his hands. "Are you willing to fight for yours?"

I turned my face away.

He continued, "We can run. You and me, right now. They'd be too busy with this war to go after us."

"You'd lose Arthur," I said, tucking a stray mint green braid behind my ear.

"I'd do it for you if you asked."

I closed my eyes and pressed my lips together then took a deep breath and looked into Lance's hazel eyes. There wasn't a single glimmer of doubt in them. He really would abandon Arthur and Camelot if I asked. My heart flooded at the idea of us together on the road again, but I squelched it as I settled on a decision. "If you'd do that for me," I said, "then I can help you defeat Charlotte."

He leaned in and gently kissed me, dimples cutting into his cheeks. "We'll be together the whole time," he said. "Arthur wants to take care of her himself. All you'll have to do is protect us, and Merlin, this is the last thing between you and Arthur's full trust."

I nodded, determination welling inside me. If Charlotte had the right to protect her family, I had the right to protect mine. I'd given her the chance to stay in Camelot. She made her choice, and I made mine.

45

YOUNG

The storm had passed along with several hours before I thought Charlotte had cooled down enough to let me explain. While I'd trained Morgana, I was confident Charlotte would eventually understand once I was able to explain. But, after seeing the hatred in her eyes as she held her dagger over me, ready to end my life, I was less confident. Still, I knew in my heart that I'd done the right thing.

I sat at the edge of Charlotte's bed as she lay facing the wall, her breaths steady and slow.

"Charlotte," I said. I wasn't sure how much time she'd give me to get this out. "She's much stronger than you think. She can save a thousand lives. She could be the difference between winning this war and total destruction."

Charlotte sat up, turning her face to me. Her stare was cold and her eyes vacant. "She's only five," she said half-heartedly. "You want her to kill people? She's just a child."

"I want her to save lives. Men who will die in this battle if she doesn't fight."

"And you would risk the life of your daughter to win?"

It was a question I'd grown familiar with. "There's nothing I wouldn't risk to win."

She scoffed and turned away.

I continued, " If we don't win, Morgana won't have a home to grow up in."

The silence between us pervaded the room and I had the urge to open the window at the head of the bed to let some of it out. I sighed. Maybe the time had come to tell her everything. "I had planned to die for you and Morgana. You were hidden in that pipe with Minseo and those guards told me they were going to kill me. I was already bleeding out. But, instead of striking me down, the guard dropped his sword and pulled me to my feet, deciding I might be worth more alive than dead."

Charlotte turned her gaze to me.

"They marched me to Bullhorn and locked me in a dungeon, promising to kill me the next day and then the next and then the next. I wasn't sure how long I sat alone in the darkness, wishing for death, but when I finally saw the light again, Drethen was no more and Camelot had taken form. That's when I met Arthur."

My hands were clammy, and I wished I could read Charlotte's thoughts because her face gave nothing away.

"He was more boy than man back then and, when he found out I was royalty, he put me in a high tower. It was a beautifully furnished bedroom with a window that filled the room with sunlight and fresh air, but it was a cell nonetheless. Locked from the outside. This time, however, I wasn't alone."

I looked down at my hands. "Another prisoner, about my age, shared the room." My throat tightened to stop me from continuing the story, but I pressed on. "Her name was Sarah." As I thought of her, I chuckled. "She was a total pain in the ass, just talked the entire day away. I assumed she was royalty since she was put in the tower, but she never mentioned where from. I figured that she'd tell me eventually, based on how quickly she burned through topics, but she never mentioned her past with any detail, and I never got the chance to ask before she died."

Charlotte's breathing quickened.

"We spent years looking out the window planning hopeless escapes, but it was a straight shot down the tower to a steep cliff and certain death. We fought all the time, too, living so closely. I think she even yelled at me for breathing too loudly. Then, one day, Arthur came to see us. He said that we would leave the next day for our respective kingdoms and that he welcomed us as the new allies of Camelot."

Her eyes began to tear.

"You see, I'd never really considered why he'd moved me to such a civil jail cell or why he'd provided me with a female companion. Sarah figured it out first, that we'd become bargaining chips for Arthur. She refused to submit. Instead, she took a chance on her escape."

Charlotte spoke softly. "She fell."

My jaw tightened. "Yes. She fell and she died a hero, saving her kingdom from the fate we now face. I could have followed her. I could have made the jump and died for you and for Vires like I said I would."

Charlotte nodded. "You loved her."

I exhaled a shaky breath. "Out of respect for you, we didn't sleep together, but I did love her."

She pressed a hand to her stomach.

"When I returned to Vires and confirmed that Sarah had been right and that my death could have prevented Vires from being lost, I knew I had to do whatever it took to dethrone Arthur. Only then would Sarah's kingdom, whatever it was, also be freed from the threat of Camelot."

Charlotte pressed her lips together, holding in a reaction I desperately wanted to dissect. After a long pause, she spoke. "Got it. So this is a grudge match between you and Arthur? So you can avenge your dead girlfriend. Young, listen to me. Putting your daughter at risk doesn't make you brave. It doesn't make you a king. It makes you callous. It makes you worse than Arthur." She stood. "And if you think I'm going to let you put my daughter's life in danger to save your kingdom, or any kingdom for that matter, know this. You'll have to kill me first."

I stood. "No, that's not it at all. I knew the second I saw you again that I still love you. We've made mistakes. But I love you and I love Morgana. Let's just get through this battle and we can give us a real chance to be a family."

She sighed. "They call them sweet nothings because they mean nothing. Young..." she said, her voice low, "if you're willing to sacrifice your child for *anything*, you don't deserve a family. A family is a place for children to be safe and protected, not used for their parents' agendas." She headed for the door and reached for the handle to slide it open. "Oh." She stopped and turned to me. "I know I should have said this before because I've thought of nothing else since I returned, but I'm in love with Minseo, and I'm going to be with him."

"Because of Sarah or because I trained Morgana and believe in her potential?"

She put a hand to her hip. "Because Minseo would rather be my husband and Morgana's father than the king."

"That's easy for him to decide when he's next in line," I spat, but she was already gone.

46

ARTHUR

I stood on the Jin Sea, the wind whipping my face as we loaded our men onto our transport ships. I'd begun this journey with a glow of pride and excitement that felt electric, but that had drained away quickly during our tedious trek to Vires. There was nothing thrilling or epic about a thousand unruly men starting fights and getting drunk every night at camp. War was slow and crowded, and my thoughts drifted to what my Uncle Roger had said when he delivered my armor.

The sea was the final obstacle between me and my legacy. Once we crossed, we'd be on Viran territory. They knew we were coming and were prepared for war. Galahad had confirmed this when he returned from his tax collection trip to Vires empty-handed. I was expecting Vires to pay if for no other reason than to buy themselves a shred more time, but they'd refused.

The only thing that kept me going through the long travel days leading to the war was an image that repeatedly played in my mind of me standing over Charlotte, in golden armor, plunging into her with Excalibur, her dragon crashing into the ground beside me.

I knew if I imagined it enough, it would come to be. I would be remembered not as a boy who pulled a magical sword from a stone but as a great king and warrior who defeated a dragon.

The boats clapped together, nearly throwing the men off the ladders as they climbed. *Ugh.*

I turned to Galahad, his greasy black hair shining even in the gray overcast. "How much longer is this going to take?" I asked.

He smiled at me, his full set of pearly teeth showing. "We're nearly there, Your Highness. Don't worry, it won't be long now. You'll have your chance," he said.

I didn't take well to being pacified but thought a battle would be a waste of what little energy I had left. I felt a hand come down on my shoulder and turned to see Jeremy standing beside me. His plain armor didn't match the stunning Excalibur replica sheathed to his scabbard.

"Your Highness," he said, "let's have Merlin cover the boats with fog."

I looked around at the empty sea in front of us. "No, tell her to save her strength. There's no need for such extreme measures."

"But Your Majesty, we're crowding our men onto a small number of ships. It would be unwise to—"

"It would be unwise to doubt your king, Lancelot."

He leaned closer. "Please, Arthur," he whispered. "It looks safe, but there's a dragon out here."

I stiffened. "Merlin!" I called, projecting my voice. "Your laziness is giving me cause to doubt you. For God's sake, conjure us some cover!"

"Yes, sir!" she said, lifting her hands to the boats.

The wind picked up, suddenly heavy and wet. A thick fog settled in around the boats. Just as a hint of satisfaction settled in, the fog began to bleed and swirl with a dark purple color.

"Merlin!" I yelled, as the violet food obscured my vision. It was so dense that it hardly let daylight through. "Merlin! What the hell is this?"

"Sorry, Your Highness. It's been a while since I—"

"You fool! You're supposed to conceal us, not put a bloody target on us."

A fierce gust nearly took me off my feet and slammed the boats together, but a moment later we stood in a colorless fog so thick the enemy wouldn't see us until we knocked at the castle door.

As the last of our men loaded onto our concealed ships, my thoughts once again turned to my Uncle Roger's final words to me: "Legends are written not by the man who endeavors to become one but by those who mourn him."

47

CHARLOTTE

The enemy has practically arrived. We'd been informed just after Arthur and his men reached the far side of the Jin Sea. It was a moment we'd been preparing for, but no one is ever truly ready for war.

I wrapped my arms around Morgana and put my forehead to hers. "It's time," I whispered. "I promise, as soon as there's no more danger, I'll come get you."

I could feel Minseo and Young watching from behind me and see the shadowed forms behind Morgana of Gabriel and Junho through wet lashes.

Morgana sniffed, her voice barely a whisper as she spoke. "You have to be safe," she said through tearful eyes.

We'd had many discussions over the last few weeks about today, but saying goodbye to her when I knew it could be the last time made my heart ache. A lump rose in my throat, but instead of melting into a puddle of tears as I wanted, I grinned. "Take care of Gabriel and Junho for me. Can you do that?"

She nodded, her curls bouncing sporadically around her head.

"Will you make sure they have breakfast and drink lots of tea?"

She nodded again, this time wiping her nose and face with the back of her hand and smiling softly.

"My turn," Minseo said, kneeling to Morgana and pulling her out of my arms and in for a hug.

"Be good," he said. But another wave of sadness hit her and a fresh line of tears streaked her cheek.

"Hey, hey, hey." Minseo lifted one arm and bent it at the elbow toward his shoulder. "Do you see this muscle?"

Morgana patted at Minseo's bicep, objectively taking a moment to appraise him before nodding.

"It's strong, right?" Minseo continued. "I'm going to keep everyone safe."

I stood to give them a bit of space as Minseo hugged her one last time. "I love you, little girl."

"I love you, Minnow," she said, her voice muffled by his neck as she nestled closer.

Next, Young stepped forward. I'd hardly spoken a word to him since our fight. It was obvious he didn't agree with sending Morgana away, but he gave little resistance since I'd overruled him. Luckily, Morgana didn't seem to sense any animosity between us, even if I'd put an immediate end to their "hiking" sessions.

Young hugged her but alarm bells sounded inside me when a whispered conversation passed between them. I knew I'd look like a monster if I intervened. Luckily, Morgana always wore her emotions on her face. I waited for her to pull away so I could read the gist of their conversation. Morgana's eyes lowered to the ground thoughtfully. Suspicion bubbled beneath my skin as I watched, but just as quickly as her face had turned thoughtful, it brightened and she waved me over for one final goodbye.

I kissed the top of her head, feeling the wisp of her soft curls on my face. I stood and walked over to Gabriel and Junho.

"So, Junho's going too?" I asked, my gaze moving between them. I knew exactly what that meant, and I wasn't going to pass up the opportunity to make them squirm as they'd so blatantly done when I first got together with Minseo. "It's about time."

Junho bit back a smile.

Gabriel said, "How do you know he's not just trying to get out of the battle?"

Junho shoved Gabriel's shoulder. "Stop," he said with a smile. "You know I feel bad about that." Gabriel reached for Junho to steady himself, their fingers locking together and lingering for a moment before dropping to their side.

My chest warmed as I watched them. They were two of the most gentle and loving men I'd known. They were the family that Morgana deserved, and I was comforted to know that if I were to die in battle, Morgana's life would continue to be filled with love and happiness.

"Gabe," I said, "thank you so much for doing this. I want you to know that I love—"

Gabe placed a hand on my shoulder. "Don't go getting sentimental. It makes me think you won't..." His gaze drifted to Morgana and snapped back to me. "You're strong. Beat them."

If he wouldn't let me say it, I'd show him. I wrapped my arms around his neck and hugged him.

"Wait!" Morgana said. I spun to see her bouncing on the balls of her feet, her eyes wide. "I didn't say goodbye to Garix."

"Garix is preparing for battle. There's no time to—"

With a powerful screech, Garix soared into view, blocking out the sun's rays before ascending. Each powerful flap of his wings sent red and orange leaves swirling around us until he gracefully met the ground beside Morgana.

I'd already forgotten she could do that. It was another reason why I was happy to send her far away from the war.

Morgana skipped over to Garix, his scales alight with determined rays of sunshine that pushed through the overcast. Morgana put her face to Garix who gave way to a gentle purr as she patted him clumsily on his lowered head.

The pit of my stomach flashed a wave of empathy from Garix that felt like the color pink. *Love.*

Morgana looked cheerful as she waved goodbye to us all one last time before climbing into the carriage. I was grateful that, once inside, she could no longer see me. I felt my strong exterior give way. As her carriage shrunk into the distance, my mind recycled one thought again and again. *This might be the last time I ever see my daughter.*

Sadness welled inside me, draining my strength like the horizon drains the sun. Everything beautiful was behind me. I could feel Minseo and Young's expectant gazes and I wondered if they shared the same pain. My balance wavered and, rather than collapse, I sat willfully on the cold ground, Garix twitching away from my sadness. *It's okay, Garix. Return to the farm for dinner.*

The gusts from Garix's wings, as he flew away, composed me a bit and, after a few deep breaths, I was ready to stand again. I sighed. It was time for me to head home for dinner. Just before I pushed myself back to my feet, I felt someone's hands curl around my legs. Minseo lifted me into the air, cradling me in his arms, and I let my head rest against his chest.

I couldn't remember the last time he'd held me, or how long since we'd even touched, but his skin on mine sent me a shot of life I desperately needed and suddenly craved.

Minseo turned away from Morgana's carriage and back towards the Vires capital, drawing my gaze to Young. I felt my heart studder at his fiery expression. But his molten gaze was not on me, it was on Minseo.

With my cheek, I could feel Minseo's heart rate double and his muscles tense. His grip on me tightened.

Young's gaze dropped to me, sending ice through my veins.

It had been weeks since I'd told Young about my decision to be with Minseo, but all of that had been pushed aside for the war. Now, as the three of us stood face to face, the weight of choosing one brother over the other seemed to hit us all at once.

Now that Morgana was safe, I had no reason to harbor ill will toward Young. The real enemy would arrive in Vires within a week. I was committed to my promise to fight and give my life to protect Young's home, as he'd once done for mine.

But if I only had a week left to live, I wanted to spend every second of that time with Minseo—to fill my final days with scarlet red before its comparable life essence was carved from my flesh.

I steeled my nerves as Young's bladelike gaze crossed with mine. My anger from his choices had dimmed and, despite the fierceness of his gaze, I knew we were not enemies but comrades in war. We had one last battle to fight together, and after, regardless of the outcome, my time with him would be at its end.

Our men were in place, our supplies were stocked, and all that remained was an excruciating wait.

48

MINSEO

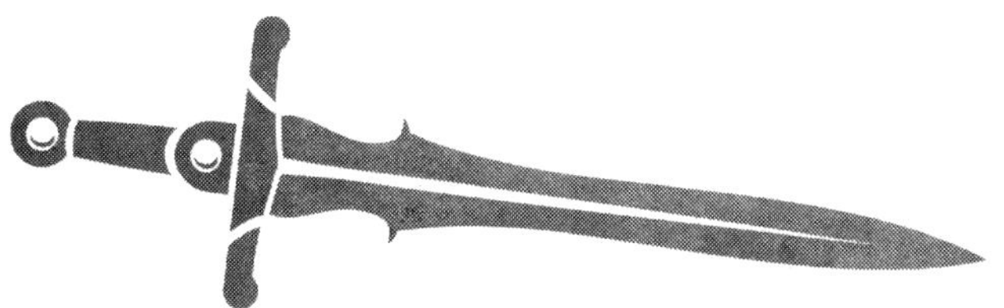

As I carried Charlotte away from Young and back to town, I imagined I was carrying her away from her old life towards a new one, but the truth was, Charlotte, Young, and I were all going to the same place. The battle. Even with all the preparations we'd made and Garix as a wildcard, the grim reaper roamed the streets of Vires and every one of us knew it. Camelot couldn't be defeated, and even if we managed to survive this battle, it wouldn't be long before Arthur tripled their efforts and returned. Our only hope, if there was one, was to kill Arthur, and there was no doubt in my mind that he would be closely guarded by Merlin. I shuddered when I thought of facing off with the earthbound goddess I'd crossed paths with before.

It was an honor to die for Vires, one I didn't want. If I was honest, I wanted nothing more than to take Charlotte, find Morgana, and disappear—away from kingdoms, thrones, and the blood that won them.

I gritted my teeth. My time with Charlotte was going to run

out, *again*. When I imagined dying alongside her, it was in a much further future.

As we neared Gabriel's empty house, I couldn't help but notice how fragile Charlotte actually seemed. She was light enough for me to lift and carry back without exerting myself. My stomach turned at the thought of her on the battlefield.

"Am I getting heavy?" she asked, jogging me from my thoughts.

"No."

Her voice was soft. "You look so serious."

We pushed through Gabriel's gate and I put her down outside the door as I unlocked it and stepped inside.

We sat by the empty fireplace, two wet logs lay charred but still whole as if the home's tenants had left in a hurry.

Charlotte's hand slipped into mine.

I turned to her, fear barreling into me. I wasn't afraid to die, but losing her, that was unbearable. "Char, I was thinking, what if we just go join Gabriel and Morgana. We can start over, find a new kingdom…"

She smiled as if there was a hidden joke I hadn't intended. She lifted her arm. "Do you see this muscle?" she said.

I nodded.

"Can you feel how strong it is?"

I patted it and nodded.

She tilted her head to the side. "We're going to win, Minseo."

"You don't think it's impossible?"

She lay across my lap, thrusting herself into my arms. "Of course I do. Absolutely impossible, just like having a magical daughter or a pet dragon."

I pulled her closer, feeling the life returning to me with every word she spoke. She went on, "And when we get married, we'll live together. Me, you, Gabriel, Junho, and Morgana."

I closed my eyes, picturing the future I desperately wanted. The one that was worth fighting for.

My eyes opened and I looked down at her. It felt as if a rock had shattered my daydream. "We can't get married, you're technically still married to my brother."

She shrugged. "We'll have to take him out during the battle."

Laughter burst from me.

She sat up. "I'm kidding." She giggled. "Seriously, that was a joke."

"I'm pretty sure that's treason."

She sighed and lay back. "Put it on my tab."

The laughter had driven out my dark thoughts. I wasn't sure if she meant any of it or if she was just cheering me up, but I got her message. We weren't dead yet and, while we still had time, we owed it to ourselves to cling to our last precious days.

I looked down at her cradled half on my lap and the half in my left arm. *Perfect.* I ran my right hand through my hair slowly and felt her shudder on my lap.

Her breaths deepened. Suddenly, a smile flashed to her face and she jolted upright. "Did you just use a move on me?"

Grasping at her, I said, "Of course not." I quickly ran my hand through my hair again.

"You just did it again."

I put my nose to hers. "Listen, Charlotte, if I wanted to make something happen, I wouldn't need a move."

I leaned in and kissed her softly and pulled away to savor the involuntary lean forward she couldn't help.

"No," she whispered. "Not gently."

My body pulsed. "Yes, my queen," I said as I stood, lifting her. I turned and pushed her back onto the couch. Heat surged through me as I slipped her dagger from her scabbard and cut through the strings on the front of her dress. I ripped her dress open and tossed the dagger aside.

She gripped me from the back of my neck and pulled me in. She kissed me hard and I matched her, taking a handful of her hair. She arched her back, the corners of her mouth turning up. My body burned, as if the fire beside us had suddenly lit. I supposed while we were still alive, she wanted to feel every sensation, to carry the weight of my touch on her body even as we stepped into battle.

But with her bare skin against mine, each taste and stroke and kiss blurred time until nothing existed but her. Five days and nights melted together and brought with it our reckoning.

Whatever awaited us in death—the next life, a long sleep, even heaven—could wait.

49

ARTHUR

I half expected us to battle our way onto the shore or for the dragon to strike us midway across the Jin Sea, despite Merlin's attempts to hide us, but we pulled our ships up to the Viran harbor without a hint of resistance or military presence. The harbor was scattered with fishermen who didn't seem surprised or impressed by our approach.

I turned to Galahad. "Have they given up already?"

He flashed a broad smile. "Virans are traditional people. They likely won't attack until you meet the king and declare war on Vires officially. "

I crossed my arms over my chest. "It seems like a waste of time. How much farther from here?"

"Not far, Your Majesty. Half a day's walk through the mountain pass."

I scanned our soldiers for Lance to no avail, but it only took a moment to spot Merlin. I waved her over and, as expected, Lance followed closely behind.

"Merlin is tired from the fog. We should let her rest a while before we—"

I scoffed. "Galahad just told me there was no risk of attack before I officially declare war on Vires. Your whole idea to have Merlin use her powers to hide us was a complete waste of time and energy." I turned to Galahad, who appeared to be ordering the twins to begin unloading a particular group of soldiers. "Galahad," I called, "let's get these guys off the ships quickly and move out."

He bowed. "Yes, Your Majesty."

Lance grabbed my arm. "Don't forget, Merlin is the one who is supposed to protect you."

I pulled my arm away. "It's everyone's job to protect me. It's also their job to follow my orders without questioning them."

I knew that if my uncle were here, he'd scold me for my impatience. But he wasn't here. All I had of him was this armor and some vague anti-war advice he'd given before I left.

The men unloaded off the ship and separated quickly into their assigned teams, each led by one of my knights. Percival and Lamorak corralled the horses off their transport ships and walked them one by one to the knights.

As soon as Lamorak handed me the reigns of my horse, I mounted it and headed for the mountain pass. I had no intention of dragging this out; I needed to get things started. I heard the scramble of my army behind me as they streamlined their preparations to catch up with me and the furious gallop of Lance and Merlin's horses as they rushed to my side.

The mountains jutted up from the earth in front of us. They were steep and covered in trees that had a navy blue hue. I felt a twinge of nerves as I scanned the foreign shore, but I certainly wasn't going to need a map to find the mountain pass. When we reached the mouth where the road met the mountains, the path was hardly five horses wide. I was glad to have most of our soldiers on foot.

The path plunged us into shade that was noticeably colder, and tunneled wind slapped at our faces as we made our way through the winding road.

We rode for almost an hour, and the road had very little variation, barring some steeper sections and stones that partially obstructed the path. I hoped that there was flat land and sunshine on the other side. When I'd envisioned this battle, as I'd done compulsively since the idea of going to war settled in, I'd never imagined it in a dark, gloomy tunnel like this, and it irked me.

My horse came to a sudden halt. Ahead, the mountains opened the road to a sunlit canyon and, even from the shadows, I could see the king on his horse at its center. *This was my moment.* A rush of fear and exhilaration shot through me as I moved through the last of the narrow path and into the rocky canyon. As my horse moved into the light, I could see rows of soldiers on the far end of the canyon behind the king, and just beyond them was another narrow pathway that I assumed led to their city.

I tallied the number of soldiers as I moved out into the canyon just enough for my own soldiers to fall in line behind me. We were in Viran territory, and by my count, we had a few hundred more than they did. I scoffed. No wonder they favored peace. They did, however, appear to be one dragon short. I sighed. This wasn't going to be the legendary battle I'd thirsted for but a mere skirmish. When the rest of my men were in position, I turned to Galahad. He nodded and I rode alone to the center of the canyon to meet the Viran king. Frustration built as I neared. He was gray-haired, his face strongly lined with age. His armor was worn from a time long passed, and he wore no flourish or crown to distinguish himself as king. He looked as if he could be quickly eliminated with a chest cold, so I knew I couldn't earn anyone's respect by striking him down with Excalibur.

I swallowed my disappointment as I stopped my horse a few feet from his. We dismounted and met at the center of the canyon.

"We do not wish to fight," the old king said. "We can spare the lives of good men. All we ask is that you let us out of your alliance and the trade tax that accompanies it."

I gritted my teeth. "You are far too old to be on this battlefield. Where's your heir?" I asked. The king's eyebrows rose.

"Where's your heir?" I repeated.

"I am the king of Vires," he said, his tone heavy with confusion.

"Prince Minseo of Vires!" I yelled. "Minseo!"

I heard the horse's hooves sound from the far end of the canyon and leaned around the king to see Minseo riding toward us. Ah. Excellent. I watched Minseo come closer into view, his body still rife with youth and vitality.

"Do not disregard me," the king said, drawing my attention. My heart stopped. The king had drawn his sword. I reached for Excalibur, but there was no time. The king lifted his sword to make his attack on me.

"No!" Minseo yelled from several yards away.

My instinct was to block my face with my arms. A clang rang out. The Viran king's sword landed on the ground at my feet, followed by the king. I blinked with disbelief as blood poured from his throat and he gurgled his last breath. Bile rose from my gut.

Minseo charged at me. "You bastard!" he screamed.

Confused and disoriented, I fumbled for my sword, the cries of both armies filling the canyon as they charged. A sudden gust of wind sent Minseo and his horse flying back across the canyon. My mind scrambled to connect what I'd just seen. Merlin had struck the king to protect me. The concentrated air had been so precise it had mortally cut the king, who was just inches away, and I hadn't even felt it.

Her larger gust had bought me time, so I mounted my horse, turned, and rode back toward my soldiers.

That's when all hell broke loose.

50

CHARLOTTE

I heard the trumpets sound, signaling the Viran archers to step up to the canyon's edge and take out Arthur's soldiers. It was Young's idea to conceal them to lull Arthur into a false sense of victory. They were only going to get a few shots before Merlin could target them. That's where I fit into Young's strategy. Once the archers attacked, Arthur's men would clump together at the center of the canyon and Garix and I could scorch them before the armies even clashed.

I pressed my palms against Garix's smooth scales. *Let's go*. We rose into the sky, the jagged peaks of the mountains below. As we approached the canyon, my heart sank. The archers were already down, and the enemy soldiers were beginning to spread as they charged across the flat of the land.

Lower, Garix, I willed. *Fire*! The pit of my stomach clenched as Garix's response slammed into me. The color black. *No.* The wind knocked out my lungs as my mind raced. What? Why? *Garix, we need you to save us.* Our whole plan depended on this.

Garix lowered us toward the Viran half of the canyon. With

one sharp twist of his body, he tossed me from his back. I landed with a crack on the rocky ground. I watched with horror as Garix flew out of the canyon and beyond my reach. Camelot soldiers charged toward us across the way. I reached for my dagger as I scrambled to my feet.

"Charlotte, what happened?" Young said, reaching a hand out to steady me.

I shook my head, my knee stinging from the fall. "Garix won't kill them. He won't listen."

"Get ready," he said.

Behind Young, Galahad raced toward us, his horse carrying him far ahead of the foot soldiers. If we had any chance of survival, we had to take out the knights first, and quickly. I could see the darkness in Galahad's eyes and the bloodlust in his wicked grin. My gaze moved to the scarlet red dragon sword raised in his right hand. Young drew his sword and I held my dagger at the ready.

Galahad's horse bucked as Minseo rode up beside him, leapt from his horse, and knocked him off his saddle. Young and I stood stunned by Minseo's sudden appearance until we jolted back simultaneously and charged in to help him.

The shuffled dirt from the canyon rose into the air like smoke obscuring my distant view of the battlefield. I'd have to judge the distance of the foot soldiers by sound.

Minseo held Galahad down, his elbow at his throat. Galahad thrashed for his sword which lay just beyond his reach. He jostled, grazing the handle with his fingertips.

I grabbed the sword as Young plunged his blade between the gaps in Galahad's shoulder armor.

Galahad's fight dimmed. His body convulsed, his mouth falling open to let out a low gurgle that came from the back of his throat. Finally, his movement extinguished. Minseo got back to his feet. My heart slammed my chest, as Minseo was badly cut across his cheek, his clothes, armor, and the exposed skin on his hands and face covered in debris and blood. The battle had hardly begun and he already looked like he was on his last leg.

I turned to Young, holding the red dragon-hilted sword to him like I had when I'd first given it to him. "Here," I said. "It belongs to you."

He smiled softly, but it didn't reach his eyes. "You keep it. You're the Dragon Princess, after all."

I turned back to the fight; they were nearly here. "I'm no princess," I said.

My heart sank as the next wave of attacks was not, as I expected, foot soldiers from Arthur's army but Lancelot, Merlin, and King Arthur himself.

Fear tore through me as my gaze locked with Merlin's. If she wanted, I would have been dead already. Why did she hesitate? Did she already expel too much energy or had she forgiven me for leaving? After all we'd been through, I didn't want her to be harmed, but keeping Minseo alive through this fight was my top priority and I'd cut through anyone to save him, even her.

Merlin's armor was scarce, her dark skin lined with intricate markings made with white paint. Her mint green braids flowed free, and her eyes were intense with focus.

Minseo squeezed my free hand, sending my thoughts to the five days we spent tangled together in Gabriel's empty home. The small, innocent gesture was a goodbye, an act of surrender I wasn't ready to reciprocate. Even if Garix was gone, the enemy was approaching, and the three largest threats had targeted my small group. I wasn't going to go down without blood on my sword. A loud clang drew my attention from the Viran side of the canyon, where Jay Hyun fought one on one with Percival. Percival's blade collided with Jay's, sending him to one knee. I turned away, unable to watch and refocusing on Merlin who was almost upon us. I clenched my jaw as I made a vow to myself not to die. We would find the will to win. *Make your move, Merlin.*

As if she'd heard me, she lifted her hand. A concentrated gust of wind pushed between Young, Minseo, and me, sending us in three different directions. I tumbled through the dirt, scratching my face on the pebbled ground. Pain rang out in my limbs and, for a fraction of a second, I considered staying down. Instead, I leapt to my feet and ran to collect my sword a few yards away. I grabbed it and turned in time to see Arthur charging at me, Excalibur raised to strike me down.

I delighted in the weight of the dragon-hilted broadsword, relished the power I felt as adrenaline surged through my body. Arthur dismounted his horse and stepped closer, as if a suitor asking for a dance. I touched the tip of my sword to Excalibur. He lunged wildly. I dodged with ease and stabbed my sword in his exposed side. My blade stopped an inch away from his body. I leaned in to notice condensed air shielding him. I looked back over my shoulder as I blocked Arthur's clumsy attacks. Merlin held back a row of Viran foot soldiers that had made it to us with a wall of wind that only slightly distorted the image of the soldiers on the other side, like a painting. With her other hand, she pinned Young down with a tornado-like gust.

How? How could she still protect Arthur? Was her power that unlimited? I'd seen her wear out before. What was she fighting for?

Arthur swung wildly at me and I stepped aside, causing him to stumble and fall.

I looked over at Lancelot who was locked in battle with Minseo. If Merlin was protecting Lancelot too, we had absolutely no chance at winning. Furious, I slammed my sword down on Arthur in a series of slices that should have killed him, but each stopped an inch away from him.

Breathless, I swung uselessly at Arthur until a sudden gust of wind from Merlin knocked me off my feet.

I landed on my back, and before I could roll away, Arthur stomped his golden-plated boot on my chest and pushed the air from my lungs.

Out of the corner of my eye, I saw the Viran soldiers breaking through Merlin's wind wall, and Young wiggled beneath the waning tornado. She was finally weakening. If she ran out of magic, we could still win. Arthur lifted Excalibur over me, his cobalt eyes wide with fear as he prepared to end my life.

Even as the Viran soldiers pushed through Merlin's gusts and Young slipped from her hold, I realized they weren't going to make it to me in time.

I could hear the clash of Minseo locked in battle with Lance. I turned my attention back to Excalibur, it's golden light reflecting gray sunbeams onto my face. I held my breath, suddenly wishing I had squeezed Minseo's hand one last time.

A dark shadow passed through the sky. I held my breath. *Garix*.

He was too late.

Beneath Arthur's armored boot, I felt my bones grind into the rocks beneath me. *So this is how I die.* Arthur's cold eyes bore into me. His hair was darkened with caked blood, his teeth gritted like a feral beast. Excalibur glinted over me, its blade thirsty for blood.

I settled into a moment of acceptance. Comfort covered me like a blanket and I felt poised to surrender to my final moment, ready to leave this world and all its darkness behind.

The ground shook with Garix's landing and Arthur lowered his blade. Suddenly, I saw Morgana. In a split second, I thought Arthur had struck, and my thoughts brought her to my mind to bid me farewell. But hurling toward Arthur was an unnaturally crimson flame and, behind it, Morgana ran towards us. Her eyes were wide with fear, her brows furrowed with determination.

"No, Morgana! Get out of here!" I screamed. But it was too late. I covered my face with my arms as Arthur lit up in a blast of red fire. I rolled just in time for a molten Excalibur to drop to the ground where I'd just been.

"No!" Merlin screamed, releasing Young and sending her hand back with a gust so strong that Arthur's charred corpse extinguished. My gaze moved from Merlin to Morgana, whose mouth drooped in the corner. Her eyes met mine as her shirt filled with the red of her blood. *How?* I leapt up, half numb to a shooting pain in my leg. I ran to Morgana and pulled her in just as her little body collapsed. I turned her in my arms and held pressure on the source of the blood. Merlin's cut of air had sliced several inches into Morgana. It marred her skin from her hip to her shoulder. My heart beat in my throat. "You're okay, honey. It's okay," I said, but her eyes were already glassy.

I looked up to Merlin whose eyes bulged with understanding. Viran soldiers clamored towards her. "I'm sorry, Charlotte," she whispered. I couldn't hear the words above the battle, but I saw them on her lips. I watched in horror as she dropped all of her spells at once, her eyes carrying the same loss and regret that raged within me. Beneath her, Young pulled himself up, the other Viran soldiers on her heels. Before she took another breath, Young's blade pierced through her. Her gaze remained on me but moved just beyond me as the light left her eyes and blood dribbled down the corner of her mouth. I traced it to Lancelot who reached for her before dropping Excalibur and falling to his knees at Minseo's feet.

Stunned, I turned away, dropping my eyes to Morgana's lifeless body. I held her to my chest, tears streaming down my face and defeat coursing through my veins. I screamed with every ounce of power in my body.

The battlefield went quiet as both sides halted their advance. "The king has fallen," I heard a voice say.

My body shook. I would not accept this. Morgana wasn't dead. *Take me instead.* I clutched my dagger. I couldn't let her die without me. I had to go with her into whichever realm she moved to. This couldn't be real. She couldn't be gone. I pulled her back to look down at her face. She was more doll-like than ever. Breathless and already growing cold. I swept a curl from her face, already missing the smile I knew I'd never see again.

"Morgana!" I screamed, my throat already raw. "Morgana!"

I sobbed, holding her to my chest.

I didn't know if the world had gone quiet or if I could no longer hear it. All was still, each second dragging into an endless eternity as my daughter failed to take another breath. She saved me. She saved us all. I threw my head back, whispering my thoughts to any deity that would listen. "Take me instead," I begged.

Why would she come here? She was safe. Had she called Garix?

I moved my gaze down from the sky to Minseo. Tears streamed down his face as he watched me, a lump of what was once Sir Lancelot at his feet.

I shook my head, willing Morgana's heart to beat again. I reached in my heart for the magic that Merlin had tried to coax from me, but there was no magic. My daughter was dead.

51

MINSEO

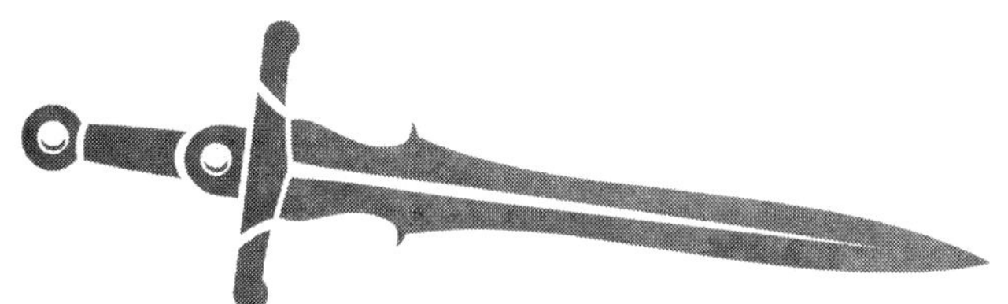

I wasn't sure what was more agonizing, Charlotte's screams or Garix's, as he echoed her pain so vividly. The crackling sound had brought the entire battle to its end, the canyon dust settling. Garix shielded Charlotte and Morgana with his tail, but it was too late. They could no longer be protected; one was dead and the other broken. I walked over to Charlotte who hugged her lifeless child. I wrenched her dagger from her hand and kicked it away. It clanged on something metal and I looked up to see Arthur's charred crown. I lifted it, warmth still embedded in the gold. I had so many questions. *Why was Morgana here?*

My thoughts drifted to the day I saw her training in the mountains. My gaze lifted to Young. The moment I saw him, I knew the truth. He told her to come. He put the idea in her mind that she could save her mother if she joined the battle.

I walked over to him, his sword still lodged in Merlin's chest, her dead eyes still open and sorrowful.

Young shook beneath my gaze. "I-I'm sorry," he said. "It's my fault."

"She's a child," I said, my thoughts blank as my emotions took over. "It's our job to protect her."

He nodded, tears falling from his eyes. He reached out and took the tip of my sword and put it to his chest. "I'm sorry, brother. I thought I could save Vires."

"You have saved Vires," I said, gesturing to the frozen battlefield. "Was it worth it?"

His face dropped as he cried. He spoke again, but his voice shook too hard to understand. "P-please," he said, pulling my sword to his chest. "It's okay."

He killed my daughter. He made every sacrifice to save his kingdom and, as I looked at the stunned armies and corpses of Camelot's leaders, I knew he'd somehow made us victorious. But the cost was too great. Many years ago, I'd raised my sword to my brother and lived to regret it, but taking his life wouldn't bring Morgana back. She was gone.

I held out the late King Arthur's crown. "Take it," I said.

His gaze rose to the charred crown and his brow came together.

"You are the new King of Vires and Camelot, if you wish. You've certainly sacrificed a lot for it. Take it!" I yelled, filling the canyon.

He shook his head, tears streaming down his blood-spattered cheeks. He took a steadying breath and took the crown, the pooling sadness in his eyes an indication he understood this was goodbye.

I took one last look at him. "We are no longer brothers."

I turned away and walked over to Charlotte. I sat on the ground beside her and put my arm around her shoulders. Morgana's curls tickled my hand. I looked over to Garix and saw the sorrow in his eyes. I could feel his heart sync with mine as I rocked Charlotte back and forth in agony.

Under her breath, I heard her mutter, "Take me instead." My stomach clenched, my whole body rife with pain, and still my heart beat in sync with Garix's. Caught in his gaze, all I could think about was how I wished I could take Charlotte's suffering away, and I too wished I could take Morgana's place. Garix laid his head beside Morgana, a whimper slipping through his fangs.

The warmth of his breath sent dust through the air around us. Sunshine beamed through the golden hour as if nothing had been lost. Garix's breaths slowed more than mine, throwing off our sync, and for a moment I thought he might've fallen asleep, but he was very still. Something was wrong. I stood, placing my hand on his body, and when I didn't feel his breath, I put my face against his scales.

"What's wrong?" Charlotte whispered, her voice gravely from screaming.

"Garix stopped breathing," I said, listening to his chest for any sign of life.

Charlotte looked at me, fear in her eyes.

Panicked, I spun. "What do I do?"

Adrenaline swelled when I heard her whisper, "Morgana?" She yelled, "Morgana?"

My attention snapped down to the child in Charlotte's arms. Morgana fidgeted then pulled herself up. Disbelief surged through me as Morgana wiped stray curls from her face. I dropped to my knees, taking her tiny hands in mine. Charlotte continued to whisper to her. "Morgana? Honey? Talk to me, please." Charlotte ran her hands up and down Morgana's body where the wound had been, frantically trying to find it. But it wasn't there. Her skin was inexplicably unmarred. "Morgana? Baby?"

Morgana reached up and touched Charlotte's face. "Is the war over? Did I do good?"

Charlotte nodded, tears running down her cheeks. "Of course, baby. We beat those bad guys. You did great!"

Morgana smiled wearily, resting her head on Charlotte's chest. "Good."

Abruptly, she sat up and looked at Garix. She jumped up and to his side. "Garry! Garry, wake up." But Garix didn't stir.

Charlotte turned to me, confusion in her eyes. "Did he...?"

I nodded, my mind going back to the moment when our heartbeats fell out of sync until his faded away completely. "I-I think... I think he gave his life for hers," I whispered.

Charlotte stared at me and took a labored breath. "Did I make him do that?"

I shook my head, unable to answer. It was possible she had and I wasn't sure if we'd ever know for certain. "He loved Morgana," I said.

I looked over to Garix, Morgana's panicked hands pushing at his scales. I sat down next to her and explained that Garix had passed on. I told her it was okay, that he loved her and was ready to go. I wiped her tears. "He came to us to be a hero. And he was."

I swallowed a mouthful of pain as Morgana fell to her knees and cried. My heart ached for her, for Charlotte, for us all.

The sudden quiet loss of Garix drained the last bit of strength in me. A gentle, loving hero had once again faded to mere myth. Even though she never said it, I was certain Charlotte blamed herself for his loss, but the guilt she carried was a price any parent would pay for more time with their child.

We sat, quiet in our thoughts of Garix, of the carnage, and of Morgana. We rested until Morgana cried herself out and we could start to think about leaving that awful place.

"Charlotte? Can you walk? Maybe we should think about leaving, going home."

She looked at me blankly. "Shouldn't we bury Garix? I mean, we can't just leave him..." she muttered.

I took her hand in mine. "I need you to take Morgana to Gabriel's. I'll take care of the rest." She nodded, lifting Morgana and scrambling to her feet. Her gaze turned to Young, and I shuddered at the darkness in her as her rage bore into him, fearful she'd attack. But Young was already broken. She passed wordlessly carrying our daughter to the safety of the Viran capital.

Among the carnage of war, I wondered if any of us would ever be the same again. Or if these vivid horrors would fade in memory and the lessons carried forward to birth a better world. Where there is love, there will always be loss. Where there are kingdoms, there will always be wars. So, when the dust settled, Charlotte and I took Morgana to a land outside the scope of kings and queens.

52

YOUNG

I sat on my father's throne, Arthur's golden crown taking its toll. Even though it had been a month, I still hadn't gotten used to its weight. I drew a circle with my finger on the armrest. There was so much still to do—decisions to make.

"Your Majesty," Hanbit said. "King Ruban of Faresa has arrived."

I waved him in and a few moments later the stubborn king stood at the foot of my throne.

"Your Majesty," he said, bowing low. "I...I don't know what to say. I underestimated you. I should have joined your cause. I'm very sorry." He dropped his gaze. "Faresa is at your mercy." He looked up to me, his posture diminished.

He was the last of the kings to arrive. The last of the five neighboring kingdoms that I'd asked to help with the war. They'd all given different variations of the same apology. Since the start of Arthur's reign, fear had been the currency between kingdoms. They'd all come in person to find out if the new King of Vires would prove to be another cruel tyrant. I handled each one with forgiveness, cementing strong alliances between their kingdoms and Vires, but I knew the truth. I *was* a cruel king. I'd made a choice, duty over love, and as my gaze gravitated to the empty throne beside me, I wondered if I'd made the right one.

I stood. "I appreciate the gesture of you coming all the way here, but I harbor no ill will towards you or your kingdom. I've dissolved Camelot's tax and I look forward to nurturing the relationship between our kingdoms."

King Ruban's face lit in surprise. "Thank you, Your Majesty." He backed away, as if attempting to flee before I changed my mind. As he got near the door, he turned back. "You know, Princess Euway of Nilith is unmarried. I could put in a good word."

My thoughts shifted to Charlotte, the pain in her eyes, the ring of her screams on the battlefield as she held our lifeless child. I swallowed a lump in my throat as I remembered the warmth of her smile, or how her soft skin felt under my fingers. "Thank you," I said, "but I'm afraid I must respectfully decline."

He nodded, giving a half-smile before he left the throne room.

I sat back on my throne, exhaling my conflicted nerves.

A woman's voice filled the room, "You're not going to try and remarry then?"

My throat tightened. "I thought you were already gone."

Charlotte walked across the room to the base of my throne. Her curls were half-pinned up but flowed freely in the back. My body tensed. She wore a simple long-sleeved dress from the west that cut wide at the neck and exposed half her shoulders. "I came to say goodbye," she said.

Frozen, I watched her ascend the stairs one by one. My pulse raced with each step until she stood in front of me, her face unreadable.

I swallowed my nerves. "I see you've come alone."

She nodded. "Minseo is with Morgana."

The way my brother's name sounded on her lips, as if he belonged to her more than to me, stung. I stood to challenge her intense gaze. "You're really going then."

"Yes." She reached out to straighten my crown and I considered kissing her. "There," she said. "That suits you."

As I watched her, I wondered if we were really so different. Hadn't she taken her young dragon into battle to save Viran lives? Didn't we share the same intentions? I took a deep breath. "Look, Charlotte—"

"Don't," she said, shaking her head. "It doesn't matter what you say now, it's already done. We've made our decisions." She pressed her lips together and tucked a stray curl behind her ear. "Now you're king. I think you're going to help a lot of people."

I took her hand and put it to my chest, my heart racing beneath her touch. "Charlotte," I said, but my voice came out as a whisper. I felt the sting of tears in my eyes as a surge of desperation washed over me. *This is goodbye? Forever*? I knew why she was leaving—she had every right. But how could I let her go? How was I going to stop loving her? "Despite everything… I just..." My voice shook. "Will this feeling ever stop?"

She paused, her gaze locked with mine. A smile touched the corners of her mouth. "Probably not," she said.

We laughed, our hands locked together against my chest. Tears slipped through my laughter, my heart grateful for one last beautiful minute with her.

She slowly pulled her hands away and, for a brief moment, she stood silently in front of me. Her eyes glistened with sadness. My heart tensed as she turned away, walking out of the throne room and my life. I had my answer. *I chose wrong*.

When I took the throne, I'd intended on forgiving every king who wronged me and now the only one left was myself.

"I love you," I called as Charlotte's silhouette filled the doorway.

And when I think of that moment, I tell myself I heard her whisper, *"I love you too."*

53

CHARLOTTE

I've heard it said that King Young of Vires is the greatest king who ever lived. They say he planned the battle where King Arthur fell, along with his knights and battle mage. King Young returned the stolen territories to their original kingdoms and ruled over Vires which prospered with the alliances of goodwill he forged. They say he's a man of honor, justice, and respect.

When I hear these things, I feel warm knowing he became the man he always wanted to be, that his world was all he imagined.

But my world is filled with the gentle whisper of unspoiled joy.

I cut the green onions and slipped them into the stew as I heard the steady knock of Gabriel cutting wood. Junho looked up from his teacup in the living room as the voices outside grew louder. "Faster," Morgana shouted.

"You're getting heavy," Minseo responded. The door opened and Minseo stepped through, carrying Morgana on his back. I smiled to myself as I continued to stir the stew.

My stomach fluttered as I felt Minseo's breath on my neck, his arms wrapping around me.

"How is my love?" he asked, kissing my neck. A chill slid down my spine.

"Very well," I said, biting back my grin.

He put his hands on my waist and spun me to face him. His lips brushed mine. Next, he bent, brought his lips to my enlarged stomach, and kissed it. "And how is my baby?" he asked.

I smiled, lifting his face back to mine. "Very well."

"Have you given the name any thought?"

I laughed, pushing his hair from his eyes. "You mean Garix? I think it's a wonderful name."

He paused, his smile fading as he searched my gaze thoughtfully. "And what if it's a girl?"

"How about Merlin?"

ACKNOWLEDGMENTS

I'd like to take a moment to thank everyone who helped make this series possible.

Trilogy Editor: Amber Richberger

Alpha Readers:

Charlee Garden
Judi Soderberg

Top Reviewers:

Brittany Smith
Christina Haynes
Shirley Cuypers
Monica Khan
Saidy Walker
Steph Pontarollo
Emily Wiebe

Amanda Arkans
Alexandria Brooks
Candice Allen

Printed in Great
Britain
by Amazon

31913732R00388